Murder School

ALSO AVAILABLE BY JK ELLEM

Stand Alone Novels
All Other Sins
Audrey Kills Again!
Murder School

The Ravenwood Seasons
Book 1 Mill Point Road
Book 2 Ravenwood
Book 3 The Sisterhood

The Killing Seasons
Book 1 A Winter's Kill
Book 2 A Spring Kill – coming soon

No Justice Series
Book 1 No Justice
Book 2 Cold Justice
Book 3 American Justice
Book 3.1 Fast Justice – A Ben Shaw Road Trip Thriller #1
Book 3.2 Sinful Justice – A Ben Shaw Road Trip Thriller #2
Book 3.3 Dark Justice – A Ben Shaw Road Trip Thriller #3
Book 4 Hidden Justice
Book 5 Raw Justice

Deadly Touch Series
Fast Read Deadly Touch

Octagon Trilogy (Dystopian Thriller Series)
Prequel Soldiers Field
Book 1 Octagon
Book 2 Infernum
Book 3 Sky of Thorns – coming soon

Murder School
by JK Ellem

Copyright © by 28th Street Multimedia Group 2022

Murder School is a work of fiction. All incidents, dialogue and all characters are products of the author's imagination and are not to be construed as real. Any resemblance to persons living or dead is entirely coincidental.

All rights reserved. In accordance with the U.S. Copyright Act of 1976, the scanning, uploading, and electronic sharing of any part of this book without the written permission of the publisher is unlawful piracy and theft of the author's intellectual property.

No part of this book may be reproduced, stored in a retrieval system or transmitted in any form or by any means, without the prior permission in writing of the publisher, nor to be otherwise circulated in any form of binding or cover other than that in which it is published without a similar condition, including this condition, being imposed on the subsequent purchaser.

Copyrighted Material

To my loving wife Jennifer,
What would I do without you.
JKE

Prologue

First Interview - Internal Affairs Bureau (IAB)
315 Hudson Street, New York.

"Can we start, for the record, by stating your full name, age, and rank."

"My name is Evangeline Morgan Sommers, forty-six years old, divorced, no children. I'm a homicide detective with the 5th Precinct, Manhattan."

Dan Miller ticked off something in the open IAB investigation file in front of him, then his pen hovered, undecided.

"It's German," the woman said, as if sensing his hesitancy. "Going back generations. It means summer, is pronounced the same. But, I was born in winter."

"Thank you," Miller said, adding a note to the file. He had already spent the previous evening reading the contents of the file, preparing for this interview. What he hadn't prepared for was the blanket insomnia he subsequently endured while tossing and turning in bed, trying to comprehend the extraordinary events that had transpired, the details of which formed nearly all of the two hundred or so pages in the investigation file.

Miller studied Sommers for a few moments. She sat expressionless, reflecting his gaze. She was pale skinned, with mousy shoulder-length hair the color of winter wheat and faded green eyes that seemed to have once been brighter. She wasn't lean, wasn't athletic looking, nor particularly muscular, more of an hourglass shape. She was surprisingly...average, forgettable. He was expecting to see Ellen Ripley sitting across from him, all taut and toned. What he got instead was Bridget Jones, a soccer mom minus the kids, which made her recent actions seem all the more incredible.

He turned a page in the file and was immediately greeted by a glossy color photo of a man lying dead in a lake of blood, the area where the face had once been—gone, replaced with a pulpy slurry of dark reds, browns, and pale grays. "You shot the victim three times." Miller was unable to tear his eyes away from the photo, trying to reconcile the gratuitous violence—of someone who was obviously unhinged—with the calm and composed demeanor of the woman who sat quietly in front of him. He glanced up. "Three times seems to be your specialty, doesn't it?"

Sommers shifted in her chair. "I used appropriate force to stop a lethal threat." Her response was measured, carefully crafted. She knew her rights, he gathered, including the legal requirements to plead a defense to homicide.

He thumbed through more pages. "So you're sticking with what you said in your signed statement? That it was 'justifiable homicide'?" He looked up again, searching her face for any change in her deadpan expression. Nothing.

"Yes."

"And yet the victim was unarmed." Miller felt a mix of disbelief and doubt in her actions and justification. "He had no weapon, Detective Sommers, and"—he flipped back to the coroner's report—"all three shots were to the face."

Sommers blinked, her stoic mask slipping slightly.

Miller gave a contented smile as he watched a glimmer of uncertainty in her eyes. He wasn't mistaken. She had hesitated, was thinking, deciding between a conservative, by-the-book legal response, or a more candid one, he believed.

After a few more seconds of deliberation, Eve Sommers, much to Miller's dismay, went with the candid response. "Maybe he should have armed himself, then," she replied.

The answer was as perplexing as it was arrogant. He made another note in the file. His eyes shifted to the plaster cast on her right hand. It extended from her fingertips, past her wrist, and up to the midpoint of her forearm.

Miller turned his attention back to the details in the file about the second victim: the woman who had survived. The medical report on her was detailed: broken jaw, shattered cheekbone, collapsed eye socket, significant facial injuries, leaving no doubt she would be in the hospital for a while, undergoing numerous rounds of reconstructive surgery and dental work. However, unlike her male counterpart, the woman—the second victim—*was* armed. And yet Sommers had chosen not to shoot her.

Perhaps she'd found it difficult, unnerving, to shoot another woman dead, preferring instead to beat her almost to death, and in the process, breaking her own hand.

Setting down his pen, Miller regarded her again. Named after summer but born in winter. She certainly was a paradox, a contradiction of sorts between her past, unblemished police record, and the more recent facts where she appeared to have spiraled into the role of belligerent vigilante.

He wanted to know more about her, specifically what had triggered such a response. Public and political opinion was divided as to her fate. Half the city wanted her thrown in jail. The other half, including her colleagues in the NYPD, the mayor and the governor, all wanted to pin a medal on her chest.

Miller cared for neither. All he wanted was the truth, so he decided to change his approach. "Tell me, Detective, about your work. Tell me how you spend a typical day."

She gave a smirk. "How do you think I spend my day?" the sarcasm clear in her voice. "During the day I'm surrounded by murderers, rapists, child molesters, and wife killers."

For a moment, Miller was taken aback by her blunt honesty. Her file said she had spent most of her adult life in law enforcement, first as a cadet police officer, then patrol officer, grinding her way up to senior homicide detective. Maybe in his report he would recommend again for her to see a department psychologist, even though she had refused the first request by her commanding officer. He made a note in the file nonetheless to follow up.

Sommers continued. "One minute I'm looking at the body of a woman who has been beaten, then strangled and set on fire by her ex-husband; the next minute I'm standing at the checkout at Trader Joe's with a basket full of frozen dinners, wondering what my life has become."

Miller nodded before double-underlining his note. She should definitely have a psych evaluation.

"And how does it make you feel?" he said. "About your job? Your career? The toll it can have on you…mentally?"

Eve stared back at the man, feeling slightly offended by his question. Was he truly ignorant? Of course it takes a toll. All cops knew that. Maybe she was just good at hiding it, controlling it.

She glanced at her injured hand and felt a rush of pride. The plaster cast was covered in scribbled pen, the well wishes of her entire precinct, and from police officers and detectives from other NYPD precincts—some she knew, many she didn't—and even the signatures of complete strangers who had stopped her in the street to thank her.

She leaned forward, and her previously dull green eyes now glowed brilliant jade. She saw sudden apprehension in Miller's eyes. Good.

"During the day I catch killers. I see, smell, feel, taste the worst humankind can do to each other. At night I go home, eat dinner alone while catching the late news, perhaps the last ten minutes of a sitcom or a cop show, believing that what I'm watching is normal, is reality. Then I go to bed where I'm hoping to sleep peacefully for six uninterrupted hours without the constant nightmares or night sweats that can't be put down to menopause." Eve paused, thinking more about the question, and the "mental toll" as he had put it. A few weeks back, she wouldn't have felt the same way as she now did. "The funny thing is, I actually count the hours until dawn, until I can return to work, to the other world." She continued staring at Miller directly in the eye. "Because that world, despite all its ugliness and mayhem, is the *normal* world, the *real* world."

Eve sat back and folded her arms. "And I wouldn't change my life for anything."

DAY 1

Chapter 1 – Murder School

Two Weeks Earlier

"Do we get extra points if we kill them in broad daylight?"

Joshua Banks smiled at the question. Finally they were getting it—or at least Victoria Christie was. "Especially in broad daylight," Josh replied.

Victoria was almost gloating as she scanned the list Josh had prepared of suggested targets. She flashed her eyes at Josh. "Good. It's too easy to kill someone in a dark alley with no one around. I much prefer an audience."

The secure video call had just ended with the other thirty or so members of this very exclusive group, and Josh's attention now turned to the three people in the room who he had invited especially for this private, face-to-face gathering of his inner circle: Victoria Christie, Tein Moriarty, and Marcus Kemp. This smaller subgroup of three, he fondly regarded as the truly rotten core of an exceptionally bad apple. Unlike the others, these three really needed no incentive, especially money. They would kill without compulsion. Winning the game was reward enough for them.

"Bonus points if it's done in a highly visible public place," Josh added. "As you can see from the list, which are only suggestions, I give you full creative license for your imaginations to run wild."

"Some of these are impossible!" a voice complained.

Josh turned his attention to Tein Moriarty, the reserved, cool, calculating strategist of the group. Moriarty did nothing without first considering the probability of every conceivable risk, contingency, and likely outcome. As a sophomore studying mathematics at Princeton, Moriarty had his eyes firmly set on Wall Street when he graduated. He was just as capable of formulating stock market trading algorithms as he was in calculating the chances of getting caught killing someone.

"That's why some have double bonus points," Josh replied seductively. Watching the three react to the little tidbit was like dangling morsels of tender meat in front of a congregation of alligators.

"Like everyone else, you three have all qualified, earned a seat at the table," Josh said, his eyes dwelling on each person individually before moving on to the next. "Moriarty, a hitchhiker. Kemp, a blind date you procured from a dating app. And Christie, an elderly woman you pushed out of a top-story window." To qualify, each member had to upload to a secure website, video footage or original photos of their joy killing, and a newspaper article as proof.

With the exception of Victoria, they all had attended exclusive preparatory schools in New York, were currently studying at the best Ivy League universities, were the prodigy of fabulously rich parents, and living privileged lives. As such, Joshua Banks knew exactly what drove each of them.

"I just want to clarify." Victoria leaned forward. "A public landmark? With tourists and everything?"

Josh turned his attention to the young woman, the dark horse of his core group. The English blonde-haired temptress had a wicked body, supermodel good looks and was a pure heathen when it came to morality and possessing any shred of a social conscience. She was a strange, unpredictable creature, indeed. Although Josh had only known her for eighteen months, compared to Kemp and Moriarty, he trusted Victoria Christie the most despite knowing very little about her background. And his quick acceptance of her into the group had created some animosity among the other two—especially Marcus Kemp.

"The more the merrier," Josh replied.

The right side of Victoria's top lip edged up subtly into a twitchy smile. It wasn't a sneer, or a smirk, but it had a certain reptilian quality to it, like she was about to gobble you up whole. She sank back into the sofa, and gazed off into the ether, smiling contentedly to herself as though it were Christmas Eve and she had the most gifts under the tree. Her eyes possessed a beguiling quality to them that had attracted, captured, and devoured many of the male species. A cold slate-gray, coupled with a permanent glint of delicious anticipation. Josh particularly loved the way—when something excited her—the tip of Victoria's tongue would slither out over her lips, leaving them glistening, before darting back over her perfectly white, sharp teeth. Josh knew for a fact Victoria was by far the bloodthirstiest of the group. Streets ahead of the others. Whoever coined the phrase, *Don't let looks deceive you*, had Victoria Christie in mind. She could suck the air out of a room just by walking into it. A devout vegan, her carnivore diet only extended to married college professors and NCAA champions.

Josh addressed the three again. "Like I said, randomness is an essential requirement. You are to select only indiscriminate targets." For Joshua Banks, there was nothing random or indiscriminate about his life. Contrary to what one might expect from a classics junior at Brown University, his life was a carefully curated construct of falsehoods. Outwardly, the young man—who some said resembled a young Christopher Walken, including the high-top hair and intense, drawn face—was a far-left extremist, despising all forms of capitalism, a staunch supporter of multiculturalism, inclusiveness, and tolerance.

However, inwardly he was the polar opposite, and had come to accept what he really was: a fascist, a racist, and a bigot. Having Tein Moriarty as part of the group served only to enhance the illusion that was Joshua Patrick Banks.

"Total strangers?" Marcus Kemp this time, sociology PhD student at Yale. At twenty-nine, Kemp was the oldest of the group, a perpetual student who seemed at home hiding in the cloistered world of academia. For Kemp, everything was either black or white, binary, zeros or ones. No filthy shades of gray. Kemp was fascinated by the controversial obedience experiments carried out by the infamous social psychologist, Stanley Milgram at Yale during the 1960s, where participants were encouraged to administer what they thought were painful electric shock treatments to other subjects in the name of researching human obedience and moral decision-making. Kemp had told Josh on several occasions he was toying with the idea of secretly reviving such experiments for his dissertation. This time however, instead of faking the electric shocks, he wanted to use only female candidates and wire them up to a live power supply.

Josh nodded as his eyes traveled across everyone in the group again. "As I explained during the video call with the other members, it is a cardinal rule. Total strangers only."

"Can we kill other members?" Kemp asked. He turned to appraise Victoria as though she was a lab rat that had outlived its scientific usefulness.

Victoria's face broke out into a wide, feline grin. "That's right, Marcus," she said, her voice low and husky. "You don't like women, do you? Do you feel threatened by us?"

"Victoria," Josh cautioned, seeing Kemp's jaw tighten slightly. She was the only person Josh knew who could breech the normally impervious, unemotional vessel Kemp lived within.

Undeterred, Victoria continued. "Was it something your mother made you do when you were a child that turned you into such a raving closet misogynist?"

One of Kemp's eyelids began to spasm, and for a moment Josh thought the Yale student had stopped breathing. He just sat motionless, unblinking, staring at Victoria.

"Victoria!" Josh raised his voice a notch.

Licking her lips, and with her eyes firmly on Kemp, Victoria began to provocatively slide the fingertips of one hand up her inner thigh. "Did she come into your little bedroom at night?" her voice switched to a sweet, childlike innocence. "Did she slip under the covers next to you, and start tugging on your wormy little—"

"Enough!" Josh snapped. "No, you *can not* kill other members."

Kemp's eyes had shrunk to razor slits, his focus still on Victoria.

Victoria threw Kemp a cheeky wink, and with a sudden movement, gathered up her backpack and stood. "Can't wait until it officially starts."

Josh gave her a roguish grin. "Who says it hasn't started already?"

Victoria said nothing for a moment, then her eyes lit up as she looked down at Josh. "Don't tell me…"

"This city has no idea of the fear and mayhem we're about to unleash on it"—Josh nodded to them all—"and the clock is ticking."

Chapter 2 – Five Pounds

Five pounds of pressure is all it would take, and Thomas Birch would be no more.

Birch glanced to his left, to a side table where a cheap photo frame sat, a priceless moment frozen in time pressed behind the glass. In the photo, Thomas was standing next to his then ten-year-old son, Justin, arms wrapped around each other, Justin holding up a yellowtail snapper freshly plucked from the warm blue waters. The photo was taken by the skipper of the charter boat, of a father and son in happier times, bright smiles and bronzed skin basking under the Key Largo sunshine.

It was the only photo Thomas had left of his son. Suzanne had taken the rest.

There hadn't been many moments like those in recent years. They used to be much closer, when Justin was in middle school. They would talk and laugh, throw ball, and eat hot dogs together. Do the fun stuff fathers and sons did. Then Justin hit his teens, and everything changed. Thomas guessed it was what just happened, when all boys grew into young men, and fathers became less important.

Thomas Birch knew he wasn't to blame. They had just grown apart. He had tried to revive his relationship with Justin—before everything had gone so horribly wrong for Birch more than two years ago. He got tickets to ball games, where they sat together in the bleachers at Yankee Stadium, the cheapest tickets with the obstructed view, because it was all a NYPD detective's salary could afford. Yet nothing seemed to work. In fact, Thomas felt the harder he tried with Justin, the farther his son slipped beyond his grasp.

Now seventeen, Justin was gone, just like everything else good and cherished in Thomas Birch's life.

Five pounds of pressure is all it would take.

Suzanne, he could live without, but Justin was his entire world. His son was all that mattered. There were no better days ahead, only worse ones to come, marching relentlessly toward him for as far as his tortured mind could see.

Five pounds of pressure, a millisecond of blinding cerebral pain, followed by total nothingness, and it would all be over for him. The appeal was too much.

The time had come.

Choking back the tears, Thomas Birch knelt a little straighter, closed his eyes, clenched his teeth, and felt the cold steel of the barrel press a little harder against his temple. He began to squeeze the trigger.

Then came a knock at the front door.

"Mr. Birch?"

A man stood there, framed in the open doorway, a large black SUV hunkered down on the dirt driveway behind him.

Birch said nothing, just looked bewildered at the man, wondering who he was. No one knew where Birch lived, except for Suzanne. Even his colleagues back at the Fifth Precinct who had disowned him knew he lived somewhere in Cold Spring—a small town an hour drive north of Manhattan—but not exactly where.

The man stepped forward. "Mr. Thomas Birch?"

"Who wants to know?"

The man gave a curt smile, then swiftly retrieved a business card from inside his dark gray suit jacket and handed it to Birch. "I represent Francis Latimer. You may have heard of him?" The man stared expectantly at Birch. "Latimer…Industries?" he continued, trying to coax a nod of recognition out of Birch.

Birch took the card, turned it over in his hand. Smooth linen texture, sharp-cut edges, raised embossed lettering. *Francis J. Latimer.* Simple. Understated. Black and white. Birch vaguely knew who Latimer was. Not personally, just by reputation due to Latimer's billionaire status.

"Mr. Latimer would like a moment of your time, if you please."

Birch continued staring at the business card, unsure as to how something so small and insignificant had interrupted something so monumental.

"Mr. Birch?" the man turned, gesturing toward the idling SUV.

Birch looked past the man's shoulder, toward the ominous shape, with its glossy black skin, impenetrable dark-tinted windows, and an accompanying low, guttural purr coming from under the chassis. "Tell him to come in, then."

The man gave a slight, embarrassed smile. "Apologies for the misunderstanding. He sent me to *collect* you."

"Collect?" The word sounded detached, almost impersonal to Birch. Collect the mail. Collect a package. Collect a stray dog that had come off its leash.

"We can be in Mr. Latimer's Manhattan office within the hour, then bring you right back here."

The man wasn't going to take no for an answer. But Birch didn't care. "No," Birch said, and began to close the door. "Now is not a good time for me."

The man stepped forward, placing his foot over the threshold. "Please, Mr. Birch." The man hesitated, like he wanted to say more. Then he did. "I was instructed to tell you it's about your son, Justin."

Chapter 3 – Eve

It wasn't the fact a dirty coffee cup sat on the kitchen counter, next to an open, warm carton of milk—even though Luke preferred herbal tea—that first aroused Eve's suspicion.

Nor was it the fact the dishwasher drawers had been pulled out, stacked high with clean plates and cups, still waiting to be put away—by Luke.

Nor was it the fact Eve—intending only to return home briefly to collect a case file she had left behind this morning after rushing off to work—needed only to use one of her keys, instead of two separate keys to open both locks of the front door of her small two-bedroom apartment. Her neighborhood wasn't a high-crime area. However, she had told a sleepy-eyed Luke before she left, to keep both locks securely fastened even when at home.

Nor was Eve's suspicion aroused when she saw the damp bath towel tossed carelessly on the kitchen floor, next to the still-empty cat bowl, belonging to Sam, her gray-and-white moggy she had rescued as a kitten from being dumped into a rollout trash can, his fur clumped in fleas and filth. Sam was staring at Eve right now, screaming silently at her through the closed glass window from where he sat on the fire escape stairs outside, an unfed look of disdain in his feline eyes.

All of these small, yet annoying indiscretions were just everyday signs that Luke—Eve's live-in lover for the last six months—was being his usual, lazy, youthful self. Eve had made allowances. After all, she was forty-six years old, divorced, with no children, and carrying a few extra stubborn pounds she put down to the daily stress and ungodly hours that came with her job. She would often tell work colleagues however, that a 9mm bullet traveled a lot faster than what she did, and that's all that mattered. While Luke, on the other hand, was thirty-years old, had the tall, sculpted physique of an Olympic rower, and told her she was beautiful, and sexy, and he wanted to have children with her: the kind of lofty promises dreams were made of for Eve. Luke's scant regard for home cleanliness hadn't discouraged Eve. A month previous, she told him she loved him too. The last time she told a man she loved him, Eve subsequently spent the next three years in marital bliss, followed by five years of trying to convince herself to leave her deceitful husband and their loveless marriage, followed by a further two years in a nasty, protracted divorce.

However, what did make the hairs on the nape of Eve's neck frizzle with suspicion as she stood in her kitchen was the sound emanating from the bedroom. It was the same sound, not less than an hour ago, Eve had made herself when she and Luke had made tumultuous, passionate, love among a tangle of arms, legs, and twisted, damp bedsheets. In addition to the groans and moans she could now hear, was the distinct, rhythmic squeaking of the ancient, coiled springs of Eve's double bed mattress.

A small ball of nausea, thick and sour, rose in Eve's stomach as she edged toward the bedroom door, the sounds getting louder, more intense. She contemplated reaching for her handgun nestled snuggly in its holster on her right hip, then reconsidered. It wasn't *her* life in mortal danger. It was Luke's—from her. Then she heard the familiar timbre of a young man's moaning reaching a crescendo, and the small ball of nausea she felt, quickly grew into a bucket-sized mass that began traveling up her throat.

She nudged the door open slowly with the toe of her shoe,

and then watched in horror as her once trusting, blissful, and secure world was thrown violently sideways. Eve immediately recognized the thin, nimble shape of the woman straddling Luke, her hips gyrating, pelvis grinding, the mattress springs squeaking, the headboard rhythmically slapping the wall. Maddy or Mandy was her name. Eve wished she had paid more attention to the young woman who lived in the apartment upstairs. The same young woman who had a penchant for walking around the apartment block wearing high-cut shorts, no bra and skimpy tight tops that could hardly contain her gravity-defying breasts. Whenever Eve saw her, the young woman gave her an insolent smile that said, *So, you're the older woman living downstairs with the much younger man.*

Sensing someone else was in the room, the young woman turned and looked over her shoulder. Their eyes locked, and she gave Eve a sly, unapologetic smile.

"Get out!" Eve snarled.

The young woman gave a high-pitched shriek as she was suddenly bucked sideways off the bed like a rodeo rider, hitting the ground with a naked, unceremonious thud. Luke, panic-stricken and horrified, rose up off the mattress in a flurry, saw Eve standing in the doorway, and stuttered the universal—and the dumbest—question of anyone who had been caught in a similar situation: "What are you doing home?"

"Get out!" Eve screamed. Her blood wasn't boiling. It had already turned into a noxious gas, threatening to kill every living thing in the small bedroom.

Quickly, Luke slipped on a discarded pair of boxer shorts while the young woman hastily found her panties that to Eve looked more like a shoelace than an undergarment.

Eve watched on as both fumbled around the bedroom.

Luke moved toward Eve, his hands raised apologetically, then said the second dumbest thing he could. "Look, I can explain. Misty came over to borrow—"

Eve silenced him with sharp glare that could cut steel. She flung back the bedroom door with such force, the handle punched a hole in the drywall. "I said get out!"

Chapter 4 – Francis Latimer

The ride in the back of the SUV was smooth, fast, and uneventful for Thomas Birch.

Fifty minutes after leaving Birch's boathouse, they were navigating within the shadows of the skyscraper canyons of Lower Manhattan, an endless tide of people and vehicles flowing around them in all directions as two million people running in a state of perpetual lateness eked out a living on a land mass twenty-three miles square, in the smallest, yet most densely populated of the five boroughs of New York City.

The SUV swung down the ramp of an underground parking garage and into the bowels of a tall edifice of glass, steel and capitalistic wealth. Flanked by two mute companions, and with the military precision reminiscent of a secret-service detail, Birch was promptly whisked into an elevator and felt his gut drop to his knees as it rocketed up fifty stories above the teeming metropolis below.

When Birch and the entourage exited the elevator, a tall woman dressed in a tight charcoal business suit stood waiting and greeted Birch. "Mr. Latimer is going to be so pleased to see you." She gave him a warm smile and asked him to follow her. The escorts dropped away as Birch proceeded to follow the swaying hips and glossy high heels down a wide featureless corridor. The only sound came from the building as concrete, steel, and glass flexed and adjusted to the outside stresses and internal pressures.

The woman knocked on a huge set of doors and stood aside, ushering Birch inside.

A shape moved from behind a massive desk, yet for some

inexplicable reason, Birch allowed his attention to be drawn to a woman who stood off to one side, statuesque, lithe, her body framed by the sun that streamed through the expanse of windows. The woman had narrow features, raven-black shoulder-length hair, blunt edges, and laser bangs. The woman stood perfectly still and watched Birch with the keen eye of someone who knew of him but had never actually met him. To Birch, the woman was a complete stranger, as was the man who rose from behind the desk.

Francis Latimer came around and greeted Birch with genuine pleasure. He had the poise and presence of someone who had supreme command of the situation, always in control.

Latimer was lean, fit looking, mid-sixties, taller than Birch, with honest, intelligent eyes. His handshake was firm, doubled-handed, confident but not authoritative.

"Please…" Latimer ushered Birch toward an oversized leather chair.

Birch remained standing. "My son, Justin?" he demanded, unable to contain his burgeoning anxiety any longer. On the ride in, Birch had tried to coax an answer about Justin from the man who had knocked on his door, but to no avail. He was promptly told Francis Latimer would explain everything once they arrived at his office, and to sit back, and enjoy the ride. If Birch could have phoned his son, he would have, to find out if he was okay. But like everyone else, Justin had severed all ties with him, his son even changing his cell phone number so his father could not contact him. Suzanne had done the same.

"There is no cause for alarm, Thomas—" Latimer paused. "May I call you Thomas?"

Birch hesitated, then nodded.

"Good. Please, sit down, Thomas."

The authoritative look in Latimer's eyes did quell some of the fear Birch felt. Reluctantly he sat down, then took in his surroundings. The wide sweeping vista of Lower Manhattan stretched below: the Brooklyn Bridge on the left, spanning the East River, and the Hudson on the right. Ferries cut between Ellis Island and Governors Island, and in the distance, the deceptively small shape of the Statue of Liberty sat proud, the symbol of freedom, enlightenment, and independence dwarfed by taller structures of servitude, moral ignorance, and greed.

The office décor was tastefully minimalistic, not the typical homage to one's self that Birch expected. Clean lines and near emptiness filled unoccupied space and lacked the usual self-indulgent display of achievement and vanity. No clues as to what business, political and social circles Francis Latimer moved in were present, nor were accolades of what he had accomplished in his sixty-six years. Latimer seemed like the kind of man who didn't need a constant reminder of his achievements.

The only photos to be seen were a small cluster of what Birch assumed were family photos, in silver frames that sat on the return of the desk. One in particular caught Birch's attention. A young woman, blonde hair, bright smile, same intelligent eyes as Francis Latimer. She had a smile and a face that could clear the worst storm clouds away. There were no other photos in the entire office. Not a single photo of Birch shaking hands with a president or mayor or film star.

"It is a real pleasure to meet you, Thomas," Latimer said, taking a seat again.

Birch regarded Latimer for a moment. The man seemed genuine enough, no fake sincerity. Birch had enough experience and a keen sense of judgment to know when someone was lying to him.

"Why am I here?" Birch's jaw ached from clenching his teeth for the last hour or so.

Latimer smiled and pointed to Birch. "I like that in a person. Straight to the point. No nonsense."

"You don't know anything about me, nor my son."

Latimer's eyes narrowed. His expression told Birch he had made a tactical error, had underestimated the man who sat across from him. Two folders sat on the desk in front of Latimer: one green, the other red. Latimer's smile broadened as he noticed Birch's attention shift to the two folders. One particular folder, the green one, was considerably thicker than the other.

"What's your purpose, Thomas?"

The question took Birch by surprise, the kind of question you ask a job interview candidate. "Purpose?"

"What do you want to do with your life, right now?" Latimer's fingers absentmindedly drummed on the red folder in front of him. "What is the one thing you desire the most?"

Birch already felt uncomfortable. The nature of these questions made things infinitely worse. He cast his mind back to the handgun he had so hastily shoved in a drawer back at his home before accepting the ride here.

"What's the purpose of you bringing me here?" Birch repeated. "I was told it was about my son."

Latimer leaned forward and the warm friendly smile vanished, replaced with a cold, granite-like stare, revealing the true persona that had got Francis Latimer to where he was today. "We've both lost someone, Thomas. In a way, you have lost your son, Justin." Latimer inclined his head. "My daughter is missing, Thomas, and I want you to find her. Maybe we can help each other to get back the only thing in our lives worth living for."

Journal Entry #4 – Lindsay

I met a young woman today.

She stepped into the train compartment where I was sitting alone.

Like me, she was traveling alone, and asked if she could share the carriage. She was polite, nicely dressed, and she had an honest smile. I didn't mind. After all, it wasn't like she was some kind of serial killer who had just escaped from jail. Definitely didn't look the type.

I wasn't looking for company. In fact, I was just happy to enjoy the trip on my own, in the solitude, so I could think, so I could write in my journal and reflect, (more like ponder) the next few years of my life. But then she walked in and everything changed.

I felt sad, depressed, even when I woke this morning. I loved the three days I had spent in Paris since the start of my trip. I could have spent weeks there, walking the cobbled streets, peering in all the lovely store windows, browsing in all the beautiful fashion boutiques, the wonderful small French bakeries, walking along the river, the museums, the amazing architecture (I hope I've spelled that right!) I loved all of it!

So, back to my new friend. At first she didn't talk much. She seemed happy staring out the window at the people on the platform, and I was happy flicking through a fashion magazine I had bought at the station kiosk.

Then, as the train pulled out of the station and gradually picked up speed, leaving behind the city for the wide-open spaces of the countryside, my mysterious traveling companion started glancing at me. Nothing too obvious at first, but then I caught her a few times staring right at me. She would then quickly look away, but I could tell she wanted to ask me something. She seemed curious about me. Maybe it was the clothes I was wearing, or the bag I was carrying. Maybe she wasn't used to seeing such quality. Maybe she thought my accent was a little strange, even though I hadn't really said much.

She made a comment about the magazine I was reading, and something about how everything seemed so expensive here, and how everyone drove crazily and how the subway smelled of piss and about all the stray cats eating out of the garbage bins in the park.

Then she asked me a heap of questions. Where I was traveling to. Where I had been. Where did I live. I don't like talking to strangers, never have. But it was good to find someone around my own age, who spoke English too. I had spent the last three days bumbling around Paris using hand signals to ask for directions and relying miserably on my year-ten French. Miss Freer, my old French teacher would have died if she had heard me.

Anyway, I kept the actual details about myself to a bare minimum. Thankfully she did most of the talking.

And did she talk! Blah! Blah! Blah!

She told me about her family, what she did, where she lived.

Time flew and I think we both must have fallen under the spell of the rhythmic sound of the train wheels on the track.

We went to the dining car and had something to eat and she told me more about her family, who she liked and who she didn't like. Then she suggested that we travel together. At first I wasn't sure; I told her I would think about it. She wants to go to Italy, and it would make sense, be safer to travel together. I've never been to Italy. I guess we could. I have no real plans. I only chose Cannes in the south of France because it's said all the movie stars go there, and I wanted to see the glamorous beaches and resorts along the French Riviera.

She's gone back to the carriage to lie down, take a nap. I've got a few more hours to make a decision before the train gets to the station.

I'm still in the dining car now, putting all my thoughts down on paper. Outside, the sun is slowly setting, and all the fields are turning golden. It really is beautiful.

I'm tired too, but I want to finish this entry, because if I don't, I'm sure my mind will explode with all the ideas I've had today.

So, I've made a new friend, and she certainly has a very interesting life, far more interesting than mine.

And, here's the strange part—listening to her has got me thinking. For the first time, I really know what I want to do with my life. For a long time, I've known what I REALLY DON'T WANT TO DO! But now I know what I want to do.

Does that make sense? I'll probably reread this later and it will sound stupid, what I've just written, but it's how I now feel after listening to her for hours.

Meeting this woman today was fate. She has given me the answer I've been looking for. The perfect solution to all my problems.

It seems so obvious, doesn't it?

Chapter 5 – Salvation

Finally, the statuesque woman spoke. "Mr. Latimer's daughter, Lindsay, has been missing for five days."

Birch turned toward the woman. In a previous life, he would have tried to get the measure of the woman, to understand what made her tick. Now, he was too tired, too far removed from the world, not just this one.

Yet, as he watched her, dusty old instincts were telling him to be cautious of her. More so than the man who sat across the desk from him, whose wealth probably surpassed most small nations.

"This is Maxine Brodie," Latimer explained. "Head of public relations for my family."

"Please, call me Max. I manage all public and media relations for the Latimer family."

"So you're a publicist?"

"Not in the traditional sense. I provide a very contrarian solution. Mr. Latimer is a very private man. He prefers to keep all family matters away from the public eye. My job is to keep the Latimer family out of the headlines. Instead of courting publicity, my role is to avoid it—at all costs."

Birch addressed Latimer. "I'm sorry to hear about your daughter. Honestly, I am. But go to the police. That's what they do." Birch needed to leave. Being here only made him feel worse. He had lost his own son, the only thing important to him, and now it seemed he was being asked to find someone else's child. Maybe at an earlier time, in another life, he could have felt stronger, be willing to help. But in his current state of mind, Francis Latimer's request only served to remind Birch of the gaping hole in his own life. Birch barely had the inclination or the energy to crawl out of bed each morning, and now the request by Latimer was another cruel twist, pulling him further down the spiral. "I can't help you," Birch said, "and you can't help me." Birch felt both relieved and deflated at once. Justin was fine, and this was a fool's errand.

Latimer said nothing, just continued drumming his fingers purposefully on the red folder in front of him.

Maxine Brodie interjected, ignoring what Birch had said. "As you can appreciate, a person in Mr. Latimer's position prefers a certain degree of anonymity. If it became widely known that Lindsay was missing, every crackpot would scuttle out from under every rock, claiming they have taken her or know something about her disappearance. It would soon deteriorate into a circus and could very well jeopardize actually finding her. Not to mention the stock market sensitivities if such information was ever made public. We need to exercise total discretion."

Birch was tempted to ask questions, but deliberately held back. He couldn't get involved. Nor did he wish to give any false hope to Latimer that he was even remotely interested in finding the man's daughter. He wasn't. But Birch was still considerate. Ignoring Max, he addressed Latimer. "Surely someone in your position has a huge amount of resources at your disposal to find your daughter." *More financial resources than the entire NYPD budget*, Birch imagined.

"I do," Latimer agreed. "I have an army of people out looking for her right now."

"All to no avail," Max cut in, directing Birch's attention back on her. "We much prefer to control such matters and the narrative in-house."

"So why do you need me?" Birch replied, hoping to convince them both that he was not the person for the job. "I'm just one man. And I don't do this kind of work anymore, looking for missing persons."

Latimer spoke again. "Pardon the cliché, but money can't buy you everything." Latimer made a sweeping gesture with his hand. "And I would gladly give all this away in return for finding my daughter. However, money can only get you so far, and when people know who you are, the money you have… they are more prone to taking certain financial liberties with my money."

Birch began to struggle. The cop inside him was stirring, getting restless, whispering to him to help the man. Another part of him was yelling at him to run, to get up and get out of this place, to go back to the serene, picturesque safety of the lake and blow his brains out, and put an end to it all. He had enough pain and suffering of his own. He didn't want to be here. There was no point. It was a world foreign to him. "I'm not a detective anymore. I can't help you. Like I said, go to the police." Birch made to stand.

Latimer finally spoke again. "I do not trust the police. It is an opinion I believe we both share."

Birch paused as an alarm went off in his head. "What do you mean?"

Latimer gestured at Birch. "You're a broken man, Thomas. People have betrayed you, and your trust, both professionally and personally. Now I'm giving you the chance to put yourself back together."

"I'm not broken, as you put it," Birch lied. "You know nothing about me."

Latimer smiled at the red folder in front of him, then began to recite from it without opening it. "Thomas Birch, forty-two-years old. Ex-detective, Fifth Precinct, southeastern edge of Manhattan. Takes in Chinatown, Little Italy and the Bowery.

You had one of the highest case clearance rates in the entire department. Two-time All American collegiate wrestler. Your mother committed suicide when you were just seven years old. She took her own life shortly after your father walked out on you both."

Birch felt like a pile driver had struck him in the gut. He had felt so ashamed of his mother's death, as though as her son, he wasn't worth living for. Latimer was telling him things Birch hadn't even shared with his wife and son.

Latimer regarded Birch with genuine sadness in his eyes. "I guess it was all too much for her to handle. It must have been horrible for you, as a young boy, to lose one parent, let alone two." Latimer gave a deep sigh. "Yet, despite all this, you endured, Thomas." Latimer resumed his recital. "Previously married to Suzanne, with one child, Justin. A Patriots fan." Latimer gave a confident smile. "Well, we're going to have to change that."

Birch tensed at the mention of Justin's name, but remained silent, shocked at what Latimer knew about him.

"You were a hardworking detective, Thomas, but never got the accolades you deserved."

"I don't go looking for accolades," Birch replied. "I know what I have done."

Latimer nodded. "Very honorable of you. Is it true in all your years in the force, you've never once fired your handgun?"

Birch jolted back in time, just a few hours, and again felt the hardwood floor under his knees, the coldness of the barrel of his own gun pressing against his temple. He came back to the present, yet his mind felt hollow, detached, unsure as to how he found himself inside the four walls of Francis Latimer's office.

"Maybe you are too honorable." Latimer continued. "You spent two years in prison after an Internal Affairs investigation uncovered police corruption directly involving you. You pleaded not guilty and vigorously denied all charges. Even some of your fellow officers and detectives testified against you. While you were in prison, your wife filed for divorce after fifteen years of marriage, took your son, Justin with her, and sold the family home."

There was no smile on Latimer's face as he described intimately the dismantling of Birch's life. "And while they now live in an exclusive riverside apartment in Back Bay, Boston, courtesy of some plastic surgeon your wife latched on to during your imprisonment, you now currently reside in a converted boathouse that you rent at a reduced rate from a charitable neighbor."

Birch's gut tightened at this new revelation. Despite trying his hardest to find out where she and Justin had gone, Birch had been thwarted by Suzanne's high-paid lawyers. While he didn't have the means or the money to locate them, Latimer obviously did, and had.

Latimer didn't relent, twisting the knife of resentment and failure Birch felt, deeper into his heart. "I guess from what you earn as a dishwasher in a local diner in Cold Spring, Thomas, means you can't compete against four thousand square feet of opulence spread out over two floors, with unrivaled views of the Charles River, *and* season tickets behind the dugout at Fenway Park."

If it were true, the answer was simple: Birch couldn't compete when it came to his son's new life.

"I could go on. There is plenty more in the file Max compiled on you."

"Compiled on me?" Birch felt a mix of shock, anger and confusion as he glared at the red folder on the desk.

"They burned you, Thomas. Your fellow detectives within the hierarchy of your own police department."

Deep in his gut, Birch knew it to be true, despite not wanting to accept it. Even his friends outside of the law enforcement community had disowned him. Turned their backs on him. Two years spent lying on an uncomfortable bunk in a tiny prison cell staring up at the ceiling gave Birch plenty of time to reflect about past loyalties and betrayals. He was totally alone. Even phone calls from his lawyer had stopped. The evidence against him, though disputed by Birch, was undefeatable. No grounds for appeal, so he was told.

Birch's eyes drifted back to the silver-framed photo of Latimer's daughter.

"You see, Thomas, I need someone like you," Latimer continued, watching Birch very closely. "Someone who has experienced such loss as I am experiencing now. Someone who is a survivor, who can be discrete, resourceful, and has connections."

"My connections, as you just put it, all 'burned me.' I have nothing."

"Loyalty is a hard trait to find these days." Latimer slid the photo frame of his daughter across the desk toward Birch. "But Lindsay, my daughter, is an only child. She is everything to me. I imagine it's the same for you with Justin."

Birch continued looking at the photo. The girl was certainly pretty, had a natural allure about her, which would attract its fair share of wanted *and* unwanted attention.

"Once again, talk to the police." Birch dragged himself to his feet. "I'm sorry, but I can't really help you." The room suddenly felt cramped and airless. Birch looked around for the exit, and spotted the office door. It seemed farther away than he remembered.

Latimer's fingers suddenly shifted from the red folder to the green one, and he pushed it a few inches across the desk toward Birch, without saying anything.

"I'm not interested in money," Birch said glancing back down at the green folder. Money wouldn't coax Justin back. Then again, Birch used to think he couldn't buy his son's trust and admiration, but apparently someone had in Boston.

"I know, Thomas," Latimer replied. "Because if you were interested in money, you wouldn't have ended up in prison."

Birch felt a building suspicion in his gut as he continued staring down at the green folder. "What's this, then?"

"Something that might sway your decision." Latimer reached across the desk and tapped the green file with his finger. "Believe me. In here is the only thing you want, Thomas, the only thing that is important in your life right now." Latimer slid the file forward a few more inches toward Birch, but just out of Birch's reach. "What I have here will bring your son back to you."

Birch continued staring at the file, bewildered.

A cunning smile slowly spread across Latimer's face. "Inside this file is your salvation, Thomas."

Birch frowned. "Salvation?"

Latimer's eyes narrowed into a devilish stare. "Total, and irrefutable proof of your innocence."

Chapter 6 – Dumpster

There was definitely a rank smell coming from the steel dumpster.

A decaying stench that went far beyond the usual overripe stink of rotting vegetables, or rancid meat.

With the heavy lid closed and the midday heat hitting eighty degrees, whatever was inside the steel box was getting well and truly cooked.

To open the lid and take a look inside, or to not open the lid, and wait until her partner returned? It was the dilemma Patrol Officer Juliana Rosa was wrestling with as she stood in the narrow alleyway behind a strip of takeout restaurants, bubble tea stores, and Dim Sum houses deep in the heart of Chinatown, a block east of Columbus Park.

She had already spoken to the restaurant owner who had called it in. He had come outside first thing this morning to empty more trash from the previous evening and noticed the foul smell coming from the dumpster. Daniel Hicks, Rosa's partner, had gone to get coffee, the result of a coin toss as to who would be the one to take a look inside the dumpster. Needless to say, Rosa had lost the bet. However, she wanted to wait until Hicks returned—just in case.

But it had been twenty minutes, and still no sign of Hicks. Rosa couldn't wait any longer. Slipping on latex gloves, she approached the dumpster, resigned to the fact it was probably a dead rat trapped inside the sweltering heat of the steel box.

The dumpster, dented, with peeling paint and blotched with rust, sat against one wall next to the back door of the restaurant. Through the screen door of the kitchen, Rosa could see shapes milling around inside, heard the clang of pots and pans being bashed, the air heavy with the hot oily smell of Chinese food being prepared for the lunchtime rush.

Rosa got within three feet before she was hit by an invisible ring of stench surrounding the dumpster. Covering her nose and mouth with one hand, she forced herself forward, wondering if her appetite for food would ever return after this.

Jeez! The smell was god-awful. Reaching out with her other gloved hand, she gripped the edge of the steel lid. A thick chain dangled loosely to one side, with a heavy padlock looped through the links.

This was no rat, Rosa thought, as she hesitated, in two minds. It had to be something larger. She felt a glimmer of dread build up inside her. Coupled with the smell, it made her want to vomit. She pressed her hand firmer over her nose and mouth. It was no use though. The smell had a solidness to it, like it was entwining itself in her hair, seeping into the pores of her face, pushing through her tightly closed fingers, invading her sinuses, and coating the back of her throat.

Rosa went to lift the lid—then stopped.

There was a sound, a metallic hum, coming from inside. Maybe it was a large cat, a scavenger that had been digging through last night's food scraps, had somehow been trapped, and was slowly being baked alive.

Rosa listened intently. It didn't sound like a cat's mournful wail, however. The sound seemed fluid, moving around inside the steel walls, resonating off the sides. The lid was heavy, and much to her disdain, Rosa now realized she was going to need *both* hands to lift it.

"Damn it!" she hissed as she pulled her other hand from her face and buried her nose and mouth deep into her shoulder, trying to escape the stench as best she could.

Rusted hinges squealed in protest as Rosa slowly hoisted the lid upward.

Quickly, her eyes scanned inside the steel box, caught a glimpse of something before she gasped in shock. Suddenly, an angry black cloud swarmed up and into her face. She felt tiny legs dance across her forehead, cheeks, across her eyes, nose, and mouth. A solid fist of stink punched her in the nose, flooded her throat before spilling deep into her lungs.

Panicking, she let go of the lid.

It slammed with a loud metallic bang as she recoiled. Rosa spluttered and coughed up one of the huge flies that had flown into her mouth. Waving her hands about her, the swarm of flies soon dispersed. She took a moment to compose herself, grateful her partner wasn't here to see her reaction.

Rosa wiped her lips and spat out the foul distaste she had in her mouth and throat. She glanced back at the steel dumpster, her mind playing back the brief glimpse of what she had seen lying inside. Green plastic trash bags piled high. Some bloated, some split open, watery yellow mush oozing out. Then a pelt of white fur, partially covered, wedged among the mound of bags. It was a cat, dead. Its body almost completely covered, the white fur along its spine just visible.

Great, a dead cat. Rosa could feel her stomach churn at the thought of opening the lid again and removing it.

Chapter 7 – Betrayal

"You were framed, Thomas," Latimer said. "Set up by people way above your pay grade. In this file is all the proof, all the evidence required to quash all convictions against you. Falsified witness statements, fabricated evidence, proof deliberately withheld from your defense." Latimer once more indicated the green file. "It's all here."

Latimer leaned forward and fixed his gaze on Birch, his voice low and coarse like gravel. "Find my daughter, bring her back to me, and you'll get everything. You have my word."

Birch didn't move. His feet remained firmly rooted to the floor. His eyes cut from the green file, to Latimer, then back to the file. "You are bluffing."

"I wish I were." Latimer reclined back in his chair with the confidence of someone who just pulled checkmate on Bobby Fischer.

Birch wasn't convinced. "Prove it." Birch glared first at Latimer, then at Maxine Brodie. "Prove it. Both of you."

Latimer nodded at Brodie.

"Carl Hagen." Brodie took the lead.

"Hagen?" Birch replied, referring to his old captain at the Fifth Precinct.

"Hagen was instrumental in your demise. You had your suspicions about him, his corrupt dealings, but you couldn't prove it." Brodie shrugged. "Hagen wanted you out of the way, to protect himself and his corrupt network."

"Why?" Birch said, his mind swirling. It was all too much to take in. "Why would he do this?"

Latimer held up a hand toward Brodie, before addressing

Birch again. "The reasons are fully explained in great detail in the information we have gathered. However, for the time being, let's just say Carl Hagen needed a scapegoat and you were a convenient one for him."

"To throw the hounds off the scent, so to speak," Brodie added. "Internal Affairs wanted a head, so Hagen gave them yours. I did the research, gathered the evidence. It's all there in the file."

"So you're a lawyer too?" Birch replied, more spite in his voice than intended. But he was angry. Two years of his life, in prison. His name, his reputation, all trashed. His career as a detective dragged through the mud, forever tarnished, labeled a corrupt cop, branded a convicted felon, a stain never to be erased. It was the only lasting memory his son, Justin, would remember him by. What Brodie had said was true. Birch had a suspicion Hagen had something to do with putting him in jail, but no one, including his own lawyer, would believe him. His lawyer said if anyone had framed Birch, then it was more likely payback by the Romano crime family from New Jersey for putting their son, Vincent, in jail for a double homicide.

Birch stared at the green file again. It was thick, full, not just with paper. It was crammed full of hope, of purpose, of a future for Birch just when he thought he had none. It was his ticket to getting Justin back.

Something worth living for.

"You have nothing to lose, Thomas," Brodie said,

Birch looked longingly at the file. He had been thrown a lifeline, tenuous, but something to cling to nonetheless. He had nothing else to lose. Except his life, which to him, had no real value, or meaning—until now.

He gave Latimer a slight nod. "Okay. You win."

Francis Latimer looked relieved. "Good. Thank you, Thomas."

"But it will be done my way," Birch added, addressing them both. "My rules." He glanced pointedly at Brodie. He didn't trust either of them, but was more skeptical of Brodie. "And I don't need anyone looking over my shoulder, questioning what I'm doing or checking up on me."

"Agreed," Latimer replied immediately. "However, you will need Max's initial help, to bring you up to speed, provide you with background information about Lindsay, her last movements, circle of friends and the like. All the same information that was provided to the other investigators."

"I will give you an update on their progress too," Max said. "Not that there is much. But it will save you the time of going back over old ground."

Birch nodded. Yet, he knew intimately as a detective, most cases were solved by repeatedly going back over "old ground," old facts, the evidence, scene reports, and reinterviewing witnesses—any and everyone connected to the victim. Rarely did anything new come to light to miraculously solve a case that wasn't already there in front of you at the beginning. Persistence, hard work, and dogged determination solved cases. Shoe leather and knuckle skin, the two things every cop in New York City should have a shortage of from walking the streets, circling back, and repeatedly knocking on doors.

"Max has been liaising with all third parties involved," Latimer added as he rose from behind the desk. "Anything you need, Thomas, please let her know. Anything."

Birch regarded the man. There was one obvious possibility Birch always considered first, in all cases like these, no matter how badly the family didn't want to hear it. "I don't want to sound bleak, but I always deal in the worst-case scenario first."

Latimer nodded resolutely. "You think like me, Thomas. All my life I have never hoped for the outcome I have been chasing. I've faced life expecting everything I do, will fail and I will lose. I have never hoped for the best. I've always planned for the worst, every time. I find the bitterness of disappointment a lot more palatable that way. And the wins, the victories, are all the more sweeter when they do happen."

"So you have no preconceptions about finding Lindsay?"

"My wife does, but I do not," Latimer conceded. "If what you're suggesting is that Lindsay could be dead, and I should be prepared for the worst outcome, then my answer is yes." Latimer took a deep breath and let it out slowly. "Life is sorrow. Here today, gone tomorrow."

Birch tilted his head questioningly.

"It's a verse from a song I'm particularly fond of, Thomas." Latimer offered a slight smile despite the morose direction the conversation had taken.

"I see," said Birch. "Then we are all on the same page." Birch indicated toward the file on the desk. "And if she is dead? What happens to me? Will I still get the information contained in the file?"

Latimer's eyes faded to a dead glaze, and a brittle iciness crept across his face. "Let's just hope for everyone's sake she isn't."

Chapter 8 – Dead Cat

"Hey, Rosa!"

With her hands on her knees, Rosa glanced sideways. Her partner, Hicks was ambling his way along the alleyway toward her, carrying two large takeout cups of coffee. "If I knew you were going to have some kind of caffeine deprivation fit while I was gone, I would have been quicker."

He must have witnessed my fight with the swarm of flies, she thought, wiping spittle from her lips.

"Ran into Riggs and Bashir on Mulberry and—"

Rosa swiftly held up a hand, like she was halting traffic, silencing her partner's endless drivel of wise-cracking comments she knew would ensue. She coughed again and spat into a nearby drain grate.

"Jeez," Hicks said, a look of concern now on his face. "What the hell happened?"

Rosa said nothing, just gestured with her outstretched hand, beckoning Hicks forward with her coffee.

Quickly, Hicks thrust one of the takeout cups into Rosa's hand.

She took a mouthful, swirled it around before spitting it out into the drain. She stood upright, took a deep breath, then swallowed a mouthful of coffee, relieved the foul taste was gone. If she could snort the coffee, to get the lingering stench out of her nostrils, she would have.

"Thanks," she said, wiping her mouth on the back of her hand. She motioned toward the dumpster. "Just got attacked by a swarm of flies from inside that thing."

Hicks smiled. "Don't they have flies in Maryland, in the town you came from?" he said with a look of smugness. "So what did you find?"

"Dead cat," Rosa said, unsure now if it was what she had actually seen. Could one dead cat smell that bad? She took another mouthful of coffee, grateful for the strong, bitter aftertaste. "Let's take a look again." Rosa finished her coffee, handed the empty cup to Hicks who placed it with his own down on a low ledge.

"This time I'll open the lid and take a look inside," Hicks said, pulling on his own gloves. "You've only been in New York, for what? Six months now? It's summer. The heat brings out the worst of the jobs we get stuck with." Hicks moved toward the dumpster, stretching latex over each hand as though he were about to perform some life-saving operation. "There was this one-woman last summer, been dead in her apartment for over a week, with the air conditioner off." Hicks shook his head. "Gotta tell ya. The smell from—"

"Hicks, let's just get this over with," Rosa said, cutting him off again.

They took up positions next to the dumpster. "Just wait a few moments though, to give the flies time to clear," Rosa said.

Hicks nodded. "Smells real bad already." Hicks hoisted the lid and they both hurriedly turned their faces away.

Another swarm of flies buzzed out, much fewer than before though.

Hicks turned back to take a look, then gagged when the full brunt of the smell hit him. "For the love of all that is holy!" Hicks cringed.

Rosa waited for most of the flies to clear before turning back and bending forward over the lip of the dumpster to take a better look inside. She saw the pelt of fur, as before, protruding up between a tumble of trash bags.

Her breath caught in her throat, not because of the smell, which was much worse now. But because it wasn't fur. It looked more like…hair. Human hair.

"Ain't no fricking cat," Hicks mumbled.

Rosa glanced at Hicks. Their eyes met. He looked pale, his face drawn tight. Rosa could tell from the look in his eyes, he knew exactly what they had found.

Just barely visible among the tumble of trash bags was a human scalp, blond-haired, the back of someone's head, the rest of them buried facedown under rotting garbage.

"Use the latch," Rosa said to Hicks as she reached out her hand, careful not to tumble in, and pulled one of the trash bags aside.

Hicks latched back the lid and together they carefully began to move aside the trash bags.

"Oh, Jeez." Hicks said, ashen faced.

They unearthed the back of a neck, bumps of a spine visible under the skin. Next the shoulders came into view: thin, supple, mottled yellow and purple, the skin lifeless, devoid of all its glowing sheen. It was a female, thin-boned.

"Wait!" Hicks pulled back. "We should call it in. Get the detectives to take a look before we disturb too much."

"You go and call it in. I'll see if I can find any ID."

Hicks nodded, then gratefully retreated away from the dumpster and reached for his police radio.

Careful, so as to disturb as little as possible, Rosa gently shifted more of the trash bags aside. The woman was definitely dead, and had been for a while Rosa guessed from the smell and the bloating. There was bruising along the backs of her arms, and some of her hair was matted with dried blood. She wore a pink top. Out of habit, Rosa felt for a pulse along the neckline.

Nothing.

Tentatively Rosa pushed aside more trash bags to reveal the woman's waist, then buttocks. She wore blue jeans, expensive, with a designer label stitched on the back pocket, where something was protruding. Rosa held her breath, stretched farther into the dumpster and tugged out a thin, pink purse wedged inside the woman's back pocket.

Rosa stepped back from the dumpster and opened the purse. Half a face peeked out from the card slot inside. A stray fly landed on the back of Rosa's hand and she angrily shook it off then slid out a New York State driver's license. The photo was of a young woman: blonde hair, blue eyes, fresh-faced, alive, smiling at the camera.

Rosa read the name.

Lindsay Latimer.

Chapter 9 – The Call

After they had both left, Eve gathered up all of Luke's clothes, shoes, and personal belongings in a large trash bag.

Next she went back into the kitchen, slid open the window near the fire escape, and grabbed Sam. She held him close, nuzzling her face deep into his soft fur, whispering she was sorry. Sam's loyalty and love was unconditional—provided he was regularly fed.

The cat wrestled free from Eve's arms and skillfully landed on all fours on the floor, and began circling his empty cat bowl, squawking.

After feeding Sam, Eve went back into the bedroom, stripped down the bed completely, bundling everything together, including pillows, into another large trash bag before marching back out to the kitchen. Pausing at the refrigerator, she tore off the photos stuck to the door with magnets, of what was once a daily reminder of how far their growing, loving relationship had come. Now Eve saw each photo as nothing but a chronology of Luke's skillful deceit and deception. Included in that was the twelve-month gym membership card she had only used twice, a gift from Luke last Christmas, a not so subtle jibe.

Eve tossed the stack of photos into a trash bag, before trudging through the open apartment doorway dragging both bags behind her. In the corridor, near the stairwell she found the large garbage cute. She grabbed the pull handle, opened the hinged door, stuffed each bag in one at a time, and slammed it shut. Somehow, the fading sound of the trash bags clanging and banging down the steel shaft, before reaching the garbage trolley deep in the basement eight stories below, felt strangely liberating and reassuring to Eve.

Marching back into her apartment, she closed and double-locked the door, went into the bedroom and sat down on the bare mattress. Sam slinked in, leapt up next to her and began sniffing the mattress. Perhaps she would burn it, get a new one, remove all traces of the treachery and her own stupidity it was now stained with.

Eve closed her eyes tightly and grimaced. How could she have been so trusting? So naive? She thought the relationship would work, despite the obvious age difference. There was a genuine connection there, between her and Luke…or so she believed. Wasn't it there? She'd felt it when they had first met. Eve had nurtured it, in this very room, in this very bed. Given herself wholly to a man as she had done before only to be betrayed yet again.

Holding back tears, she opened her eyes and glanced toward the window, heard the reassuring commotion of the city below. It was Eve's antidote, always had been—the city. She would allow it to smother her again, feel its protective embrace, let it distract her from the darkness and sadness she had felt at times. She would throw herself deeper into her work too, swim farther below the surface, mask the personal pain she now felt with the pain felt by others. It usually worked, except on those rare occasions when she went too deep below the surface, swam at the depths where the worst of the bottom feeders roamed, the creatures who rarely ventured toward the daylight unless they were caught then dragged up to the surface by Eve.

In a few days she would feel better. Work always served as a reliable distraction from the flaws and imperfections of her personal life.

Eve wiped her eyes, then scratched Sam behind the ears as he brushed up beside her. She didn't have time to feel sad or depressed. That would come later. When her anger had subsided and was replaced with sadness.

Eve's cell phone rang and she unclipped it from her belt without checking the caller ID. "Detective Sommers," she said.

"Sommers, it's Captain Hagen."

Eve's skin bristled; her mind clicked into gear. "Yes, Captain."

"Where are you?"

Eve could sense a rare tinge of strain in her boss' voice. "East Village."

"Good. You need to get over to a crime scene. A woman has been found dead in a dumpster near Columbus Park."

Eve listened as Hagen relayed her the location. It was just two blocks away from the Fifth Precinct, and six blocks from where she lived. But why was he calling her? She had a full caseload, and this sounded like a routine job one of the junior detectives in Homicide Squad could handle. It was usually the chief of detectives who assigned cases. "Sir, shouldn't—"

"No, Sommers," Hagen cut her off, as though he had anticipated her question. His voice sounded annoyed, a forced whisper, like he didn't want to be overheard. "You are a senior detective, Sommers. I want you to personally take charge of this one."

Eve could tell there was something personal for Hagen about this particular case.

"Report to me directly on what you find." There was a pause before Hagen continued. "The dead woman has been identified as Lindsay Latimer."

The name didn't ring any bells for Eve.

"She is the daughter of a very prominent New York family. Francis Latimer, is her father," Hagen continued, frustration evident in his voice as though Eve should have known who Francis Latimer was.

Now it made sense to Eve why Hagen had called her directly and not the chief of detectives. Hagen had intervened in the allocation of the case. He was well within his rights to do so as commanding officer of the precinct. However, it was highly unusual and a first for Eve.

"I want you to tread very carefully with this one," Hagen warned. "This case will be sensitive."

To Eve, a body was still a body, another crime to be solved like any other. It was true the case could attract additional media attention, including political interest. Cases involving the rich and influential always did, as if the wealthy were somehow insulated from everyday crime. However, for Eve, no special treatment would be dished out to the Latimer family. But she wasn't about to tell this to Carl Hagen. There were well-founded rumors Hagen had political aspirations of his own.

"I'll be there," Eve said before ending the call.

Chapter 10 – Hagen

Carl Hagen slid the cell phone away and regarded himself in the mirror as he finished buttoning up his shirt.

It was the right decision, to appoint Eve Sommers in charge. She was new to the precinct, had been there only six months after transferring from Brooklyn, but that was an advantage. She knew very little about him, could be molded into a real asset in the future—if she played her cards right.

Another smile in the mirror. Truth be known, he couldn't give a damn about Lindsay Latimer, other than her untimely, or rather timely death, presented another opportunity to escalate his plans.

He hadn't come this far just to come this far. The chief of police position was his next upward step, and certainly not his last.

Careful management of the case, and of Eve Sommers, was going to be essential if any possible stumbles along his carefully planned path were to be avoided.

The sound of the shower running in the bathroom stopped, and Hagen continued to preen himself in front of the mirror. He had a good wife, solid and loyal. His two children, a son and a daughter, both in college studying reputable degrees rounded off the picture-perfect family persona voters loved. Solid, conservative, decisive. Crime was out of control in this city, there was no question about it, and the hierarchy of City Hall had no clue how to bring it under control. The current chief of police was weak, too compliant. Likeable enough, but a man with no ambition who had been promoted into the position simply because he was a safe, impotent alternative who dutifully nodded his head, followed orders, and didn't ruffle any feathers. A puppet for the mayor and the governor, both of whom pandered to the minorities and allowed the city to be overrun by the criminals and civil libertarians. A return to strong family values and firm policing was what was needed. And Carl Hagen was just the right person to deliver.

Hagen slid on his cuff links and tugged on each shirt cuff to smooth out any creases. He turned one way, then the other, admiring himself again in the large mirror. At nearly sixty years old, he couldn't help but think he looked good. Very marketable for the political arena. Tall, lean, and fit, he cut a striking figure. He always thought of himself as a modern-day Cary Grant but with gray hair. However, time wasn't on his side if he was going to become mayor first, then, governor. The stepping-stone to police chief was just that; a step out of law enforcement and into the arena where the real power was.

And then? Hagen smiled to his reflection. Pennsylvania Avenue.

The bathroom door opened, and a young woman padded out wearing only a cheeky grin. Reaching Hagen, she wrapped her arms around his waist from behind, and whispered into his ear. "I don't know where you get the stamina from. You were like a raging bull."

The remark pleased Hagen to no end. He looked, felt, and performed like men half his age. He knew it, the string of young lovers he kept on tap knew it, while his wife didn't. Making love to his wife was like sleeping with a corpse. Something no man, especially one of such high political ambition, should endure. Washington didn't only offer conquests of the political kind for Hagen.

The young woman nibbled Hagen's ear while he knotted his tie.

"There's something for you on the nightstand to help pay for your college tuition this semester," Hagen said.

Immediately the young woman peeled away and went to the bed. There on the nightstand, next to the room-service menu, sat a pile of crisp, smooth bills she greedily picked up, and began counting. "This is more than usual," she said with delight, her eyes fixated on the ten faces of Benjamin Franklin.

"I pay well," Hagen replied, turning to her. "And I expect your continued loyalty and discretion in return."

The woman turned front-on to Hagen, unabashed by her total nakedness. "Of course."

Hagen nodded, feeling as though he was performing his civic duty as well as fostering America's college education system by financially supporting a number of fine young women, like her. "Don't forget to use the service elevator when you leave."

"Sure."

Hagen slid into his jacket and paused at the door, turning to the young woman. "You vote don't you?"

The woman shrugged. "I turned eighteen last year. Haven't given it much thought."

"I'm running for mayor soon. Make sure you vote for me."

The young woman smiled brazenly, battered her eyelids and fanned herself with the hundred dollar bills. "You keep paying me like this, and I'll vote for you all the way to the White House," she replied in a thick, southern belle accent, unaware of how foreshadowing her comment was.

Hagen gave her a wink, "That's my gal."

Chapter 11 – Abuse

"Would you say she is rebellious?" Birch asked.

"I wouldn't say 'rebellious,' more like she is strong willed, has a certain moral standing," Maxine Brodie replied.

"I'm just asking for your honest opinion of her." Birch drank his coffee as they sat in a booth in a coffee shop a block from the Latimer offices where Max had already given Birch a summary on Lindsay Latimer. Lindsay was a Sociology Sophomore at NYU, twenty-years-old and lived in a company paid apartment in East Village. Lindsay enjoyed the money and limelight associated with being a Latimer, but preferred not to live in the sprawling, ten-thousand-square-foot family penthouse on Park Avenue.

"And what makes you think she has actually disappeared, not just gone to ground, or perhaps run away?"

"Because this is so out of character for her." Max went on to explain that Lindsay and her father are very close, so much so, they would communicate by text, three to four times a day. Nothing dramatic, just how the day was, questions about university, when would she next be over for dinner to see her mother. Then five days ago all communication ceased. Nothing. Her cell phone went dark.

"What about her friends?" Birch asked.

"She keeps a close circle of people around her. We did ask them but they all said the same thing: they too had not seen nor heard from her in five days. It was as though she suddenly ghosted everyone."

"Kidnapped?"

Max shook her head. "No one has contacted us."

"Boyfriend?"

"Not that the family is aware off. Lindsay is very dedicated to her studies." Max leaned forward. "Lindsay told me once she's not interested in any kind of relationship at the moment."

"Things may have changed. Maybe she recently met someone, someone different who influenced her."

Max nodded. "Perhaps. However, the other investigators have found nothing that would suggest a serious relationship."

"So what exactly have they found out about Lindsay's disappearance for the money the Latimer family is paying them?"

"Not much. Nothing concrete. I'll have the reports delivered to your apartment so you can go through them." She had given Birch the keys to a corporate apartment in the city, one of several the company owned and made available for executive staff and VIPs. "It's all standard lines of inquiry they have been following. Remember, we're trying to do this as quietly as possible."

"What about her apartment," Birch said. "I'd like to take a look it."

Max nodded. "It's been gone through. Still no clues as to where she's gone. I'll get you the key and address." Max hesitated, something on her mind. "We're at a dead end at the moment," she finally confessed. "We simply do not know where she is."

"Why did you pick me?" Birch asked. "I don't even know how you or Francis Latimer even know I exist."

"I didn't know anything about you until I started researching you."

"Then how did you compile all this information of me? Surely it would have been more than five days ago, before Lindsay went missing?"

Max nodded. "I cannot tell you anything much, other than

about three months ago, Francis gave me your name and asked me to look into your background, and why you were sent to jail."

"Does he know Carl Hagen personally?" Birch asked. "Are they enemies or something? I can't believe Latimer would be doing this out of the goodness of his heart for me; he doesn't seem like the type."

"I'm not privy as to what his motivations are, other than finding his daughter." She looked Birch in the eye. "Find Lindsay Latimer, and all your questions will be answered."

"What about sexual abuse?"

"No!" Max almost yelled, as though someone poured scalding hot coffee on her hand.

A few customers turned and looked in their direction.

"Definitely not."

"How can you be so certain?" Birch asked, lowering his voice. "Plenty of people run away because of family abuse. They vanish, start a new life, and assume a new identity."

"You mean abuse by her father?"

"Or perhaps by another close family member."

"No," Max said firmly. "I can't imagine her father would..." her voice trailed off.

"It could explain a lot," Birch said. "Did Lindsay keep a diary or a journal? Maybe she wrote down how she had been feeling, if she wasn't happy and why."

"I don't know. I certainly didn't see her carrying one or writing in one. Then again, I really haven't seen much of her in the last twelve months." Max frowned, thinking back. "Her parents have been seeing less and less of her over the past twelve months. She's become somewhat of a recluse."

"You said she was in daily contact with her father."

"All by text," Max replied. "I remember Francis making a

comment a few months back saying Lindsay kept cancelling family dinners and events. She had told him she wanted to concentrate more on her studies at NYU."

"Being withdrawn, avoiding family gatherings is a classic symptom of abuse," Birch suggested. "Maybe there is more to this father-daughter relationship than anyone wants to admit."

Chapter 12 – Size 9

Moving deftly past the suspicious eye of the white-gloved doorman, Birch crossed the gleaming marble lobby, and using a spare keycard Maxine Brodie had given him, rode the elevator up to the fourteenth floor.

Stepping out into the private entrance, Birch quickly surveyed what eight million dollars crammed into a three-thousand-square-foot corner apartment looked like.

The apartment had the classic, elegant feel of new wealth, without the gaudy, fleeting vanity of fast money. There was a living room with gas fireplace, separate dining room, galley kitchen, guest bathroom, and a north wing with three large bedrooms—two with adjoining bathrooms—all walled with an abundance of glass windows, furnished in clean natural colors and textures, sandwiched between high ceilings, crown moldings, and rosewood herringbone floors.

Donning latex gloves and moving with infinite care, Birch searched every drawer, closet, cabinet, nook and cranny. The bathroom off the master bedroom had only a few cosmetics, not the usual plethora of bottles and tubes Birch would have expected. In a cabinet under the sink he found bleach, bars of soap, and a bottle of contact lens solution.

Fruit and vegetables, bruised, wilting, and shrunken sat in the drawers of a Sub-Zero refrigerator in the kitchen. Plant-based dairy and opened jars of Moroccan and Indian curry pastes, all well past their expiration dates, formed neat rows on the shelves.

Returning to the master bedroom, Birch sat down on the bed and looked around the room again. Absent were the usual laptop or cell phone cables plugged into the wall sockets. Except for the outdated contents of the refrigerator, the place looked lived-in, *still* lived in. There was a faint, fragrant smell, the smell of Lindsay Latimer, he surmised. Subtle, not overpowering, like the beach, fresh and clean. Nothing seemed out of the ordinary.

A paperback book sat on the bedside table and Birch picked it up. *Animal Farm* by George Orwell. He had read it himself in the tenth grade, written an essay on it too. The name of a bookstore was on the price sticker on the back cover.

Getting up, Birch walked into the walk-in closet again. Pairs of shoes in various styles were neatly pigeonholed in a tall, custom-built rack. Taking several pairs out from the top row, Birch examined them. It seemed Lindsay Latimer was a size seven. Placing the shoes back in their slots, Birch turned his hand over and rubbed his fingers together.

Dust.

He pulled another pair out from the next row down and held them up to the light. The straps and toes were covered in a fine layer of dust. It was then he noticed an empty row lower down in the rack, at waist height. Below, more shoes were neatly stored. Reaching down, he pulled out and examined the shoes from the lower section, noticing the style of shoe in this section was slightly different. Less heel, less strappy, less extravagant—all still extremely expensive-looking—but more practical. And none were covered in dust, their surfaces clean and shiny.

Birch pulled out all the shoes from the lower section and lined them up on the plush carpet.

Every pair was a size nine.

It was six blocks in a straight line, down East Fourth Street, heading west toward where the New York University campus sat at the southern edge of Washington Square Park.

At a moderate pace, the half a mile walk would usually take just over ten minutes. But Thomas Birch wasn't walking at a moderate pace. He wanted to take everything in, see the world through a young woman's eyes. How would she walk with a backpack slung over one shoulder, headphones covering her ears, shutting out the cacophony of bustling life around her? Did she favor one particular side of the street? Where did she stop? What stores did she pause and stare in the front window? What took her fancy in the myriad of coffee shops, juice bars, takeout food, and delis that lined both sidewalks?

These were all important questions that needed answering if Birch was going to build a profile, a mental picture of Lindsay Latimer's daily life, her habits, her routine, that could lead him to her.

Birch was still a cop, would always be despite not having the ability or resources to now go door to door, badge in hand, with authority to get answers, demand access to security camera footage. The harsh reality was, this was a new experience for him. He was walking the streets alone, hoping to catch a break, and was going to have to become more inventive, less orthodox if he was going to find her.

A bohemian-looking coffee shop sat across the street. With a colorful swirling façade of neon yellow, orange and red, and a bright chalkboard menu on the sidewalk, Birch wondered if this was where Lindsay Latimer bought her coffee. He pictured her sitting at one of the windows tables inside, watching the world pass by while reading about Mr. Jones, the owner of Manor farm, and the three pigs, Old Major, Napoleon, and Snowball, marveling at the subtle cleverness of George Orwell and his allegory of the Russian Revolution.

Lindsay Latimer didn't have a car, and to Birch she didn't seem the type to bike the short distance to NYU. She seemed more likely to enjoy the walk among the smells and sights, feel and touch the East Village from a more granular perspective.

He preferred walking the streets when he was cop too, discovering an entirely different world as he often did. New York had varying layers to it, different levels of social topography you couldn't see from the limited view of a squad car window or tourist bus or from the balcony of an Upper East Side apartment dominated by a Central Park view.

Two years was a long time in New York, while Birch was in jail. Much had changed, and some things hadn't. New high-rises clawed skyward, some impossibly narrow, rising precariously, seeming to teeter on the verge of toppling over, as the city pushed its burgeoning population vertically. Heat rippled off the concrete and back up into Birch's face as he tried to say in the shadows of scaffolding as much as possible, his ears throbbing from the constant noise of jackhammering and car horns blaring. The air was hot and misty with plumes of construction dust billowing out from the interior of gutted facades, the city in a constant flux of death and rebirth, tearing and rebuilding.

He sidestepped plastic trash bags heaped almost waist high on the sidewalk and continued his journey.

There was a Whole Foods four blocks farther south, and the Fifth Precinct lay another mile beyond. Despite New York being so huge and varied, Birch knew most New Yorkers rarely ventured beyond a few blocks of their home. They were creatures of habit, buying coffee from the same store, where the barista knows your name. Shopping locally at the same deli or convenience store. Visiting the same grocery stores, buying and eating the same staples week in and week out. It was these daily, weekly habits and rituals, the endless wash, rinse, and repeat loop of human nature that made detective work easier. Not that it was ever easy in Birch's mind.

Birch continued walking in Lindsay's footsteps, noting the distinct lack of security cameras in the store fronts he passed. Farther along, Birch stopped again. Diagonally across the street, wedged in between a jujitsu studio and a travel goods store, was a large bookstore.

It was worth a shot. Dodging traffic, he crossed the street and was about to enter the bookstore, when his cell phone rang.

"Thomas, it's Max."

Birch paused under the store's awning. Despite the noise all around him, he could hear the dread in Maxine Brodie's voice. And when she spoke again, it was Birch who felt as though he had just plunged down an unsuspected rabbit hole.

"It's Lindsay—she's dead."

Chapter 13 – The Body

"Get her out of there, now," Eve said, addressing the two crime scene technicians.

All three of them stood at the dumpster, peering in at the body. To Eve, the sight was so much more disgusting than the smell. The thought of a person being left in a dumpster, discarded like trash, made her blood boil. No one deserved to be treated like garbage, and it made her even more determined to find who had done this to the young woman.

Farther back, the two patrol officers, Rosa and Hicks, stood watching proceedings. Police tape cordoned off both ends of the alleyway, preventing any likely traffic or nosy onlookers from entering.

"But shouldn't we wait—" one of the crime techs started to say, before Eve cut him off.

"Any evidence will be inside the dumpster. Removing her will make no difference. You won't be disturbing anything. I want to take a proper look at her."

Both techs exchanged glances, further infuriating Eve.

"I'll take full responsibility. Just get her out of there, now," Eve snapped.

The techs reluctantly nodded, spread out plastic sheeting on the ground around the dumpster to catch any debris that might dislodge from the body.

While they worked, Eve walked over to the two patrol officers. She had briefly spoken to them when she first arrived. She was pleased both officers had the sense to wear gloves.

"Who found this?" Eve held up the purse retrieved from the body.

Rosa spoke up. "I did."

"And you touched nothing else on the body?"

"No ma'am."

"Don't call me ma'am," Eve replied. "Detective will suffice."

"No, Detective," Rosa corrected herself.

"What about you?" Eve said, turning to Hicks.

"We touched nothing, Detective, just shifted a few trash bags aside to make certain she was dead. We found the purse in her back pocket."

Eve had already gone through the purse. Except for the driver's license, there was nothing. No cash. No credit cards. Nothing. "What about a cell phone?"

Rosa shook her head. "We didn't search the body any further. Just called it in."

A small crowd had gathered at one end of the alleyway, curious onlookers no doubt. Then Eve recognized one face: the man, who was standing next to a tall dark-haired woman, both of them looking on anxiously.

Eve addressed the two patrol officers. "Okay, I want each of you stationed at either end of this alleyway. Police tape means nothing. People will still try and come in."

Both Rosa and Hicks nodded and went to take up positions at each end of the alleyway while Eve approached the man and the woman.

"Detective, my name is Thomas—"

Eve cut Birch off with a look of annoyance. "I know who you are. You're a convicted felon. I read the newspapers too."

Maxine Brodie stepped forward. "I represent Francis Latimer; perhaps you've heard of him?"

Eve swiveled her irritation toward Brodie, then her brain suddenly registered the name. "No, I haven't heard of him," she lied, wondering why was it just because someone had money and influence should people automatically assume you know their name. The more alarming question for Eve was, how the hell did word get out about the victim's identity? She had barely been here a few minutes herself. Eve glanced over at Officer Rosa who was standing out of earshot. Their eyes met before Rosa hurriedly looked away.

"All we want to know is if the person you have found is a young woman called Lindsay Latimer," Brodie asked.

Eve was infuriated. Someone leaked the name, but she wasn't about to confirm anything with anyone. She rounded on Brodie. "Look, I don't know who *you* are or why you're here. But this is a police investigation. Stay away." Eve turned and began to walk back toward the dumpster, then called back to Birch and Brodie. "Either of you cross that tape, I'll have you *both* arrested."

The two techs had erected a crime scene barrier, shielding the dumpster from view, and had lain the body face up on the plastic sheeting. Eve squatted down beside the body, her attention drawn to the head and facial area first. Blonde hair was plastered across the face, stuck in place by blood that had dried to a crimson thatch. More dried blood trailed down one side of her neck and there was heavy bruising across the throat. To Eve it seemed as though someone had first struck the woman hard on the side on the head, then while she was down and disorientated, they proceeded to strangle her to death. An autopsy would reveal the cause of death.

Eve's eyes tracked farther downward. The woman was thin, too thin, in Eve's mind. Long limbs, narrow hands, the skin textured and creased, all veins and sinew. Eve paused and studied the body more closely. Then, with one gloved hand, she gently pulled away a clump of hair obscuring the face.

"What the…?" Eve breathed.

Moments later, Eve was dialing Hagen. "It's not her."

"What do you mean, 'it's not her'?"

Eve stood away from the body, her cell phone pressed to her ear, and watched as the crime scene techs went about their business. "It's not Lindsay Latimer." She could hear Hagen give an audible sigh of relief on the other end of the call.

"Good," Hagen replied.

Good? Eve gritted her teeth. There was nothing good about finding a dead person inside a dumpster or anywhere else for that matter. She held the driver's license in her hand, the fresh-faced, Lindsay Latimer smiling back at her.

"Who the hell said it was her, then?" Hagen asked, sounding slightly annoyed now, like he had been deliberately misled. He still hadn't asked Eve who the dead woman was. Eve knew it didn't matter to Hagen; it was unimportant. "A rookie mistake," Eve replied, looking at the driver's license in her hand. They had similar blonde hair, but that was where the similarities ended. The yet to be identified dead woman was older, mid-to-late-thirties perhaps, and certainly not a twenty-year-old as indicated by the driver's license. She was thin, almost emaciated, wore heavy makeup, either to camouflage the onslaught of ageing or to hide an abrasive life spent on the streets, surround by poor choices and an unforgiving environment. Eve had taken several photos of the woman with her cell phone. "My guess is the deceased is a hooker who stole Lindsay Latimer's purse, then met with her own fate by being robbed herself. All I found inside the purse was a driver's license."

Was it a pissed-off client? Maybe her pimp? To Eve it seemed like robbery, maybe even premeditated murder with any cash or credit cards a bonus. Someone may have intended to kill her.

The act of striking her on the head was designed to incapacitate her just long enough to do what the killer had planned. The final act of tossing her in the dumpster like trash was exactly that: the killer considered her to be garbage, and there were no security cameras in the alley.

"DNA will tell us who she is, if she is on the database," Eve said to Hagen. "Maybe we can pull some prints off the purse."

"Flick the case to a junior detective," Hagen said. "You have more important cases to work on."

"But, Captain, you asked—"

"It's not Lindsay Latimer," Hagen cut her off, his voice stern now. "Don't waste your time on this one." The line went dead.

Eve pulled her cell phone away and stared at it as though it had just bitten her on the ear. She glanced back to where Birch and Brodie were standing.

Eve made her way over and said bluntly to them both, "Who tipped you off? Either word travels fast or someone inside the police department contacted you to tell you a body has been found in a dumpster and it is Lindsay Latimer."

"Is it Lindsay?" Brodie asked.

"No it isn't," replied Eve. "Who told you it was?"

"It is a private matter," Brodie replied. "And thank you, Detective, for telling us it isn't her."

Eve noticed Brodie's eyes drop to the purse she was holding.

"Is that Lindsay's purse?" Brodie asked.

Eve held up the purse. "Do you recognize this as belonging to Lindsay Latimer?" Eve held Brodie's gaze for a moment, both women sizing each other up. "Her driver's license was found in it."

"Perhaps," Brodie replied.

"And why are you here?" Eve said turning to Birch.

Again Brodie took the lead. "Mr. Birch has been engaged by the Latimer family. Once again, it's a private matter." Brodie held out her hand. "Can I have a look at the purse?"

Eve shook her head. "It's evidence now. And where is Lindsay Latimer?" she asked. "I'm going to want to talk to her, find out how come her purse ended up in the possession of a dead woman."

"So this is a murder investigation?" Birch asked. "Who is the dead woman you found?"

"Why don't you tell me?" Eve replied, her voice abrasive. "You seem to think it was Lindsay Latimer. Where does she fit into all this?" Eve rounded on Birch. "Come to think of it, where do you fit into all of this?"

Brodie touched Birch's arm, pulling him away slightly, before giving Eve a cordial smile. "Thank you, Detective, for letting us know. Mr. Latimer will be pleased to know it wasn't his daughter."

"But it is someone's daughter," Eve replied. "And it matters to me."

Brodie conjured up a smile of condolence, that to Eve, seemed false.

"Not so fast," Eve replied. She affixed Birch with a cold stare. "I don't know why you are here or what private family business you are working on, but stay out of my lane, Birch."

Brodie stepped forward, angling herself between Eve and Birch. "Like I said, Detective, thank you for your help." Brodie nodded at Birch and they both turned and walked away.

Approaching the body, Eve noticed one of the crime scene techs motioning toward her. "There's something inside her mouth."

Eve squatted down next to the tech as they tilted the head of the woman and pulled down her jaw.

"It's wedged pretty well right at the back of the throat."

Eve took out her flashlight and shined it into the opening. She caught the glint of a round object pushed deep inside, something metallic, with sharp serrated teeth. "What the hell?"

Chapter 14 – First Kill

One side of the woman's top lip rose up into a lopsided smile, as she regarded Evan Brinkmeyer.

Evan turned and smiled at her awkwardly, trying not to think about the woman's firm breasts pushing up against him. Admittedly, the Roosevelt Island Tramway was crowded this time of day, and people were squashed together like sardines. Yet, he got the distinct feeling she was deliberately rubbing up against him in such a provocative manner, it was causing him to sweat nervously.

More people squeezed in, then someone yelled out to move away from the closing doors. Bodies compressed together to make room for more passengers, and someone pushed against Evan's arm. He adjusted his stance, pivoting slightly toward the woman behind him, feeling the back of his arm distinctly pressed up against her breast. The young, blonde woman behind him didn't move. In fact, to Evan's nervous surprise, she pressed her firm body further into him, molding herself into the shape of his spine and buttocks, as though she was spooning him while standing.

Evan closed his eyes and swallowed hard. Newspaper headlines flashed across the inside of his eyelids: "Middle-aged man caught molesting young woman in public!" What would he tell his mother? He'd done nothing wrong. It was the woman who was brushing up against him like some feline creature wanting to be fed.

She was so close he could feel her warm, tantalizing breath on his neck, and a subtle, fresh smell of her perfume that reminded Evan of candy floss and trips to the beach. Not that he had been to the beach lately. Last year he went with a few work colleagues to Coney Island, but it was too hot and too crowded. So he'd spent most of the day red-raw and sweaty, sitting in the shade eating ice cream, wishing his skin wasn't so deathly pale while his tanned, oiled, and chiseled coworkers swam, sunbathed, and played beach volleyball like a bunch of fighter-pilot jocks from a movie he'd once seen.

Finally the doors closed and Evan opened his eyes. Gripping the overhead-loop strap tighter, he tried to relax as the tram slowly lifted up and away from the Roosevelt Island terminal and began its four-minute trek across the gray expanse of the East River toward Manhattan.

The tram shuddered as it passed over the first tower and Evan felt the woman behind him press her pelvis into his buttocks. Not that he minded. It was the closest he had been to any woman in more than a year. He tried not to turn and look at her directly, but the urge was too much. When he did, he was greeted with disappointment. She had turned her head away and was looking out the window.

What did he expect? A chance encounter with a beautiful young woman would be anything more? After all, women like this, unless they absolutely had to, didn't get this close to him. Why would they? He was forty-six, bald, an accountant who had to move back into his parents' house in Queens, because he could no longer afford to live in Manhattan since his employer had to cut back his work to just three day a week.

What little savings Evan did have, had been chewed up on an online bridal site that promised to find the 'woman of his dreams'. A week after setting up his profile, any hope of finding a Belarusian wife, together with three thousand dollars of Evan's money, had vanished. The image of the tall, curvaceous, twenty-eight-year-old schoolteacher from Minsk, whom Evan had his heart set on, was promptly replaced with a "404 Website Not Found" error on Evan's computer screen.

The tram dipped as it reached the middle of the East River, and Evan's mind drifted to Tania, the schoolteacher from Minsk. With her glossy dark hair, liquid brown eyes, snow-white skin and more curves than the Nürburgring racetrack in Germany, she never strayed far from his thoughts.

It was almost as though they were destined to be together. Tania loved chocolate—so did Evan, but only dark chocolate—traveling, and going to the movies. She wanted to meet "an intelligent, loyal and generous man, thirty-seven to forty-five, who wanted to get married and have children." Evan wanted children too, and age was still on his side. He read somewhere men could father children well into their eighties. And having a young, child-bearing bride like Tania seemed perfect. He didn't know about 'generous' now though. After the bridal site debacle, what little money remained, Evan promptly blew during a mild bout of depression, on online cam girl websites, where young naked women inserted all manner of paraphernalia into all manner of bodily places. He wasn't going to reveal that little secret to his parents though. His mother would crucify him, while his father would want to know the website addresses his son had visited.

Maybe it was all women were interested in these days: Money! The problem was Evan was too trusting, too gullible. He knew it too, but he couldn't help himself. He always saw the good in people, not the bad.

The tram began to slow as it approached the Manhattan terminal. Old people merrily chattered, while the younger ones silently thumbed their cell phones or were listening to music through earphones.

The woman was still there, attached to him like a remora stuck to the underbelly of a shark.

Suddenly Evan could feel the bodily pressure of the woman behind him ease off as the tram began to slow further. Over the sea of heads he could see the red structure of the approaching terminal.

Then two things happened simultaneously: Delicate, yet powerful fingers clamped tightly around Evan's mouth from behind, muffling any attempts at a scream, and a sharp shard of pain pierced Evan's right thigh, like a spear plunging deep into his leg. He tried to pull his hand out of the loop strap above his head, but it wouldn't slide out.

He tried desperately to turn, to break free, to face the woman behind him. But she had gripped him like a praying mantis, was leaning into him, hooking one leg around the front of his left leg, her forearm coiled around his neck controlling his head and neck as her hand crushed his mouth, stifling his panicked cries. His eyes looked desperately at the faces around him but no one returned his gaze. Heads were down, or turned away, focused on other things. Evan could feel warm wetness run down one trouser leg, and thought he was urinating himself. The sour taste of bile rose in his throat, his vision a watery blur.

The tram shuddered to a stop and the doors hissed open.

People began to surge and move around Evan, like a school of determined fish swimming around a rock in a stream. Evan felt himself wilting, his life draining out of him, the loop strap around his wrist the only thing holding him up.

The hand over his mouth released, and the grip around him slipped away.

Evan's body sagged.

A woman screamed. A man slipped in a pool of red that was spreading out beneath Evan's feet.

Another scream.

People repelled from Evan's dangling form. Confusion gave way to fear, then mass hysteria as the flow of people became a tsunami of blind panic and self-preservation as they spilled out of the tram and onto the platform.

Walking quickly, the young woman with the lopsided smile exited the tram, the sound of screaming and shouting fading behind her as she hurriedly made her way down the pedestrian ramp and onto the street level below, skillfully avoiding any security cameras as she went.

Next, she headed west along East Sixtieth Street, walking a block before cutting into Bloomingdale's. Emerging on to Lexington Avenue, she crossed the street before disappearing into the bowels of the subway station on the other side.

An hour later she made it back to her two-bedroom apartment just in time for the six o'clock news. She grabbed a shot glass from the kitchen cupboard, slid out a thin bottle of Stolichnaya Elit vodka from the small freezer, and poured herself a measure. She threw back the shot, then poured herself another.

Taking the shot glass with her, she went into the living room and sat down cross-legged on an old, worn sofa, picked up the remote control and turned on the television.

Victoria Christie hadn't felt so alive in months. All her nerve endings tingled and her skin shimmered. This was much better than the last time.

While waiting for the news to come on, she contemplated touching herself, to heighten the wonderful surge of energy she felt coursing through her body, then thought otherwise. Later, much later, she would go out to a local bar she often frequented, find some nice man, go back to his place and break him. Breaking men. That was her specialty now. Physically and mentally. Married or single. Young or old. Sons or fathers. It made no difference. It was her purpose in life, what she had been placed on this earth to do: to break the male spirit, one Y chromosome at a time.

The newsreader came on the television screen, a stock picture of the Roosevelt Island Tramway behind her. "A man was brutally murdered today on the crowded Roosevelt Island Tramway. He was stabbed in the leg and bled out in a matter of minutes and died at the scene."

Raising her second glass of vodka, Victoria toasted the TV presenter before throwing it back, savoring the instant viscous burn in her throat and sensual heat building in her loins.

So much blood. So much blood.

They'll be scrubbing the floor for days to get it all off, she thought. Placing the shot glass down, she noticed a red speck of blood on her wrist, and promptly licked it off in one, delicious swipe.

"The victim has been identified as Evan Brinkmeyer, an accountant, aged forty-six from Queens." A photo of Evan filled the TV screen.

Victoria looked up and smiled, then blew a kiss at the screen.

"Police say it's too early at this stage as to any likely suspects. However, they believe this was an apparent random act of senseless violence. And despite the tram being packed during rush hour, there were no apparent witnesses as to who committed this brazen and highly public killing."

Victoria pulled out her cell phone and shot off a short text: "Bonus points, please."

Chapter 15 – Shock Treatment

The alligator clips were heavy duty, rugged steel construction, with spring-loaded jaws more than capable of puncturing human skin.

The palm-sized portable hard disk had a rubberized bright orange outer shell, making it drop, shock, rain, dust, and crush resistant. Perfect for taking backup files with you while camping or for the urban tech geek on the go. But looks can be deceiving. The internals of the drive had been removed and replaced with custom-made variable shock battery. At three milliamperes you would feel just a mild shock. Between ten to twenty mA you would begin to experience muscle contractions and moderate pain. Above thirty mA, you would start to suffocate. And above ninety mA, you would go into full cardiac arrest. The modified device was capable of delivering up to two hundred milliamperes, enough to bring down an adult rhinoceros.

Picking up the shock battery, Marcus Kemp admired its beauty. Just holding it gave him a sense of delicious anticipation. He hadn't yet fully tested it, as it was only delivered to him two days ago from a reliable source he had used before, a nameless person who specialized in building such devices of pain.

He had planned everything for tomorrow with meticulous detail, including two additional escape routes if needed. Kemp had his parents five-story Brooklyn brownstone all to himself. Each year, they went on vacation to Europe.

Kemp's cell phone buzzed as a text landed. He thumbed the screen, read the message then gave what best could be described as an annoyed smirk. The little English whore Victoria Christie had surfaced, struck first, made the main news channels too.

Marcus didn't bother with watching the news. It was all biased drivel anyway. He had anticipated the overly ambitious Christie would be first out of the gate, the first to kill. She looked as though she practically was having an orgasm when Joshua had explained about his little devious game. Joshua Banks may be the leader of their group, but to Kemp, Christie was the "show," the entertainer, always wanting the attention, seeking the limelight. She would do anything to win. Even eat her own kind if she had to. *Joshua better watch his back*, Kemp thought as he pocketed his phone.

He had a plan, though, which guaranteed Victoria Christie wouldn't win. The plan was simple logic really. After all, she was the biggest threat. So what do you do to the biggest threat in a game you also wanted to win at all costs?

Malicious images of a bound and gagged Victoria Christie began to seep into Kemp's demented head. Almost immediately his heartbeat started rising, the draw of his breath became increasingly shallow, and one eyelid broke into an intermittent spasm. Seconds later, a fail-safe triggered inside his mind, and the wave of images began to gradually recede.

Kemp blinked.

His mind switched back to the task at hand, to what needed to be done tonight. He pulled out a heavy brass key and stared at it thoughtfully while tapping it against his palm. Then, with the shock battery in his hand, he picked up a pair of the alligator clips and made his way down the stairs to the old stone basement.

He needed to fully test the device before tomorrow—on a real, living test subject.

Chapter 16 – 3:00 a.m.

It was nearly midnight by the time Eve sat down on her sofa, peeled off the lid from the takeout container, and began to slowly eat dinner in silence.

Despite Hagen's insistence that she flip the case of the murdered woman in the dumpster to a junior detective, Eve had decided to keep the case for herself until she knew more. Back at the precinct, she had told no one about finding Lindsay Latimer's purse and driver's license and had logged both as evidence. The body had been sent to the morgue and, hopefully by tomorrow, she would know more about how the victim died, and more about the strange object lodged in her throat.

Eve ate with the television on, and sound muted. A police procedural crime drama was playing, where two cops with supermodel looks had just solved a homicide within an hour, excluding ad breaks.

The act of eating felt mechanical to Eve, the food tasteless. But it served a purpose, filling a hollow space inside her. She looked down as Sam brushed against her leg, while his wise eyes peered up at her. "Looks like it's just you and me," she said.

She couldn't face the bedroom, not wanting to sleep in there. So she made up a bed on the sofa, and shared it with Sam who was content to curl up at her feet.

But sleep evaded Eve. She fought with the bed sheets, then lay awake listening to sounds of police sirens swelling then fading in the night, wondering what horrors and heartbreak they were heading to.

It was around 3:00 a.m. when sleep finally pulled Eve under. She found herself trapped inside a dumpster, surrounded by eternal darkness, buried under a mountain of slippery trash bags oozing rancid warm liquid and mushy rotting food. Her desperate cries for help were drowned out by the excruciating sound of thousands of tiny claws scratching on rusted steel. The lid of the dumpster seemed as distant to touch as the dark, empty heavens. Every time Eve managed to pull herself above the muck, the dark heavens above would split into a thin ribbon of bright light and more trash bags would rain down on her, pushing her under again.

Suddenly a hand gripped Eve's ankle from below. She could feel herself sinking even farther, being hauled downward by someone below, the person using her as leverage to free themselves from the muck and escape toward the surface.

A body slithered up next to Eve, with a bulbous, translucent skull, hairless and spidery with veins. The neck slowly twisted, the face of a man gradually revealing itself one scarred inch at a time, with sunken cheeks, swollen lips stained with blood, and finally, the emptiest, coal-black eyes she had seen before. Uri Goff.

Goff's face erupted into a heinous grin, his teeth gray and twisted. "Hello, Eve," he rasped.

The body of a dead child bobbed to the surface next to Eve, bloated and wide-eyed in death. Then another…and another until she found herself floating in a sea of dead children.

"You couldn't save them! You couldn't save them!" Goff shrieked at Eve. He grabbed the nearest child, a young girl, her pale face matted with blonde hair that he began to stroke with his bony fingers, his eyes never leaving Eve. "This one was particularly tight…but I broke her, and on the inside." He gave a little shiver as his eyes rolled back into their sockets. "Boy was she juicy!"

Suddenly Eve could feel multiple fingers clawing at her ankles and shins, and with an abrupt tug on both her feet, she gave a last gasp before she was violently wrenched under the surface.

And as she sunk deeper and deeper, she could hear the taunting, watery rasp of Uri Goff float down through the darkness toward her.

"You…couldn't…save…them."

Two men were arguing with the waitress who stood behind the counter. Something about politics or celebrities preaching climate change while jumping in their fuel-guzzling armored SUVs or flying about the country in their private jets. One of the men was a shift worker, the other an Uber driver taking a break.

Birch couldn't sleep. Maybe it was the apartment. Too unfamiliar. Too empty. Too sterile. Too big. So he had rolled out of bed at 3:00 a.m., got dressed, grabbed the file on Lindsay Latimer, plus the book he had taken from her apartment, and found the all-night diner to drown his insomnia in coffee.

Now ensconced in a booth near the window, and on to his third cup of coffee, he read the file for the third time. It was slim pickings. The progress reports from information gathered and conclusions reached by the various investigators on the disappearance of Lindsay Latimer were thin on detail and heavy on speculation. Perhaps Francis Latimer was right when he had said he was being taken advantage of.

After confirming the body found in the dumpster was not her, yesterday Birch had left Maxine Brodie, preferring to go it alone. He returned to his apartment and spent the rest of the afternoon and evening going through the two Bankers Boxes of information he had been provided on the life of Lindsay Latimer.

Everything from her birth certificate to her latest cell phone bills. And yet, as he pored over the information, Birch got the distinct feeling nothing of real value was going to emerge.

Birch glanced out the window of the diner. The streets were empty, cold, lonely, like how he felt right now, as the gravity of finding Lindsay began to sink in. What if the file Francis Latimer had was a fake, all lies designed to lure him in? Birch was placing a lot of faith in what he had been told, by two people he didn't really know. He hadn't actually seen any of the evidence Latimer and Brodie purported was in the file.

And now the task at hand seemed enormous, especially without the law enforcement resources he once had. The detective he had met earlier, Sommers, had a better chance of finding Lindsay than he did. Yet, Francis Latimer had promised Birch the full support and resources of Latimer Industries. But what could he do with it? He was just one man.

Partway through his fourth cup of coffee, his thoughts drifted back to Justin, his son's face always on his mind, sometimes close and clear, other times the features obscured behind a gauze of distrust and betrayal. Also, finding Lindsay Latimer, and trusting what Francis Latimer was claiming was the only option Birch had if he were going to clear his name and have any chance of redeeming himself with his son.

The waitress came and refilled his coffee cup, then gave Birch an almost smile of pity. "Animal Farm?" she said noticing the book on the table, the one Birch had taken from Lindsay's apartment. "Sounds intense."

"It can be," Birch replied. "I read it a while ago, back when I was in high school. It's about the Russian Revolution."

"Sounds like the perfect solution for insomnia, Hon."

Birch smiled. The woman had a kind, warm face. "Maybe I

should have started reading it again last night."

"Maybe," she replied, touching his arm with reassuring pat. "It would have put me to sleep for sure." The waitress gave another smile, then whirled away.

Birch thought for a moment, then picked up the book, reading the address again of the bookstore printed on the inside. The cover showed an illustration of a pig dressed in a military uniform holding up a pitchfork as a weapon. The cover was more graphic, more stylized than the version Birch remembered reading years ago.

He fanned through the pages, front to back.

Then something fell out onto the table. Birch picked it up.

It was a blank postcard. No writing, no address, used as a bookmark, he figured. It showed a painting, old Baroque style, depicting a woman upending a man, throwing him into what looked like a well. Birch turned to the back of the card and read the tiny print at the bottom. While it was written in Italian, he could decipher the museum and city the postcard was from:

Naples.

DAY 2

Journal Entry #11 – Timoclea

Today we visited a wonderful museum in Naples where I saw a painting by an Italian artist, Elisabetta Sirani, called, *Timoclea Killing Her Rapist*.

I carefully noted down all the details from the painting's placard, as the man in the painting reminded me of my Uncle Cyrus. Except he didn't end up at the bottom of a well with his head smashed in with rocks. Still, he will never lay his grubby hands on me again.

I bought a postcard of the painting from the museum gift store. I use it now as a bookmark. It serves as a constant reminder. I'm looking at it right now as I write this, thinking about this courageous woman, Timoclea, who lived hundreds of years ago. Whoever she was, she has become my hero, my guiding light to never allow what happened to me to ever happen again.

My mother is a weak-minded fool, blinded by so much self-doubt and self-pity, who I now know for a fact allowed my father and my uncle to take advantage of me.

My own mother? STUPID FUCKING COW! I thought she would help me when I went to her, first told her what my uncle had done to me. I can remember the day as clearly as though it was yesterday.

My mother was standing in the kitchen in front of the sink, washing up dishes, rinsing then off then placing them carefully on the drying rack next to her. She had her best crockery out and didn't trust anyone else with washing them.

For a moment I thought I saw her tense, almost look up as though she knew what I was going to say when she saw my face, my cheeks glistening with tears. But then when I told her, she simply went back to washing the dishes, adding more detergent, and smiling out the window at the bright sunshine.

She didn't believe me, said I was making it all up, saying I'd had a bad dream and I must have suddenly woken up dazed and confused, still half awake and still half asleep in the nightmare. She brushed it off as nothing more, went on washing up, making sure none of her precious damn cups and plates were damaged. They were more important to her than her own daughter.

Then she told me to never mention it again, to tell no one what I had told her. She said it wouldn't be right. Those were her actual words. "It wouldn't be right." I thought she would save me from the horror. But she didn't. She refused to accept it.

Afterward, I soon realized no one was going to save me. I was going to have to save myself. As I sat alone in my bedroom, with the door closed, I thought about putting a chair up against the door at night, because there was no lock. It was then I decided to take matters into my own hands, because my father, my mother, everyone, had abandoned me.

I was an abandoned child.

Chapter 17 – Maya Zin

Despite the bright morning sunshine, Eve strode inside the NYU Langone Medical Center, one of three forensic pathology centers in the city, with a dark heart.

The Office of Chief Medical Examiner or OCME, has wide authority when it comes to death. Its primary responsibility is to investigate all deaths that are a result of criminal violence, accident, suicide, or deemed suspicious or unusual. And in New York City, with a staff of more than seven hundred, covering all five boroughs, it is the largest OCME in the country. As well as serving as the city mortuary, its laboratories act as the centralized hub for all DNA testing, physical evidence analysis, and post-mortem toxicology reporting.

The victim from the dumpster was still yet to be identified. No cell phone or personal belongings had been discovered after sifting through the contents of the dumpster.

Eve found Dr. Maya Zin, in her office at her computer. Everything about the thirty-two-year-old forensic pathologist spoke vintage. From the short bob cut of her raven-black hair, brilliant red matte lipstick, and plaid swing dresses and skirts she often wore, to the tortoiseshell cat eye-shaped glasses behind which sat a pair of owlish, intense brown eyes. Even when out on the town at night, which was a rarity for Maya, Eve had never seen on Maya's feet anything other than her pair of floral pattern Dr. Martens boots, an otherwise jarring contrast to her classic wardrobe ensemble.

Eve had attended dozens of autopsies, and despite knowing Maya for only three years, Maya now looked after all of Eve's cases, rather than the other medical examiners she had dealt with in the past.

"Hey, babe," Maya said affectionately without looking up. "Be with you in a tick, Eve."

"How did you know it was me?" Eve said, loitering in the doorway, her arms folded.

Maya gave a slight smile, still not meeting Eve's eye. "Your fragrance precedes you. Tom Ford, Fucking Fabulous." Maya finally looked up at Eve. "I don't know any other cop who can afford to wear anything with his name on it."

"It was a gift."

"From Luke?"

Eve resentfully nodded,

Maya leaned back in her chair, a sly, quizzical look on her face. "Tell me Eve, doesn't Luke have to go back to school? Your relationship with him reminds me of an old Rod Stewart song."

Maya's sarcastic banter was nothing new to Eve.

Maya's office was perfectly neat, tidy yet functional, with no personal mementos or framed photos, nothing to remind Maya of a life she had outside of work.

It was much more than a job to Maya, and that's what had caught Eve's attention when they first met. Maya took each case personally, as though those who had the misfortune to lay on her examination table were her own family, lost souls with a piece forever missing from the last moments of their lives, pieces Maya had to reconstruct then slot back into the victims stories to explain how they arrived at their ultimate destination: death. Maya once told Eve she felt indebted to the dead to tell the living exactly how they died and why. Eve thought it was an eloquent way to describe what was a very harrowing and distressing job. On the curve of Maya's right hand, between her thumb and forefinger Maya sported a tattoo of a triquetra, a three-corned intertwining loop. It has many symbolic meanings; however, Maya told Eve it represented the three stages of a person's existence: birth, life and death—apt for someone in her profession.

What Eve loved most about Maya, apart from her technical brilliance, unbridled pursuit of the truth, and keen eye for detail, was her almost detective-like approach to the work. Unlike some of her colleagues, Maya wasn't afraid to share her thoughts on homicide cases, on the victim's possible killer and motive.

"Blunt force trauma to the side of the head, followed by strangulation," Maya said returning to her computer screen, the glare reflecting off her lenses.

Maya continued tapping away on her keyboard. "I came in early, did her then. It was relatively quiet in here at five a.m. Less distraction."

"I owe you one," Eve said as she took a seat across the desk from Maya.

"A Moondog," Maya replied.

Eve nodded. "The drinks are on me, next time. And not just one." Maya's favorite cocktail bar, in East Village, was aptly named Death & Co.

On occasions, especially when Eve and Maya found themselves at the end of a particularly harrowing day they would rather forget, they would meet and, while ensconced on a velvet sofa within the dark and moody interior of the bar, drink their colorful concoctions of choice while comparing murder notes.

"So how is the ever-youthful Luke?" Maya asked, her eyes growing wide behind her glasses. "I want to know all the sordid details." Maya waved her hand about. "All the men I know who are hard and stiff tend to be dead."

"Don't ask," Eve replied, a coldness in her voice.

Maya raised an eyebrow. "I told you so," she said. "He was way too young for you."

Eve made a conciliatory face, pleased Maya hadn't phrased

her comment about their age gap the other way: it was *she* who was too old for him.

"Like I said, most men are bastards," Maya said.

"No," Eve gave a sigh, "just the ones I tend to meet." The idle banter soon vanished, as Eve learned forward, her face deadly serious. "What else can you tell me about her?"

Maya slid a tablet across the desk toward Eve. "All her vital stats are there. DNA and toxicology should be back from the lab by tomorrow."

Eve scrolled through the two-page report and accompanying photos. No real surprises there, confirming what Eve had thought all along. The woman was a drug user, and likely prostitute. Mid-forties, malnourished, her limbs an epitaph of syringe puncture marks, old scars, nicks and cuts, all signs of a hard life spent on the streets. One photo showed the injury to the side of the woman's face, the hair matted to the scalp and cheekbone by a viscous mass of dark red.

Maya opened her drawer and pulled out a sealed evidence bag. It made an audible clunk as she dropped it down on the desk, startling Eve. "This is what you're really here about, aren't you?"

As Eve looked at the object in the plastic bag—traces of blood and tissue clung along two serrated curves—she tried to imagine the mechanical thing wedged in the back of the woman's throat. Eve's jaw tightened as she continued to stare at the object, unable to tear her eyes away from it.

"Hard to believe isn't it," Maya spoke, noticing the horrified look in her friend's eyes.

"This was what was in her mouth?" Eve said. "It looks too big to fit in there."

Maya's face turned grim, "Took me nearly an hour with a scalpel to remove it without pulling half her throat out with it."

Chapter 18 – Bookstore

It wasn't the most recent photo, but certainly the clearest of Lindsay Latimer that Birch could find in the files.

He slid it across the counter, and waited patiently while the bookstore assistant, a young man named Billy with long unruly hair and a pinched face, scrutinized it. Birch guessed, from Billy's facial expression, he was more interested in how attractive the woman was in the photo than if she had actually been into the bookstore recently.

"Well?" Birch asked, drumming the counter with his fingers. "Have you seen her?"

Billy slowly nodded but didn't look up. "Yeah. She's been in here a few times. I remember the face."

"When was she last in?" Birch asked, wishing he still had his detective's badge, so he could flash it and garner a quicker response. But he didn't. So he had to tread a fine line between being an ordinary citizen, and coming across too strong and raising suspicion.

So he decided to lie. "She's my niece," he added. "She's been missing for almost a week now. I need to find her." That part was definitely true.

Birch placed the tattered copy of Animal Farm on the counter, hoping to add credibility to his line of questioning. "She purchased this book from here. So I thought she would be a regular customer."

For the third time, Birch glanced up at the security camera on the wall behind the counter, wishing he could get access to the video footage.

Billy finally looked up, noticed the book on the counter.

"Maybe a week ago she was in here I remember." He handed back the photo. "I only work here three days a week. So maybe she's been in when I wasn't here. Can't say. But she usually browses the shelves then orders a coffee and sits down out the back."

Off to one side, behind the counter was a small in-store café with wooden tables and chairs where a few people sat, mainly college kids, laptops open and ear buds in, large coffee cups within reach. Behind a big stainless-steel espresso machine on the café counter, a young woman wearing a green apron moved back and forth with smooth efficiency as though she had four arms, grinding beans, turning knobs, releasing steam, and frothing milk.

"Did you ever see her in here with anyone?" Birched asked, bringing his attention back to the store assistant. "Like with a guy, maybe a boyfriend?" Birch tried to sound casual, not like he was interrogating the young man, which he subtly was.

Billy's deliberate show of thinking made Birch want to reach across the counter, grab him by the collar and shake some sense of urgency into him.

"Not that I can recall. She always seemed alone," Billy said.

Birch took the book back. In a past life, he would come back with a warrant, ignored everyone, and demanded to see the security video footage for the last few weeks. Now he had to change tack. Having no authority was going to take some getting used to.

"Thanks for your help," Birch said with a sarcastic twinge, which Billy mistook as genuine thanks.

It took Birch less than three minutes from sitting at a café table, drinking his coffee, watching customers and staff move about the store, to formulate a new plan of attack. It was risky, and he could end up back in jail, but he had no choice.

Draining his coffee, he plucked a book from a small display stand on the café counter—some erotic bestseller with a semi naked woman on the cover, bound and gagged about to be whipped by a bare-chested man—and tucked it under his arm. He assumed the demeanor of a literary snob and made his way to the back of the store, pausing every so often to pluck a book off the shelves then frown in horror at the sticker price, before hastily returning the book to the shelf and moving on.

He passed under a security camera positioned high on the back wall, its red light blinking down at him. The camera was pointing back toward the café and took in part of the front section of the store. There was a narrow corridor, with a restroom sign on the wall. Birch casually glanced around. The corridor and washroom area beyond was a blind spot, not covered by security cameras.

As Birch made his way along the corridor, an older woman suddenly emerged from a side door in front of him. Birch smiled at her as he continued walking past, giving a cursory glance at the sign on the door she had just stepped out from.

Staff Only.

Sixty seconds later, Birch emerged from the restroom with clean hands, went straight to the office door and entered without knocking. He found himself in a storeroom and was greeted with the fresh smell of new books neatly stacked on shelves, and cardboard boxes were stacked up against one wall.

Past the shelves a large corner desk was positioned, with a computer, and three widescreen displays. One display screen showed what looked like an inventory spreadsheet. Another screen had the bookstore's Facebook page up, and the last screen was split into four sections—multiple views of the store security cameras. Also on the desk sat a brick-shaped box with a blue winking light on the front and cables plugged in the back.

Birch went straight to the brick-shaped box, reached out for it then paused. Glancing at the security feed display, he saw the older woman he had passed in the corridor. She was now standing next to Billy at the cash register, talking to a customer. There was no sound, but judging from the animated display of the customer, they were none too happy; the older woman was obviously the store manager.

This gave Birch more time.

He quickly studied the external hard drive on the desk. It was about the size of a thick paperback book. He glanced at the security feed display again. The manager was still trying to pacify the customer. Birch picked up the box, and studied the cables plugged into the sockets at the back.

He glanced at the security camera feed display again.

The manger was gone from the cash register counter.

Quickly he unplugged all the cables, shoved the hard drive into his jacket, and made for the door. Just as he reached for the handle, the door swung inward.

Standing there staring at him was the store manager.

Her expression went from one of alarm to one of suspicion. "What are you doing in here?" she demanded, her wide girth blocking the doorway.

Birch jumped in mock fright, clutching his chest, one hand holding the hard drive hidden under the jacket. "Sorry! You gave me such a fright."

The woman held her ground. Her eyes narrowed to slits. "This is a staff-only area."

Birch made a pleading face, brought his knees together, like he was distressed. "Sorry, I was looking for the restrooms. I have a weak bladder and if—"

The woman's face softened, and she instantly stepped aside. "Turn left and they are at the end of the corridor."

Birch gave an exaggerated smile of relief, thanked the woman and stepped out into the corridor and began walking toward the restrooms.

No sooner had he heard the office door close behind him did he perform an about-face and promptly walked back out of the corridor, into the store and past the café, only stopping briefly to deposit on the cash register counter—in full view of a nun Billy was serving who was purchasing a Bible—the erotic book he had taken from the café.

The nun glanced down at the book, then disapprovingly at Birch.

Birch made a pious face. "Anyone who reads this filth should burn in hell," he said to the nun, before hurrying out of the store.

Chapter 19 – Autopsy

"I've never seen anything like it inserted into the mouth cavity," Maya said. "Or anywhere else in a human body, and I've seen some strange things in my day."

Eve picked up the object in the sealed bag, slowly turned it over in her hand, feeling its ice-cold metallic touch through the thin plastic. From its design, Eve had an idea as to its originally intended use, far from the brutal purpose for which it had actually been used.

"No prints on it, nor the victim's body," Maya added.

"Please tell me this...thing was inserted into her throat *after* she died," Eve asked, placing the bag down, sliding it away from her, feeling repulsed. "It definitely wasn't the cause of her death?"

Maya shook her head. "You could easily choke to death on it. But no, she died from asphyxiation. Was strangled to death by powerful hands." Maya prodded the plastic bag with her pen, as though it contained a poisonous insect. "The delightful thing was inserted post-mortem, as a cruel and deliberate afterthought."

Eve began grinding her teeth. Who would do such a thing?

"It's a spring-loaded climbing cam," Maya explained, "which has been modified in this instance."

"Modified?"

Maya picked up the plastic bag. "Rock climbers use them to secure a climbing safety line into a crevice or large crack. You squeeze the trigger to make the device smaller, slip it into the crack, then release the trigger and it springs back to normal size." Maya demonstrated without removing the device from the bag. She gripped the small handle along the shaft of the cam then pulled the trigger, causing the four metal curved lobes to slide inward on themselves like the petals of a flower closing, making the device smaller, almost half its normal size. "So you insert this into the crack when it's contracted," Maya said. "Then release the trigger." Maya eased off the trigger and the four metal lobes expanded outward like wings. "Except the killer had sharpened the edges of each cam so it cut the insides of the victim's throat. When it was in place and fully expanded, the killer, is some sick act of cruelty, removed the handle and sling just to make it much harder to reach in and pull the trigger so it could be easily removed."

"The killer was making a statement." Eve whispered what Maya was probably thinking. "He knew her or knew of her. This was personal." Eve called up the photos on the tablet again. "The killer is confident," she began. "Approached his victim front-on."

"The blow to the side of the head," Maya noted, "And not to the back."

Eve agreed. "He was facing her. She felt safe, not threatened by him as he stood in front of her. They could have been talking."

"She felt no compulsion to flee," Maya started. "Could be a customer of hers."

"And he felt no compulsion to sneak up from behind," Eve finished.

Both women were in sync, their mental reconstruction of what led up to the murder in alignment.

Eve studied the head injury photos again. "Do you know what the weapon was?"

Maya gave a shrug, "Could be a number of objects. It was blunt, and it was solid, that's all I can tell you. It left no particular pattern, no distinguishing impact shape on the skull."

"Hard enough to stun her, but not hard enough to kill her,

so he could then strangle her to death," Eve continued.

"Up close and personal," Maya added.

"Vengeful?"

Maya picked up the plastic bag, looking at the object as she spoke. "Sending a message, as you said. Strangulation is such an intimate method of killing someone." She put the plastic bag down again. "He wanted to look her right in the eyes as he was squeezing the life out of her."

"He wanted his face to be the last thing she would ever see."

"And you didn't find any ID whatsoever on the victim or at the crime scene?" Maya asked.

"Nothing," Eve replied. "Just someone else's purse. I'll send it over to you for analysis."

Maya frowned. "Stolen by the victim?"

"Seems likely."

Maya leaned forward. "Since you're here, I want your thoughts on the body of a male that came in late yesterday. They needed a rush on the autopsy, otherwise I would have done your Jane Doe yesterday. He was traveling toward Manhattan on the Roosevelt Island Tramway around five-o'clock when someone decided to stick a blade into his thigh."

"And he died from that?" Eve asked.

"He's in the fridge right now," Maya said, nodding with her head past Eve and outside the doorway. "From his size and weight I estimated he bled out in under ten minutes, well before the cops got there."

Eve vaguely remembered something on the morning report, where crimes across the city were tabulated from the previous day and shot out to all precincts. The tramway was located around the intersection of East Fifty-Ninth Street and Second Avenue, the turf of the Nineteenth Precinct. Eve knew Kathleen

Walsh, the commanding officer there. She was a good woman, a straight shooter who didn't mince her words.

Eve was curious now. "So tell me about the case."

"The victim was an accountant, forty-six, single, living in Queens. Parents are coming in later this morning."

"And the weapon?"

"Something thin, and very sharp, almost needle-like. Maybe an icepick. I've seen the guys behind most cocktail bars use them to hack up large ice blocks for drinks. I think the killing was purely random, had no real motive."

"Like on the spur of the moment?" Eve asked. "Only the crazies would carry an icepick around with them just in case they suddenly felt the urge to stab someone."

"It's not that," Maya said thoughtfully. "There were no other puncture wounds, just a single entry wound in the thigh. He wasn't stabbed anywhere else on the body. The act was intentional, stealthy and whoever did it knew exactly what they were doing, knew exactly where the femoral artery was. They didn't fluke it. They didn't have to second guess. They hit it once and hit it right. Death by exsanguination or bleed out."

Eve thought for a moment. The tramway would have been packed with commuters that time of day. "And no one saw anything? No witnesses at all?"

Maya shook her head. "Spoke to one of the detectives this morning just before you arrived. They've already combed through all of the security camera footage in the vicinity. Nothing."

"Everyone probably scattered. The killer would have fled the scene hidden among the crowd." To Eve it was almost as if the killer, by choosing that place and time of day, had made it particularly hard for themselves not to be caught. Like it was a challenge for them.

"If I was going to kill someone," Maya said. "For whatever reason—greed, lust or loathing—I wouldn't choose to do in such a public place, like a crowded tram or bus or on the subway. I'd wait, pick my spot, someplace less conspicuous, a quiet street, a dark alleyway, or deserted parking lot. Not in broad daylight during rush hour."

"Remind me not to get on the bad side of you," Eve joked.

"It's mostly blind bad luck when people get stabbed in the femoral artery," Maya continued. "It's difficult to intentionally do it when you're alone with someone, and almost impossible when you're in a crowded place, surrounded by so many people while trying not to get caught."

"And why not just stab them in the stomach or the chest?" Eve asked.

"Too easy or too obvious," Maya replied.

"Or to make a statement. More messy. More shocking."

"True," Maya said. "The average person has around ten pints of blood in their body. From the body stats of the victim, I'd say half of his blood ended up on the floor of the tram."

Both women looked at each other, their brain waves again in sync. The killer was cold and clinical, intentional, deliberately chose a crowded place to make a spectacle of it. To Eve it seemed like they wanted the attention, to showcase how cunningly clever they were. And a killer with no apparent motive was the hardest to catch.

Maya finally spoke. "I could be wrong but…"

Eve looked at her friend and saw something was troubling her. "What?"

"The killing of the man, its pure, random simplicity, could be just the start of something dark, and sinister."

Chapter 20 – VIP

"Hey! If you're going to scan my bag, it will set off every alarm in the place."

The guard manning the security checkpoint conveyor looked up at Marcus Kemp. "Sir, we need to make sure there are no explosives or weapons in your bag. It is standard procedure." The guard gave Kemp a quick once-over, noticing the uniform he wore. "Unless you'd rather be denied access."

Disrespectful prick, Kemp thought.

"Hey buddy," came another voice this time, from a short, sweaty fat man who was standing behind Kemp in the line. "What's the holdup? And how come he gets to go to the head of the line?" The man pointed his finger at Kemp. "There are other people here as well you know. Why is he so special?" he said with a sarcastic drawl.

Ignoring the man, Kemp stepped through the metal detector arch and watched the computer screen of the x-ray machine as his bag disappeared into the scanning tunnel, only to emerge a few moments later on the conveyor on the other side. Kemp collected the plastic tray with his shoes, phone, belt and wallet, and was about to grab his duffel bag when a female security guard pulled it off before he could, took it to a side bench, and unzipped it.

Kemp waited patiently to one side as the woman rummaged through the contents of the duffel.

"Won't be a moment, sir," she said. "Just need to make sure." Satisfied there was nothing other than what she had expected to find inside the bag, she handed it back to Kemp.

Kemp joined the long line to the bank of elevators in the

crowded lobby. Judging by the number of people ahead of him, it would be ten or so minutes until he progressed to the front. No problem. He was in no rush, and he used the time to scan the sea of people for suitable candidates. Laughing tourists, stressed parents with excited children pulling at their arms, elderly people with walking canes waiting patiently, couples with selfie sticks capturing the moment—the lobby was filled with the din of anticipation, and a little fear too. *Good*, Kemp thought as he watched, thinking of the fear he was about to bring to the unsuspecting.

Unlike other visitors, Kemp didn't need a ticket. The landmark attracted more than four million people each year, transporting them up a thousand feet above the bustling New York streets, then safely back down again in a well-oiled, precision display of herding people without them feeling like they were cattle.

At the head of the line, ushers firmly but courteously directed the hordes toward each available elevator car.

The line moved and Kemp shuffled forward.

Suddenly Kemp felt a hand grip his shoulder. He turned to see a security guard, older, maybe in his seventies, next to him. "Is there a problem?" Kemp asked, forcing a smile while trying to remain calm.

The man said nothing, his watery eyes searching Kemp's face before his gaze dropped to the logo on Kemp's shirt. Then he turned away from Kemp, and spoke, addressing the usher at the head of the line who was checking tickets. "Hey, Pam!"

Pam looked up.

"Let this gentleman in will ya? He shouldn't be waiting in line."

Raising her hand, Pam beckoned Kemp over.

The security guard turned back. "There you go, sir. A man like you shouldn't be made to wait. You're got the most important job in the whole damn place," he chuckled.

Kemp looked down, saw the name badge on the guard. "Thank you, Raymond. Much appreciated."

Raymond gave Kemp a wrinkled smile, leaned in, then whispered, "Truth be told, I've got eight grandkids. When I bring them here, I use my authority to jump the line too." He patted Kemp on the shoulder. "Get going. Pam will look after you."

Kemp thanked the man again and made his way to the front of the line, much to the ire of onlookers.

Once there, Pam unhooked the rope bollard and ushered Kemp through.

As he stood first in line for the next available elevator, Marcus Kemp couldn't help but think his obedience to authority experiment was off to the perfect start.

Now to the next, lethal stage.

Chapter 21 – Beatriz Vega

For what seemed like almost a full minute, Thomas Birch stood in the alleyway behind a tired and dilapidated-looking building, staring up at the small dome security camera perched high on the crumbling brick façade, making certain his face was clearly visible.

In front of him stood a steel door; to the untrained eye, it looked like any other service entrance door one would expect to find at the rear of a commercial building. While the door's outward bland appearance was designed not to draw attention—like the rest of the building—there were subtle nuances to it Birch did notice: the thicker hinges with steel shields and tamper-proof screws. The reinforced doorjamb with metal folded inserts, and the all-metal frame surround.

Finally the door unlatched with a heavy mechanical click, and Birch passed into a small passageway where a red dot winked at him out of the gloomy ceiling.

Another camera. This one infrared.

The passageway led to an antique freight elevator with vertical sliding steel doors. Stepping inside, Birch closed the doors behind him and pressed the button. Somewhere in the darkened shaft above, mechanisms whirled and clunked, as ancient cogs, pulleys, and counterweights began to move in unison. The elevator lurched, then settled into its rickety ascent. The inside of the elevator was like a steel box, the walls dented, the paint peeling in some places back to the bare metal. The once-varnished floor planks were rubbed down to raw wood by countless feet over the decades.

Moments later, the elevator jolted to a halt and Birch pulled open the sliding doors.

A woman stood facing him, a gun pointed at his head: Beatriz Vega, thirty-one-years old, a native of Lima, Peru. Short in stature, but towering with presence, she had coal-black hair, olive skin and impatient, brown eyes. Vega said nothing, just regarded Birch, with the eye of someone contemplating whether to pull the trigger or not.

Birch kept his hands in plain sight.

Finally she spoke, but the gun remained aimed straight between his eyes. "I thought you were in prison."

"It looks like you live in a prison."

"It's to keep people out, not in." She stepped forward, her aim dropping a fraction. Her arm relaxed, her face softened. Her eyes gave him a once-over. "You look thinner."

"Prison tends to do that to you." Birch spread his arms wide. "I'm not armed."

Vega smirked, then she lowered her gun. "You're standing in what effectively is a large metal detector."

Birch glanced around the walls of the elevator.

"If you were armed, I would have known." She nodded above Birch's head. "And you'd be dead by now."

Birch followed her gaze, noticing the small holes drilled into the ceiling.

"Since I last heard from you, who else have you told about me? What I do, where I live?" Vega asked.

Birch shook his head. "No one, like we agreed."

Birch had crossed paths with Vega five years ago during a child homicide case he was investigating which ultimately led to a large, complex pedophile ring, courtesy of Beatriz Vega's help. Birch received an anonymous email containing the names, addresses, Internet IP addresses, and enough damning evidence to put all of the perpetrators behind bars for the rest of their sick, perverted lives.

"Did anyone follow you here?"

"I'm not worth following, Beatriz," Birch admitted, his shoulders slouching a fraction as he reflected on the broader meaning of his own words. "Everyone disowned me once I went to jail. I have no friends anymore. I didn't even think you would open the door."

"Well…" Vega's aura of cautious indifference softened slightly, "maybe you still have one friend left in the world." She turned and walked away.

Birch took her movement as permission to enter. Stepping out of the elevator, he followed her, walking only a few steps before the space opened up into a cavernous interior. "I see you've done some more renovations since I was last here." Birch paused, taking his time to look around at the converted warehouse. "A lot more security precautions too."

"You were here more than four years ago," Vega said over her shoulder, making her way to a large open-plan kitchen. The space paralleled Vega's own personality; Bare concrete walls with exposed brickwork in places, overhead sprinkler pipes, ventilation ducting, sheet metal, rust-stained girders, lashings of rivets and bolts, and raw wooden-plank floors. Industrial chic meets high-end technology set amid a camouflage of shadowy grays, blacks, and charcoals. Practical, functional, unpretentious. Tall glass windows framed in thin black steel ran the entire length of one side of the warehouse. A long custom-made desk, made from repurposed wood salvaged from an abandoned wharf, stood against the windows, with a solitary flat-panel display taking pride of place sat at its center, the screen a messy maze of scrolling text, symbols and numbers.

"Coffee?" Vega's voice came from behind a stainless-steel commercial espresso machine that hissed and spat as she worked knobs and ground coffee beans.

"Thanks."

"You can put down on the desk whatever you're carrying in your jacket," she said, looking up at him, her face obscured by a mist of steam. "It did register, but not enough to be a gun."

Birch smiled. Vega was as observant as ever. He slid out the external hard drive he had taken from the bookstore and placed it on the desk, then sat down on a long soft leather sofa. "Can't keep secrets from you," he replied.

Vega came out of the kitchen carrying two coffee cups and handed one to Birch. "I trade in secrets," she said, taking a seat on an opposite sofa. "Secrets and the information they contain is the most valuable commodity of all, Thomas. You should know."

"It's the reason why I'm here, Beatriz." Birch took a sip. "Not just for your excellent coffee."

When Beatriz Vega was just a precocious twelve-year-old, she caught the attention of her mathematics schoolteacher, as a gifted, intelligent child, with an acute ability to create complex algorithms and data structures to rival the skills of the best university professors. When she turned sixteen, a representative of Peru's National Directorate of Intelligence paid her parents a visit and offered Beatriz a fast-track career path in their Cyber Protection Division. After ten years of working for the Peruvian government, including a stint with the military, Vega left and struck out on her own.

Now she was a freelancer, with a select group of legitimate private clients, and despite her sometimes fiery Peruvian blood and proud heritage, Vega had refused all subsequent governmental approaches for her services. She didn't hate governments, but a ten-year career of working for one had left Vega with a healthy distrust of them—all of them. She now preferred to put her unique skills toward more altruistic endeavors, like tracking down global pedophile rings and sex-trafficking networks on behalf of international charities and interest groups who lacked the daunting resources, capabilities, and stealthy reach Vega had acquired over the years.

But money talks. It loosens lips and points fingers, and provides names and addresses—both digital as well as physical—of where evil hides and masquerades as decent, honest citizens.

So the money to finance Vega's operation came courtesy of her secretly wading, with a bucket in hand, into the virtual river of digital money that flowed illegally into the offshore bank accounts of various tax havens around the world. In her mind, she was taxing the tax cheats and repurposing the money for more humanitarian purposes. It had also allowed Vega to "vanish" off the face of the earth, purchase the disused building where Birch was now sitting, and convert it into a fortress where she now lived.

"What's on the hard drive?" Vega asked, watching Birch carefully as she stroked her hair with one hand. It was a subconscious habit she had whenever something or someone aroused her peculiar interest.

"Video footage," Birch replied. "I'm looking for someone. A missing young woman." Birch gave Vega an abbreviated bio on the Lindsay Latimer case. "I need to know if she was filmed during the last few weeks at a bookstore she sometimes frequented."

Vega tilted her head. "And how did you come by this video footage?"

"I stole it," Birch replied. "From the bookstore in question." Birch made an uncaring smirk. "I'm a criminal now. What can I say?"

"You were never a criminal," Vega countered. "The people

whom you worked for in the police were the criminals. I told you long ago, but you refused to listen."

Birch didn't want to get into the past, preferring to focus on the task at hand. "Can you take a look at it? I'll pay you."

Vega stood up. "No need to pay me. You kept me out of prison on more than one occasion."

Birch nodded. "Because you were invaluable to me, the information you provided over the years. What you do is for the greater good."

Vega gave a curt nod, appreciating the compliment, then went to her desk, picked up the hard drive and plugged it into a cable hub. She sat down at the screen and Birch joined her, preferring to stand. He laid the photo of Lindsay Latimer next to the keyboard.

"Attractive," Vega remarked, giving the photo a sideways glance. "If you like the American homecoming-queen look. Clearly not as attractive as Peruvian women."

"Clearly," Birch responded, knowing Vega's remark wasn't malicious—well maybe just slightly—but more from self-belief.

Vega took the photo, scanned it, and opened up facial recognition software she had created. She uploaded the scanned image of Lindsay Latimer into the software then began typing on the keyboard, opening windows and closing others, her fingers racing across the keyboard. "There's about six months' worth of video footage on this drive," she said, accessing the content on the hard drive.

"How long will it take?" Birch asked, watching as the facial recognition software went to work. A swarm of small green squares appeared on the computer screen, then rapidly jumped from face to face of the bookstore customers as the video footage was played at speed. The software was searching out a facial match between customers inside the store and the facial topography map it had built from Lindsay Latimer's scanned photo.

"I'm going in reverse," Vega replied. "Starting with the most recent footage. What else can you give me?"

"Like what?"

Vega looked up. "Driver's license details, any credit cards, cell phone number. I'll do a separate search. See if there has been any recent activity."

Birch thought for a moment. The other investigators had already done an exhaustive search of such things, all to no avail. Lindsay's credit cards, like her cell phone, all went dark around the time she had vanished. But it didn't hurt if Vega took another look, just to be certain. "Sure," Birch said. "I'll email over what I have."

Vega gave Birch a generic email address. "Do you have a computer?"

So far Birch had no need for one. His own laptop was back at the boathouse by the lake. "No," Birch replied. "Do I need one?" He was going to get Max Brodie to email directly to Vega what digital financial and cell phone records she had on Lindsay. Now that option didn't seem like a good idea.

"It would help if we're going to work together on finding her," Vega replied.

Birch felt relieved. He needed someone with Vega's skill set. He thought he could go it alone, but it was proving to be more difficult. "So we're working together?" Birch asked slowly.

Vega stopped mid-keystroke, and swiveled in her chair so she was facing him. She gave him a tragic look. "You're not a cop anymore. You have no resources, no access to law enforcement databases or records, and probably no friends either. Your problem is you are too trusting, Thomas. Too honest."

"How can someone be too honest?" Birch asked.

Vega shook her head. "Even now you still don't get it." Vega's chair creaked as she tilted toward Birch. "I told you this before," she said, almost infuriated. "You always play by the rules, and yet you're trying to catch killers who don't play by the rules. How can you possibly compete?"

Being locked away in a tiny jail cell afforded Birch plenty of time to think about the exact same question. He'd gone to jail because he had played by the rules. Was put there by people who didn't. He had lost, they had won.

Birch held up his hand. "I get the picture. You're right. I need your help in finding her," he said steering the conversation away from him, and back to Lindsay Latimer.

Vega rolled her eyes, muttered something uncomplimentary in Aymara—a native language also spoken in Peru—rather than Spanish, so Birch would not understand, and went back to work.

As Birch stood up, Vega swiveled around to him again.

"What?" Birch could sense she wanted to ask him something.

"What if she's not truly missing? Did you ever consider that?"

"Yes, I have."

Vega nodded. "Who told you she was actually missing?"

"Her father." The thought had crossed Birch's mind when he first met Francis Latimer in his office. Vega stroked her hair slowly. "We all have our own reasons for hiding, for not wanting to be found—especially by our parents."

Chapter 22 – Perfect Subjects

"Is everything okay?"

Marcus Kemp looked sideways. The man standing next to him in the elevator was a little too close for Kemp's liking. He could smell the remnants of a chili dog on the man's breath, mixed in with the sour stench of sweat wafting up from the damp patches under the arms of his shirt. The man had a pudgy, red face, with thinning, damp hair, and small beady eyes, distorted into the bulging size of two hard-boiled eggs thanks to the thick lenses of the eyeglasses he wore.

A young girl, perhaps no more than ten years old, with pigtails, stood clutching the man's hand. She too wore similar thick eyeglasses that magnified her inquisitive gaze as she also stared up at Kemp.

Poor genetics obviously ran in the family, Kemp thought as he regarded them both, his utter contempt for them both masked behind a cordial smile.

"It's just my daughter is scared of heights. I'd hate anything to go wrong," the man said. His hard-boiled-egg eyes swiveled to the logo on Kemp's shirt, the motion reminding Kemp of an owl clock with moving eyes he'd once seen advertised on a cable shopping network.

The young girl smiled up at Kemp, a set of braces running across her front teeth.

"Everything is just fine, sir," Kemp replied in the most reassuring tone he could muster, while also wondering how much of a dent in the elevator aluminum wall he could make with the man's head. "It's just routine. Nothing for you to worry about." Kemp nodded at the little girl, suppressing the immense urge he felt to lean down and straighten her crooked teeth himself—with his fist.

The elevator slowed and the excited chatter inside the space increased.

Kemp gripped the handles on his duffel bag a little tighter, and watched as the illuminated number on the floor-indicator panel finally came to rest on eighty-six. The elevator doors parted and bodies surged forward.

Kemp stepped aside, allowing people to pass, then gestured toward the father and daughter duo. "After you."

The man nodded, "Thank you, and have a nice day."

"You're very welcome," Kemp replied, watching them as they exited the elevator and were soon swallowed up by the mass of people outside.

Kemp gave a devious little smile.

He had just found the perfect subjects for his experiment.

Chapter 23 – The Shadow

"She's got a shadow."

Birch swiveled away from the elderly couple sitting a few feet away from him at the same window counter of the coffee shop and lowered his voice into his cell phone. "What do you exactly mean 'a shadow'?"

"Lindsay Latimer," Vega said impatiently on the other end of the call. "She was in the bookstore fifteen days ago. It was the first hit I got on her face, the most recent. A Friday morning. So I continued running the program back from that day. Three days prior, the Tuesday, she was in the bookstore again, in the afternoon. Then nothing again until a week prior. On that day she sat at a table at the coffee shop inside the store. Ordered a drink, opened up a book, then sat there for fifty-two minutes. During the two more recent visits she just was browsing the shelves, purchased nothing. I'll send you the shortened footage. I've edited down, so you will see."

Birch inserted earphones. His cell phoned pinged. "Got it." He opened the attached video file and began playing it, while Vega narrated in his ear.

"On the Friday, a man entered the bookstore after she did. Tall, dark jacket and jeans, wearing a hat and scarf. Can you see him?"

Birch watched the edited footage as it jumped camera angles between Lindsay Latimer strolling among bookshelves, then passing the front counter, just as a tall man wearing a jacket walked through the front door. The man kept his distance from Lindsay, but Birch could tell from his posture and the turn of his head, he was watching her. A ball cap was pulled down tight around his head, with the brim angled downward, and a shemagh scarf—popular among military and civilians as sun protection—was wrapped fashionably around his neck. His chin was tilted downward, making the man's jaw line and mouth subtly but cleverly hidden behind the folds of the scarf.

The man walked to a side display table, selected a book, then appeared to be reading the back cover, holding the book particularly high, almost at head height so he could stealthily watch Lindsay Latimer over the top of the book as she stood at the opposite end of the store, browsing at a display of writing journals and diaries.

"Sneaky bastard," Birch muttered.

"Totally," Vega breathed into his ear, like she was inside his head.

As Lindsay moved on, so did the man, closing the book and placing it back on the table. His movements were subtle, but always keeping her in his line of sight, running a course almost parallel to her like an orbiting moon but maintaining his distance so she wouldn't notice him.

"This is not his first rodeo," Vega said.

"I agree," Birch replied, engrossed in the footage. At times the man used other customers to shield his surveillance from afar, while other times he used the aisles, squatting down to peer through gaps between the books. The high placement of the cameras afforded a birds-eye view of all of this unfolding inside the store. It was like watching a lion hiding among the tall grass stalking an unsuspecting gazelle.

Lindsay disappeared momentarily down an aisle and the camera angle switched, showing her browsing the nonfiction section; "Political Science," the sign on top of the shelf said.

The camera angle switched again, showing the man briefly

looking up in her direction, before slowly making his way toward a parallel isle. Once there, he looked as though he was searching for another book, absentmindedly running his fingers along the upright spines, pausing when there was a gap to peer through to the other aisle.

"I agree. He's shadowing her," Birch finally said. The video footage jumped to an early time frame. It showed Lindsay sitting at a table in the coffee shop inside the bookstore, almost at the same table where Birch had sat. She took out a thick book from her bag, opened it, then began writing. Birch had mistaken Vega's description that Lindsay had opened up a book to read. From what Birch could tell, Lindsay was writing in some kind of thick, journal or diary. The man who was watching Lindsay during the previous footage was nowhere to be seen on this particular day when she was captured by the in-store security cameras. "Did you manage to enhance the man's face?" Birch asked Vega.

No sooner had Birch said the words, then his cell pinged again.

"Already did," Vega replied drily. "He did a good job concealing his face with the scarf and cap most of the time. But as he left the store, after Lindsay had gone, he looked up at the camera on the wall above the door."

Birch opened up another attachment and scrolled through the images on the screen. It was a montage of six cropped and enhanced photo stills of the man's face, taken from the video footage and at various camera angles. In the first five photos, the man's face was cleverly concealed by the scarf and brim of the ball cap. However, it was the last photo that brought a smile to Birch's face. "I see you," Birch said softly as he studied the man's upturned face closely. The man stood at the front door, one hand reaching for the handle, his face tilted up toward the camera above the door, his eyes staring right into the lens. The motion of him looking up had caused the scarf to fall away from around his mouth and jaw, revealing a sly but knowing smile across his face as he stared up at the camera.

"Couldn't resist, could you," Birch said as he looked right into the eyes of the man who may have abducted Lindsay Latimer. "Confident snake, aren't you."

"More like a rat bastard," Vega retorted. "I haven't gone back in-depth to check the other times she was in the store, to see if he was also there," Vega said. "I just wanted you to see some of the footage I found of him before I went further."

"Good work, Beatriz. So she had a stalker."

"Someone was definitely following her," Vega replied. "And judging from the footage so far, I'd say he wasn't an admirer either."

Birch had to agree. The man had come prepared, was experienced, had done this before, perhaps plenty of times before. His method and his manner all shouted bad intentions to Birch. "Thanks, Beatriz. You're a genius."

"It's what I do, Thomas," Vega said breezily.

From her tone, Birch could visualize the warm smile of contentment on Vega's face. Openly, she would never seek praise or affirmation of her abilities. But deep down, Birch knew she craved it—and rightly so. Her unique skills and talents were what he desperately needed right now to catch this guy.

"Find him, Beatriz," Birch said. "Find him for me." Lindsay Latimer's stalker could lead Birch right to her.

"Don't worry," Vega replied, her tone icy cold. "I'll find him." She ended the call.

Birch took a moment to finish his lukewarm coffee while

studying again the last photo of the man, recalling what Vega had just said about him not being an admirer. There was something all too familiar about the way the man moved, how he carried himself, his sly tactics. He was cold, calculating, and confident, almost to the point of being arrogant when he'd looked up at the camera above the door and smiled. This man was laying the groundwork. Getting ready.

He wasn't admiring Lindsay Latimer from afar. He was hunting her up close.

Chapter 24 – Yellow Cab

Like the unexpected phone call in the middle of the night, Eve got the distinct feeling something terrible was about to happen, as she reached for her cell phone.

Pausing on the steps outside the Langone Medical Center, she took the call.

"Eve, where are you?" It was Andy Ramirez, his voice a tight whisper.

At just twenty-five, Ramirez was the only child of a widowed mother who had raised him since his father died in a car accident when Andy was just three years old. He had risen through the ranks from the bottom, as rookie patrol officer, then in a supporting investigative role for Eve. He practically begged Eve to take him on so he could get the necessary eighteen months experience needed working in an investigative unit before being considered for third grade, or junior detective role. He showed plenty of promise, was quick-thinking, took initiative, and was a whiz when it came to anything IT.

Eve looked toward her unmarked police car parked across the street in a loading zone. "Just finished up at the autopsy." She could sense the urgency in Ramirez's voice.

"Where exactly?" Ramirez hissed.

"NYU Medical Center." She spotted a street sign on the corner of the block. First Avenue and East Thirty-Fourth Street. Why?"

"There's a situation unfolding not far from you."

Eve tensed. "What kind of situation?"

"Don't know exactly. But the Internet has just been bombarded with livestream footage of some kind of hostage situation six blocks from you."

An attack? Six blocks? "Where? Which direction?" Eve demanded, hustling down the steps, looking around wildly, trying to orientate herself. North, south, or west of the present location were the only options. A block east was FDR Drive, then the East River.

"West," Ramirez confirmed. "Straight down East Thirty-Fourth."

Six blocks in late morning traffic would take her under three minutes with her lights and siren blaring. She reached the street intersection just as Ramirez relayed her the exact location. Facing west, Eve squinted down the length of East Thirty-Fourth Street, her heart tightening in her chest as she did. She tried to focus into the distance along the narrow trench of space between the towering wall of skyscrapers on either side of the street. Eve's focus slowly tracked upward, cold dread building in her gut. Her eyes cleared the tops of the buildings and she looked toward the clear blue sky—at the tall, majestic building a mile away rising above all else.

Eve began to run toward her parked car.

Driving fast and watching livestream footage on a cell phone at the same time took some effort by Eve as she hurtled toward her destination. The vision was jerky, screams coming from all directions; dark silhouettes moved in and out of the frame. A woman's face filled the screen, wide-eyed in panic. She screamed at the camera, "He's got a gun!" The woman's face suddenly whipped away, and was gone. The view abruptly tilted with more jerky movements, a glimpse of sunlight pouring through tall glass windows, the metal curve of the suicide barrier beyond. Then came another voice, very close. Eve guessed it was the owner of the cell phone who was shooting the livestream. "It's not a gun!" A man's voice was tinged with fear, but obviously not enough fear for him to stop filming and run like everyone else. "He's holding something in his hand. Could be a bomb." The vision bounced as someone ran into him, before settling again. "Hey, what's with those wires he's got?" the man's voice came back again.

As she hurtled down East Fifty-Fourth Street in her car, Eve's attention switched back and forth between her own cell phone sitting in the dash cradle, watching the livestream feed on the screen that Ramirez had sent her the link to, and the chaotic traffic in front of her.

"What the hell? He's got the wires connected to a little girl," the man spoke. Eve shot a look at her cell phone. Little girl? Urgency flooded Eve as she pushed the accelerator harder, her car weaving in and out of traffic, narrowly missing a pedestrian. "Get out of the way!" she screamed at a food delivery cyclist as they wobbled into her path before dramatically peeling away to the side, the front fender of Eve's car missing them by mere inches.

"There's another man standing beside the girl. No, he's kneeling, like he's praying or pleading. I can't tell."

Eve shot a quick look at the cell phone screen. The vision was cut in half, the camera partially jutting out from the edge of a wall. "Where the fuck are the cops?" A voice in the distance demanded.

Eve was only two blocks away, closing the distance fast. She cut across Park Avenue, dodging traffic, people, and cyclists flowing like ants in all directions. Suddenly she jerked the steering wheel, narrowly missing a cherry-red convertible Mustang with the top down. It had cut in front of Eve, a young blonde woman behind the wheel, who promptly flicked Eve the finger as she went past.

One block to go, Madison, then Fifth Avenue, Eve thought. *Nearly there.*

She raced down a bus lane, swerving to avoid a parked delivery truck. *Little girl? Wires connected to her? A bomb? Suicide jacket?* Eve's mind tumbled with sickening images of an aftermath too ugly to imagine. She gripped the steering wheel harder. She had her handgun, two spare magazines, and body armor in the trunk. It was a race against time.

Craning her neck, Eve glanced up through the windshield, saw the vaulted building loom skyward in front of her. She was close, very close.

Out of the lower portion of her eyes, a blob of bright yellow swelled. Then Eve felt an almighty thump and everything turned face-numbing white.

Moments later, Eve staggered out of her car, cell phone in hand, disorientated and stunned, blood dribbling from her nose, her feet crunching on glass. Looking down at the front of her car, she saw the hood crunched inward, buried into the side of a yellow taxi cab. The taxi driver was standing off to one side, screaming and shaking his fist at her, a ring of bystanders gathered around, cell phones pointed at her.

Eve recoiled, then saw the saggy white airbag draped over the steering wheel of her own car, the cracked windshield, steam and smoke seeping from under the crumpled hood, and green engine coolant spreading out from underneath.

"Dumb bitch drove right through a red light," a heavyset man growled at the others in the crowd. "I saw the whole thing."

Eve shook her head, trying to clear the fog of concussion. She took a few drunken steps away from the wreckage.

"Hey!" said the same man. "Grab her, she's trying to escape."

Eve shook her head again, took a deep breath, then drew her gun.

Instantly the circle of onlookers scattered outward, away from Eve. "She's got a gun!" A woman screamed. "Someone call the cops,"

"I *am* the fucking cops!" Eve snarled back at the crowd.

Ignoring the sharp pain in her spine and neck, Eve looked up, found the building she wanted against the blue backdrop of sky, then plummeted headlong into the crowd of onlookers, elbowing her way through before finally breaking free and running, leaving wide-eyed faces and the cursing taxi driver in her wake.

Chapter 25 – Live Feed

The muffled sound of people yelling and screaming caught Vega's attention.

Across the top of her computer screen were the photos of the man who had been shadowing Lindsay Latimer in the bookstore. In one corner of the screen, she had opened a fictitious Facebook page window, one of many cloned profiles she used to trace people she was after.

She turned and watched the livestream that had sprung into her feed. Jerky camera movements, punctuated by a man's unsteady voice, a mix of fear and macabre excitement, synonymous with most viral live videos shot and shared of deplorable things. As Vega watched on, she saw a man appear in the distance, standing on what looked like an outdoor balcony, the Manhattan skyline in the background. The man was holding something in his hand, something boxy with wires snaking down and out of frame. There was something about the man…

Vega quickly swiveled her chair and grabbed her mouse, clicked on the window, enlarging the live feed window, then sat back and watched intently. A shard of sunlight hit the man's face for the briefest of moments, and Vega jolted upright, almost toppling off her chair. Quickly, she hit a key and began recording the livestream, then leaned closer just to make certain.

The man's face became blurry, distorted, but she could make out his side profile against the backdrop of blue sky. Then sunlight hit him again and his face came into focus. Vega quickly moved the computer mouse, rapidly drawing multiple cropping grids over the man's face and screen-shooting them before dragging the images to the side, placing them under the row of profile photos she already had. She worked for the next twenty minutes on the screen shots, enhancing, rotating, comparing them to the bookstore images, while all the time keeping one eye on the livestream.

Finally she sat back and regarded her handiwork. The distinctive jaw, the high cheek bones, the neck and shoulders. They seemed to be similar. Not a perfect match, maybe sixty percent.

She glanced back at the livestream, but the transmission had been terminated by the social media platform.

Vega got up, went to the kitchen, turned on the espresso machine and leaned against the kitchen counter, assembling her thoughts while it heated up. An idea came into her head, ludicrous as it was, but it might just work. She made herself an espresso, went back to her desk and worked on enhancing the images some more, before choosing the clearest of them. Next she compared the best two images again, side-by-side, one taken off the livestream, and the other from the bookstore security camera. Vega was more convinced now. Maybe as much as 80 percent convinced. It was enough for her to email the images to Birch to see what he thought, together with a separate idea she had.

Sixty seconds after sending the email, her cell phone rang,

"So what do you think?" Vega asked, a tiny knot of excitement in her gut, the feeling she usually experienced in an assignment when on the verge of a breakthrough on the person she was hunting.

"There are similarities," Birch admitted. "But without seeing his eyes clearly, it's hard to say."

"It's the closest thing I've got so far in identifying our shadow." Vega explained about the livestream she had just seen.

Nothing of great detail had appeared on the mainstream media feeds she was also monitoring, other than there was some kind of "unfolding incident" at the Empire State Building and it could be terror-related. There was also live footage from news choppers circling the outside of the building, however there was nothing to see.

"The police have also cordoned off a six-block radius north and south, and a three-block radius east and west—including shutting down all subway stations within the cordon," Vega added. She had tapped into the NYPD network and was monitoring police as well as fire department chatter. "What do you think of my other idea?" Vega asked.

"I should have thought about it before," Birch confessed. "I just didn't think."

"It could work, Thomas. It's worth a try."

Birch agreed. "But there is no way I can show my face there again."

Vega smiled. "I will go. It is my idea after all."

"But what do we do once we have it?" Birch asked. "Assuming you manage to find the right one. Someone may have taken it or moved it."

"Let me worry about that," Vega replied. She ended the call, then went to bedroom area of the warehouse and stood in front of a tall framed mirror lying against the brickwork. She regarded herself for a few minutes before talking to her reflection. "Now, how do we make you look different?"

Chapter 26 – Stairwell

It took Eve just sixty seconds after she entered the lobby of the Empire State, to grasp the total confusion, utter mayhem, and absolute panic of the situation.

Security guards were trying to corral people in an orderly fashion out of the building while they were streaming down the fire escape stairs like a stampede of wild horses. Eve could see several people had been injured in the process. Some had minor head wounds, a few limped with twisted ankles, others more serious from where they had fallen and had been trampled on by the mob. One woman had gone into labor from the ordeal and was being rushed outside in a wheelchair, clutching her swollen belly.

Eve managed to forcefully pull aside one of the security guards who was reluctant to tell her anything until she flashed her badge at him. She was told the police had arrived; a few patrol officers on foot were nearby when the call came through. They were forced to begin the arduous climb up using the stairs because power had been cut off to all the elevators, trapping some people inside. There was no way now of getting up or down using them.

A fellow security guard, who was swapping shifts with another guard on the eighty-sixth floor observatory level, had managed to get into an elevator before the power was cut, and had radioed back that he had made it up to the eighty-fourth floor with a group of passengers. The guard managed to get the elevator doors open on that level and get the other passengers safely into the lobby on the floor. But the guard had gone silent since, despite repeated attempts to rouse him again on the radio.

"There must be another way I can get up there!" Eve grabbed again at the same security guard who was now helping an elderly woman who had a gash on her forehead. Eve stared at the row of indicator lights above the elevator banks, the numerals frozen on various floors. She noticed one was illuminated on eighty-four, while the others were stuck above and below eighty-six. There was no elevator on eighty-six.

"Service elevator," the guard yelled back over his shoulder at Eve. "Go through the lobby, past the restrooms." Then he shrugged off Eve's hand and escorted the elderly woman outside toward several EMC trucks pulled up haphazardly in the street.

Not willing to wait for more police to arrive, or the Emergency Service Unit, Eve took off at a run, shouldering her way through the river of people who were flowing in the opposite direction.

Eve stepped out of the service elevator on eighty-five, one floor below the observatory level, preferring to take the fire-escape stairs up to reach the floor above. She didn't want to suddenly arrive on eighty-six, have the elevators doors open only to immediately face a threat.

The lobby on eighty-five was deserted. She went straight to the fire escape door and found herself in a narrow concrete stairwell on the other side. She drew her handgun, partially pulled back the slide, checking that a round was in the chamber, then fist-thumped the magazine baseplate making sure it was rammed home. She did this every time she drew her weapon. The last thing she wanted was for it to jam during a firefight and then end up being shot dead. She closed her eyes and brought her handgun to her chest, gripping it in silent prayer. It was just her, alone.

Eve snapped open her eyes, brought her gun up, took aim at the edge of stairs above her, and began to climb.

Halfway up the next flight of stairs, she stopped.

Thin strands of blood dribbled down from the cement edge above her head and splashed on to the metal handrail next to her. She learned out, craned her neck to look up the stairwell, but couldn't see the source of the blood.

Gripping her gun harder, she tensed her shoulders and arms, then continued her ascent, keeping her aim focused on the stairs above her.

Reaching the next landing, Eve immediately pivoted her aim up and around, almost expecting someone to be standing there. But the next flight of stairs was empty. She was between floors, and still couldn't see the fire-escape door to the eighty-sixth floor. More blood dripped down from above.

Relax. Keep breathing, she told herself.

Eve relaxed her grip on her gun, then applied it again and continued upward. As she slowly climbed, one step at a time, something came into view. First, a hand, draped over the top step, then a person's head, then the entire body, laying faceup on the landing above.

She stood perfectly still, and listened. More voices echoed up from below, and the clang of doors being opened, then slammed. More people fleeing down the stairwell in panic, Eve imagined.

Glancing up and to her left she spotted the fire door to level eighty-six. Next it, near the floor, a small metal box was attached to the wall; the front of the box was open, wires dangling out.

Switching to a one-handed grip on the gun, Eve aimed at the center of the fire door, then crouched and reached out with her other hand to the body to feel for a pulse.

Nothing. But his skin was warm, very warm.

He had gray hair, and vacant eyes that seemed to slowly dim even as Eve looked at them. The front of his security guard's uniform was soaked in blood, and a vile, deep cut went clean across his throat, the larynx partially sliced open and exposed.

Eve tasted sour reflux in her throat as she glanced at the name tag on the man's uniform: Roy.

Stepping over the body, careful to avoid the pooling blood, Eve reached the landing and stood in front of the fire door then pressed her ear against it.

Silence.

Gently she pulled on the handle, easing the door open just a few inches and looked out into the lobby of level eighty-six.

"Please help me!"

A man staggered toward Eve, clutching a blood-soaked cloth to his face, his hair disheveled, suit crumpled, the front of his white business shirt and necktie speckled in red. The side of his face not covered by the bloodied cloth was blackened and charred.

Eve lowered, then holstered her gun.

The man looked wildly around the lobby of the eighty-sixth floor, then back over his shoulder whence he staggered. "It was madness," he stuttered. "People…everywhere…running." He turned back to Eve. "Thank God." He grimaced, squeezing the one visible eye shut in pain.

"Sir, can you tell me what happened?" Eve asked.

He staggered forward some more. "I was pushed," he said. "Fell into a glass…" His words trailed off.

Eve could see he was confused and dazed.

"An explosion," the man then spluttered, swiveling one eye at Eve.

Explosion? Eve tensed at the word. A bomb? Eve stepped

forward, and instantly the man cowered away from her.

"It's okay," Eve said, wanting to get past him, to see for herself. There could be other lives still in danger, the perpetrator still here. "Sir, you need to get out. The elevators aren't working," Eve continued, taking hold of his arm and praying the service technicians were on their way to get the elevators working again.

The man pulled away.

"Don't worry, I can get you out." Eve said. "There's a service elevator waiting on the floor below." Eve guided the man through the lobby. "Are there any others on this floor?" she asked.

The man avoided Eve's eyes. "Others?" His voice was hollow, vacant, like he didn't understand.

"Other people," Eve repeated. "Is there anyone else injured back there? Who did this?"

"I...I don't know," the man stammered. "There was a man, he had a hostage or something. I couldn't really see. I must have passed out when I hit my face. People said he had a bomb."

She hurried the man along. "Go down the fire escape to the next floor, there's a body in the stairwell. Don't worry about it, just go around it."

"A body!" the man shrieked.

Eve nodded. "Stay inside the stairwell on the next floor below. Don't go outside. Walk past the fire escape door on eighty-five, and you'll see another elevator further along. Stay there and wait for me. There may be others I need to bring out," Eve said, hoping the service elevator was still waiting on the floor below.

"Thank you," the man said as he staggered off.

Eve drew her gun again and moved cautiously past the bank of elevators, up a short flight of stairs, and into the wide observatory area. Rope barriers lay strewn, tossed aside, and broken glass crunched under Eve's feet as she cautiously moved forward, sweeping her gun left to right, then back again. The place seemed empty, silent except for the moan of the wind from beyond the expanse of glass wrapped around the outer perimeter of the room where sunlight poured in from, the Manhattan skyline beyond.

Eve moved down a ramp, pushed open a heavy glass door, and went outside.

Eve heard the roar of an engine from above and a NYPD police chopper swooped down out of the sky toward her. A police sharpshooter was strapped to a harness, his body tilting out of the side door, both feet resting on the chopper's skid. The sharpshooter brought his rifle to bear directly at Eve, aiming at her head. Eve was instantly doused with a relentless wave of rotor wash. Looking up, she brought her hands up, displaying the police badge dangling around her neck.

The sharpshooter paused then lowered his rifle, said something into his mouthpiece. The chopper pulled away and began a slow circle of the building.

Eve was halfway around the outside area of the observation deck when she saw the two bodies.

A man and a young girl.

Chapter 27 – Phobia

She glided between the shelves, tables, and other customers like a bored shark contemplating a school of trapped mackerel.

She was looking—careful not to touch anything—for something in particular, and was acutely aware the store assistant behind the counter was watching her out of the corner of his eye. From studying the security footage so many times beforehand, she knew the layout and where her prize should be located.

Stopping at a table, she looked down, then took her time, making certain the geometry of the neatly stacked books on the table and the angle of where she was standing matched the mental scene she had memorized.

Satisfied she had found her catch, she discretely pulled out a pair of latex gloves, slipped them on, picked up the chosen book, and carefully placed it into a Ziploc bag.

She waited patiently by the cash register while the store assistant finished serving another customer, until it was just her alone. She smiled at the young man and held out the book in the plastic bag.

The young man frowned as he took the book, then glanced at the latex gloves the woman was wearing.

"I have a germ phobia," the woman explained, handing over cash for the book.

"I think this is the only copy we have in stock I'm afraid." The young man looked around, then whispered to the woman. "I can wipe it clean for you with an alcohol wipe if you wish?" he offered, with a look of complete understanding. "I do it with all my books. You never know where people's fingers have been these days."

Suppressing a bout of mild panic, the woman replied, "That won't be necessary, thank you."

The man nodded, rang up the sale and placed the plastic bag containing the book into a store paper bag and handed it over.

"Keep the change," the woman said graciously.

Outside, the woman quickly crossed the street, then from under the shadows of a flower-store awning, placed a phone call.

A man answered after the first ring. "Yes?"

"Got it."

Outside the Empire State Building, Marcus Kemp spotted a paramedic approaching him, a young black woman with dreadlocks, wearing an EMS jacket and latex gloves.

Perfect.

His limp suddenly became more pronounced as she took him under the arm and steered him through the mayhem of people milling around. Police were running in all directions and a growing crowd of bystanders were filming with their cell phones. Kemp ducked his head down, covering his face more with the bloodied cloth. Once they were past the police barricade and heading toward the open double door of an ambulance truck, Kemp slowed, his one visible eye swiveling about. Then his prayers were answered. "Hey Casey, can you help me with this one!"

Kemp saw another paramedic struggling with an older woman with a bone protruding from her leg.

"It's okay," Kemp said motioning toward the other paramedic. "I'll just sit down for a second."

"Try to remain conscious, sir?" the young female paramedic said as they reached the back of the EMS truck. Kemp slid his arm off her shoulders and sat down on the rear steps of the truck. "You go and help the woman; she looks a lot worse than me."

The paramedic nodded, appreciating the unselfish gesture.

"I'll stay right here," Kemp called after the young woman as she jogged over to help her colleague.

Kemp looked around, still holding the cloth to his face. When satisfied no one was looking, he stood, slipped down the side of the truck and out of sight.

Walking quickly now with no limp, Kemp was a block away from the police cordon when he cut down a narrow side street where he quickly tossed the bloodied cloth into a trash can and washed away his blackened face under an outside faucet. Then slipping out his cell phone, he shot off a quick text. "Expect extra bonus points."

Then from his jacket pocket he pulled out the device he had used on the father and daughter. The experiment had been a complete success, but he wanted to test the device further, push it to its limits—and he knew the perfect candidate.

DAY 3

Journal Entry #16 – Milan

Somewhere between Paris and Milan, I knew if I was going to live, then she needed to die.

It was never my intention at the outset. Sure, I had thought about it after the first day we met, but soon discarded it as just some crazy idea. However, as I got to know her more, the idea didn't really seem that crazy after all.

I can honestly say it's her fault for planting the seed in my head in the first place. Like a fool, she has told me everything about her life, including hundreds of photos she has on her phone. Her parents live in a huge Manhattan penthouse overlooking Central Park.

Fourth of July last year, she spent at the sprawling family beach house, sailing their yacht in some place called Erin's Bay. I have no idea where the place is. Then there was Christmas at the family cabin in a place called Aspen, where I believe the rich go skiing. From the photos and from what she's told me, the place has eight bathrooms! Why the hell would you need eight bloody bathrooms! The place looks more like a castle than a cabin.

And all the talk about how much she loves her father. It's starting to make me sick.

Her undoing is going to be her own error, and she is so blind to it.

My moment of crystal-clear certainty came today as we drank coffee in the Piazza del Duomo, under the shadow of the Milan Cathedral. Once more I was listening to the everyday minutiae dribble out of her mouth, picturing one of the Cathedral spires breaking off, falling from the heavens, then impaling her through the top of her head.

She has no appreciation for what she has, seems almost bored by it, her safe, want-for-nothing life living on the Upper West Side of New York City.

God, I even look like her! But I'm not her.

But I could be…

She knows nothing about my life, what I've had to endure, suffered, what I'm running from. I have kept those secrets hidden from her. I've told her a few facts, and plenty of lies about my past.

Milan is such a beautiful place. I certainly wouldn't have visited it myself, and these last two weeks have definitely been an education for me, the sights, the food, the shopping, (not that I have bought anything). But she has bought so many clothes, and insists I follow her into every boutique, stand near the change rooms so she can come out and perform a cringe-worthy ballerina twirl and ask my honest opinion. Bollocks to her! So I lie, tell her she looks like a princess.

We're close to the same size too, and she has bought me a few dresses as well. She insists on paying for everything, the restaurants, the cafés, the accommodation. I am truly grateful to her, in more ways than she could ever possibly know.

Today she wanted us to go to the hotel spa, but I refused. I had other, more devious plans… While she was gone from the room for two hours, I tried on her dresses. They were a little tight. I just need to lose a few pounds and they'll fit like a glove. I tried to put everything back in the boxes exactly as they were so she wouldn't get suspicious.

Her shoes do not fit me and no amount of dieting will change that fact. It's not that I have large feet, it's just mine are not as small as hers.

She left her purse behind too, preferring to charge the spa treatment to the room. Too trusting, she is. My god! She has so many credit cards!

She has kept all the receipts for the dresses and the shoes. I'll keep the dresses. They'll be my incentive to lose some weight, but I'll return the shoes and get refunded in cash, which is good, as I'm almost out of money. I don't think she suspects it. I took some Euros from her purse while she was in the shower yesterday. She had such a thick wad of cash in there anyway. I'm certain a few bills missing would go unnoticed.

I deserve better. I want more. Pure survival and the desire for a better life is now what drives me. Meeting this young woman, my traveling companion, my new friend, has shown me what I truly want, how I want my life to be, minus the constant moaning I must endure as I listen to her each day. If she only walked a day in my shoes, seen what I have seen with my own eyes, then maybe she wouldn't complain so much.

Killing her won't be a problem. But how do I get rid of the damn body?

Chapter 28 – Under the Bus

"He must have had a change of clothes," Eve said. "The blood I imagine was purchased from some theatrical store, as was the black powder he used to darken his face, to make it look like he had been caught in an explosion."

Disappointment and regret were two words not in Eve's vocabulary. But she felt the bitterness of emotions right now. For the last hour, both she and Andy Ramirez had stood in Hagen's office, with the door closed, listening while he ranted as to what had transpired yesterday.

"I've got a press conference at ten a.m.," Hagen said from behind his desk. "And what exactly am I going to tell them?" His furious eyes cut between Eve and Ramirez before finally settling back on Eve.

Eve met his gaze. "Tell them the truth," she replied calmly. Truth was, Eve wanted to yell at her boss. "Tell them he got away," she continued. "There was no bomb, no explosion, and the perpetrator had disguised himself as an elevator technician so no one questioned his authority, plus it gave him unfettered access to wherever he chose. Tell them we found an electronic device patched into the elevator master-control cabinet allowing him to remotely control the main elevators and to cut power when he did." A duffel bag was also discovered stuffed under tiles in the ceiling above a cubicle in the men's restrooms. Inside the bag were an assortment of tools, and a discarded uniform, the shirt emblazoned with the logo of a nonexistent elevator maintenance company.

Eve had already explained all this to Hagen.

"Offer your deepest sympathies to the families and loved ones of the security guard, who had tried to apprehend the perp, and of the father, both of who were brutally murdered, and whose daughter is now in hospital after being tortured by apparent electrocution. Then tell them the daughter is expected to make a full recovery." Eve finished what she thought was an eloquent summary of a hopeless and embarrassing situation for all involved.

Andy Ramirez remained ramrod straight and mute, preferring to avoid Hagen's eyes and stare straight ahead at the row of framed commendations, perfectly lined up on the wall behind the captain.

Hagen leaned back in his chair, his anger subsiding for a moment as he regarded his senior detective. She was practically giving him his speech for the press who had been assembling in the foyer downstairs since dawn.

Eve's picture had been snapped by an opportunistic journalist on their cell phone last night while she stood on the street talking to other police officers and being treated for mild concussion and a facial wound. Her photo was soon plastered all over the internet with the story that, Eve Sommers, a detective from the NYPD Fifth Precinct, was the first senior officer on scene, after first T-boning a yellow cab in her police vehicle. It was then reported that—after ignoring her own injuries—Detective Sommers ran the remaining block to the Empire State Building, where, without waiting for further backup and disregarding her own safety, she bravely rode up in a service elevator to apprehend a likely terrorist. Multiple cell-phone footage soon emerged, and had gone viral, of Eve stumbling out of her car wreck, brandishing her police-issued Glock before taking off down the street. She had become an overnight online sensation both for good and bad reasons. Some were saying she was extremely courageous and unselfish, and more police should take action like she had. Others—the inevitable online haters and trolls who had crawled out of the cyber swamp—called her actions reckless, immoral, and she should be locked up in jail.

"Tell them all occupants were successfully evacuated from the building without any further loss of life or major injury," Eve paused, seeing the glimmer of excitement in Hagen's eyes that wasn't there an hour ago, just two huge burning coals of fiery rage consuming most of his face.

Perhaps it was jealousy from Hagen that it was *her*, and not *he* who the press were talking about. But Eve didn't want the limelight. She had always shunned it. She was just as enraged as Hagen, more so, that the killer had slipped through their fingers. All she wanted was to focus her anger on catching him.

And now for the icing on the cake, Eve thought. "Tell them if it wasn't for the quick thinking of one of *your* senior detectives—whom you have personally mentored—the body count could have been much worse." The last comment wasn't for Eve's benefit. She knew Hagen desperately needed an opening to get his own name into the rapidly unfolding news cycle before it was too late. That's why he had so hastily announced this morning's press conference, to steal the attention away from other law enforcement services and other precinct captains, just like a coyote urinating to claim ownership, to mark and defend its territory.

Hagen sat upright. His eyes narrowed, his jaw twitched. The old coyote had finally seen the injured deer Eve had just placed in front of him. "And what do I tell them when they ask about the identity of the killer?" Hagen asked. "That we have an accurate description of him, a facial composite we are going to release?"

Eve was mildly surprised by this line of questioning from Hagen, that she practically had to hand-hold him through the process of using spin to explain failure. Maybe he wasn't political material after all. "You tell them it's too early in the investigation," Eve replied. "Your officers, under your direct supervision, are working twenty-four seven, poring over security footage and witness statements, and it will only be a matter of time before the identity of the assailant is known."

Hagen's facial expression almost morphed into a smile—almost.

So Eve went for the jugular. "And neither you, nor any officer under your command will sleep a wink until an arrest has been made, and"—Eve paused again, knowing she was treading a fine line between controlled emotion and reckless ambition, the latter of which she knew Hagen had plenty of—"you have personally taken command of this case and New Yorkers can rest easy that the villain will be soon caught."

Hagen slowly nodded thoughtfully.

Eve could see the cogs of self-interest slowly turning inside his head. She wasn't only appeasing her boss, she was also laying the path for her own involvement. It made Eve's blood boil knowing the villain had hoodwinked her into thinking he was a victim, had then ridden the service elevator down to the lobby only to waltz right past the hordes of police, firefighters, and heavily armed ESU officers, before vanishing into the bright sunshine outside.

And yet, last night after going for a long walk to calm her frustration, only to then toss and turn in bed, alone in her apartment, waiting for the first rays of sunshine to cut through the bedroom blinds, Eve couldn't see how she would have reacted any differently. It was such a convincing act the man had played on her. Eve had tried to jot down some notes on how he looked, but he had used the bloodied cloth to hide half his face to great effect, and the dark makeup obscured the other half. The only real thing she knew about him was he was extremely cunning, meticulous, and very inventive.

Eve looked past Hagen toward the wall behind him, her chin and jaw thrust out defiantly. She passionately wanted to lead this case. Not for the accolades. She wanted retribution, to hunt down the ruthless killer who had fooled her, murdered two innocent people, and tortured a helpless child. It wasn't her job. It was her life. An unquenchable fire raged inside her to catch such people.

"I want this," Eve broke her silence, and glared at Hagen. It was her turn to vent her anger. "I want to be the lead detective on this case."

Hagen's smile widened as he watched Eve.

For a split second, Eve wondered if Hagen's wide smile was because she had finally convinced him to see the opportunity to further exalt his public persona as the savior of the people—or if she had inadvertently provided him with a body to throw under the bus if it all turned to crap.

Chapter 29 – Romance

Back at her desk, Eve picked up an envelope lying on her keyboard. "What's this?"

The homicide squad room resembled five movie sets squashed onto one small soundstage, besieged by myriad diverse actors all playing their differing roles at once. Some detectives sat hunkered behind cluttered desks, phones cradled to their ear. Others stood at the water cooler, verbally jousting with their colleagues, reenacting a particular tragedy—fingers shaped into a gun or a knife—welcoming a second opinion. The air in the room sat heavy under the humidity of stale coffee, yesterday's takeout dinner, slept-in clothes, and the hollow sound of computer keyboards being brutally tortured by two-fingered antagonists.

All signs of undying dedication.

Andy Ramirez swiveled around from his desk to face Eve. "It was dropped off this morning to the duty sergeant at the front desk," Ramirez replied. "So I was told."

Eve examined the envelope, her name in neat script on the front. Inside she found a slip of paper. She read the message and frowned, then crumpled it up and threw it angrily into the wastebasket. She sat down with a heavy sigh, not wanting to look at the pile of paperwork in her desk tray, for fear it would topple over at the slightest glance.

Ramirez's cell phone rang. He glanced at the caller ID then answered the call, swiveling back around at his desk and speaking in hushed tones. "I said not to call me at work," Ramirez said into his phone.

Eve glanced at Ramirez's back as he spoke.

"No, I can't make it tonight," Ramirez said, shifting in his seat, trying to cup the mouthpiece with his hand, making it obvious to all was a personal call.

When Ramirez ended the call, he turned back to Eve and she could see the embarrassment on his face. "Woman problems?" Eve asked, enjoying watching the young man turn an even darker shade of red.

"Just a new girl I started dating," Ramirez replied. "She calls me all the time, wanting to know what I'm doing almost every minute of the day. She can be kind of smothering."

Eve gave a smirk. "Enjoy the attention while you can; just don't let it interfere with you work."

Ramirez nodded.

"What I don't understand is how did our killer get a knife through security screening at the Empire State?" Eve asked.

"You mean what he used to kill the security guard?" Ramirez asked.

Eve stared off into space. "Think about it. He poses as an elevator technician, has a bunch of tools with him in the duffel bag, which he then leaves behind."

"A box cutter?" Ramirez offered. "I know plenty of people who carry them around under the seat of their cars or when they're out at night."

"It's still considered a concealed weapon," Eve said, thinking. "And security would have taken it off him when they x-rayed his bag." Eve gave Ramirez a look that said get to work. "I want a full inventory of the duffel bag they found in the men's restroom."

Ramirez grabbed a notepad and started writing.

"Find out what tools could have been used to cut the guard's throat." Eve began drumming her desktop with a pen. "I doubt he left the weapon behind." They were yet to locate the murder weapon used on the security guard whose throat had been slit, nor the device he used on the father and daughter. "But check it out anyway."

Ramirez nodded. "Sure, boss."

Eve glanced back into her wastebasket, thinking about the note she had screwed up and tossed away. Forensics had told her it could take weeks to fully process the scene at the Empire State Building, and at the moment, they had nothing solid to go on. Another team was working on the security footage and online videos shot by the public, but until then, the investigation was going nowhere. By nature, Eve was an impatient person, not willing to sit around during an investigation and wait for a break. She needed to make things happen.

She called the hospital to check on the young girl. A nurse told Eve the girl was stable, but hadn't regained consciousness. Eve decided it was best to post a police guard outside her hospital door so she quickly organized it. Right now the young girl may be the only real witness they had.

Eve checked her watch, then stared at the wastebasket again. She grabbed her jacket off the back of her chair and slipped it on.

"Where are you going, boss?" Ramirez said, glancing back at her.

Eve gave him an anxious look. "To do something I might later regret," she said. "Call me if you find anything."

Chapter 30 – Unlikely Alliance

"I can't begin to imagine how many fingerprints you will have to comb through and analyze," Birch said with a look of empathy Eve didn't believe.

"Not to mention the multitude of partial prints you'll waste time on reconstructing, hoping to find a match." He drained his coffee cup. "It could take years to wade through it all."

"What do you want, Birch?" Eve asked. "You didn't arrange to meet so you can tell me what I already know." As she regarded him properly, up close for the first time, Eve couldn't help see some damage there, behind his eyes. He was unshaven, with short messy dark hair, finger-combed at best to create a look most men would pay a stylist good money to achieve. He was tall, lean, boyish, like a man caught between youthful exuberance and stoic maturity. She was unsure if his relaxed, unkempt look was just how he was or if he just didn't care anymore. She felt it was the latter. He was jittery too, bouncing one leg incessantly up and down under the table.

Birch smiled, "I take it you haven't identified the killer yet. Plenty of witnesses I imagine, but no accurate physical description worthwhile pursuing."

Eve drummed her fingers on the table, next to her untouched coffee cup.

Birch continued, "No clear security footage either, but plenty of grainy online footage that's poor at best, even after you've cleaned it up."

"What makes you say that?" Eve didn't like her investigation being deconstructed, then fed back to her by an outsider, even if everything Birch was saying was true.

"You wouldn't be sitting here if you thought otherwise," Birch replied.

Eve tried not to show her annoyance. Hagen had already called Eve again on the way over to her meeting at the park café with Birch, to see what progress she had made. He was placing undue pressure on her and the team to have something tangible to go to the mayor with or announce to the press.

Eve studied Birch for a moment. He had been a senior detective, and had cleared more cases than her. But the past was the past. "Like I said, what do you want, Birch?"

"To help you, Detective Sommers," Birch replied.

"To help *me*?" Eve stifled a laugh as she looked around the park. Birch wanted something. Something he didn't have and couldn't get either. Then it hit her. "Lindsay Latimer," Eve nodded slowly. "So she really is missing and you want something from me to help you find her." Now it was her turn to put her skills of deduction into play, just as Birch had done to her. "You've hit a brick wall, haven't you?"

"Not exactly a brick wall," Birch replied.

"And you're flying solo. You don't have any of the resources you once had as a detective." Eve gave a smile of contentment.

Birch gave a nod of agreement, even though not fully true. He had Beatriz Vega. She was worth ten detectives to him. "I give you something and you give me something in return."

"What could you possibly give me that has any value to my case?" This time Eve couldn't stifle her laugh. She shook her head slowly. This was a complete waste of time. She wasn't about to bow to Birch's game of cooperation. He was a convicted felon after all. Eve leaned forward, gave a sarcastic smile. "How about I just arrest you for obstructing an investigation into a multiple homicide."

Birch shrugged. "Because it wouldn't stick. And you know it. I'm not obstructing anything. I'm just sitting here in the park having a cordial conversation with you. No harm in that."

"Withholding evidence for starters," Eve countered, the smile gone from her face.

"You haven't seen what I have to offer."

"Not interested." Eve pushed her chair out and stood. "I value my job enough not to give police information to a convicted felon."

Birch reached down to the backpack at his feet, and pulled out an object wrapped in plastic. He placed it on the wrought-iron table in front of Eve, and said nothing.

Eve looked at the book inside the sealed plastic bag. "What is this supposed to be?" She felt disappointed. To think she actually had a fleeting belief Birch had some actual solid information as to who the Empire State Killer was.

Birch tapped the book with his finger. "Let's just say a person of interest to me may have touched this. His fingerprints could be on it."

Eve didn't move. "And you think it's the same person as the Empire State Killer?" Eve detested using the term the press had labeled the perpetrator. The press were also speculating there could be a link to the killing on the Roosevelt Island Tramway, that it could be the same person. Two highly visible, seemingly random murders in two days, at two popular tourist attractions in the city, with no apparent motive. The similarities weren't lost on Eve.

Birch held Eve's gaze. "I've seen the video footage of the incident yesterday. There are distinct similarities between the person I'm interested in and the man who killed those people at the Empire State."

Eve cocked her head. Birch wasn't telling her everything. "And what were you comparing the Empire State Building video footage to? What else do you have?"

"Do we have a deal?" Birch asked. "If you manage to pull a decent fingerprint off the cover of this book, I want his name. I want to know who he is."

Eve picked up the book, studied it closer. Now she was interested. The book cover had a smooth, glossy finish, perfect for retaining the sweat and oil from a person's fingertips. "Plenty of people could have touched this book." She looked at Birch.

"But not as many as those who have visited, trampled and touched your current crime scene over the weeks, months, even years. Hundreds of thousands of grubby little fingers on every door handle, lift button, windowpane." Birch indicated toward the book in Eve's hand. "This could narrow your search down considerably. Save you a lot of time."

"You're forgetting one thing, Birch."

"No, I'm not. I fully understand this will only work if *your* killer and *my* person of interest have been previously arrested."

"If their fingerprints are not already on the database, then all bets are off," Eve said, looking down at Birch. "And if I do get a hit, and it leads my investigation nowhere, then you get nothing in return. No name."

Birch shrugged. "Then we'll both have nothing, and we'll both just have to wait until…" Birch left his words hanging.

Eve sat back down. Still holding the book, feeling the weight of it in her hand, she looked around at the people in the park: couples hand-in-hand, joggers pounding the footpaths, older people content to take their time, a dog chasing a Frisbee. A woman was pushing a young girl in a stroller, her little legs kicking to her own beat as she lovingly licked an ice-cream cone.

Everywhere Eve looked she saw innocence, trust, and faith that, on balance, the world around them was generally safe, and they were protected. She imagined it was the same belief people had on the Roosevelt Island Tramway and at the Empire State Building—until terror hit.

This was *her* city, *her* people and she needed to protect them. Yet, the events from the last two days had left her feeling useless, unable to do her job. She thought back to what Dr. Maya Zin, the forensic pathologist, had said about the tramway victim. *This could be the start of something truly dark and sinister.*

Eve turned back to Birch. He was watching her with hopeful eyes.

"Deal," she said.

Birch scribbled down his cell phone number and handed it to her.

"And keep me in the loop about your person of interest." She stood up again and began walking away. "I want to know everything and anything you find out about him," she said over her shoulder.

No sooner had Eve departed when Birch's cell rang. It was a restricted number. He answered the call.

"Thomas?"

Birch's heart stumbled a beat. It was a woman's voice, a voice intimately familiar to him from fifteen years of marriage.

"Suzanne?"

The line went silent, and for a moment Birch thought he had lost the signal.

Suzanne Birch's trembling voice came on the line again. "It's Justin. He's gone missing."

Chapter 31 – Images of Death

"So you think the Empire State Building murderer's fingerprints are on this book?" Dr. Maya Zin looked down at the book inside the plastic bag Eve had placed on her desk.

"Maybe," Eve replied. "I'd like you to rush the testing. DNA too."

"I'll personally walk it to the labs, get Dalton onto it ASAP," Maya replied.

"Thanks, Maya. I really appreciate it." Eve knew she could confide in Maya, and the conversation they were having would go nowhere else. She was on Eve's team, part of the small inner circle of people she could trust. Apart from being extremely dedicated to her profession, Eve knew Maya was extremely confidential. The young forensic pathologist was instrumental in removing a number of staff members, senior ones too, for leaking autopsy results and forensic case details to the press. Maya wouldn't tolerate such behavior in her lab. "At the moment we've got nothing, not one lead as to the identity, or motive of the killer."

Maya's eyes narrowed behind her glasses. "Surely there would have been plenty of witnesses?"

Eve shook her head. "We're combing through everything, but the killer just blended in. Even the online footage I've seen so far hasn't given us much to go on."

Maya glanced at the book in its plastic bag. "Prints, we'll get started on within the hour. DNA, if there is any, we'll know within twenty-four hours. But, from what you've told me, it's a brand-new book from a bookstore." Maya picked up the book in the plastic bag and studied the front and back cover. "Unless your person of interest bled, ejaculated, licked, urinated, defecated, or left some other form of biological material on the surface, then we won't have anything to test for DNA."

Eve smiled at Maya's clinical yet candid summation of the biological material used to determine a DNA profile.

"But, I'll do my best," Maya added.

"That's all I can ask for. Look it's just a hunch, from a source of mine."

Maya gave Eve a dubious look. "Could end up being a wild-goose chase." Maya clicked on her keyboard. Instantly the large flat touch screen on the side wall lit up. "Now let me share with you what I do know about your two victims from yesterday's killing."

They both got up and walked over to the screen. "By the way, how's the young girl going?" Maya asked.

Eve gave a helpful smile, "Thanks for asking. No improvement so far when I called the hospital this morning. It's touch and go. She took a massive electric shock I was told by the doctors."

Maya nodded, an almost parental look of concern on her face. "Hey, did you hear?"

"Hear what?" Eve asked.

"Uri Goff is dead."

Eve said nothing.

"Eve?"

"What?"

"Uri Goff is dead," Maya said again. "He was found this morning in some alley, shot three times. Someone had clocked him, execution style."

Eve shrugged. "Looks like there is justice after all."

"Wasn't he one of your arrests, the child-killer who had just been released after his conviction was overturned?" Maya persisted. "How many children did they claim he tortured and killed? Ten? Fifteen?"

"Twenty-three." Under Maya's scrutinizing gaze, Eve could almost visualize the cogs turning inside the young pathologist's head.

"Twenty-three," Maya repeated slowly.

"Let's look at Raymond Chandler," Eve said, changing the subject, "the security guard's autopsy first before we discuss the father of the little girl."

Maya broke her gaze, touched the screen and pulled up large, bright photos taken during the autopsy of Chandler.

Eve folded her arms as she watched the screen, her own face covered in the glow of the raw, brutal images of death.

"As you know, and as you can see, the victim was slashed across the throat. Thin blade, right-handed stroke, the killer standing front-on to his victim." Maya turned to Eve. "Still no sign of a murder weapon?"

Eve shook her head slowly. "We're still looking. He may have taken it with him. Even if we do find it I doubt if we'll get any prints of it. He's too clever, too careful."

Maya returned to the screen. "So am I." She zoomed in on one particular photo that showed the neck region under the chin. The victim's head was tilted back so much from the brutal cut, it reminded Eve of the hinged head of a Pez candy dispenser. "He died in seconds. The cut was deep enough to expose the trachea. Your killer didn't hesitate. He used one sweeping arc intending to kill."

Eve thought back to all the blood dripping down the fire escape stairs.

Maya turned back to Eve. "It takes some skill, and I believe he has done this before."

"Why do you say that?"

"It's not easy to do," Maya explained, "to slash the throat like this. It requires a certain level of confidence, and experience. Not for the squeamish either. Much easier and less aggressive to just stab someone in the abdomen. I've seen hundreds of mortal knife wounds, not so many throat slashes. And this is one of the cleanest I've seen. Suffice to say your killer is confident and experienced in such things or he is one extremely sadistic individual who takes the time to master his craft of killing."

Eve pointed at the photo. "He is right-handed you say?"

Maya nodded. "From my examination of the wound, I can tell you the blade swept right to left from the killer's perspective, and he was standing directly in front of the victim."

Eve nodded and turned back to the photo.

Maya waited patiently but said nothing. So Eve probed her, wanting Maya to extend her line of thinking. "Anything else you can tell me about the killer?"

"The victim had no defensive wounds. The kill was quick and unexpected. The security guard had no idea. He was standing right in front of the killer, within arm's reach, so to speak, without any fear or concern. It was someone the guard either knew or trusted."

The fact the killer had posed as an elevator technician hadn't been made public yet. Eve imagined the security guard had crossed paths with the killer in the stairwell, thought nothing of it, then had his throat cut.

"The killer wore the uniform of an elevator technician," Eve finally revealed. "That's how come he got so close to the victim without raising any suspicion." Eve turned to Maya. "That fact hasn't been made public yet."

"Understood."

"So it happened so fast the guard didn't have time to react."

"Seems likely," Maya added.

"What can you tell me about the next victim?"

Maya tapped the screen and the ghastly images disappeared, replaced by photos of a pale naked male laying on a mortuary examination table, the skin of the torso blotched with ugly dark blemishes.

"Not much to say with this victim, the father of the young girl," Maya began. "He died from electric shock. The blackened areas are where the skin was burned and the tissue damage is consistent with electric shock being applied. In these blackened areas I also found tiny punctures in the skin, pincer marks where I believe alligator clips had been attached."

Eve stepped closer to the screen and slowly looked over the photos. There were two significant dark patches where the skin was singed to the deep gray-black hue of charcoal. "Is it usual to see such discoloration from electric shock?" One dark patch was under the left breast, the other along the fatty area of skin near the stomach. The dark patches were the size of dinner plates, Eve estimated.

"Unlike the first victim, this took longer."

Eve turned sharply toward Maya. "Longer?"

Maya used one hand to expand, then zoom in on the burn mark under the left breast. "Only exposure to prolonged electric shock would result in this severity of burnt skin and tissue."

Maya faced Eve. "Your killer took his time with this victim," she said. "His heart didn't seize up from one massive shock. Rather, he was slowly tortured, I would imagine with ever increasing voltages until his heart finally gave out."

Eve concluded her meeting with Maya Zin, by reluctantly agreeing to meet her for drinks tonight after work. Maya said she would get off work at around 9:00 p.m. and would meet her at their favorite cocktail bar in East Village, take a break from the recent death and mayhem. By then Eve was hoping Maya would have some good news about the prints and DNA testing of the book.

It was a long shot, but Eve was scrambling at the moment.

Chapter 32 – Suzanne

It took Birch almost a full minute to convince his ex-wife, Suzanne, to calm down so she could explain what had happened.

Her voice was completely different now compared to the last time he had spoken to her, just before she had walked out on him, taking Justin with her. Back then, she was forthright with her words, stinging in her condemnation, and confident in her tone, all the qualities that were now lacking in her stymied speech.

"He's been missing for six hours now," Suzanne said, her voice sodden with tears.

Birch pressed the cell phone closer to his ear, trying to block out the noise around him.

"We have tried calling his cell phone," Suzanne moaned. "But it keeps going to voice mail. And we've contacted all his friends and none of them have seen or heard from him either."

In the background of Suzanne's voice, Birch could hear the muffled echo of another person. Then it sounded like a hand covered the mouthpiece, some arguing, raised voices—before another, unfamiliar voice came on the line.

"Listen, Tom," came a man's voice now.

Tom? Off to a bad start already, Birch thought. He hated being called that.

The man on the other end continued with an aloof, condescending tone. "This is Dr. Oliver Sloane here, Suzanne's partner."

Finally, Birch thought. A name he could put to the faceless person who had taken his wife and son away from him.

"Ordinarily," Sloane continued, "There would be no need for you to be involved."

Involved? Birch gritted his teeth, imagining some pompous ass of a plastic surgeon on the other end, head raised, looking down his nose at Birch. Birch *was* involved, always would be when it came to his son, Justin. Birch was his father after all. Who was this arrogant prick on the other end? "Put Suzanne back on," Birch said, with a subtle growl in his voice.

There was a short pause, then, "I speak for Suzanne," said Sloane, his voice dripping with even more arrogance, like he was the kind of person who didn't like being questioned, his authority being challenged. "Justin has just been acting a little strange lately…but it doesn't concern you."

Birch squeezed the cell phone harder.

Sloane continued. "It's just this morning, Justin said something strange. We were having an argument."

"What kind of argument?" It took every ounce of effort for Birch not to swear at the man on the other end.

"Nothing to bother yourself about," Sloane replied, dismissing Birch as though he were a speck of lint. "Let's just say we had a slight disagreement…a difference of opinion…Justin and I."

"What kind of disagreement?" Birch wanted answers.

"And then Justin just stormed off," Sloane replied, ignoring Birch's question.

Birch's patience was almost gone. Whatever had happened, whatever Justin had said was enough of a concern for Suzanne, his ex-wife, to pick up her phone and call Birch after more than two years of ghosting him.

Suzanne came back on the line. "Thomas, Justin just got angry. Then he took off." There was a pause, and Birch could feel his ex-wife was struggling to tell him more. Then she did. "He said he was going to New York."

Birch's heart leapt.

"He said he was going to find you."

Chapter 33 – Finding Justin

"And you trust this detective you've given the book to?"

Birch stood in Beatriz Vega's kitchen, cradling a cup of coffee she had just made for him, contemplating the question she had just asked.

"We don't have any other choice," he replied.

Vega stood with her arms folded, her face looking as though she was watching a snake slowly swallow an impossibly large cow.

"You and I don't have the resources to test for prints or DNA," Birch continued.

"And you believe she will share with us the information, if she finds a match to the person we are looking for?"

Birch made a hopeful expression. "We'll see. In the interim, what else have you found out about Lindsay Latimer's trail from the records I gave you?"

Vega voiced her disapproval of Birch's decision with a clicking sound of her tongue, before launching into her findings. "Cell phone records I cannot get access to, and as far as her digital footprint is concerned, there is no recent activity. Social media, credit cards, nothing. It all went dark around the time she disappeared."

So they had reached a dead end; the trail had gone cold. For Birch, Eve Sommers now seemed like their only hope, unless something new came to light. "What about the rest of the video footage from the bookstore?"

Vega shook her head. "Lindsay went in there a few times over the earlier weeks, but the man we saw wasn't following her. He only appeared recently."

On the way over to Vega's place, Birch had been preoccupied

with Justin, and what Suzanne had said about him coming to New York to find him. Perhaps it was just a threat, a barb shot in anger just to get a reaction from his mother. Yet, deep down, Birch was hoping it wasn't an idle threat, that his son actually wanted to come and see him. Maybe as he got older, Justin had begun to see through the toxic sludge his mother had been feeding him over the years about his father. Maybe Justin wanted to see for himself, talk to Thomas.

Birch didn't have Justin's cell phone number and Suzanne had refused to give it to him even when he asked, telling him it was pointless, she had already tried calling Justin numerous times and it kept going to voice mail. Birch had told Suzanne if she managed to reach Justin, to tell him to call him. Suzanne reluctantly agreed. She had little choice; her son could be coming to a city of eight million strangers. All Birch could do now was wait for his cell to ring with any news.

"I need you to search for someone else for me," Birch finally said to Vega.

Vega pushed off the countertop. "Who?"

Birch paused, then looked her in the eye. "My son, Justin."

If Vega had a reaction to the request, she didn't show it, nor did she ask. She just waited patiently while Birch told her about Suzanne's phone call earlier and how she and Justin had left and gone to live in Boston while he was in jail. He didn't provide Vega with all the details, just enough to get her started.

To Vega's credit, she just listened, no expression on her face, no judgment in her eyes. "Do you think he will go to your home upstate?"

"I hope not," Birch replied. "I'm hoping he will call me first. I have a neighbor, a woman who keeps an eye on the place for me while I'm away. She has my cell phone number."

"Maybe you should give her a call and let her know, to keep a lookout."

Birch agreed, and called his neighbor while Vega drifted back to her computer. "Boston to New York, by bus or train will take about four hours. He would be here by now if you said he left home six hours ago."

"If he came straight away," Birch replied. He stood next to Vega while she sat down and began furiously typing away on her keyboard. "I'll check the bus and train companies, see if they have a booking. If it was a spur-of-the-moment decision, he may have paid by cash at the bus depot or train station." The Amtrak website came on the screen and Vega set in motion software she had written to hack into the reservation system. Lines of code and symbols soon dribbled down the computer screen that made no sense to Birch as he looked on.

"Leave it with me for a while," Vega said over her shoulder as she opened other windows on her screen, and began searching for Justin Birch through other bus and train companies.

Following Vega's wishes, Birch wandered to one of the large windows and stared outside at the landscape of buildings with water towers perched on top, thinking that out there, somewhere, was his son trying to reach him. He stared down at his cell phone, willing it to ring, praying for it to be Justin calling him, to hear his son's voice after all these years. The thought of speaking to his son both thrilled and terrified him. It's funny how you yearn for something so much, think about it constantly night and day to the point where it consumes your entire life. And then, when there is the possibility of it happening, self-doubt and fear begins to slowly creep into your dreams, turning them into nightmares.

Chapter 34 – Kill Dozens

"There she is," the salesman said excitedly while mauling the side of his face with spindly, nail-chewed fingers.

"The source came from a fracking company in Pennsylvania," he stuttered. "Plenty of it left lying around when the company went broke. Use the stuff to punch big-ass holes through solid rock."

Moriarty leaned in to get a closer look. Sitting snuggly within the foam-cut interior of the hard case was a stainless-steel sphere, about the size of a soccer ball. He could see his own face, distorted and swollen in the shiny, mirrorlike surface. "Will it work?" Moriarty said, captivated by the thing.

"'Course it will work," the man giggled, with a toothy grin. "You got the money?"

Money wasn't a problem for Moriarty, thanks to rich parents who had made their wealth in Hong Kong by establishing a chain of commercial laundries well before the territory was handed back to China in 1997. Reaching into the trunk of the battered sedan, Moriarty felt the cold, smooth aluminum shell under his fingertips, pictured the raw carnage waiting to be unleashed from within the sphere—and smiled. He slipped out his cell phone and wired the money directly using the bank account details he had been given.

The salesman's own cell phone pinged as a notification landed. He squinted at the screen, his mouth twitching as though someone was pulling at the corners with invisible thread. "Sw…sweet."

Moriarty stood back and appraised the salesman, knowing full well, within a week at the most, the ten grand he'd just wired him would be blown on booze, babes and drugs.

The next few minutes were taken up by the salesman explaining how the device worked.

"Is that it?" Moriarty said in disbelief when the salesman was done.

Another toothy grin and a face scratch. "It ain't rocket science to use it. The rocket science went into making it."

Moriarty glanced around the Walmart parking lot, making sure their dirty deeds had gone unnoticed. He shut the case, lifted it out of the trunk, and placed it into the trunk of his own rental car parked alongside, making sure he didn't allow the salesman the opportunity to look at what else he had inside his own trunk. Unlike the salesman, Moriarty's own sedan didn't have the luxury of a hidden panel. He had something much better, just in case the police decided to pull him over during the three-hour drive back to the city, and ask if they could take a look in his trunk.

Shutting the trunk securely, Moriarty opened the driver's-side door.

"Don't forget what I said," the salesman giggled. "Twenty-eighty."

Moriarty frowned.

"Twenty seconds to get at least eighty feet away from it."

As he drove out of the parking lot, Moriarty smiled at his reflection in the rearview mirror.

Victoria Christie had killed just one person. Marcus Kemp, two, maybe three.

He was going to top them all.

He was going to kill dozens all at once.

Chapter 35 – Death & Co

They sat together on a blue crushed-velvet sofa, under the golden hue of subdued lighting, surrounded by warm, dark wood panels. It was after 9:00 p.m., and the hip cocktail bar, Death & Co, was throbbing with customers.

"So let's break this down," Eve said, almost having to yell. "The woman in the dumpster is yet to be identified. No DNA match, no prints on the purse I gave you either. She was strangled to death after being hit with a blunt instrument."

Maya nodded, taking a sip from her colorful cocktail. "And unless someone comes forward, a friend or relative, she'll be buried in an unmarked grave. What about the fact the purse you found belongs to Lindsay Latimer?" Maya asked. "How does she fit into this?"

As a courtesy, Eve had also left several messages for Francis Latimer to call her back, with no success either. She knew she was being ignored so she left it at that. "There is no police involvement until the parents officially lodge a missing-persons report," Eve replied. "And so far, they haven't."

There was no trace DNA on the book; however, forensics had managed to pull three clear prints and two partial prints from the cover. Maya told Eve she would be the first to know if they had a match in the database.

Eve continued with her summation. "Still no luck identifying the tramway killer. Same with the Empire State killer. Both seemed to have vanished like ghosts. And no one can give us an accurate description of them."

"Do you think it's the same person?" Maya asked.

It was something Eve and her team were considering.

"Perhaps. But what's the motive? Both victims were unrelated as far as we can tell."

"So my theory is correct?" Maya said.

Eve shook her head. "That these seemingly random killings are somehow connected?"

"They seem related in how *unrelated* they are."

"We need a clear motive, hun," Eve replied. "People don't just go around randomly killing other people unless they are completely crazy."

"And yet," Maya said. "In both crimes the act seemed premeditated, the killer was careful, planned an escape route, and avoided all security cameras as best they could before vanishing into thin air."

"So it rules out a maniac just killing just for the sake of it." Eve took a sip of her soda water. Technically she was off duty but in her mind she never was, especially given the current situation. The entire precinct had been put on high alert. She wanted a clear head when there was a breakthrough, no matter what time of day or night.

"But even then they have a motive—enjoyment," Maya said before draining her glass.

"Seems like a pretty sick motive to me if that's all it boils down to in these cases," Eve responded.

Maya shrugged her shoulders. "Maybe, but I think the woman in the dumpster is the odd one out. She seems completely unrelated."

"I agree," Eve replied. "No audience. Too easy. The body hidden in a dumpster. We may never have found her." Then it dawned on Eve after hearing her own words above the din of the crowd. Three killings—one highly concealed, two highly visible.

Maya nodded, as if knowing Eve was thinking the same.

"Whoever committed the two highly visible killings could be playing a game."

"Catch me if you can..." Eve said softly, almost to herself.

Maya smiled. "It seems like it to me. Think about it. On the surface you have two random killings in very visible, public places. Tourist attractions. Can't get any more visible than that. So why take the risk?"

Eve thought about it for a moment. "A test," she said. "Make it difficult. See if you can get away with it."

Maya nodded. "A challenge, as I said, a game."

The waitress came over and Eve ordered another drink for Maya. It felt good to relax even though they were still talking about work, and Eve enjoyed Maya's company. Maya looked different out of her white lab coat and face shield, not leaning over a corpse or looking through grisly photos. She had styled her hair and had swapped out her vintage glasses for discreet contact lenses.

"So how is your love life?" Maya asked unexpectedly.

Eve almost choked on her soda water. "I have trust issues, so men are the furthest thing from my mind at the moment. What about you?"

Maya made a face. "Too busy with work. Plus smelling of formaldehyde all the time is a big turn-off for men."

Eve laughed as she looked around at the pulsing crowd. It felt good being here, a few precious moments reprieve from the death and mayhem of both their worlds.

And yet, when they weren't working for the dead, they picked a place to meet and have drinks that was aptly named after the dead.

Eve just hoped it wasn't a bad omen.

Chapter 36 – "Miffy"

Patrol Officer Steve Roberts handed back the driver's license to the man, but he wasn't done yet.

There was something about the driver that didn't sit well with Roberts. For starters, his eyes had a look of indifference to them. No concern, no fear, just bored complacency. Then there was his smug smile, as though he almost wanted to be pulled over.

Roberts thanked the man again, then performed a slow walk around the vehicle as it sat pulled up on the shoulder of the road, noticing as he did, the man was watching him closely in the side mirrors. At the rear of the car, Roberts paused, running his fingers across the surface of the trunk. Then he returned to the driver's-side window.

"Can I take a look in the trunk?" Roberts asked, resting both hands on his duty belt.

"Sure," the young man replied, much to Roberts' surprise.

"Is there anything in the trunk you need to warn me about first before you open it?" Roberts cautioned, as he followed Moriarty around to the rear of the vehicle.

"No," Moriarty said innocently. "Like I said before, I have no weapons, not carrying any drugs or anything illegal. I was just returning to my home in the city from a short day trip upstate."

"So what was the purpose of your trip up to Binghamton?" Roberts asked, watching Moriarty for any sudden movements.

Moriarty didn't seem to hear the patrol officer's question.

He just stood next to the closed trunk, the remote raised in his hand, pausing for effect. He could have easily popped the trunk using the release on the side of the driver's seat...but it was better this way. Planned misdirection. Also he wanted to see firsthand was the impending look of shock on the cop's face. Moriarty gave a slight smile and pressed the trunk release button, ready to enjoy the cop's reaction.

The lock gave an audible hollow clunk and the lid of the trunk slowly raised upward on silent hinges. The small internal light switched on, offering not much, but enough light to see clearly what was inside.

Moriarty didn't move his feet, rather, he leaned around to better see the cop's facial expression.

The cop leaned forward and peered into the trunk, then suddenly jerked back in fright. He quickly covered his nose and mouth with one hand and swore, his face aghast at the sight of the thing inside the trunk.

Moriarty stepped up next to the cop, his voice now tinged with well-practiced sadness. "Miffy had been missing for over a week now," he said mournfully, both of them now looking at the dead body of a hundred-pound adult German Shepherd as it lay wrapped in a plastic sheet in the trunk.

"Christ!" the cop muttered, as he studied the dead animal that almost took up most of the trunk. "What happened to its head?"

"Hit by a car I'm afraid," Moriarty said with deep remorse, his voice hollow and distant. "Ran over her skull, crushing it." Moriarty paused and inhaled deeply. "Thankfully she died instantly. Didn't suffer a long and torturous death."

The cop tentatively reached out to touch the bloodied dog collar and tag around the dog's neck, then quickly thought better of it and whipped his hand back.

Moriarty continued his death-in-the-family tone. "A good

Samaritan found her on the side of the road. Called me when they saw the dog tag on her collar with my cell phone number on it."

The cop slowly shook his head. He had seen plenty of injured and dead animals on the side of the road before. Family pets, deer, the odd squashed squirrel, but nothing like this. It was almost as though something had beaten the poor dog with a tire iron.

Moriarty let out a sigh. "Judging from her other injuries, the people who found her said she probably had been laying on the side of the road for a few days now. Birds and forest animals had more than enough time to do that to her. Thankfully she was already dead."

The cop looked away in disgust, reached for his flashlight, then reconsidered.

"Sorry about your dog," he said, indicating to Moriarty to hurriedly close the trunk lid.

"I'm going to take her home," Moriarty said, wiping away an imaginary tear from one eye. "Give her a proper burial at the Pet Haven Cemetery in the city." He turned to face the cop. "I had a plot picked out for her when I first got her as a puppy. A nice cedar box and everything."

The cop nodded solemnly, as though he had misjudged the young Asian man. "Thank you, sir, for your cooperation and have a safe journey back to the city."

Moriarty thanked the cop, then climbed back into his own car, and watched as the man got back into his police cruiser, pulled out from behind and accelerated away, the red taillights of the cruiser eventually swallowed up by the darkness.

Moriarty started the engine and checked his mirrors before pulling back onto the road himself, an evil little smile on his face.

After disposing of the dog's body wrapped in the plastic sheet in a dumpster a block away from the car rental lot, Tein Moriarty spent the next ten minutes deodorizing the trunk of the rental car with the strong aerosol sprays he had brought with him.

With the trunk and the rear-seat passenger area only smelling vaguely of takeout hamburgers, he returned the car back to the rental lot, handed the keys to the sleepy attendant, and paid extra for the interior deep-cleaning service.

Then he made his way home on foot carrying the hard case inside a backpack slung over his shoulder. Once inside his apartment, he placed the hard case on the top shelf in his wardrobe and took a long shower.

Half an hour had passed, when standing in his kitchen preparing a light meal, there was a gentle knock on his front door.

Standing in the hallway was his neighbor, a middle-aged woman whose name always eluded Moriarty. He did remember, though, she had once told him she was an aspiring melodrama actress who had fled Los Angeles, jaded and disillusioned about the film and television industry and now resided in New York City, having reinvented herself as a self-taught life coach. More like self-taught *con artist*, Moriarty had thought to himself at the time.

And as he stood there looking at her, he was reminded again of everything he detested about LA. Her exaggerated sex-doll features; the trout-pout lips, the swollen Botox face, her fake, gravity-defying boobs, and her constant perky manner as though her life was one continuous audition for a Tampax commercial.

"Hi, Tein!" the woman said.

Moriarty dragged up his warmest smile, while gripping the chef's knife he was holding behind his back a little tighter, visualizing plunging it into the top of her bleach-blonde skull.

"Hi...Emma," he said, almost forgetting her name, before suddenly remembering it sounded like enema. "What can I do for you?"

"Look, you haven't seen Miffy, my dog, have you?"

Moriarty switched to a look of deep-seated concern. "No, why?"

Emma's shoulders slumped and her face took on a downtrodden look. "It's just she's been missing for nearly a week now. Somehow she managed to get out of my apartment." Emma twirled a loose strand of hair. "I can't imagine how she did get out though. I've searched the entire neighborhood." She shoved a piece of paper at Moriarty, so close to his face he could have blown his nose in it. "I've been knocking on doors and handing out these flyers just in case people have seen her. I can't imagine she would just run away."

I would run away from you too if you were my owner, Moriarty thought to himself, taking the flyer and pretending to read it. He looked up at Emma. "Sorry. I haven't seen your dog at all. But I'll keep a look out for her," he said, noticing Emma was now looking over his shoulder, trying to look past him and into his apartment.

Moriarty began to close the door, shrinking the background view she had. "Thanks for the flyer. I'll stick it on my refrigerator as a reminder."

Emma gave a hopeful smile. "Thanks. And also—"

Moriarty closed the door, cutting off Emma's words and the sight of her bubble face.

Returning to the kitchen, he crumpled up the lost-dog flyer, popped the trash-can lid with the foot pedal, and tossed it in. "Who calls a large German Shepard 'Miffy' anyway?" he muttered to himself, taking pleasure in knowing Emma would never know what really happened to her precious Miffy—until photos from an anonymous sender arrived in her mailbox in a few months' time, graphically revealing the dog's painful and protracted death, all in full, hi-res glossy color.

Chapter 37 – Night Shift

She knew it was too good to last.

Eve's cell phone rang on the nightstand. She groped for the illuminated object, fumbling with the buttons as she did, before answering the call.

"Detective Sommers? This is Officer Paul Rimes."

Eve raised herself up onto one elbow, her heart throbbing. A call in the middle of the night was never a good thing. "What?" she demanded.

"We have a homicide"—the man's voice trailed off, then came back—"you may be interested in. Just happened. Paramedics are on scene. One deceased."

"Who else is on the night shift?" Eve asked, still groggy, feeling worse than she did before she had managed to drop off to sleep. Surely there were other detectives who could handle it. Why were they calling her? Unless…

Eve sat bolt upright, checking her watch. It had just gone 2:00 a.m. "What's the address?"

The officer read it out and Eve's heart fell to the pit of her stomach.

It was Maya Zin's apartment.

Twenty minutes later Eve was standing in the street out front of a small block of apartments, the flashing lights of three squad cars and one paramedic truck throwing blasts of red and blue off the surrounding neighborhood buildings. The police had cordoned off the sidewalk on both sides in front of Maya's apartment block and a few bystanders were mingling around, or standing on the steps of their own building looking out to see what was happening.

Eve ducked under the police tape and saw a young police officer deep in conversation with another.

Looking up, the young police officer saw Eve and immediately ended the conversation, then met Eve at the foot of the stairs leading up into Maya's apartment building.

"Detective"—

Eve sidestepped him, took the steps two at a time, and went straight into the building.

Maya's apartment was on the third floor. She badged her way past another police officer stationed at the top of the stairs, then paused in the corridor outside the open door to Maya's apartment.

Slipping on latex gloves, she took a few seconds to compose herself. Then taking a deep breath, Eve stepped forward toward the open doorway—and stopped dead cold.

Running down the wall just inside was a long, weeping slash of red.

Rain beat relentlessly against the tall windows of Vega's apartment as Birch watched lightning fracture the evening sky. They hadn't been able to find any trail of Justin's movements with any of the bus or train companies, and now Birch was worried sick for his son.

Suddenly his cell phone chimed as a message landed. Staring at the screen, Birch read the message, and immediately felt a temporary reprieve from the anxiousness and worry that had consumed him the entire afternoon. The message was from Justin, but the caller ID had been blocked. Justin told him not to worry, he had spoken to his mother and he was staying at a friend's place for a few days. He just needed time to think, to sort a few things out.

The text message filled Birch with hope. Maybe there was a slender chance of reconciling with his son after all.

It pained him he couldn't call Justin, or reply to his text. But at the same time, he didn't want to scare his son off, seem too forceful, too eager. Justin was an adult now, independent, a young man, searching for answers about his father. At least he had reached out to Birch, made the first move. It was a good start.

As Birch stared out the window into the darkness beyond, he made a vow to show restraint, give his son the space he needed, allow him to come to his father on his own terms.

Chapter 38 – Daffodils

The first sign of blood was the spray on the wall next to the front door.

It slashed across a mirrored hall stand, staining it and the walls on either side.

Eve inspected the front door. No sign of forced entry. Alarm panel silent. Security chain still intact. Through the slash of blood in the mirror, she saw her own reflection. Her eyes were ringed with dark circles, tears of blood-red running down her face and neck, her facial muscles sagging, heavy with the burden of what lay ahead.

A vase of pure white roses sat on the hall stand, its base wreathed with dead brown petals. They were Maya's favorite: white roses. She bought a bunch each week from a local grocery store that displayed rows of fresh flowers in water buckets along the sidewalk.

Eve looked at herself one last time in the mirror, silently willing her reflection to stay calm, to remain composed, to be professional. She had to do this. She had to see it through. This was her friend. She owed it to Maya.

Looking down, Eve noticed the hall runner was askew and bunched, like a building fabric wave. Carefully she walked down the small hallway, reaching the first evidence marker: a small, numbered wedge of yellow plastic. No matter how many times she saw evidence markers at crime scenes, they always reminded Eve of bright, cheerful daffodils growing up from the ground. The first marker was positioned near a large skid of blood, where someone had possibly lost their footing, slipping on the slick viscous liquid.

Another yellow marker sat a few inches farther along, against the baseboard, a bloody handprint at chest height on the wall above.

Right handed.

Eve stifled a gasp. Maya was right handed.

Eve's eyes went from the handprint on the wall, down to the skid mark on the floor, then up and further back to the arterial spray across the hall stand behind her, assembling a likely scenario in her head as she went: Maya had been slashed at the front door, retreated, then slipped in her own blood as she hemorrhaged, steadying herself by placing one hand on the wall before staggering off again, trying to escape from the killer she had allowed into her home.

The frequency of the little yellow markers increased the further Eve went, a veritable garden bed of daffodils now, she thought. Another spray of blood across the right wall, another handprint, this time lower, knee height maybe, the hall runner there soaked so dark with blood it seemed to form a pool of black above the fibers.

Then a flock of handprints taking flight up the wall, red fading to pink as they climbed.

More arterial spray on the opposite wall.

Maya had fallen here, stayed down longer this time, her strength fading, her life seeping out between her fingers, holding her neck with her left hand, clawing at the wall with her right hand, desperately trying to get back to her feet. Maybe her cell phone was in the kitchen at the back of the apartment. Maybe her trauma kit was there too. Maya had once told Eve she always kept a fully stocked trauma kit at home, capable of treating anything from a simple cut, to a gunshot wound. Just in case.

Eve looked back along the hallway from where she had come,

toward the front door, then back the other way to where she had yet to go, her mind visualizing her dying friend staggering toward her, then past her. Eve's jaw began to tremble and her vision began to blur, but she pressed on.

Ahead, a grim-faced patrol officer stood near an archway on one side, his hands clasped in front of him, guarding the opening leading into the living room where random flashes of light were coming from.

The cold rawness of death was close. Eve could feel it. It was the threshold she had to cross.

The patrol officer gave a slight nod at Eve just as a hooded man dressed all in white came through the archway, a sealed plastic bag in his hand, scalpel inside, razor-sharp blade with stainless-steel handle all covered in red. On seeing Eve, he paused, hesitated. Then he offered her the plastic bag to inspect.

Through his goggles Eve could detect a hint of uncertainty in his eyes. "The killing weapon used," he finally said.

Eve studied the scalpel inside the bag.

"The victim had their throat cut," he explained. "Bled out in a few minutes."

Eve thought back to the tramway victim and what Maya had said, how the victim had bled out so fast. She handed back the evidence bag.

"Where is the victim?" she asked, knowing the answer, but somehow still not accepting it was Maya, her friend. God, she was just with her hours ago, laughing and sharing drinks, Eve thinking how lucky she was to have a work colleague as well as such a good friend all rolled into one. Theirs was going to be a lifelong friendship, growing old together. Now it had been brutally torn away.

"In the living room through the archway." The man jutted

his thumb over his shoulder. "Mind the blood," he added. "There's a lot of it in there."

The tech headed outside and Eve stepped cautiously through the arch and into the living room beyond.

Immediately Eve's senses were assaulted. A blinding flash of light momentarily stole all her vision, all color from the room. Then came the squealing sound of a camera flash recharging.

Then another flash.

Eve turned her head away. After a few seconds, shapes and colors slowly came back into focus, the blinding white receding. In her peripheral vision she saw where Maya's body was on the sofa, pale limbs, forearms gloved in red. Eve averted her eyes, not wanting to look fully at her dead friend yet, wanting to hold on to the living memory of Maya for a few more precious seconds.

Instead, Eve turned her attention to the middle of the room. Upended coffee table, soft furnishings thrown about, a smashed picture frame on the rug. Two more white-suited techs were crouching with their backs to Eve, their attention focused on the floor next to a toppled chair, blood everywhere, the room a torrent whipped up by a person in the throes of death, desperate to live.

So much blood.

One of the techs stood and moved away—from the body on the floor.

Another body, bulkier than Eve had expected, a boxy yellow handgun clasped in one bloodied hand, thin wires like fishing line dangling from the barrel and coiled around the wrist and forearm.

Eve blinked. Her head throbbed from the camera flashes, her eyes still scalded white.

Then a familiar voice, tinged with sarcasm, spoke to Eve from the sofa. "No need to perform an autopsy on that one."

Eve turned and looked directly at what she had been putting off looking at—her dead friend.

Confusion gripped Eve. Her eyes cut back to the body on the floor, then back to the person sitting, not lying, on the sofa. Eve's heart began clawing its way up her throat, desperate to unfurl wings, fly out of her mouth, and soar joyfully high above her.

Maya was sitting very still on the sofa, a blanket draped across her shoulders, the edges of the blanket stained from her blood-covered hands.

She gave Eve a fierce look. "Because I know exactly how he died."

DAY 4

Chapter 39 – Scalpel

"His name is Marcus Kemp."

"I know," Eve replied. "We found his wallet and ID inside."

It was 7:00 a.m., and Maya and Eve were sitting in an interview room. Crime scene techs had spent the early hours of the morning scouring Maya's apartment, and the body of Marcus Kemp was in the morgue, another forensic pathologist assigned to perform the autopsy. After Maya had been checked out by the paramedics and forensically processed at the scene, she had taken a shower, placed all her clothing in evidence bags she was provided, changed into a fresh set of clothes, and accompanied Eve back to the precinct.

Despite Eve insisting, Maya had refused to be driven to the nearest ER for a thorough examination, telling Eve she had no injuries, nor did she require any counseling. She just sat quietly in the interview room under the watchful eye of a patrol officer until Eve was ready to interview her without interruption and get the full story as to why she was attacked in her own home by Marcus Kemp.

"He came prepared," Eve said as she watched her friend closely. Like Maya, Eve hadn't slept at all. She was running entirely on coffee and adrenaline.

"Tell me again what happened," Eve said, reaching, but failing to grasp Maya's hand as it was quickly pulled away.

With her shoes off, Maya was sitting with her legs pulled up, her heels resting on the edge of the chair, and her hands wrapped firmly around her shins. "I've already told you," Maya said, staring at the scuffed linoleum floor. "You dropped me off in front of my apartment. I went inside. Moments later there was a knock at the door." Maya finally met Eve's eyes. "I thought it was you coming back, like I'd left something in your car or you wanted to tell me something. But it wasn't."

Maya was in shock, Eve could tell. Her friend's face was pale, leached of all warmth and color.

"Death followed me home," Maya said, her voice robotic, detached, lacking any feeling. A car GPS would have spoken with more emotion.

"How did he know where you lived?"

Maya shrugged. "Maybe he'd been watching me for a while. We dated a couple of times maybe eighteen months ago. But he never knew where I lived, or worked. I made sure." Maya went back to staring intently at the scuff marks, as though there were bloodstains. "It was a brief relationship. He was obsessive, so I broke it off. I just got this feeling something was wrong with him—not right."

"How did you meet?" Eve asked.

Maya shrugged. "That's probably the most embarrassing part, and why I never told anyone." She looked up at Eve. "I had a momentary lapse of reason. One lonely night, after too many drinks I stupidly joined a dating app. I was curious, that's all. Then he found me, and after one swipe right, I was drinking an Irish whisky cocktail with him at the Dead Rabbit two days later."

Eve knew of the Dead Rabbit, an Irish pub located in the historic district of Lower Manhattan.

Maya went on to explain how, while they dated, Marcus Kemp would constantly make snide comments about other women he'd see in public while out with her. Derogatory, disturbing remarks, revealing a side to him she somehow knew was always there. "Turns out he was a misogynist," Maya continued. "I could tell, so I broke it off. I just ghosted him, even changed my cell phone number. I know it sounds bad, but I just got this really dark feeling about him after a few dates, as though he wanted to do something…nasty to me."

"Did he hurt you?" Eve asked softly.

Maya gave a thin smile. "You've seen firsthand what happens when someone tries to hurt me."

"And the knife?" Eve asked, her mind flashing back to all the blood inside Maya's apartment.

"Scalpel," Maya corrected her. "Kept in the hall-stand drawer by the front door. He had a Taser in his hand. He fired just as I slammed the door on his arm, so he missed. It gave me just enough time to grab the scalpel and slash him. He kept coming, though, pushing his way inside."

Eve slowly nodded. Somehow the prospect of someone breaking into your home holding a Taser, rope, or duct tape seemed infinitely more chilling than them just holding a weapon. Eve could only imagine what Marcus Kemp intended to do with Maya—before he killed her. And he was going to kill her—afterward. There was no doubt. Kemp wore no mask, and was carrying a backpack when he entered Maya's apartment, was still wearing it when he staggered down the hallway after her, relentless, determined, getting caught up in the Taser wires after he deployed the electrode darts, before finally collapsing in the living room where he died, bled to death after his throat had been expertly slashed by Maya.

Inside the backpack Eve found what could only be described as a kidnapping kit; cable ties, rope, heavy-duty duct tape, handcuffs, and drawstring hood. His plan wasn't to kill Maya in her apartment, despite the hunting knife and gun she had also found. His intention was likely to immobilize Maya first with the Taser, then bind her for transportation elsewhere. They had no fixed address for Kemp but were following up on several leads as to where he was residing.

"Why a scalpel?" Eve asked, making notes in her file. She didn't want to seem like she was interrogating her friend, but Eve had a job to do, follow proper procedure. "Why not keep a gun nearby?"

"Have you ever seen me *use* a scalpel?" Maya remarked, smiling properly for the first time since last night at the cocktail bar. "Maybe next time you should come earlier, and I'll show you," Maya said. "You always miss the actually *cutting* during my autopsies."

"No, thanks," Eve replied. "I'll pass." Eve leaned forward and squeezed Maya's hand, her own eyes blurring up as she spoke. "I thought you were dead, that you were the homicide victim I had been called out to. You scared the hell out of me."

"I didn't mean to, Eve," Maya replied meekly, as though a child in trouble. "Honestly. I guess I was still in shock. I sat on the sofa while the crime scene techs processed the scene."

It was remarkable how calm and composed Maya was when she spoke to Eve after seeing her sitting very much alive on the sofa. She was cold, clinical, keenly watching and giving instructions to the crime scene techs on how to gather the evidence off the body and from her own body.

Eve sighed. "Well, it is obvious Marcus Kemp knew where you lived, somehow found out, and was stalking you."

Maya nodded. "He was hell-bent on revenge, for being rejected I imagine. I really didn't provoke him and never heard from him after I broke it off."

"Granted, it's an extreme reaction," Eve said. "And I do believe you didn't provoke him. Something just triggers the rage inside some people."

"Patient too," Maya added. "For eighteen months he could

have been waiting and watching me, controlling his rage, bottling it up inside him."

It certainly made Eve wonder what else they were going to discover about Marcus Kemp by the time the full investigation had run its course.

"Do you have a place to stay?" Eve asked. "You can stay with me if you like."

"I have an apartment," Maya replied. "Don't you remember?"

"Surely you can't go back there?" Eve said in disbelief, the images of blood-spattered walls and the blood-soaked rug still vivid in her mind.

"I have every intention of going back there," Maya said with conviction. "It is my home and no one is going to drive me away from it. I'll scrub the floors and walls, get the blood out myself if I have to. I can do a better job than any cleaning contractor ever could."

Eve didn't doubt it. If it was her, Eve would only return to gather up her personal belongings, then leave, move out, get a moving company to pack and shift the rest of her stuff to a new place far away from the horrors of the old.

Maya continued, her face suddenly becoming cold and hard, "It is my home," she said, pressing a solitary finger into the tabletop, stressing each point. "He came into my home. Into my space, and I defended myself. I'm not going to run away in fear, Eve, if that's what you're thinking."

Eve held up her hands defensively, "Okay, I'm just saying, I'm here if you need me. Not as a cop, but as a friend."

Maya's stoic face began to soften, crumble, and for the first time since this whole ugly episode began, Eve saw some heartfelt emotion there: a single glistening tear trickled down the cheek of her friend.

Chapter 40 – Under Pressure

After the interview, Maya left to return to her apartment and Eve returned to the squad room.

"Where the hell is Ramirez!" she said to no one in particular, looking around.

"He's in with Hagen," came back the answer. Roy Beckman, one of the senior detectives, popped his head up from behind a workstation partition. Eve liked Roy. He was gruff, old-school beat detective three months shy of retirement. Roy took meticulous notes in pencil, and always wore a sports jacket and tie, even at the height of summer.

"And the Captain also wants to see you, pronto," Roy added.

Eve gave a nod. "Thanks, Roy."

"Hey, Eve," Roy said as Eve walked past his workstation on the way to Hagen's office, "did you hear Uri Goff is dead?"

When Eve didn't answer, Roy shrugged and went back to the case file he was reviewing.

Hagen was prowling restlessly near the window of his office. He looked up, saw Eve outside, and waved her in.

Eve's cell phone rang as she reached Hagen's door. "Detective Sommers," she answered. Eve caught Hagen's attention and held up one finger—*wait one minute*—then turned away and took the call. It was the forensic labs. They had the test results back from the book Thomas Birch had given her to analyze. They had a hit on a fingerprint lifted from the book cover. When she was told the name, she felt a mix of shock and confusion.

Eve thanked them and ended the call. She really needed to talk to Birch now about this new development, but Hagen was glaring at her through the glass.

"So what have we got?" Hagen said impatiently as Eve entered, closing the door behind her.

Eve filled Hagen in on what she knew from interviewing Maya but held back on the news about the matching fingerprint from the book belonging to Marcus Kemp. She needed time to fully digest what it meant in the overall scheme of things. She sped through her report with Hagen, wanting urgently to call Birch. But Hagen would go ballistic if he knew she was in communication with him on what looked now like a possible a link between the missing woman, Lindsay Latimer, and the deceased, Marcus Kemp.

"Is that all?" Hagen said, his eyes wide, jaw clenched. "What about the Empire State Killer?" he demanded, looking at Eve intently. "I don't need to remind you the pressure I'm getting from the mayor's office," he said. "Not to mention from the governor too."

Eve took a deep breath, and decided to throw Hagen a morsel, albeit a small one. "Marcus Kemp could be connected to what happened at the Empire State Building."

"You think there's a link between this guy who attacked this medical examiner and the Empire State Killer?" Hagen asked skeptically.

Ramirez shot a puzzled look at Eve but said nothing.

"Maybe," Eve replied, cautiously. "We haven't confirmed a direct link. We're trying to find out more about Kemp, especially where he lives. We pulled Kemp's details from the DMV records and traced him to an old address in New Jersey where he used to live more than three years ago."

Hagen nodded but wasn't satisfied. "And?"

"We'll follow up the address," Eve replied. "But until then, we have no solid connection yet."

This seemed to appease Hagen for a moment.

"He had a cell phone, but it's proving a bitch to crack the code. The tech guys told me the phone has some type of military-spec encryption software on it, but they're working on it as we speak."

Hagen rubbed his forehead, and Eve could see his was trying not to explode.

With a low, even voice he said, "What happened at the Empire State Building will have ramifications for this entire city. New Yorkers will be terrified to go outdoors. Tourists will stop coming here. Businesses will suffer."

"I agree, sir," Eve replied, knowing full well it was the mayor's and the governor's words she was hearing from Hagen's mouth. His own political aspirations didn't extend to caring about tourist numbers or the welfare of New Yorkers in general. "We are doing our best. But so far we haven't been able to directly ID the perpetrator at the Empire State. His face was obscured, and he vanished into the crowd afterward."

Hagen glared at Eve. "I need solid progress, Detective. Solid evidence, not speculation." He threw his hands up dismissively. "It looks bad for the department. I need to call the mayor back with something more tangible other than 'we don't have a clue'!"

"Understood," Eve said. She needed to talk to Birch. Until they could find out more about Kemp, Birch's line of inquiry seemed to be the only one offering a possible breakthrough in the case. "As soon as we find out where Kemp was living, we'll get rolling." Eve went on the offensive. "And when we do, sir, I don't want any red tape holding me back."

"Do whatever you need to do, Eve," he said with a dismissive wave. "I'll take care of the paperwork, and the D.A." Hagen continued. "Just get me something more solid than what we already have, okay?"

Eve nodded.

Back at her desk, Eve swung into action. "Ramirez, I want you to find out everything about Marcus Kemp."

Ramirez was already at his computer, pulling up information and doing searches on the police databases. "You never said he was somehow linked to the Empire State murders," Ramirez said over his shoulder as though he were sulking.

"You're not a detective yet," Eve replied. "You don't get to know all and sundry. I want a current address, where he has been living. I want to know everything about him: who he associates with, who his friends are, family, distant cousins, I don't care. Get it all."

"I'm on it," Ramirez said, typing furiously at his keyboard.

Eve abruptly stood and slid her jacket off the back of her chair. It was time to go on the offensive, not wait around for another person to end up dead. "Call my cell when you find something," she said over her shoulder as she rushed out.

Chapter 41 – Kemp's Lair

"We found fingerprints on the book you gave me. They belong to a man named Marcus Kemp," Eve said, drinking her coffee while watching Birch—and occasionally glancing over his shoulder, scanning the street and the late-morning crowd in the small diner.

"What do you know about him?" Birch asked.

To Eve, Birch looked a little preoccupied, a little glum.

"Information about him is a little sketchy at the moment," Eve continued, "and we have his DMV details but with an old address. He is a sociology PhD student at Yale. Twenty-nine years old, wealthy parents, both lawyers, no other siblings we can determine at this stage. We're trying to track down an address for the parents' home; maybe he's living with them."

"Any priors?"

"Intentional assault of a female jogger in Central Park last year," Eve replied. "I haven't gone through the file in detail yet, but he was processed, his prints taken, then was let off with a fine. The female claimed he was filming her while she and a girlfriend were jogging. She confronted him, went to take his cell phone, and he struck her. That's all we have on him."

"Can I have his DMV photo?"

"Who is Marcus Kemp to you?" Eve said flatly, ignoring his question.

"Where is he now?" Birch replied, ignoring her question in return.

"Don't play games with me, Birch," Eve said, her jaw firming. "Quid pro quo. Isn't that what we agreed on? First you tell me about this book and how Kemp happened to get his fingers on it. I also want to know how Lindsay Latimer is involved, and more importantly do you have information I don't have that can identify Marcus Kemp as the Empire State Killer?" Eve leaned forward, her voice hushed. "I'm taking a huge risk telling you what I know so far," she said, stabbing the table top with her finger. "Tell me everything *you* know about Marcus Kemp." Eve didn't want to tell Birch just yet about Kemp's fate, in case Birch would then clam up about what he knew.

"I don't know anything about him, other than what you have told me."

"Crap!" Eve hissed, looking around. She had deliberately chosen a corner booth, farthest away from other customers. "You're lying. Our paths are now crossed. I thought there were two separate investigations; now I believe there's a link between Lindsay Latimer and Marcus Kemp. And if Kemp is our man, I want to know about the link."

"All I know at this point," Birch said, "is this guy—Kemp—was following Lindsay Latimer. I have video footage of him in a bookstore she frequented. He was stalking her. That's all I know."

"So he touched the book in the store, you grabbed the book, and brought it to me to test." There were pieces still missing Eve couldn't see. Birch was being too tight lipped and it made her angry, like she was being played, used.

"I gave you the book on the presumption the guy in the bookstore could also be the Empire State Killer," Birch replied. "Now it looks like he very well could be."

"What made you think Kemp was—" Eve's expression suddenly changed, her eyes narrowed. The missing pieces of the puzzle finally slotted into place in her brain. "How did you get hold of the bookstore security footage of Kemp?"

Birch picked up his coffee mug and regarded Eve over the rim, "I have my methods," he replied, before taking a sip.

"Illegally, you mean?" Eve scoffed.

Birch shrugged.

"I want to see the footage you have."

"Give me your email address and I'll have it sent to you."

Eve thought for a moment. It was becoming apparent Birch was one step ahead of her in her own damn investigation. "The video shot by bystanders at the Empire State Building that's plastered all over the Internet is poor quality," Eve said, thinking out loud. "We haven't been able to clearly make out the killer's face, even after spending a day trying to enhance it. How come you managed to?"

Seeing the slight gloating look on Birch's face only made Eve more infuriated.

"Let's just say the friend who is helping me may have better technical resources than perhaps the NYPD."

Eve frowned. As far as she knew, NYPD had the best resources to enhance video footage, unless… Then it dawned on her. "Military," she slowly said. "Or intelligence service."

Birch smiled. "Look, we can both help each other find this killer."

"I want your footage too," Eve demanded. "The enhanced one your nerdy friend worked on."

"You'll have it, I promise. Then you can compare," Birch said. "It's not perfect, but there are similarities. I believe it's the same guy. We both don't have much else to go on, so it's worth a shot."

Eve was pleased but hid the fact. Now she was getting somewhere. She would tell Ramirez to also focus on Lindsay Latimer as part of the investigation. Eve sat back for a moment. "Tell me about Lindsay Latimer," she finally said. "Everything."

Eve listened intently while Birch described meeting Francis Latimer at his office, about his missing daughter, Lindsay, and Maxine Brodie, the woman Eve had seen at the dumpster. "So who tipped Latimer off about Lindsay Latimer's purse being on the dead woman we found?" Eve asked, wondering if Birch had told her everything. His story seemed a little edited, condensed, as though parts had been skipped over.

Birch made a face. "The guy is a billionaire. He's probably worth more than the entire NYPD annual budget. I'm sure he has his sources."

Eve wanted to know more but had to tread cautiously. She didn't like the idea of outside interference in her case. It was becoming an all too familiar fact of life in law enforcement these days when dealing with the rich and famous. People like Francis Latimer seemed to hire their own private army of investigators and security consultants more and more, bypassing traditional policing functions, running interference and making her job just that much more difficult.

"So you agree we should work together on this?" Birch concluded.

Eve gave him a puzzled look. "I've agreed to nothing."

"We need to share information," Birch insisted. "You said yourself, 'our paths have crossed,' and we seem to be chasing the same person. You want to find Marcus Kemp, and so do I. He is the only tangible link I have in finding Lindsay Latimer."

"He's dead," Eve said definitively.

"What?" Birch sat up suddenly. "What do you mean 'dead'?"

"Dead—as in *not* breathing." There, she had said it. It was too late now to unring the bell as they say. She had to tell Birch. He would find out sooner or later from the newspapers in the coming days. "He was killed last night."

To Eve, Birch's face seemed to collapse in on itself. "My one and only lead is dead?"

Eve nodded, "Afraid so."

"How?" Birch said, sagging slightly.

Eve explained what had happened at Maya Zin's apartment—obviously leaving out her friend's personal details.

Birch sat back, looking deflated and beaten. Finally he sighed. "Motive?"

"Don't know yet."

"So this woman, who killed Kemp, had no connection with him?"

Eve pursed her lips. "They had a past relationship, a while back."

"What kind of relationship?"

"A brief one. I don't think it ended amicably." Eve had tried pressing Maya on more details about her relationship with Marcus Kemp, but she refused to say any more and had retreated to her apartment. She would call later, check in on her.

"I don't mean to take anything away from the woman who was attacked by Kemp," Birch said. "But if Kemp and the Empire State Killer are one and the same, it seems like him trying to kill a past girlfriend was an uncontrolled, knee-jerk reaction. It doesn't really fit in with the highly visible crime he may have committed."

Again, Eve tried not to say too much, preferring not to tell Birch about the theory Maya had about the tramway killing and Empire State incident being somehow linked. "We'll know more once we find Kemp's lair."

Birch gave an amused smile. "Lair?" Then his face turned deadly serious, and Eve saw a spark of excitement kindle in his eyes.

"Where he could be holding Lindsay Latimer," he said.

Eve's cell phone buzzed. It was Ramirez.

He had an address for the Kemp family home.

Outside the diner, Birch watched as Eve hurriedly took off down the sidewalk.

His cell phone chimed.

It was a voice message, and his heart softened when he heard the voice. It was Justin checking in again with him this morning, saying that he was okay, and he was thinking of coming to see him but would call first. Birch's heart had leapt at the suggestion. It was certainly good news, and coupled with what Eve had just said, Birch felt he was making real progress with his son and with finding Lindsay Latimer.

Chapter 42 – Chamber of Horrors

The door was as beautiful as it was intimidating. Hewn from a single piece of oak from the Southeast plains, there was no glass window, nor peephole, and was finished with dark iron studs and a thick handle giving the door the look of a medieval battlement entrance.

A keypad and intercom panel were affixed to the stone wall under an ornate portico entrance drooping with dark ivy.

Eve crouched on the top step, her cell phone pressed up hard against her ear, face scrunched. Heavily armed ESU officers were bunched up behind her, a swarm of lethal red dots hovering over the door's surface, instant death just a finger-press away. Eve listened intently, waiting on the line. Hagen had called the D.A. who then called a district court judge.

Minutes ticked by as she waited.

Behind her, she could feel the bristling wall of violence she was holding back. All eyes were on her. Grips on triggers adjusted, breathing slowed, heartbeats sped up, muscles relaxed, then tightened again.

"Yes?" Eve suddenly said into the phone. She listened some more, then her lips broke out into a grim smile. "Thank you, Your Honor."

Eve ended the call, drew her own gun, muzzle down, stepped aside, turned to the team leader, a man called Bain, behind her and nodded.

The door came off its hinges, blown inward by a fistful of high-explosive charge strategically placed. The entry team swarmed past Eve then she followed them inside.

As warning shouts echoed throughout the house, Eve broke

off from the team, and ignoring the plush furnishings and expensive decor, she frantically searched for internal stairs that would lead down to the bowels of the sprawling house. Her logic was sound, based on years of experience: bad things and secrets were almost always hidden at the very bottom, not toward the top of a building structure. Basements, root cellars, boiler rooms and the like were the playground of the evil and the demented. Maybe it was because such dark, damp, earthy places were closer to hell than the light, airy upper floors.

Shouts continued to echo throughout the house, growing distant as the team spread out to the upper floors, clearing each room as they went. No shots fired. It was a good sign, Eve thought as she searched.

In a hallway off the kitchen she found a locked internal door. She paused, studied the door structure, lock and hinges.

No time to search for a key.

"They can bill me," Eve muttered to herself as she stepped back, then swung one leg up and forward, hitting the door squarely with the heel of her foot. The door crushed inward, the lock pulled clean from the mounting plate.

The light from behind her only reached the first step of a staircase, a rectangle of darkness below.

Eve smiled. "Bingo."

Her fingers found a switch on the wall, and the solitary overhead light bulb cast a faint yellow dimness, not enough light to fully illuminate the stairs, let alone push aside the darkness pooling below, giving the illusion they descended under the surface of a black, oily lake.

Eve hesitated as she heard voices from above and the heavy thump of feet. She felt the thick darkness below calling to her. Something was down there, tugging her forward. Eve flipped on the flashlight attached to the underside of her handgun barrel and instantly six hundred lumens of white cut through the uncertainty below. Slowly, one step at a time, she began to descend the narrow stairs, feeling the temperature drop with each creaking step she took.

At the bottom, Eve panned her gun around. The beam of the flashlight illuminated wine racks full of bottles, storage boxes, cold gray walls, and dusty cobwebs. It was a wide space, with a raw cement floor and dull unpainted cinder-block walls. The ceiling was low and overhead pipes hissed and creaked.

The air smelled fresh, not dank or musty, as Eve expected.

Her skin tingled as she looked around. The air smelled *too* fresh. Almost to the point of being scented. She swore she could detect the faint trace of lemon and pine needles, an unnatural odor.

Behind the stairs she found more storage boxes filled with old clothing, toys, and photo albums. A steel workbench sat against a wall and Eve panned her flashlight over it. No rust. The framework and legs shiny like new. An assortment of hand tools were neatly laid out on a rubber mat according to function. Cutting tools were grouped together: box cutter, serrated duct knife, small hack saw, tin snips, and cable cutters. Next were crushing tools in a row: electrical pliers, needle-nose pliers, pipe wrench, hand vice. There were alligator clips, small spools of electrical wire, a soldiering iron unplugged with its cord neatly wrapped. A magnifying desk light was clamped to an overhead shelf. Eve flipped it on, and a wedge of light illuminated the bench top.

Eve felt her throat constrict. Suddenly the innocent, commonly available hardware tools took on the appearance of surgical instruments glinting under the light of an operating table.

Eve panned her flashlight under the shelf and saw a diagram of the Empire State Building, a visitor's guide, unfolded and pinned to the wall. farther along the bench she found a slim laptop. She opened it and was greeted with a password-protected screen.

Leaving the workbench, Eve did a complete loop of the entire basement.

Empty. No one was here.

More feet thumped from above, closer this time. Then footsteps belted down the wooden stairs, as hunched shapes swept down and into the basement.

"It's just me!" Eve yelled. "Detective Sommers."

The beam of a flashlight swept over Eve's torso, settled for a second, then moved on toward the dark corners of the basement.

A dark silhouette loomed toward Eve, and for the first time, she saw Bain's young face, and his scowl. He wrenched up his goggles onto the top of his helmet. "Nothing here, Detective. No one is home."

She should have waited for his team to clear the basement before she entered it. If she were injured or was killed, then his ass would be in a sling. But Eve hadn't been willing to wait.

"Same down here," Eve said. "But we're in the right place. Kemp is our guy." Eve showed Bain the workbench, the assortment of tools, the diagram of the Empire State Building, and the laptop computer.

"Well, well." Bain began rummaging through the bench and the shelf above. "Hardly bomb-making tools, but someone was tinkering around with something down here."

Looking up, Eve noticed a sagging line of electrical conduit loosely secured to the low ceiling with plastic fasteners. Leaving Bain, she followed it with her flashlight. The conduit ran along the ceiling away from the stairs and toward the far wall. Eve moved slowly toward the far end of the basement. Bain's team had finished their sweep and had moved back upstairs leaving just Eve and Bain.

"Got some blood here," Bain said behind her, but to Eve his voice sounded dialed down, distant, as she focused on the overhead conduit. It ran under a wooden beam, then up and over an overhead waste pipe before continuing all the way to the far wall, where it threaded its way into a small hole at the top of the wall before vanishing.

"What looks like a clump of hair too." Bain's faint words floated to where Eve was now standing.

She studied the hole in the top of the wall and then touched the cinder block in front of her with her palm. It felt cold, solid.

Taking a step back, she walked the length of the wall, panning her flashlight along the top and bottom edges. The mortar between the cement blocks was old, faded, cracked and missing in some parts—all except in one section at the far end where the wall sat ninety degrees to the exterior wall. In that section of wall, the mortar lines seemed shallow, and the blocks were a lighter shade of gray.

"Hey, what's in this box?" Bain's voice again.

Eve touched the section of wall. It felt different. She pressed her palm against it, hard. It wasn't solid, had some give. Wood made to look like cement perhaps?

Eve tapped the section wall section.

Definitely hollow.

"Christ!" Bain swore.

Eve turned to see him holding up in the beam of his flashlight what looked like a small hot-dog sausage.

But it wasn't.

"Human finger," Bain said with a smile that was half grimace, half amusement. "Cut clean through the second joint. Red nail polish too."

Eve turned her attention back to the section of wall in front of her, anxiety slithering and building in her gut, and began searching the section of wall, looking for a seam, a gap, anything.

"Bain get over here!" Eve yelled.

Bain dropped the finger back into the shoebox and hustled to where Eve was.

"This section of wall is not like the others."

Bain stepped up to the wall, felt it, thumped it with his fist. "Drywall disguised as cinder block." He searched along the edges. "Nothing. No latch, no hidden release mechanism."

Eve saw him speak into his throat mike. "Cain, Vasquez, get your asses down to the basement and bring a couple of sledges, pronto."

Moments later the basement stairs shook and two huge members of the team appeared, each carrying a massive sledgehammer.

Bain shone his flashlight at the section of the wall. "Punch it open. It's a false wall."

Both men smiled at each other, then attacked the wall with huge, powerful swings, smashing a large hole in the drywall. Clouds of white dust billowed, and wooden joists splintered then shattered as they hammered relentlessly. When the hole was wide enough, Bain called them off and nodded to Eve. "Your show."

Leaning forward, Eve first pushed her gun into the dark, gaping hole, then squeezed her shoulders through the ragged edges. She panned the gun flashlight around. "Oh my god!"

She turned and screamed back over her shoulder. "Call paramedics! Now!"

Chapter 43 – Off Message

"We can say with near certainty Marcus Kemp, whose parents' Brooklyn townhouse we raided, is the Empire State Killer."

A tsunami of noise cascaded around the conference room where local, national, and even international affiliate network journalists, reporters, and TV camera crews were crammed in.

Eve waited for the commotion to die down. She had already advised everyone she would take questions after the conclusion of her formal statement.

At the table next to the podium where Eve was standing, Captain Carl Hagen sat between the chief of police, and the mayor herself. Hagen was dressed in full uniform like a proud peacock: his teeth freshly whitened, his hair immaculately cut, his ego overly inflated. His gleaming smile possessed a subtle smugness to it as his eyes scanned the room, seeking out which TV camera he believed to be focused on him so he could present his best angle.

For Hagen, there had been praise from the chief and rapturous handshakes from the mayor. Even the governor had called Hagen offering his congratulations for the fine piece of police work that resulted in catching the perpetrator. To Eve's dismay, some of the announced "facts" had been reshaped, spun by Hagen to suit political gain and bolster a more favorable public opinion. Such as the fact Marcus Kemp had not been caught by police but had instead been killed during an unrelated incident. That fact had been completely glossed over by Hagen. Or the fact it was not "superior police work" that had led Eve and her team to Kemp's parents address to find a wealth of damning evidence confirming he was indeed the culprit. In Eve's eyes, they were just doing routine follow-up on where Kemp could possibly be living and happened upon his basement of horrors.

Eve took a sip of water, then continued, reading from the statement she had initially prepared which was heavily edited by Hagen. "We discovered in the basement of the Kemp family townhouse significant physical evidence linking Marcus Kemp to the Empire State case." Eve paused and looked around the room, knowing the next part of her statement was certain to bring a flood of questions. "We also found the body of a young woman." A ripple of murmurs spread around the room. Eve pushed on, raising her voice so she could be heard over the growing disquiet. "The woman had been taken hostage and kept in a secret hidden room in the basement. The woman's family has been contacted."

Looking up from her notes, Eve stared straight into the row of TV cameras in front of her. "It is with great sadness and with the condolences of the entire New York Police Department, that our heartfelt sympathies and our prayers go out to the family and loved ones of this new victim."

Eve took a breath, as a barrage of questions bombarded her from all directions. She cast her mind back to the horrors she saw in the secret room in the basement. The fire department had cut down the entire false wall to reveal what police now believe was a purpose-built torture chamber. These gory details, for the sake of the victim's family, were not made public, including the fact they had found not one, but three cages in the secret room, one occupied, two empty, leaving Eve with no doubt Maya Zin was destined to end up in one of the cages. Police were still trying to contact Marcus Kemp's parents who, according to a neighbor, were avid mountain climbers and were in Nepal on a climbing trip where the cell phone coverage was nonexistent.

Eve waited again until the clamor settled down.

"Our investigation is ongoing and we believe Marcus Kemp acted alone." Even as Eve said the words, she didn't believe them. There was a niggling feeling at the back of her mind during the last twenty-four hours, a detective's intuition perhaps, making her believe Marcus Kemp's actions were part of something bigger, and she was beginning to agree with what Maya Zin had said.

"We also found a device, disguised as an external hard disk drive, that we believe was used to electrocute the father and the daughter at the Empire State Building."

Eve nodded at the restless crowd. "I will now take questions."

Through the throng of shouts, a female reporter pushed her voice out from the press pack and toward Eve at the podium. "Detective Sommers!" she almost yelled. "Can you say what alerted you to Marcus Kemp in the first instance? Was he already a suspect on the NYPD radar?"

The question drew nods of approval from the other reporters in the room.

Eve glanced at Hagen. He turned his head and stared directly at Eve, a cool look of expectation in his eyes. He had anticipated this, and many other questions like it when he and Eve had rehearsed prior to the press conference. The agreed answer was, "we were following several promising leads at the time, and we had identified Marcus Kemp as a key person of interest."

Eve faced the female reporter. "Marcus Kemp was killed by a young woman two days ago." Out of the corner of her eye, Eve could see Hagen shift violently on his seat, as though he had just been given a colonoscopy without any aesthetic. "During an apparent break and enter unrelated to the Empire State Building case. It appears to be an act of self-defense on the part of the young woman, who Kemp knew." Eve continued undeterred, despite feeling Hagen's scorching eyes on her. "However, I believe Marcus Kemp's actions at the Empire State are part of wider acts of violence against the people of New York City."

Eve saw the mayor's face take on a constipated look, then watched as the mayor turned and whispered something to Hagen as if to say, *what the hell is all this crap about?*

Eve gave Hagen a defiant stare as the room erupted.

Hagen cornered Eve in the hallway outside. "What the hell do you think you're doing?" he hissed, taking her by the elbow and steering her away from the scrum of reporters who were jostling out of the doorway of the conference room. Moments ago he had jumped up to the podium, almost pushing Eve aside, and hastily ended the press conference.

"That is not what we agreed on."

Eve shook off his clawing hand, not happy he had manhandled her like some disobedient toddler. She rounded on him. "I am the lead detective on this investigation," she seethed. "It is my call." Eve pointed back down the hallway toward where reporters were being held back by a line of police officers.

Hagen pulled Eve around a corner and out of sight of prying television cameras which had emerged into the corridor. "You had no right whatsoever to tell them you believe Kemp's actions were part of something bigger."

Eve threw up her arms, pushing Hagen away from her. "Like hell I don't." Eve straightened her jacket and dusted off the disheveled sleeves, as though Hagen had contaminated the fabric by his touch. "I have every right to voice my opinion as lead detective if it's what I believe is true. The public has a right to know."

Hagen placed his hands on his hips and slowly shook his head, a heinous smile spreading across his face, devoid of any ounce of warmth or joy. "The public has a right to know only what I believe they have a right to know!" he snarled. A vein on the side of his temple pulsed under the skin, his face growing redder by the second. "I decide what you say to the public." Hagen stabbed his chest with his finger so hard Eve thought he would break it. "Me! Not you!" Hagen's face contorted. The muscles in his jaw and throat bulged, as though his true face were trying to force its way out from under the mask he wore.

Eve's eyes narrowed, a tirade of abuse poised on the tip of her tongue, infuriated that her boss wanted to manipulate the truth so he could bask in the glory of an alternate reality that better suited his ambitions.

But Eve was better than this, above the schoolyard intimidation and bullying tactics Hagen was employing. "I believe there is more to Marcus Kemp, and what he did," Eve replied, trying to keep a lid on her fury, "than just some random act. I think it is linked to the Roosevelt Island Tramway—"

Hagen held up his hand. Then as fast as the torrent of anger had risen, it drained away from Hagen's face. The swelling subsided, the clenched teeth vanished, the pit bull snarl eased back, and his normal skin color returned. "You have a lot to learn, Detective," Hagen said coolly, adjusting his collar and subconsciously smoothing down his rigid hair. He then swiveled on his heels, began walking away, stopped, turned back, and pointed a long, boney finger at Eve, as though casting a spell on her. "You're off the case, Sommers. Reassigned to other duties. The case is closed, finished. So will you be if you don't toe the line and continue chasing some absurd notion."

Hagen threw a well-rehearsed politician's smile at her before sauntering away toward the waiting cameras.

Chapter 44 – Bad Catholic Girl

With a click of the remote control, the TV screen went black.

For Joshua Banks, the news was only a slight inconvenience, nothing more. Everything was going to plan. He stared at the ghosted outline on the screen of the detective who was just speaking at the press conference.

"Bleedin tosser," Victoria Christie sneered. "He deserved to die." She sat on the sofa, one leg draped over Banks's thigh. "Fancy going after some ex-slapper! The fool was told not to target anyone personal. He knew the risks; now we're all exposed."

"Who is she?" Banks asked in a calm voice. "This 'young woman' who apparently killed Marcus." Within minutes of the police press conference, the news was trending all over the Internet: "Empire State Killer Caught!"

"Don't know. Don't really care either," Victoria replied as she regarded the freshly manicured nails on one hand. Fire-engine red is what she had asked for. She had damaged a nail driving the needle so hard and so deep into Evan Brinkmeyer's thigh; she thought she would treat herself with a full set of custom acrylics. And how sweet and scary they were. "I can only guess she is an ex-girlfriend or some woman he wanted to shag who didn't feel the same way. I can imagine Kemp breaking into her place carrying a pear of anguish, not a bunch of roses."

Banks looked at Christie. "What's a pear of anguish?"

"Look it up."

"Aren't you at least saddened at all about Kemp?"

"Kemp was your friend, not mine," Christie continued, now studying the workmanship of the nails on her other hand. "I never trusted him. He had long fingers."

Banks gave her a puzzled look.

"Never trust a man with long fingers," Christie said airily. She turned her attention back to Banks. "Is it going to be a problem?"

"What? Kemp being killed?"

"You said you didn't want anything to be traced back to our little group or the main group."

Banks shook his head. "Impossible. All communication is encrypted and the chat room we use is impenetrable." Banks had paid good money to ensure their covert, devious little game was well hidden.

"Where's Moriarty?" Christie asked.

"He was in the chat room a few hours ago," Banks replied. "Said for us to keep monitoring the news cycle, as he's got something big planned."

Christie rolled her eyes. "I doubt it. The only thing 'big' in Moriarty's life is the erection he has for himself."

"Find out who she is."

Christie made a face. "What? The woman who killed him?"

"I want a name and an address. If they were in a relationship, I don't want it coming back to us."

"Too late now," Christie scoffed. "The police will be crawling all over his place."

"They'll find nothing about us." Banks thought for a moment. The entire Murder School architecture was virtual, it only existed in cyberspace and he controlled everything with only his cell phone. The designer who had built it had assured Banks not even China or Russia could hack the hidden site. And surely Kemp wasn't dumb enough not to encrypt his cell phone and computer. Still, this latest news gave Banks pause for thought.

Systems didn't fail. It was people who failed. History had proven it time and time again.

"Just find her," Banks snapped.

Christie threw her arms up. "Fine!"

"And that detective woman too," Banks added.

"No problem." Christie untangled herself and stood up, then paused, looking down at Banks. "How come you've never made a pass at me?"

Banks did a double take. "What?"

Christie prodded his knee playfully with her own knee. "You know," she gave him a wicked smile. "Tried to sleep with me."

Banks held her gaze. At times he had no idea what went on inside her pretty little head. She ran hot and cold, yet always had the knack to defuse any stress or tension he felt by going off on one of her little tangents. "I guess I think of you more like a sister, than a lover."

"So?" Christie replied, her voice low and husky. "That could work."

Banks gave a weary smile. "Are all the sweet, innocent English girls back home just as shamefully perverted as you?"

Christie tilted her head. "Only the Catholic ones."

Chapter 45 – No Choice

The outside of the precinct building looked as though a bomb had detonated. Part of the street was buckled and torn apart, the sidewalk innards wide open, revealing bright red veins of cable. A cracked pipe was bleeding murky water, as burly men in hardhats were yelling at each other.

Navigating around a pile of fresh rubble, Eve quickly walked alongside a row of bright orange plastic posts wrapped in ribbons of stripped tape blowing in the hot, dusty wind. She ducked into a temporary plywood tunnel, emerging on the other side before turning into a quiet alleyway to escape the endless construction that was New York City.

Turning her back on where she had come from, Eve brought her cell phone to her ear. "Birch, it's me." She glanced down at the small fabric case she was carrying in her other hand. "How fast can your friend crack a password-protected laptop?"

"That depends," Birch replied. "But she's extremely good."

Eve thought for a moment. She was going out on a limb here, could end up severely disciplined, even sacked and charged with stealing police evidence. But she couldn't ignore what her instincts were telling her. After what Hagen had said, she knew the laptop would only be buried in some evidence locker, tagged and shelved because it didn't suit the narrative he was peddling to the press. The Empire State Killer had been stopped; the case was closed according to Hagen.

"Where can we meet?" Birch asked in her ear. "I just saw the press conference you gave a few minutes ago."

Eve looked around. "No," she replied. "I'll come to you. I want to meet your friend."

"That won't work, Eve."

She could hear Birch moving, then he came back on the line, his voice hushed. "The girl who works for me won't allow it." There was a pause. "She values her anonymity above everything. She won't agree to it."

Eve could feel the case of the cell phone bend in her grip. "Listen to me, Birch" she replied. "I've got Marcus Kemp's laptop in my hand right now. I've just broken the chain of evidence. I could lose my badge, even end up in jail like you did. I'm taking a huge career risk just by talking to you, let alone telling you before the press conference about the raid on the Kemp family brownstone and what we had found. You need to take some risk too and convince your friend to meet me in person at her place."

"The answer is still, no," Birch replied. "We can meet anywhere but here."

So Birch was there right now, Eve thought. "We're wasting valuable time," Eve countered. "No meet-and-greet. No laptop. No chance of finding out what Kemp knew about Lindsay Latimer. All the answers could be on his laptop."

"What about his cell phone?" Birch asked.

Eve threw her head up skyward, wanting to yell at the gathering storm clouds. The air was hot and sticky, rain was coming, Eve could smell the thick and heavy ions of energy. "We haven't been able to crack it, yet. We may have better luck with the laptop." Eve only had a certain amount of time before Hagen officially took her off the Kemp case, effectively banning her from accessing any of the seized material held in the evidence locker.

There was a muffled sound on the end of the line as Eve waited for Birch's response to her demand. After what seemed like an eternity, the line cleared and Birch came back, his voice sounding harassed. "Meet me here." He gave Eve the address. "Come alone and don't come armed if you value your life."

Chapter 46 – Dog Cage

Eve felt as though she were standing inside the jaws of some giant steel trap. She had parked her car a block away from the address Birch had given her, locked her handgun in a safe locker in the trunk and made her way on foot, not pleased with the fact she would have to defend herself with her bare hands should someone decide to steal the laptop bag she was carrying.

She felt naked without her gun, but Birch had insisted. When pressed as to why, he simply repeated the warning to come unarmed.

The elevator jolted to a rickety halt, and Eve slid open the door.

Birch stood there, but Eve's eyes went past his left shoulder to the young woman standing behind him, drumming her fingers on her thigh.

"Thanks for—" Birch started to say, but the young woman cut him off.

"Is that the laptop?" she asked abruptly, stepping forward, and jutting her jaw at the bag Eve was carrying.

"This was Marcus Kemp's," Eve said, trying to get the measure of the woman in front of her, who looked like she was also sizing Eve up. "He attacked my friend. He also killed two innocent people, slit one's throat and electrocuted another and tried to kill a young girl who is still in a coma." Eve thought she saw the young woman's face tighten, but she could have mistaken it for partial indifference.

"Eve, this is—" Birch started speaking, appearing to want to break the tension in the air between the two women, but Vega cut him off again.

"You are never to mention me to anyone, where I live or what I do," Vega said, addressing Eve. "Is that clear?"

"Absolutely," Eve replied. "What's on this laptop could help you find Lindsay Latimer, and I need to know who else Kemp was involved with."

Vega said nothing, just stood stony faced.

Eve slid out her cell phone. "I want to show you something," she said, thumbing the screen. "This was footage I took of the basement of Kemp's parents' home, where we found..." Eve offered the cell to Vega. "You can see for yourself."

Vega took the cell from Eve.

"Just press the red—"

"I know how to use a phone," Vega said, a hint of annoyance in her voice.

"Just mute the sound," Eve suggested. "Otherwise you'll just hear a whole string of expletives from me."

Eve saw a slight smile grace Vega's lips. Vega said nothing for a few moments while she watched the video, her face unmoving. Thirty seconds later, Vega's brow furrowed ever so slightly, and Eve saw her visibly inhale.

Instinctively Eve knew where Vega had reached in the footage.

"Is that a dog cage?" Vega asked without looking up.

"I believe so," Eve replied. "Large enough to fit the girl we found inside. She was alive when we found her...but died on the way to hospital."

Vega's shoulders momentarily stiffened, and her lower jaw began moving sideways, back and forth. She was grinding her teeth. Vega looked up, pausing the video. "Her breasts, her buttocks?"

Eve slowly nodded. "Alligator clips used to apply electric shock. She was tortured."

The two women stared at each other, their eyes locked

together for a moment, a silent understanding between them. An alignment of common goals.

"There could be others," Eve finally said, "more like her. Maybe even Lindsay Latimer is held somewhere."

Vega returned her attention back to the screen to watch some more. Seconds later she stifled a gasp.

Eve could see something flare in Vega's eyes.

Vega looked up. "He removed her…?"

Eve slowly nodded.

"But he is dead?" Vega asked. "This man called Kemp? The woman who you spoke of in your press conference, she killed him, no?"

"Slit his throat. She's a good friend of mine."

Vega smiled at the news. "Butchered and bled him like the pig he was." Vega handed back the cell phone to Eve. "I understand now." She took a deep breath, and looked as though her entire demeanor toward Eve had changed. Gone was the tightness from her jaw and stern face. Her shoulders relaxed, and her face brightened, transforming her into a compassionate, yet still fiercely determined looking woman.

"My name is Beatriz Vega," she said offering her hand to Eve, who shook it. "And I would very much like to meet this friend of yours one day," Vega said. "Buy her a drink."

Eve smiled, surprised by the strange, but perhaps not so absurd suggestion. "Maybe one day you will," Eve said, pocketing her cell.

"Coffee?" Vega asked Eve.

"Thanks, black, no sugar."

Vega nodded. "Then we will get started, see if we can find Lindsay Latimer, and also these others whom you speak of, and then…"

Eve watched as Vega's face slipped back again into the cold, hardness she had been initially greeted with.

"Do to them what was done to the poor woman in the cage?" Eve suggested.

"Correct," Vega affirmed.

Chapter 47 – Proof of Death

"How will you crack the password?" Eve asked, standing behind Vega, watching the young woman plug a cable into Kemp's laptop.

"I won't," Vega replied as she focused on the huge wide screen of her own computer, clicking the mouse, opening multiple windows and dragging and dropping files.

"What do you mean 'you won't'?" Eve was still coming to terms with the short answers, riddles and broken sentences Vega tended to speak in. Most people would have interpreted Vega's abrupt manner as simple rudeness. However, Eve saw it as Vega's disdain for having to constantly explain, handhold, and guide those who couldn't keep up with the steep incline and pace she had personally set for herself. Clearly she was someone of high intellect, extreme focus, didn't suffer fools, and had little patience for the unimportant and irrelevant.

Eve glanced at Birch who was standing off to the side, leaning against the edge of a deep, wide windowsill, and gave him a questioning look.

He responded with a look of his own: *trust her, she knows what she is doing.*

Vega gave a satisfied nod, muttered something Eve couldn't make out, then swiveled around in her chair to face Eve. "It will be much quicker if someone else cracks the password on the laptop. My time is much better spent searching through the rooms of a house than picking the lock on the front door."

"Who?" Eve demanded, concern flaring in her eyes. "I can't let anyone else access—"

Vega raised a calming hand. "You have nothing to worry

about." Behind her, the computer seemed to have sprung to a life all its own as a flurry of icons and lines of code began filling the screen like a spreading virus.

Vega explained, "People get invited to crack the code. They see it as a challenge, competing with each other. Once someone solves it, they will immediately get kicked off and the connection will go dead. They won't have access into the contents of the laptop once we're in."

"Good." Eve gave a sigh. "Do you pay them?" Eve asked, more curious about this new world she had entered. "For their help?"

"It's a credit system. We barter our services. Other services are paid for, but this is low-level work."

Low level work? Eve thought to herself. *How amusing.* "Might as well get comfortable for the long wait," Eve said, walking to the sofa and settling into it. She closed her eyes and began massaging her temples with her fingers.

Moments later, Vega's computer gave an audible beep and the screen went blank.

"It's done." Vega started again on her keyboard.

Eve's eyes flew wide open. "What?" She glanced at Birch who just gave her a look of, *I told you so.*

Eve sprang to her feet and joined Birch as they both took up position behind Vega.

Vega's computer screen lit up with the desktop mirrored from Kemp's laptop. Vega was inside the laptop but using her own screen as the display, yet the desktop seemed empty—no clutter of folders, shortcuts, or icons. Nothing, just a wallpaper image of a jungle swing bridge tapering off into a wide expanse of lush tropical rainforest. Eve squinted at the screen, then noticed a single file almost hidden in the top right corner among the green foliage. "Entry?"

Vega clicked on the file. It opened into a library of what looked like hundreds of tiny folders with a mix of names, random numbers, and dates. Vega made a sound of disappointment with her tongue, then arranged the files alphabetically and scrolled down to the letter "L" for Lindsay or Latimer. There were no files named as such. Unperturbed, she then did a search of the hard drive for the same key terms for Lindsay Latimer, and the computer churned away. "This might take a while. There are a lot of files on the hard drive."

As the computer searched for the key terms, Vega did a slow scroll, top to bottom of the first layer of files.

"What's that file?" Eve said over Vega's shoulder, bending down and pointing at the screen.

"Which file?" Vega asked, her mouse pointer hovering among the rows of files.

"Providence," Eve said slowly. Eve had been once investigated the murder of an art dealer who was later discovered to have sold several high-quality forgeries—to a New Jersey crime family. "Providence," Eve repeated. "It means to authenticate, to prove. Like if a piece of art is real, not a fake."

"Let's see." Vega doubled-clicked on the file to reveal two dated video files and another folder labeled "VC."

Birch and Eve exchanged looks, but it was Eve who recognized the significance of the two dates on the video files. "The file on the left is dated when the incident at the Empire State Building occurred." They were just one click away from proving beyond a doubt Marcus Kemp was indeed the killer. "Play that video first."

For five minutes, no one spoke as they watched in morbid silence.

The video started with the bumpy, jostling point of view of

Marcus Kemp. His hands were busily working on the wiring of what look like some electrical junction box he had open. Eve recognized the location. Kemp was crouching in the stairwell on the eighty-sixth floor at the open control box she had seen and where she had found the dead security guard. Kemp had been wearing some kind of spy camera on his chest, maybe a GroPro, Eve gathered as she watched the footage.

Footsteps could then be heard echoing up the stairwell.

"Hey!"

The camera jumped, then panned around, to behind Kemp.

A security guard came into view coming up the stairs. Eve saw it was Raymond Chandler; husband to one, father to three, grandfather to eight. "Did you cut the power to all the elevators?" Chandler sounded none too happy.

But Kemp didn't use a box cutter to slice the throat of the security guard. Maya Zin was right, Eve thought, as she watched what happened next. It was the blade of a multitool. The video footage was extremely graphic and shot in high resolution.

Vega advanced the footage until it showed Kemp's point of view as he held hostage the father and the daughter, then electrocuted the father to death using the same handheld device they had been found in Kemp's basement. Wires could be clearly seen being attached by Kemp's own hand to the father first, telling the man he would execute his daughter if he didn't comply.

"Let's take a look at the next video," Eve said, knowing full well what was coming next. The time display counter indicated the full length of the footage was forty minutes, and they had only watched ten minutes.

Vega double-clicked the second video file and they stood and watched in silence again. This video was shorter, the time display counter indicated just under ten minutes.

"It's footage taken of the killing on the Roosevelt Island Tramway," Eve said as she watched.

Birch and Vega said nothing. Again the footage started bumpy but then settled. Unlike the first video, this one looked different in how it was shot. The view was vertical, not horizontal, but still crystal clear.

"It has been shot on a cell phone," Vega said. "Held vertical, hence the narrow field of view and the black edges, not full-screen width like the first video."

The screen panned slightly left, then right, capturing disinterested passengers, some sitting, others standing in the crowded interior of the gondola. The screen then focused on a man standing directly in front of the person holding the cell phone. He had his back to the person, but his head was slightly turned, revealing one side of his face.

"Evan Brinkmeyer," Eve breathed. "The man who bled to death after being stabbed in the leg." A melting pot of conflicting emotions spun around Eve as she watched: disbelief, anger, helplessness. She knew she was witnessing a homicide that had already happened, but she still wanted to scream at the video, yell at Even Brinkmeyer to turn around, to move, to get away as though he still had time to save himself.

As the tram rumbled over a support tower, the footage bumped then settled again. The passing scenery through the wide windows began to slow as the gondola began to descend toward the Manhattan terminal.

"It's not the same," Vega said, pausing the footage, then running it again. "It's been shot differently."

"Maybe Kemp decided to just use his cell phone for this killing," Eve said. Yet she wasn't convinced by her own suggestion. Something didn't sit right with her after viewing the second video. It had a more creative feel to it.

"Take a look at the other file," Eve said, pushing aside the niggling feeling.

Vega double-clicked on the file labeled "VC."

The screen exploded, immediately filling with hundreds of photo files.

Eve watched as Vega began to open each photo file.

"Christ!" Birch exclaimed.

"La hostia," Vega muttered.

"Fuck," Eve whispered.

Journal Entry #19 – Arm

I took a black felt-tip pen and drew a line, marked my skin, no more than three inches, I measured, along my forearm.

The paring knife came from a culinary store I happened across while exploring the old part of the city today. It's almost an omen for me, how these cities are divided into old and new, past and present, and how easily it is to move between the two.

I sit here now writing in my journal, under the soft flicker of candlelight, a glass of local red wine within reach. The smooth, velvety liquid reminds me of the blood I spilled today.

The knife was incredibly sharp. It had to be. I also drank a few shots of local Grappa, more to numb my fear and to bolster my courage, then used it to sterilize the knife and the wound afterward. I think it's a lie when you see it in the movies when someone takes a swig of alcohol to numb the impending pain.

But I wanted to feel the pain, to feel the burning cut of the blade as I slit open my skin and cut into my flesh. It was also served as a bloodletting, draining out the impurities tainting my insides, purging the past and the people I once trusted.

Yet I know some of the impurity remains, and it is a good thing.

I cut myself over the bathroom washbasin in my hotel room,

watched as the blood dripped bright red into the white sink, then as it slowly trickled into the rusted plughole.

When it was done, and I was satisfied, I patched myself up as best I could, wrapping the wound in a small towel, burying my forearm beneath a shawl, then made my away to the small clinic I had seen the previous day, where I paid some listless doctor fifty euros in cash to suture the wound. To my mild surprise, he didn't even question why the cut was so clean, so straight, so precise. Perhaps he believed the lie after all, that I had fallen off my rented Vespa, had gone too fast across the narrow cobbled streets and misjudged the turn into the piazza.

When he was done, he handed me two small plastic bottles, and in heavily accented English told me one was painkillers, and the other was antibiotics to stave off possible infection. He assured me the sutures would dissolve in seven to ten days.

I would need to wear long-sleeved clothing until then.

Then with a sad face, he told me the news it would leave a permanent scar.

It was difficult for me not to smile upon hearing such wonderful news. My foray into self-surgery had been a success.

The things we do...

Chapter 48 – Obsession

Hundreds of Lindsay Latimers flooded the computer screen: Lindsay walking along the sidewalk. Lindsay coming out of a Starbucks carrying a takeout cup. Lindsay sitting at a picnic bench in a park. Lindsay standing on the sidewalk texting. Lindsay getting into a car, maybe an Uber.

All of the photos were taken from a distance, and none were of Lindsay posing or looking directly at the camera.

"He's stalking her," Eve said, "and she's completely unaware he's photographing her."

Birch nodded. "She was his obsession."

Eve looked at Birch, saw his face go pale. "Sorry, Thomas. But she's either dead or he has her locked up somewhere and soon will be. Lindsay Latimer has now become a police matter. We need to find her."

"If she was already dead, then why is there no video footage of him killing her?" Birch asked, the agitation in his voice obvious. He began pacing back and forth, running his fingers through his hair as though wanting to pull it out by the roots. He glared back at Eve. She could see the strain in his face, bloodshot eyes circled by dark puffy rings.

"He seems to enjoy filming the people he is about to kill or in the act of killing them. So why nothing of Lindsay?"

"Maybe her video is somewhere on the hard drive," Eve offered, knowing her words sounded grim. "Lindsay Latimer was being stalked by a psychopathic killer who has already murdered three people for no apparent reason other than to get his thrills. He also nearly killed another two: the young daughter of the father he killed at the Empire State, and my friend."

"I'll find it, if there is any video of her," Vega cut in. "If she's in here, on the hard drive, I'll find her. I just need time."

"Time is what we don't have," Birch said turning away again. "If Marcus Kemp abducted her, and she's still alive, then her location has gone to the grave with him."

Eve thought about it for a moment, picturing in her mind Lindsay Latimer trapped in some dark, hole in the ground, running out of air, or chained up in a room like how she found the other woman. No food, no water, and where no one could hear her muffled screams as she took weeks, perhaps months to slowly whittle away and die. In killing Kemp, Maya Zin may have also inadvertently killed Lindsay Latimer. From the sheer quantity and voyeuristic nature of the photos on Kemp's laptop, it was clear to Eve that he had been planning for a while to abduct Lindsay Latimer.

Eve touched Vega's shoulder gently. "Can you please scroll through the photos and the rest of the hard drive for anything else about Lindsay Latimer or where Kemp could have been holding her. There could be clues in the photos. A building. A Room. Backgrounds. Anything. Utility bills. Lease payments for property. You can reach me on my cell if you find anything." Eve gave her the number.

"On it," Vega said, swiveling around, then attacking her keyboard.

Eve made for the door.

"Where are you going?" Birch asked, as though suddenly he was very alone and seemingly lost.

"To find out the truth about Lindsay Latimer. To do what I should have done from the very start."

"The truth?"

"Yeah," Eve said. "Like I said before, Thomas, this is now a police matter. Lindsay Latimer has walked right into the Marcus Kemp case. *My* case. She's now part of it."

Birch hung his head and Eve felt sorry for him. The man was slowly unraveling before her eyes. "You're being played, Thomas." Eve touched his shoulder, her grip firm yet reassuring. "I don't believe you've been told everything about her."

Eve caught Vega looking over her shoulder at her.

"I'm going to pay her father, Francis Latimer, an official visit whether he or the rest of the family likes it or not," Eve continued. "And together, the three of us are going to find her and anyone else who is involved with Kemp."

Vega gave Eve one of her rare, barely perceptible nods of approval.

Chapter 49 – The Nanny

"Mr. Latimer," Eve continued. "I believe your daughter is in grave danger. Otherwise we wouldn't be here."

Eve and Birch agreed on the ride downtown, that Eve would take the lead, in an official, but uninvited capacity. They had left Vega to scour Kemp's laptop to see what else she could find.

Francis Latimer sat silent for a moment, his head nodding slightly, deep in thought.

"How could you possibly know this?" Maxine Brodie snapped, her gaze falling on Eve. Brodie wore a tight, all-black suit with a high collar and tasseled epaulettes, reminiscent of some futuristic military dictator. While Latimer didn't seem angry Birch had arrived at his office with an NYPD detective to discuss the whereabouts of his daughter, Brodie was positively furious.

Eve ignored Brodie's question. "We have reason to believe, Mr. Latimer—and this is all totally confidential—your daughter may have come to the attention of Marcus Kemp, the man responsible for the Empire State killings."

"That sounds absurd!" Brodie scoffed. "Lindsay would never—"

Latimer held up a hand, cutting off his head of public relations. With a soft calm voice, he then indicated toward Eve, "Please proceed, Detective Sommers, with what you were saying."

Eve gave a slight nod of appreciation. *Chalk one up for me*, Eve thought, *and not for the Nazi bitch in black*. "We have found compelling evidence that Marcus Kemp was stalking your daughter prior to her disappearance. We believe he may have abducted her. Time is critical, Mr. Latimer, if we are going to find her."

Maxine Brodie quivered like a volcano about to erupt.

"We just want to find Lindsay and bring her home safely," Birch added. "Detective Sommers was following a separate investigation regarding Marcus Kemp when she found photos of Lindsay on his laptop computer."

"But I read in the press Marcus Kemp is dead," Latimer said.

"That is why we need to know more about your daughter Mr. Latimer,"Eve continued. "And this is by no means a forced intrusion into your family's personal lives. Another team of detectives is working now as we speak on uncovering everything we can on Kemp: his habits, friends, connections, where he could have possibly taken Lindsay if he indeed did abduct her. Time is really critical."

Eve glanced at the photo of Lindsay Latimer in a silver frame on the desk. Blonde hair, intelligent eyes, lopsided smile, and a fresh-faced exuberance that made Eve suddenly feel old and very tired. With her own hair a mess, her eyes feeling like gritty cement balls in their sockets, and her crumpled ten-year-old jacket, Eve could only imagine what she must have looked like to the bright-eyed, youthfully tanned Francis Latimer in his perfectly fitting suit and brilliant white teeth. But looks could be deceiving.

"Do you have any other photos of your daughter?" Eve asked. "When she was younger perhaps?"

"I have plenty of photographs of Lindsay," Latimer replied. "But I can't see how it will help with you finding her."

"Nonetheless," Eve said, "I'd still like to see them."

Latimer nodded toward Brodie, who remained firmly planted

at Latimer's side. She looked down at Latimer. "Francis, as your advisor, I strongly suggest—"

Latimer began to raise his hand at Brodie, but Eve beat him to the punch, her voice firm and full of authority. "Let me assure both of you, whatever confidentiality agreement you have with Thomas"—she looked Latimer straight in the eye—"extends to me also. I promise you, nothing we discuss will ever leave this room."

Latimer seemed to consider what Eve had said, a thoughtful expression on his face. Then he leaned forward. "Thank you, Detective. As you can imagine, this is a delicate situation given my position, my company. But it's not worth what my daughter is, so please proceed."

"I fully understand," Eve said. "We just want to find Lindsay." She clasped her hands together. "Now, can you tell us more about Lindsay while Ms. Brodie locates some photos of your daughter."

Latimer nodded at Brodie who reluctantly left the room.

"Everything we have is in the files we gave you, Thomas," Latimer said.

"I mean we want *you* to tell us about your daughter," Birch explained. "Her childhood, her upbringing. More about how she was as a child. Her schooling when she was much younger, and your relationship with her over the years. Things that weren't necessarily in her file. A deeper look into her past, that I didn't consider relevant before, I now do."

Eve took a sideways glance at Birch, curious as to where his line of questions was going.

Latimer contemplated Birch for a moment, then spoke. "Lindsay was a very precocious young girl. She takes after her mother."

Both Eve and Birch took out notebooks and began to write.

Eve looked up in the ensuing silence from Latimer. He was looking at the notebook in her hands. "Like I said, Mr. Latimer, we will treat everything with the strictest confidence."

Latimer nodded. "How far back would you like me to go?"

"Perhaps her early childhood," Birch replied.

"She was born in England," Latimer said.

"England?" Birch queried.

"My wife is English. We first met when I was there on business when one of my companies was drilling in the North Sea. We have an estate in Cheshire. Lindsay went to private school there, spent most of her early childhood growing up on the estate. She loved horses and learned to ride. But Lindsay lost all of her accent after we moved here when she was eight years old. She sounds like any other New Yorker now."

"The files you gave me mentioned nothing about Lindsay's childhood," Birch said. "They only went as far back as the start of her university days. Was there anything from her childhood that stood out?"

Latimer made a show of thinking. "Nothing significant comes to mind. She was always well behaved, good at school. Lindsay is an A-class student since elementary school, all the way up to senior high school. Top grades, all her teachers had nothing but praise for her."

"All the way up to senior high school?" Eve asked, quoting Latimer's words. "Did something change after that?"

"She seems to have struggled when she started at NYU. Almost failed the first year." Latimer sighed. "Look, I don't see how any of this is really relevant in finding her."

Birch held up his hand. "Please, just bear with me." Eve watched as he referred back to his notes. "Nothing medically happened to Lindsay?"

Latimer shook his head. "Nothing sticks in my mind, but I will have to check with my wife. She would know a lot more than me about Lindsay when she was younger." Latimer gave a conciliatory smile. "I was away a lot on business."

"Does Lindsay wear glasses?" Birch asked. "Contact lenses?"

Latimer shook his head. "No. She's always had perfect eyesight, even as a child." Latimer brought his hand to his chin. "Come to think of it, she did break her arm." His face clouded over. "Yes! She had a fall." His eyes lit up. "That's right. When she was perhaps thirteen or fourteen years old I believe."

"At home?" Eve asked, trying not to sound accusatory. She had experienced her fair share of incidents of domestic abuse.

"No, no," Latimer replied. "Lindsay was in her last year of middle school here New York, and we were all vacationing in the UK for winter break. The Cheshire estate became our winter home. We return there each Christmas for my wife to visit her family, go gift shopping at Harrods, Fortnum and Mason, and the like. I remember, because we were concerned about her starting high school the following year with a broken arm."

Eve had only heard of Harrods and did most of her Christmas shopping online. "So how did it happen?"

"Lindsay was out riding, alone I believe, and her horse was spooked by a badger or rabbit in the fields. It reared up and threw her off. She had to have a plate inserted into her forearm, her left arm I believe, to pin the break together. The surgery left a decent scar."

Eve scribbled all this down in her notebook. "And do you still have the medical records?"

"I'll have to ask my wife I'm afraid. She usually keeps the medical records. But it's going back a long time, mind you."

"What about her DNA?" Eve continued. "Do you also know Lindsay's blood type?"

Francis Latimer's face darkened, the connotation of what Eve was asking not lost on him. "In case you find…" his voice trailed off.

"We just want make sure," Eve quickly cut in. "Be thorough. Just in case."

Latimer looked down at his hands. "I'll get her medical records to you."

"Thank you," Eve replied. She glanced up just as Maxine Brodie walked back in carrying a Bankers Box. She placed it down none too lightly on the desk in front of Latimer.

He opened the box and began to shuffle through the contents, a smile breaking out across his face. He held up one photo and slid it across the table toward Birch. "This was taken when she was twelve years old."

Birch took the photo and looked at it before handing it to Eve. It showed a young girl standing next to a horse in front of horse stables. The date was written in neat script on the back.

"My wife dates all of the family photos," Latimer said, "It's just a thoughtful habit she has. I guess you lose track of time and dates as you get older."

Over the next ten minutes, Latimer dug up several more photos of his daughter when she was a teenager, reminiscing about each one as he pulled them from the box.

"When was that photo taken?" Eve said, pointing toward the photo in the silver frame on the desk.

"It is the most recent. Just after she came back from Europe. Why?"

"Can we take these photos?" Birch asked, holding up the bunch of photos in his hand. "We'll take good care of them and will return them."

Latimer nodded and slid the entire box file across the table.

"There's more inside. Take them all if you wish."

"Can we have the one in the silver frame too?" Eve asked, "since it's the most recent photo you have of her."

Latimer handed the silver frame across to Eve. "Anything to help you find my daughter."

Eve studied the photo for a moment. "It's a lovely diamond pendant necklace she's wearing." Eve looked up at Latimer. "Was it a gift from you?"

Latimer shook his head. "A friend she made while in Europe gave it to her. She wears it constantly. Lindsay said it has sentimental value."

"Some friend," Eve muttered, looking at the photo again. The necklace looked expensive. A male friend no doubt, from a holiday romance. Eve made a mental note to follow it up.

Eve nodded at Birch to say she was done. They both rose together, thanked Latimer, and Brodie, who threw them both a frosty glare in return.

They were at the office door, about to leave when Latimer called out. "Oh, there was just one thing."

Both Birch and Eve turned back toward Latimer.

"I just remembered something," he said, a vague expression on his face. "I don't know if it's relevant, but it's worthwhile mentioning."

Eve exchanged looks with Birch. Every little detail was important, no matter how minuscule.

"It doesn't really relate to Lindsay...directly. But..." Latimer paused, undecided if he should mention it or not.

"Mr. Latimer," Eve said. "Everything could be important in helping us find your daughter."

"It was such an awful event, and yet I had up until now forgotten completely about it," Latimer continued.

Eve and Birch waited patiently.

"When Lindsay was maybe six months old, we employed the services of a nanny, who was also like a live-in housekeeper. She looked after Lindsay, especially when my wife and I were away. The woman practically raised her I guess."

"And?" Eve said, wishing Latimer would just get to the point.

"Well, she died." Latimer said. "The nanny that is. She fell from an attic window of our house in England."

Birch stepped forward. "How old was Lindsay when this happened?"

"It was two years ago, and Lindsay had just turned eighteen, had just come back from Europe after taking a gap year off before starting university here in the States. The housekeeper, Mrs. Bates, continued to be employed by us after Lindsay grew up. She managed the estate while we're here in New York."

"Fell from an attic window you said?" Eve asked, her interest aroused.

Latimer shook his head. "I shouldn't really say 'attic.' We converted it into Lindsay's nursery just before she was born. As it was located at the very top of the house, it was perfect, so we wouldn't be woken during the night. Mrs. Bates would feed Lindsay or get up and tend to her in the middle of the night if required. Her own room was right next door to the nursery so it was convenient." Latimer paused, his eyes looking into the past. "It's quite a fall from up there. Police said it was likely an accident. She was cleaning the windows, had opened one, and unfortunately lost her balance and tumbled out."

"Where was Lindsay when this happened?" Birch asked.

"My wife and I had moved back to New York by then, after spending Christmas in the UK. Lindsay had just returned from Europe and was staying on the estate only for a few weeks after we had left. We never saw her when she returned. She was planning to come across to New York. It was just her and Mrs. Bates on the estate when the tragic accident happened."

"Is there anything else about the incident you can recall?" Eve asked, taking out her notebook and jotting down the details.

"The strange thing was," Latimer spoke again, "the upper story of the house, where the nursery was, had been closed for years. Mrs. Bates had no reason to go up there. In fact all the nursery windows had been key locked for safety reasons."

Chapter 50 – Mary Poppins

Outside Francis Latimer's office, Eve's cell phone rang.

It was Ramirez. "Eve, where are you?" he said, almost in mild panic.

"Downtown, following up on a lead," she replied. "Why?" Eve paused at the bank of elevators, Birch next to her.

"The tech guys have cracked the password on Marcus Kemp's cell phone." Ramirez was whispering now, and she could hear the excitement in his voice. "And you're not going to believe what's on it."

Eve and Birch agreed to split up, Birch returning to Vega with the photos of Lindsay Latimer, and Eve heading back to the precinct, first making certain Hagen wasn't there. Officially, she was off the case. Unofficially, she didn't care what Hagen thought or had said. A security guard with his throat slashed open, the burnt corpse of a father, his young daughter unconscious in a hospital bed, and the brutally tortured young woman she had found in the basement of Kemp's parent's house was enough to convince Eve she had unfinished business. Marcus Kemp may be dead, but his ghost still haunted her.

The squad room was full and noisy when Eve entered and motioned to Ramirez. "What have you got?"

Kemp's cell phone was plugged into Ramirez's computer. "The tech guys gave it back to me about half an hour ago," Ramirez said, typing away on his keyboard, bringing up files from the cell phone.

Eve hunched behind Ramirez, glancing around making sure Hagen didn't suddenly appear. There were other less important cases she was working on with Ramirez, so she could use as an excuse for being at his desk intently studying his computer screen.

"The call log has been deleted, and there were only a few texts to unknown numbers we can follow up on," Ramirez said.

Eve hadn't mentioned to Birch about Kemp's cell phone now being accessed. Let him pursue the Lindsay Latimer angle. She wanted to concentrate on Kemp, and whoever he may have been colluding with prior to his death.

"Then I found this file," Ramirez said proudly, clicking the mouse. "It's not really a file with anything inside," he said. "It's a portal into a hidden chat room with a detailed history of communications between members."

"Members?" Eve said, wishing Ramirez would go faster.

"I went in to take a look, logging in as Kemp, just to browse past conversations, history, to see who Kemp was communicating with. I thought at first it was a dating site or something. The password was saved already at the login screen for future use." Ramirez, seemingly please with himself, turned and gave Eve a gleeful smile. "Kemp wasn't acting alone. It's like some kind of game being played, and Kemp was part of it. One of the members."

"Game?" Eve asked. "Played by who?" So many questions flooded Eve's brain and she wanted answers to all of them at once. Leaning closer she saw lines of condensed text, like a movie script, flowing down the computer screen.

Ramirez nodded. "A killing game as far as I can figure out, and heaps of people are involved, maybe thirty or more. From what I can decipher, it seems like points are awarded for killing people. The more public, the more graphic the kill, the more points you earn." Ramirez pushed his swivel chair sideways. "Here, take a look."

Eve pulled up a nearby chair and sat next to Ramirez as he

controlled the computer mouse.

"They call it Murder School," Ramirez said.

Eve felt the first roots of dread beginning to take hold and grow inside her. "Murder School?"

Ramirez nodded. "I've only just started reading some of the conversations between members. They all use handles, like anonymous names when they talk."

"I know what a handle is," Eve replied. "I'm not *that* old."

Ramirez gave a smirk. "Like I said, as far as I can tell, overall this Murder School has maybe thirty or so members. But Kemp was part a much smaller group, a subgroup of Murder School, a kill team of four."

Eve's head was swirling. *Murder school? Kill teams? Points awarded for killing people?* If what Ramirez was saying was true, then Kemp definitely wasn't acting alone. But, in her wildest nightmares, Eve never imagined she could be dealing with up to thirty killers.

Ramirez turned to Eve. "And get this. That murder that happened on the Roosevelt Island Tramway three days ago?"

"Evan Brinkmeyer," Eve replied, feeling her excitement grow. She had deliberately kept Ramirez in the dark with what she was doing with Birch and Vega. It wasn't a matter of trust, she just didn't want anyone else finding out until she was certain what the hell was going on.

Ramirez nodded. "His murder was all over the news. Well from the conversations in the chat room around the date of the murder, it was another person, a different member of this smaller subgroup who killed him. Someone called 'Victoria' who uses the handle, *KillMaryPoppins*, took credit for killing Brinkmeyer. She announced it to the entire Murder School and asked for bonus points."

In all her years of being a detective, Eve Sommers thought she had seen it all. Apparently not. The Internet and social media had created an elevated platform for all crimes, no matter how vile, so they could be put on public display, to be celebrated, and endorsed by an increasingly perverted global audience.

"But how did you find her real name is Victoria?" Eve asked. "I thought the reason why you use a handle is so your identity remains hidden?"

Ramirez shook his head. "Apparently not within this smaller subgroup. Only they can see each other's online names as well as their first names. No surnames are used."

"They know each other more intimately than those in the wider group," Eve said thoughtfully. "They're friends, whereas those in the larger group could all be strangers."

"That's my guess," Ramirez said. "This special group seem to know each other."

It was now apparent to Eve that Vega was right about the difference between the two videos she had watched earlier with her and Birch on Kemp's laptop. Both seemed to be shot differently because they were taken by two different people, two different killers: a woman called Victoria and Marcus Kemp.

"I'd really like to get a look at Kemp's laptop you found in his basement," Ramirez said. "Maybe I'll follow it up with the tech guys to see how they're going with it."

"No! No, leave that to me," she said quickly. "I'll follow it up with them. You just stick to what else you can find on Kemp's cell phone."

Ramirez gave a shrug.

"Are you certain Kemp was part this Murder School?" Eve asked, trying to distract Ramirez away from thinking about Kemp's laptop, "and not just some sick spectator, joining in the chat and was not actually an active member?"

Ramirez shook his head. "Kemp went by the handle, *EmpireState88* and took credit for what happened up there. He's definitely part of the smaller group."

"We need more proof," Eve said. "And are you certain it's not some hoax competition open to all gaming sickos who can come in and participate?" Eve had to be absolutely certain this was real, not some virtual game where headline hunters took credit for actual killings around the city.

"As far as I can tell, Murder School is a closed group. No one else can join. They're not publicizing their kills online, just sharing it among themselves through this secure portal."

Eve couldn't believe what she was hearing, but she needed compelling proof. If she took this to Hagen with anything less, she'd definitely lose her job and the respect of the entire force. "I need to see more," Eve said. "Uploaded pictures and videos of members taking part in actual killings. If this is real, then members would have to provide some form of confirmation. I can't go public with this until I see solid evidence."

"Understood," Ramirez replied. "I need to do a lot more digging. I haven't seen any uploaded video footage or photos yet, and there are areas within the chat room I can't get access to."

"Keep this quiet too, don't breathe a word of this to anyone until we know more," Eve warned. "And drop everything else you are working on; stay on this," Eve insisted. "I want to know who these people are, starting with the smaller subgroup you said Kemp and this woman, Victoria are part of. I want her full name."

"Victoria…" Ramirez muttered.

Eve could tell he was thinking. "What?"

Ramirez shook his head. "No, it's nothing."

"What about her cell phone? Do you have those details?" Eve fired questions rapidly at Ramirez, not waiting for him to answer. She was craving to know practical details so she could go after them.

"I've got the full name and cell phone details for just one other in this subgroup, a man called, Tein Moriarty. It seems like he hasn't taken credit for killing anyone—yet."

Eve felt a pang of excitement. If they had a cell phone number, they could track him.

"It seems Marcus Kemp and Tein Moriarty had a closer friendship than with the others," Ramirez said. "They sent several private messages back and forth outside of the smaller subgroup. That's how I managed to pull his name and cell number."

"Good," Eve replied. "Start with him."

"He goes by the handle, JohnnyMo."

"Johnny Mo?"

Ramirez looked at Eve as though she should know the name. "Johnny Mo... as in the movie, *Kill Bill*."

"Whatever," she said with an annoying wave. "I want you to find out who this Moriarty person is." At least they had a name and cell number for one member of the group Kemp was part of. They needed to focus on finding him, and hopefully it would lead to finding the identities of the others.

"Moriarty was planning something big for his part in all of this," Ramirez added.

"Big?" Eve asked. "How big?" Eve felt a spike of fear grow inside her.

Ramirez scrolled up the page of text. "Moriarty was in the chat room yesterday. It was the last conversation I can find for him." Ramirez highlighted the last line of text and turned toward Eve. "And what he said doesn't sound good."

Eve squinted at the computer screen and slowly read the words: *How many bonus points do I get if I kill more than fifty people at once?*

On a scale of one to ten, Eve's fear instantly jumped to an eleven. She took a moment to compose herself, suppressing the urge to blunder forward. She needed hard facts, not speculation. Then she spoke in a clear, calm voice. "I need you to track down Moriarty. See if you can triangulate his cell phone signal from the towers. Find out where he is right now. I want his DMV photo too."

"Already onto it," Ramirez replied, reaching for his keyboard.

Eve's cell phone rang and she drifted back to her desk. It was Maya Zin. "Maya, are you okay?"

"I'm fine Eve. I'm keeping myself busy cleaning my apartment."

Eve shook her head in disbelief. Maya was certainly strong willed and that's what she loved about her.

"Look, the reason why I'm calling, Eve, is that forensics just called me. They've managed to pull a partial print off the spring-loaded climbing cam I found in the throat of the woman in the dumpster."

Eve sat down. More good news. Things were starting to pick up pace. Then Eve's hopes were quickly dashed when Maya spoke again.

"The bad news is there's no match."

"Not to Marcus Kemp?"

"Sorry, Eve," Maya said. "We ran his prints first. Came up with nothing. Whoever killed the woman is a clean-skin, no prior criminal record on file and no match to unknown prints on the database either."

Eve had all but forgotten about the woman in the dumpster.

There was a connection to Lindsay Latimer. But Birch could follow up on that lead. At the moment Eve's investigation was moving fast in another direction. "Thanks Maya."

"Sorry I could not be more helpful."

"You've been more than helpful. And take it easy. You've been through hell lately." Eve ended the call just as Hagen entered the squad room. His vulturelike eyes picked out Eve and he scowled.

"Working on other cases, with Ramirez," Eve threw at Hagen before he could even get his mouth open to ask.

"Good," Hagen replied, before heading toward his office.

Moments later, Ramirez said, "Got him!" He glanced over at Eve. "Moriarty, I've got his signal up. Found him. He's on the move."

Eve jumped up and hunched behind Ramirez's shoulder.

On the screen was a detailed satellite map of New York City, with a red pulsing dot: midtown, two blocks east of Bryant Park, one block west of the Chrysler Building.

Eve felt she was having heart palpitations when she saw the exact location of the pulsing dot—a place where you could easily kill hundreds, even thousands of people all in one, highly concentrated area. A place where more than seven hundred fifty thousand people pass through each and every day.

This was no hoax. Moriarty's threat to commit mass murder was looking very real.

Chapter 51 – I Love NYC

The silver spinner luggage case was purchased from one of the many souvenir stores on Eighth Avenue.

The blue and red 'I Love NYC' rubber luggage tag completed the authentic look, making the spinner case look like any other of the thousands of similar cases seen every day being wheeled, pulled, dragged, kicked, thrown, and cursed at along the crowded sidewalks and traffic-choked streets of New York City—day and night, by tourists and backpackers alike.

The case first started its journey this morning arriving at the St. George Ferry Terminal on Staten Island. Along with its owner, the case then boarded the ferry for the twenty-five-minute trip across Upper Bay to the South Ferry Station on Manhattan. From there it was a quick three-minute walk to the Bowling Green subway station and onto the 4 train heading Uptown to its final destination.

Tein Moriarty stood under the star-filled heavens, masses of people, like shoals of fish, swirled past him in a chaotic but somewhat deliberate pattern. To his right, a huge Stars and Stripes hung, as if to remind people which country they were in. In front of him, bright sunshine flooded into the cathedral-like space through three huge arched windows, bathing the concourse in an ethereal glow.

From above, Orion kept a watchful eye, who—according to myth—had once threatened to kill every animal on Earth.

Moriarty noticed a few army grunts standing on the outer edges of the Main Concourse. Dressed in urban camouflage with thick-soled boots, their attention was turned elsewhere.

Glancing ahead, Moriarty saw the information booth topped

with its iconic four-faced brass clock.

Time, Moriarty thought. Unlike those who scurried past him, he was in no hurry. He had plenty of time and intended to savor every moment of it. After all, he was going to leave an indelible bloodstain on the city that would not be washed from people's memories for a very, very long time.

He set off again, navigating through the streams of commuters, wheeling the innocent-looking spinner case behind him.

Chapter 52 – Faces

"She looks different," Vega said to Birch as they sat in front of Vega's computer.

She had taken the photos Francis Latimer had given Birch in the file box, including the most recent taken from the silver photo frame from the billionaire's desk, and had scanned them into her computer, then had spent the last hour or so manipulating and enhancing the images. Vega had cropped, enhanced, and then magnified each photo utilizing specialized software so only the face was visible for comparison.

Now Vega had the clearest of the earlier photos, taken when Lindsay Latimer was in high school, just before she went to Europe, and had positioned them on the left of her wide screen. On the right side of the screen sat the single enhanced picture of Lindsay, taken from the silver photo frame. This was the most recent photo of Lindsay.

Vega looked from left to right, then back again, her eyes like huge orbs, peering through her glasses at the images, her lower lip curled under her top row of teeth in concentration. Vega sighed, then sat back. "So what do you think?"

Birch leaned forward on his chair next to her.

"It's the best I can do without pixelating her face," Vega said as she continued comparing the photos. "Then they will become too grainy, and blurry."

Birch said nothing, his eyes shifting between the images.

"What is the approximate age difference between when these were taken?" she asked. Vega pointed at the group of photos on the left. "And this most recent photo?" Her finger shifted to the photo on the right.

"Two, maybe three years," Birch replied. "The photos on the left were from her last year at high school. Lindsay would have been seventeen years old. The photo on the right, the most recent according to what Latimer told me, was taken last year when she was nineteen. She had come back from Europe and was about to commence her first year at NYU."

"So she was seventeen when she graduated high school, then took a gap year and traveled around Europe where she turned eighteen, went back to England, then enrolled the following year at NYU when she had turned nineteen?" Vega said.

"Correct," Birch replied, trying to get the timeline aligned with the sets of photos. "Now she's a sophomore and is twenty."

"So what do you think?" Vega asked. "About what I said that she looks different."

Birch studied the photos some more. "We all look different over time."

"Yes, I know, but there is only a two-year difference between her high school photos and the photo taken last year," Vega replied. "Your facial appearance doesn't really change much in just two years."

"Perhaps she put on some weight while traveling around all those European cities?" Birch suggested. "Eating in all those restaurants and cafés."

"That's what I originally thought," Vega replied. She took the mouse and drew a thick red circle with the pointer around Lindsay Latimer's face on the photo on the right. "The bone structure is slightly different in this photo taken last year. She may have put on some weight, but it's her facial structure I'm talking about. Cheek bones, jaw, around the eyes. Not the skin and flesh, but the bones underneath."

"How do you know all this?" Birch asked.

"Because it's my job!" Vega shrieked. "I find people who don't *want* to be found. And let me tell you, people go to great lengths to alter their facial appearance when they're on the run or in hiding."

"So you think Lindsay Latimer altered her facial appearance?"

"Perhaps."

Birch found Vega's ensuing brooding silence unsettling. "What?" he finally said. "What are you thinking?"

"It's left field."

"So?" Birch said. "In case you haven't noticed, you and I don't exactly live in a 'right-field' world. Tell me your opinion. We need to find her and we don't have much time."

When Vega replied, her voice had suddenly taken on a vacant, empty tone. "When I said 'left field,' what I meant was we may be no longer be standing in the entire ballpark anymore."

Now Birch was totally lost. "Explain, Beatriz."

"We haven't so much as been looking in the wrong places either," Vega continued. "But I believe we've been only seeing what our eyes want us to see, and it's the biggest mistake you can make when you're hunting someone down."

Then Birch heard a certain sadness in Vega's voice. "There is no doubt Lindsay Latimer traveled to Europe, took a year off between high school and college. But she didn't come back from Europe—someone else did. The Lindsay Latimer who went overseas is not the same Lindsay Latimer who returned home—literally." Vega paused.

Birch urged her to continue. He wanted to hear her theory, no matter how absurd it might be.

Vega took a deep breath and continued. "I believe Lindsay was killed by someone, and that someone took her place, and is now pretending to be her."

Chapter 53 – Hunting

Eve went from helpless to complete helplessness as she entered the Main Concourse of Grand Central Terminal and was pulled, pushed, and jostled as a tide of humanity swirled around her.

With her cell phone pressed hard against her ear, Ramirez was feeding her the location of the moving blip that was Tein Moriarty.

"There's like a million people here!" Eve yelled into her phone, her head swiveling all directions, faces streaming past her. "I need his photo, Ramirez."

"Sending it to you now."

Seconds later the DMV photo landed on Eve's cell phone. Conscious of suffering the wrath of angry glares, Eve pulled out of the river of people and leaned on a nearby wall while she studied the photo of a young Asian man: round faced, with dark cynical eyes seeming to view the world and all the people in it through a distrusting lens.

Eve glanced up, her eyes rapidly flipping across the face of each person as they streamed past, her brain quickly becoming overloaded, trying to compare the photo of Moriarty she held in her hand with the overwhelming flow of passersby around her. It was like trying to locate a single asteroid in a universe made up of thousands of heavenly bodies all moving at once but all in different orbits.

Undeterred, Eve pushed off the wall and began to walk as calmly as she could through the Main Concourse, scanning faces as she went, trying not to look like a panicked mother who had just lost her child at the Super Bowl, but that's exactly how she felt. Her handgun was concealed under her jacket, as was her police badge.

Ahead she spotted two MTA police officers dressed in Kevlar helmets, tactical gear with assault rifles slung across their chests, one holding a huge German Shepherd on a leash. Eve felt a jolt of anxiety as the dog turned its huge head and affixed her with two coal-black eyes. Quickly, she veered away, changing direction, shielding herself behind a group of lost tourists wheeling identical Pokémon spinner cases. Eve was treading a fine line, not wanting to alert the transit authorities either without definite confirmation Moriarty was here, and he was a clear and present threat to public safety. If she did incite unnecessary mass panic, Hagen would bounce her out of the force so fast and so far, she'd end up as a mall cop somewhere in Alaska armed with nothing more than a can of pepper spray, and a sour face.

Two National Guard soldiers dressed in operational camouflage stood on the balcony directly ahead of Eve, their heads rotating like tank turrets, scanning the crowds below. Another quick course correction and Eve found herself heading toward a pair of NYPD patrol officers talking to each other while standing next to a platform entrance. Eve turned again and ducked her head down. "Where is he?" she hissed into her cell phone.

Ramirez's voice buzzed in her ear. "The signal is coming right dead center in the building. Are you certain you can't see him?"

Eve suddenly had to take evasive action, sidestepping a young woman who was coming straight at her, wearing oversized pink headphones, and eyes intently focused on the massive cell phone she held in her hand.

Eve stood still. It was impossible for her to see every face clearly as it went past. Looking around, she gauged she was standing in the middle of the concourse again, but no Moriarty.

"I can't see him!" She caught partial glimpses of faces, the backs of heads, some faces covered with face masks, others obscured with ball caps, all whirling around her so much so she was starting to feel dizzy. Slowly she began circling toward the information booth, noticing a small line of tourists at one of the ticket windows.

Eve stood off to one side and did a slow 360-degree turn, smiling into her cell phone like she was talking to a best friend. "He's not here," Eve growled, her mouth fixed into a forced smile.

"He's right there," Ramirez buzzed in her ear. "Look around."

"I am looking around!" Eve snapped.

"Hold on," Ramirez said. "I'll refresh the signal."

Eve waited and kept scanning the people as they flowed past—then she froze.

Thirty feet away a man was standing still, staring up at the main display board. Next to him sat a small spinner case. He turned his head and Eve caught a glimpse of the side of his face. Quickly she looked again at the DMV shot of Moriarty on her cell phone.

She looked up at the man again, then slowly edged forward toward him, her cell phone pressed to her ear. "I've got eyes on him."

"Eve, it's—"

Eve slid her cell phone into her jacket pocket, twisted her neck loose, and pumped her fingers as she advanced toward the man, her right hand hovering just outside the flap of her jacket where her gun sat hidden.

Twenty feet away from the man, Eve angled to her right, circling around so she could get a better look at his face.

The man turned and began walking away from her, wheeling the luggage case behind him. Eve sped up, and brought her hand up to near her appendix, ready to sweep her jacket aside and draw her weapon.

The man stopped again, then suddenly turned toward Eve.

Eve tensed, went for her gun—then stopped.

It wasn't Moriarty.

Eve's shoulders sagged and she cursed, quickly covering her holstered gun.

Eve had only gone a few steps when she felt someone touch her shoulder from behind. She whirled around. There was no one standing behind her—but she had sensed...something...someone. Suddenly Eve felt cold, as though a window in her imagination had been left open and a sinister, icy draft had floated in and brushed over her. Then, for some reason, she looked up toward the west balcony level that led to Vanderbilt Avenue. Her eyes searched long the length of the stone balustrading where people were mingling, posing for photos, or seated at tables of the bar overlooking the Main Concourse. The unnerving feeling intensified, as though it were coming from that direction.

"Eve!" Ramirez's voice screamed from her jacket pocket.

She pulled out her cell phone again.

"He's right there. Not moving. You're almost standing on top of him!"

Eve spun around, looking back toward the center of the concourse. The crowd momentarily thinned, but there was no sign of Moriarty.

Then it hit her. "Damn!" She felt her gut tighten as she started moving again, toward the stairs that led down to the lower-level dining area. Ramirez wasn't wrong when he said Moriarty was standing in the center of the concourse—just not the Main Concourse at ground level. He was standing directly below Eve—one level down.

Chapter 54 – Chasing a Ghost

Birch sat quietly and listened as Vega explained the meaning of her cryptic comments and the theory behind them.

They had shifted to the kitchen, where Vega had replenished their cups with a fresh batch of her specially brewed coffee. She stood behind the counter, while Birch sat opposite on a stool.

"People who assume a new identity are extremely difficult to find; believe me, I should know. They make up the bulk of the assignments I'm given." Vega began pacing back and forth in the kitchen. "False passports, fake driver's license, even forged birth certificates are almost impossible to detect these days with the naked eye, even if you know what to look for." Vega stopped her pacing and looked at Birch. "Everything has become more sophisticated and so much easier to create a new life for yourself you can easily slip into and vanish. It is the tactic adopted by most of the people I hunt. But it is still a fairly thin cloak you can cover over your old self with, to hide from your previous self."

"Like undercover cops," Birch said. "You tend to create a backstory that goes back only three or four years."

"Agreed," Vega said. "But there is a type of illusion, an extremely rare one I have only encountered once before, when I was tracking a sociopathic killer, on behalf of the families of the victims after the police investigation had stalled for more than five years. This type of illusion is almost foolproof, extremely simple when you think about it, but requires genius levels of cunning, deception, confidence, and self-belief."

Birch waited patiently, allowing Vega her moment of cleverness.

"What if the villain is hiding in plain sight?" she whispered.

Birch frowned.

"What if they're standing right in front of you and you see them, but you don't see them for who they really are."

"Now you've lost me."

Vega became more animated, waving her arms about in either frustration, excitement, or both. "What if you are looking at someone, like how we have been looking at Lindsay Latimer, her photos, the video footage from the bookstore, but…you're actually looking through the eyes and into the mind of a completely different person?"

Birch went to say something, then closed his mouth when the notion of what Vega was saying finally dawned on him. She had seen something in the photos he hadn't noticed. He stood up, almost knocking the stool over, and quickly walked back to Vega's computer and stared at the screen, at the photo of Lindsay Latimer, fresh faced and smiling back at him. Then he saw it, behind the eyes, like a curtain had been partially opened, revealing something blurred and hidden in the shadows of the backstage. But it was the slightly upturned corner of one lip, a discerning smugness, like she knew a secret the world didn't. "Is it possible?" he breathed, looking deeper at the photo. Vega had brought with her a fresh perspective, a different angle of viewing the same object. Now she had opened his eyes to it as well. Birch was so engrossed in the face, the eyes, the faint mocking smile, he was unaware Vega had walked up behind him.

"I'm sorry, Thomas. I made a terrible mistake. All this time we've been chasing a ghost. This is why I believe Lindsay Latimer is dead, and she died while in Europe."

"Then who is this?" Birch asked, pointing at the most recent photo, the one taken from the silver frame on Francis Latimer's desk. It was a possibility too incredible to consider. "And the woman in the bookstore? And the one who has been living in her apartment, and going to NYU and the young woman visiting her parents?"

Vega's eyes narrowed, and her nostrils flared like a hound on the scent of a fox. "An imposter. A shape-shifter. A woman who not only killed Lindsay but did it so she could kill her own past and adopt a new future."

Chapter 55 – Cubicle

With her head down, and her eyes focused intently on the red blip on her cell phone screen, Eve rounded the corner—and bumped right into a woman coming the other way.

"Sorry," the woman said before hurrying off.

Farther along the corridor, Eve spotted the sign for the men's restrooms and, without stopping, barged right in, pushing the swing door almost into the face of a young man exiting on the other side. The man's eyes did a double-take as Eve tried to negotiate around him. "Line too long in the women's restroom?" he said with a snicker.

"Get out of my way," Eve said, pushing past him.

There were three cubicles inside the restrooms. Two vacant and one occupied. Two men stood at the urinals, their heads turning in unison as Eve walked in. "Hey!" one man said in a gruff voice. "Wrong place. You want next door."

Eve flashed her badge, placed a finger on her lips and jerked her thumb toward the door. Then she drew her gun.

Hurriedly, the two men zipped up, then almost ran for the exit.

Taking slow, deliberate steps, Eve traversed across the white tile toward the occupied cubicle, at the end of the row. The sound of her knees cracking was amplified inside the small room, making her grimace, as she squatted down and craned her neck to look under the cubicle door.

She saw a pair of white sneakers, the toes speckled red, blue jeans riding up over the ankles and white crew socks—and something else, something Eve hadn't noticed immediately. The left sneaker was sitting in a puddle, not of urine but something else. A red viscous liquid seemed to sit on top of the white tile.

Eve sprang up, took one step back, and careened forward with a front kick into the cubicle door. Pain instantly shot up her ankle, knee and hip, but she ignored it. The cubicle door slammed back on its hinges.

Tein Moriarty, sat on the toilet seat, his eyes, like two marbles of dull gray staring up at her. His mouth was ajar in mild surprise, and something thin was sticking out of the left side of his head, a thick ribbon of red oozing down his temple.

Eve kept her gun pointed at Moriarty's head, her mind trying to process what she was seeing and what she had previously seen. The film inside her head quickly reversed: people walking awkwardly backward and away from her, faces drawing level with her own face, before shrinking into the distance in front of her. All sights, sounds, smells, and faces her brain had subconsciously recorded just moments ago.

Now she played the footage forward again.

The woman who Eve bumped into. A swirl of blonde hair, a flash of blue eyes, a rushed, almost begrudging apology.

Eve backed up, ran to the door, yanked it open and was confronted by two burly, transit police. Both their eyes went to the gun Eve was holding in her hand and they instantly drew their guns and started yelling at Eve. "Put the gun down! Put the gun down!"

Eve dropped her gun. It was always easier that way, to immediately obey. Trying to explain first as to why she was holding a gun would have cost her a hail of bullets in the chest.

A man's head bobbed up from behind the two transit police. "That's her! That's her!" a sneer across his face. "She kicked me out while I was taking a piss! Told you she had a gun."

Bringing her hands up into clear view, Eve tried to look past the transit officers, but the blonde woman had fled.

Eve hung her head.

Chapter 56 – The Shape-shifter

"We are hunting an extremely dangerous, cunningly clever, and totally ruthless killer," Vega said.

"A 'shape-shifter' as you termed it?" Birch said.

"A figure of speech. The term 'shape-shifter' is used predominantly in modern-day commercial fiction, like horror and fantasy. The term is grounded in mythology and folklore, the ability of someone to change literally their biological shape through magic, sorcery, and spells. I prefer the recognized term 'chameleon' to describe this woman who changes her appearance, not in any magical way, but so she blends almost perfectly into her current environment."

"Thank goodness," Birch said. "I thought for a second we were looking for a werewolf or something."

Vega didn't smile at the remark. "Don't get me wrong, Thomas. Monsters do exist in the real world, but not in the literal sense. I'm a realist, and like you, I have seen some of the worst, most heinous, evil things people can do to each other and to children. They are monsters—the child killers, pedophiles, mass murderers. On the surface, they look human, but it doesn't stop me from calling them living monsters, because in my mind, below the surface, under their skin, they are monsters masquerading as human beings."

"So someone is masquerading as Lindsay Latimer?"

"Yes. That is my theory."

"So tell me how this woman…chameleon, became Lindsay."

Vega began counting off on her fingers. "Firstly, and apart from the slight physical differences I have noticed between photos, you said Francis Latimer told you Lindsay had been more distant during the last two years since she returned from Europe. Our chameleon wanted to limit direct family contact, less chance of someone scrutinizing her up close." Vega raised another finger. "Secondly, according to her parents, you told me Lindsay was an 'A student' since elementary school all the way up to senior high school. Then she almost fails her first year in college, even though her parents hardly saw her much during then, and when questioned, she told them she was busily studying. Her recent poor academic results seem out of character, don't you agree?"

"Maybe she met a guy," Birch offered. "Maybe she got pregnant and hid from her parents until she could have an abortion. It happens."

"Maybe," Vega said, her tone telling Birch she was unconvinced by his explanation. "Thirdly, she is the sole heir to the Latimer fortune."

"Okay," Birch said, trying to hard understand. "So this chameleon is driven by greed, money; that's her motive? She intends to kill both the parents and inherit the lot?"

Vega twisted her lips. "I don't know what her motives are yet."

"I'll guess we'll know once we find her, then question her."

Vega gave a thin, tight smile. "This is the type of person would rather chew off her own handcuffed hand than be caught, Thomas. She will do anything to evade capture. She will kill without compulsion, or remorse."

"So you're a behavioral psychiatrist now?" Birch said.

Vega's eyes narrowed to slits. "You forget I have a Bachelor of Arts majoring in forensic psychology."

Birch hadn't forgotten the fact Vega had dragged herself through an undergrad degree at John Jay College of Criminal

Justice, a senior college of the City University of New York. "My apologies, Beatriz," he said.

"And doing what I do has also given me a unique insight into human behavior. I know this kind of person. I've seen them once before."

"But only once."

"Once was enough."

"Then tell me about the case."

"I can't divulge specifics about a case."

Birch felt disappointed.

"But, based on that case, I can tell you what likely happened to Lindsay Latimer and the type of person we are now looking for."

"So you don't believe Marcus Kemp abducted Lindsay, then either killed her or has her held captive somewhere?"

"Let Eve follow up on the Kemp angle," Vega said. "Just hear me out on an alternate theory I have."

They moved to the leather sofa and Vega pulled her legs up and under herself and got comfortable. She then began describing a likely scenario of how Lindsay Latimer may have been targeted while traveling through Europe. As he listened, Birch felt as though Vega was blending into the narrative actual facts of the previous case she had mentioned, without directly divulging any names or places, thereby keeping her vow of confidentiality intact.

"Lindsay would have appeared like any other tourist," Vega explained. "A wealthy one, wearing nice clothes, perhaps jewelry as well. And the best way to travel throughout Europe and see the sights would have been by train."

"She was traveling alone too," Birch added, according to what Francis Latimer had told him.

"The perfect opportunity," Vega responded, "for her to unfortunately cross paths with our chameleon."

"So you're saying it was premeditated? The person intended from the outset to seek her out to take her place? If not her, then it would have been some other unfortunate, unsuspecting victim?"

Vega shook her head vigorously. "I believe it was purely opportunistic. No one decides to wake up one day with the intention of finding, killing, then assuming someone else's identity. Even the person in my past case wasn't that predatory. They were driven however by pure desperation to completely erase their past, to completely vanish, and start again."

"But as someone else," Birch replied listening intently. It fascinated him how someone could do what Vega was suggesting.

"Correct, "Vega replied. "I believe someone first befriended Lindsay."

"Someone who bore some resemblance to her in the first place."

"An essential requirement," Vega replied. "Make it easier for them to make the leap from just an idea to actually acting upon it. They would have been a complete stranger at first to Lindsay, maybe they shared the same train carriage together, or got talking while in the line outside a tourist attraction. The person befriending her, then gains Lindsay's trust. They could have become traveling companions."

Birch could picture it. "Women traveling together would be safer than a woman traveling alone."

"Correct," Vega Agreed. "Most young people who travel through Europe have no fixed itinerary. You plan it as it comes. Traveling alone can be boring too, lonely, even if Lindsay does seem like a fairly strong-willed and independent young woman."

"So as they travel together their friendship grows."

"Exactly. As they got to know each other, Lindsay would have opened up more, let her guard down, told this person more about herself, about her family, personal, intimate details. Our chameleon may have grown envious of Lindsay and her privileged life. As time passed, the seed was planted in the head of our chameleon that she could take over Lindsay's life, assume her identity, and the belief began to grow. On the outside, she still would have appeared to be Lindsay's new friend, perhaps the sister Lindsay never had but always wanted. But inside, this woman slowly shifted her agenda, began making plans to step into the role. She became a student of Lindsay."

"She began to study Lindsay more you mean?" Birch asked.

"Correct. Watching her closely, her mannerisms, how she spoke, any unique expressions or terms she may have used. As well as memorizing everything about Lindsay's life. Her family, friends back home, every minute detail would have been noted, and written down to be studied later I imagine. Lindsay would have thought her friend sitting across from her was writing notes in a travel journal about the trip or the sights they had seen together."

"But she was actually writing down all the details Lindsay was telling her about herself and about her life," Birch said.

"Correct. Lindsay would have been totally unaware. She thought she was sharing intimate details about her life, whereas in fact she was inadvertently revealing everything about herself, and her entire family, to a person who was going to kill her, then become her."

"She would have enjoyed the attention too, to talk about herself," Birch said. "Confiding in someone who ended up being a coldhearted killer."

"I disagree with the assertion," Vega shook her head. "The person would likely not have been a killer in the first place, but was driven out of sheer desperation to change her life, to hide from her past."

Birch frowned. "You said at the beginning this person was an extremely dangerous, cunningly clever, and totally ruthless killer."

"I meant how they are now, what they had to become, transform into in order to vanish, to hide, to survive and erase their past."

"It's quite a leap, Beatriz," Birch said. "To go from innocent person to ruthless killer in the space of a few days or weeks."

Vega looked deep into Birch's eyes and uttered one word. "Fear."

"Fear?"

Vega nodded. "Despite what most people think, love is not the most powerful emotion. Fear is."

Birch sat back and thought about what Vega had just said. It was fear of a life spent without his son, Justin that had driven him to almost kill himself. Not love. Birch did love his son, more than life itself—more than his own life. Yet fear had sent him down the path to where he now found himself. Maybe it was fear for what would happen to Justin that had led Birch to just accept his fate, do the time in jail, give up the fight, sacrifice himself, knowing it meant at least Justin would be safe.

Birch looked up. "So what specifically can you tell me about this woman? This chameleon?"

Vega took a moment before replying. "Based on the previous case I mentioned, the killer's life was in reality the complete opposite to the victim's. She wanted the victim's life because her own was so dismal."

"Pretty extreme though," Birch said, "to kill another person for it."

"People have killed for much less."

Birch had to agree. A life was cheap these days. "So our killer had a pretty dismal life?"

"Perhaps," Vega replied. "Poverty could be one element. A broken family unit. Maybe sexual abuse. I'd say she was raped, and maybe she killed or wished she could kill her rapist as a form of retribution." Vega stood up, went to her desk and returned with the postcard Birch had given her to research. She placed it on the table. "You found this inside the copy of the book you took from Lindsay's apartment," Vega explained, "a book whose themes are about inequality, class struggle, the unfairness of society, the divide between those who have power and money and those who don't."

Birch closed his eyes. It was all starting to make sense. "Like the pigs in the book, rebelling against the farmer, she's rebelling against the hardships she has had to endure, the injustice of it all."

"Just like Mr. Jones, the farmer in the book, he represents the ruling class in the eyes of our chameleon. So did Lindsay Latimer, and her family and what they stood for."

Birch opened his eyes. "You read the book?"

Vega shrugged her shoulders like it was nothing. "Last night. It was a quick read."

Birch picked up the postcard. Then he held it up, pointing at the woman in the painting, upending the man into the well. "So I guess she sees this woman as herself?"

Vega nodded. "The painting is a depiction of a woman killing her rapist. She lures him to a well, pushes him in, then drops rocks on to him as he lies at the bottom, killing him."

"Retribution," Birch whispered to himself.

"Many elements, when added together, all lead to one, overpowering motivation."

Birch nodded. "Fear." Birch thought for a moment. "But the fear this woman felt must be extreme, almost a phobia?"

"No. Our chameleon would have to have psychopathic tendencies to start with. Not enough for her to act out. However, when you add real fear, it would be like adding fuel to a fire, accelerating her evolution into a cold-blooded killer. She has the same, basic, primal survival instincts we all have hiding inside us, Thomas. There are only two options when we experience a traumatic event. We either do nothing, and live in fear for the rest of our lives, or we do something; we take action, so it never happens again."

It made sense to Birch, what Vega was saying.

"We are all just one fearful encounter away from shifting from mammal to animal."

Birch stood and stretched. "Now you're really sounding like a psychiatrist."

"Thomas, I'm giving you a summary of the psychological and psychiatric reports I read as part of the case I mentioned, about the subject I was assigned to track down."

"And did you?" Birch asked. "Catch him?"

"Her," Vega corrected Birch. "I did. Afterward, I requested the reports of the subject after she had been extensively interviewed. There was just one issue the doctors did not anticipate," Vega said.

"What?"

"The woman I'm referring to first killed out of fear, to escape her past life and to assume someone else's life. But she continued killing. She didn't stop, even when she thought she was completely safe in her new life."

"Continued killing?"

Vega nodded. "She developed a liking for it—the killing, that is. She couldn't stop, it become fun for her. She truly transformed into a killer."

"She became what she feared," Birch said. "She became the villain."

Vega leaned forward, her voice barely a whisper. "They said, if we hadn't caught her when we did, she would have continued killing for no reason whatsoever, until the day she died."

Chapter 57 – Touched by Evil

It wasn't the fact of seeing a man slumped on a toilet seat, his back resting against the cistern. Nor the fact he was clearly dead, as evidenced by his grayish skin, lifeless marble-white eyes, drooping jaw, and lolling tongue.

Nor was it the fact dried blood had obviously dribbled down the side of his face, past his jaw, onto his shoulder and had dripped off the tip of his elbow, forming—what look like to Beatriz Vega—a dark red hole in the white tiled floor near his feet. What did however capture Vega's attention was the thin, needlelike object protruding from the dead man's temple.

"You're kidding me," Vega said for the second time now, studying the various photos Eve had taken with her cell phone of Tein Moriarty in the toilet cubicle. Vega turned from her computer screen and looked up at Eve who was standing behind her. "A cocktail swizzle stick?" Vega said. "She actually killed him with a cocktail swizzle stick?"

Birch was standing next to Eve, his arms folded across his chest.

"She's more ruthless than I first thought," Vega said, looking past Eve, her eyes drifting off into space. "My god, she could have used anything, but she chose…that?"

Eve thought she saw a thin smile touch the corners of Vega's mouth. "You sound as though you admire her," Eve said. "Hold her in awe."

"I admire her…inventiveness. Her resourcefulness," Vega said. "*How* she kills reveals more about her character than *why* she kills."

"And you believe it was Lindsay Latimer who killed this man, Moriarty?" Birch said, to Eve.

"I can't be certain," Eve faltered. She had just spent the last twenty minutes telling Birch and Vega about what had transpired at Grand Central Terminal, and what Ramirez had found on Marcus Kemp's cell phone; the messages in the members only chat room: Murder School, how someone named "Victoria" was responsible for killing Evan Brinkmeyer on the Roosevelt Island Tramway as part of some sick game, and Moriarty's cryptic message hinting he was contemplating mass murder to get him ahead of everyone else in the competition.

"Like I said," Eve continued, "maybe Lindsay Latimer isn't the sweet, innocent homecoming queen her father thinks she is." Eve looked at the image of Moriarty. Before coming to Vega's warehouse, Eve had spent the last two hours at the crime scene in the men's restroom. The entire lower level of Grand Central Terminal had been closed off and was crawling with police and forensic technicians.

"All I know is, on the way to the men's restrooms to catch Moriarty, I passed a woman, practically ran into her. I only caught a fleeting glimpse of her. I didn't think anything of it. Then I found Moriarty dead. In hindsight, the woman did bear a resemblance to Lindsay Latimer. She had blonde hair, blue eyes and did look like the photos of Lindsay Latimer her father had shown us. But at the time, my brain didn't register it, I was too focused on finding Moriarty before he carried out his threat."

Birch and Vega exchanged looks. The movement wasn't lost on Eve. "What?" Eve said. "I know it sounds strange, but I now believe Lindsay Latimer isn't the victim we all thought she was. She wasn't abducted by Marcus Kemp. She is somehow part of this Murder School, a group of sick college students trying to outdo each other by carrying out highly visible, random killings, as I've already explained to you."

"Murder School," Vega said. "School's out and so are the killers."

Birch addressed Eve. "Eve, you said before you think there may be thirty members of this Murder School."

"As far as we can tell."

"And this woman, Victoria, is one of just four members of a smaller subgroup, a kill team as you put it."

"Perhaps," Eve replied. "All I know is this smaller group are pretty tight. They all seem to know each other more than the members of the larger group and can see each other's first names that other members outside this particular group can't."

"It's possible," Vega said. "And easily done. A system administrator can assign certain levels of access, user rights and identity reveals to particular members who have formed a group or team. It's no different to playing online computer games in teams. Members of a particular team can see details of other members in their team that others can't."

"And how do you make the leap that Lindsay Latimer and this Victoria woman are one and the same?" Birch asked.

"It was no coincidence she was there," Eve replied. "Lindsay Latimer knew exactly where Moriarty would be. She was tracking him like I was. That and the fact that Moriarty only shared his question about bonus points for killing fifty or more people, with this smaller group of four he was in." Eve massaged her temples, before continuing. "Lindsay *is* Victoria, and she *is* one of the four in this kill team. A woman wouldn't just randomly kill Moriarty. She was taking out the competition."

"It's a tenuous link," Birch countered.

"And taking out one of her own?" Vega said.

Eve shrugged. "You both weren't there. I was, and that's what I believe."

"So we have Marcus Kemp, Tein Moriarty, and Lindsay Latimer," Birch said. "Then who is the fourth member of this group?"

"I don't know." Eve rubbed her neck, could feel the start of a massive headache coming on. She popped two tablets, washed them down with the now cold coffee Vega had made for her. She was running on caffeine and practically no sleep for the last forty-eight hours. "We haven't been able to establish the fourth person yet. But we will. We're still going through Kemp's cell phone and a team is tossing Moriarty's apartment as we speak. But I believe Lindsay is going by the name of 'Victoria' instead." Eve turned to Vega. "When we watched the two videos from Kemp's laptop, you said they looked like they had been taken by two different people, because they *had* been killed by two different people. And the folder you found on Kemp's laptop, labeled 'VC' with the numerous photos of Lindsay Latimer."

Vega nodded. "The 'V' could mean 'Victoria.'"

"So that supports my view they are one and the same person," Eve said.

"But what does the 'C' stand for?" Vega asked.

Eve gave a weary smile. "I can think of a word, none too complimentary."

Eve's remark brought a smile to Vega's lips.

Birch rubbed his jaw, seemingly unconvinced. "If Lindsay—or Victoria, is part of this group, then why was Marcus Kemp following her? Stalking her in the bookstore? Aren't they supposed to all be on the same side?"

"He obviously didn't care," Eve replied, "Perhaps like Maya, my friend who killed him, Lindsay and Kemp had past history together. This smaller subgroup all seem to have known each other before the game started. Maybe in the past Lindsay rejected him or taunted him, so he started stalking her months ago, taking all those photos of her, preparing for her to be his next victim well before this game started." Eve looked at both Birch and Vega. "I'm sure both of you have a wide circle of friends, not all of whom you like nor get along with?"

The exchange of blank looks between Birch and Vega made for an awkward silence between all three of them.

Vega finally spoke. "Put a bunch of killers in a room and I guess some will form relationships, bond, admire one another—"

"While some will view others within the group as a threat," Birch cut in.

"Correct," Eve replied. "Lindsay was planning to win the game at all costs, even if it meant killing off the competition. So when she saw Moriarty's comment, she knew he was planning something big, something that could catapult him to the top leaderboard so to speak. She was also hunting Moriarty at the same time I was."

"Except she got to him first," Birch added.

Eve nodded. "Kemp may have been planning to do the same thing to Lindsay all along. But then he got sidetracked, allowed his emotions to cloud his judgment, made it more personal."

"So he went after your friend," Vega added. "An old flame, someone not in the game, to make it look like her death was part of the game, blame her death on another member of the wider group."

"I think my friend and Lindsay Latimer were going to be neighbors in the cages in Kemp's torture chamber we found in his parents' basement," Eve said. "He had another killing agenda that the game conveniently provided cover for."

"Bent bastard," Vega muttered.

"And what motive would Lindsay Latimer have in being part

of this Murder School? She just doesn't seem like…" Birch trailed off.

"What?" Eve raised an eyebrow. "What doesn't she seem like?"

"The type," Birch replied, throwing up his hands. "It seems so out of character."

"Stop protecting her!" Eve snapped. "She is a cold-blooded killer, like the rest of them."

"I'm not protecting her!" Birch yelled.

Vega held up her hands. "Calm down people."

Eve took a deep breath, counted slowly to five, then spoke again. "The most vile, murderous killers often hide within the most harmless, innocent-looking people we see every day."

"I still need a solid motive," Birch muttered, staring at the floor.

Eve sighed. It was something she had wrestled with since realizing she may have bumped into Lindsay Latimer outside the men's restrooms. "I haven't been able to establish a motive yet," she said to Birch. "And I don't know what Tein Moriarty was planning or what drove him to want to commit mass murder. Maybe they're all just a bored bunch of sick college students who get their thrills from killing people." Eve faced Birch. "This could be one of these rare occasions where there is no clear, concise motive that fits neatly within expected criminal psychology." The sudden rush of events was happening so fast for Eve that she felt her tired brain couldn't keep up. "I can't make sense of it, but I will."

"It seems all too well planned, this Murder School," Birch said. "Too well orchestrated just to be a bunch of bored college students getting their kicks."

"I agree," Eve replied. "There must be more to it, something I haven't seen yet."

"And you found nothing on Moriarty?" Vega asked. "No device, no bomb?"

Eve shook her head. "We're going through security footage now, but we're talking about Grand Central Terminal here. Thousands of people go through there every minute of every day. There simply aren't enough cameras to track everyone's movements, especially when everyone there is either carrying or wheeling a bag or a case with them."

Birch chimed in. "So he goes to the perfect location to commit such an atrocity, and ends up being murdered himself."

Eve agreed. "By a fellow competitor."

"How ironic," Vega added. "Almost cannibalistic. Eating your own species."

"Species of cold-blooded killers," Eve replied, rounding off Vega's thought process. The more time Eve spent with the young Peruvian woman, the more she liked her. They were in tune, on the same wavelength.

Eve glanced once again at the image of Moriarty on the computer screen, and then thought about the video of Evan Brinkmeyer. Both killings were efficient, brutal, ruthless, without hesitation. Maya Zin was correct; it was a game after all, to see who could carry out the most challenging kill. Tein Moriarty was on public display, like a work of art sitting in some macabre murder gallery, while Brinkmeyer was a public exhibition of cunning and daring cleverness. "It seems like two completely different women though," Eve said, "Lindsay and Victoria." Eve massaged her temples, thinking her brain was getting overloaded with more questions than answers. "It's like a puzzle. All the pieces are there...yet I feel something is missing...or not right." Eve's voiced trailed off.

Birch and Vega exchanged looks again, as though privy to

something Eve wasn't. "What?" Eve said, her eyes going between the both of them. "What aren't you telling me?"

Vega shrugged, "Maybe it's two puzzles, placed into the same box. Some of the pieces fit together and make sense, and others don't."

Suddenly it dawned on Eve they were talking about two different things. Eve faced Vega. "When you said moments ago, 'she is more ruthless than you first thought,' who exactly did you mean? Lindsay Latimer?"

Vega looked at Birch. "It's your party, you tell her."

"Tell me what?" Eve said. She pointed at the photo of Moriarty. "Who do you think killed him? I want you to tell me right now."

Birch rubbed his chin. "It's just a theory. Like your 'two puzzles in the same box' idea, some parts of it make sense, other parts seem like they don't belong."

"My theory," Vega said to Eve, touching her leg, nodding approvingly. "Not his."

"Then tell me who the hell this woman is who killed him, and Even Brinkmeyer," Eve said to Vega, trying to keep her anxiety in check.

Birch gave Vega an approving nod, and Vega spent the next few minutes telling Eve about her chameleon theory, about Lindsay Latimer befriending someone during her travels in Europe, only to be killed by them before assuming her life. Vega showed Eve the two sets of photos for comparison and explained the slight physical differences that lead her to believe they were of two different women. When Vega was done, no one said anything for a moment.

Eve slumped into a chair and rubbed the side of her head; her headache had returned with a vengeance. "It's an interesting theory," Eve finally spoke. "About a woman killing another so she could assume the other's identity and escape or hide." Eve looked up at Birch. "This isn't some ploy cooked up by you both to draw attention away from the possibility Lindsay Latimer could be a murderous nutjob?"

Birch shook his head. "We still don't really know. And we're really just basing this on past photos and what her father told us…"

"What did he tell you?" Vega asked, her head pivoting back and forth between Birch and Eve.

"The nanny," Birch replied.

Vega frowned. "What nanny?"

Eve suddenly felt her gut turn. Now the pieces were starting to twist and lock into place, forming a disturbing, almost abstract picture. "She killed the nanny," Eve whispered, coming to the slow realization it could be a distinct possibility. At first, she had dismissed it. Now it could be true after what Birch and Vega had shared with her about a woman taking Lindsay's place and returning to the family home in the UK.

Vega let out an impatient breath. "Will someone *please* tell me about the nanny."

So Birch did.

When he finished, Vega sat back. "Maybe the nanny discovered it wasn't Lindsay who had come back. She looked like her, but it wasn't the same person she had known from all those years of raising her."

"Thinking about it now, your theory does make some sense, Beatriz," Eve said. "Lindsay Latimer—the real Lindsay Latimer—just doesn't fit the profile of what this group is doing." Then she remembered something when she was at Grand Central, about the cold creepy feeling, as though someone had touched her while she stood in the Main Concourse. "She was there, whoever she is," Eve finally said. "Watching me." Eve's gaze swung back and forth between Birch and Vega. "She would have known what I looked like from the newspapers, the press conference I gave the other day."

Vega sat up in her chair. "You said you never really got a good look at her."

"I didn't. But I felt her there, watching me." Eve then told them. "She was on the east balcony, I couldn't see her, she was hidden, like a ghost, an enigma."

"She probably sat at the bar on the balcony, stirring her cocktail with a swizzle stick while she was watching you," Vega said. "She's not an apparition or some ghost. She's just flesh and blood, like any of us—the devil nonetheless, but unlike the devil, she is not possessing Lindsay Latimer's body. She has *become* Lindsay Latimer."

"According to your theory," Eve added, trying to understand—not fully accept, just understand—what Vega was saying. Eve nodded at Birch. "What do you think?"

Birch exhaled slowly. "Look, after what you've told us today, I don't know what to believe anymore. But I know one thing for sure. I want to find Lindsay or Victoria or whatever her damn name is."

Eve did too. She wanted to find this mysterious blonde woman. "You know I've never felt something so…malevolent as when I was standing in Grand Central Station today." Eve felt a shiver just thinking about it again. "It really felt as though something truly evil had laid its hand on me."

She smiled at Vega. "I know you said she's just a woman, evil, though, but still human. Yet, I can't help thinking now, after what you have said about her, if she does really exist, that she's always been there, in the background, watching and waiting." Eve looked at both Birch and Vega. "Closer than what we think…almost within touching distance."

Chapter 58 – Headmistress

It had taken a late cancellation for Andy Ramirez to secure a table at the exclusive restaurant that normally had a three-month waiting time.

And despite the events of today, and the past few days, he desperately needed a time-out, to get out of the office, to decompress and clear his head if for only a few precious hours. At Eve's behest, he'd spent most of the afternoon at Tein Moriarty's apartment, watching the crime scene techs and canvassing the other tenants in the building, all to no avail. They had found nothing in his apartment and all the neighbors said the young Asian man was quiet, courteous, and basically kept to himself. There was one neighbor however, a middle-aged woman named Emma, who seemed more worried about her missing dog than about possibly living next door to a killer.

Andy shook his head to clear his mind, not wanting to think about work for just a few hours. He took a sip of water as he waited patiently, watching the servers clad in crisply starched white shirts and chocolate-brown aprons ferry plates the size of manhole covers, with a slither of food in the middle. Well-dressed patrons, husbands and wives, business associates, and married men with other men's wives, sat and drank and fondled among the sound of clinking cutlery, chinking glassware and hushed tones, plotting and coercing.

Andy checked his watch for the fifth time.

She was late. Her lack of punctuality was the only predictable thing about her.

He leafed through the wine list again, turning each heavy page, trying to decipher the Italian and French wording and searching for a bottle with a price tag that didn't resemble a ZIP code—then quickly closed the leather-bound book.

But she was worth it, Ramirez thought to himself, adjusting his necktie—the only decent one he had—so it didn't feel like a noose around his throat.

He had only known her for a month now, however he could honestly say it had been the most thrilling, exhilarating, and at times precarious, four weeks of his entire life. And maybe the most expensive.

She was an enigma, and maybe it was why he'd found her so alluring. When they were together, all he could think about was getting away from her, as though she had invisible tentacles wrapped around him, strangling him. She was as intoxicating as she was dangerous to his health, possessing a sexual appetite that—while at first had been mind-blowing—was now physically taxing on Andy's body. On several encounters he had limped away battered and bruised. On the last occasion, he needed to consult a chiropractor to reset a few vertebrae in his lower back.

And when they weren't together, all he could do was think about her, counting down the hours until he would see her again. She was like a drug: you know it was bad for you, but after a brief taste, you craved more and more, your life spiraling out of control, willing to do anything just to get the next sweet hit, experience the next blissful high. And yet, actually he knew very little about her. He knew her parents lived in New York, and she had no other siblings, and she worked for some ad agency off Madison Avenue as a junior account executive. When questioned further by Andy, she had the uncanny ability to steer the conversation away from herself and toward him. Not to say Andy didn't mind. Most women he had dated either talked incessantly about themselves or just played with their cell phones, waiting for an excuse to end the date.

Andy's cell pinged. He glanced at the screen.

Just arriving now.

Andy felt a shiver of anticipation. Moments later the hairs on the back of his neck prickled as a subtle, amorous fragrance enveloped him. Fingers lightly caressed the back of his shoulders, then a warm breath touched his ear. "Sorry I'm late, Andy." Moist lips pressed against the side of his face, and he could feel an impression being left there after they pulled away.

Andy looked up as the woman circled around from behind his chair and sat down opposite him.

Instantly he sensed eyes at nearby tables looking across at him, men who had temporarily lost interest in their appetizer—and their own dinner companion—to take more than a cursory glance at his new arrival.

Andy smiled. It made him feel good knowing men were jealous of him. Sadly, it had been lacking with his past exploits. Usually it was his date who garnered the attention of women looking on with pity in their eyes. Now women and men alike stared at Andy, perplexed as to how he had ended up with such a blonde-haired temptress with supermodel good looks.

"I hope you haven't been waiting too long," she said.

Andy noticed how her tongue slithering across her perfectly white teeth when she spoke, a habit that gave her both a predatory and erotic demeanor. Not to mention her sexy British accent Andy found so painfully arousing.

Andy shook his head. "No, not really," he said. Staring into her alluring slate-gray eyes suddenly made all the stress and pressure of his workday vanish in puff of lewd possibilities.

The woman reached out and gave Andy's hand a squeeze.

He glanced down at her hand. Delicate and soft, cool to the touch. "Bright red," he commented.

The woman let go, splayed her fingers to admire her nails. "Just got them done." She graciously thanked the server as he unfolded the crisp white napkin, placing it across her lap, then she ordered a drink. Vodka. And when the server had gone, she tilted forward, gave Andy a sultry look—and a full unashamed view of the firm, hemispherical mounds of flesh stretching at the edges of her low-cut dress.

"I hope you like them," she breathed, the corner of her top lip rising.

For a moment Andy was perplexed as to what she was referring to.

She caught his wondering gaze, then followed it down toward her own chest. Looking up, she raised an eyebrow at Andy. "My nails silly," she said. "Fire-engine red. They're sharp too," she whispered. "You'll find out how sharp they are later." The woman sat back contentedly and watched as Andy hurriedly took a sip from his glass, spilling some of the water onto the white tablecloth.

"Now Andy," the woman said, her accent shifting, mimicking the deep baritone of an English, matronly headmistress. "Tell me all about your day, every little detail." Her eyes widened in delicious anticipation. "And leave nothing out."

Andy let out a sigh. "You know I can't discuss the specifics of what I do, Vicky."

The woman suddenly gave Andy's hand a playful slap. "Now what did I tell you, Andy?" she said, the English headmistress tone now scolding. "I hate how you Americans feel the need to abbreviate everyone's first names." She leaned forward and lowered her voice. "I may have to keep you in after class, teach you some manners, young man." The woman gave Andy a lopsided smile. "My proper name is Victoria."

DAY 5

Journal Entry #22 – The Suitcase

I couldn't believe how simple it was to kill her.

I was admiring the new diamond pendant necklace she had just purchased and was wearing around her throat. As I held the pendant in the palm of my hand, her fragile neck just inches away, something triggered; I was overcome, and before I knew it, I had wrapped my hands around her throat, breaking the chain. I didn't plan it. It just kind of happened. Something inside just took over.

First, I saw the initial look of confusion in her eyes, then shock, and finally the gasping horror as I tightened my grip, her face just inches from mine as I squeezed and squeezed. Her eyes ballooned so big and round I thought they were going to pop out of her head.

She fought, but I was the stronger. She kicked and clawed and lashed out, desperate to cling on to what life she had left. But, I was more determined to live than she was determined not to die.

She sunk to the floor, I followed her there, pressing harder and harder, almost forcing her head through the floor, pushing her further down. And as I stared deep into her eyes, I saw through them to a wide canvas of misery that had been my life. I wasn't killing her, so much as I was killing my past, killing my memories. Memories of when I was ten, the hunched shape of Uncle Cyrus slinking into my bedroom in the dead of night. Memories of my mother ignoring my pleas, scolding me, telling me I was lying about him, hot tears running down my face as she hit me. Memories of ungodly, searing pain that tore through me, then having to wash my bloodstained underwear in the toilet bowl, not the laundry tub because I was too ashamed someone would see me. Memories of going hungry at night, even after my mother had given me almost all her portions of food. For her, food was easy to give. Her motherly love and protection she couldn't give.

I saw memories of me as a child walking to school in the snow, my feet wet and numb from the holes in my school shoes and my body shivering in the threadbare sweater two sizes too small for me.

I saw memories of my father returning home, his breath reeking of alcohol from his so called 'efforts' to try and find work, taking what little money we had and wasting it on drink.

These were all the bitter memories I saw today as I looked into Lindsay's eyes, past her contorted face, her teeth clenched, pale blue lips drawn back, her tongue thrashing about inside her hollow mouth.

Then my memories began to fade, and so did she. The glimmer went out of her eyes, the movement in her face beginning to slowly settle into a fixed picture.

I didn't kill her. It is what I truly believe. I liberated her. I simply took her life—something so precious and cherished yet taken so much for granted —and made it my own.

Much as I hate to admit it, after it was done, I was actually aroused. I can't explain why. It just…turned me on, like a switch being flipped deep inside me. I know it sounds perverted, but what can I say? Maybe the switch is within us all, hidden somewhere in the darkness as we fumble through life trying to find it. Some find it. Some don't. Today I had found mine, and now I can see clearly everything and everyone around me.

I'm not a bad person, really, I'm not. I've just had bad things done to me. So in order to survive, I did what I did, and I will do it again if I have to.

Afterward, I couldn't believe I had wheeled her right past the hotel reception and through a lobby full of people, with just a courteous nod from the hotel concierge, and an offer to help. To him it must have looked like I was taking some spare luggage out to our rental car in the parking lot. I told him I could manage, but was tempted to let him help me, just for the fun of it.

And as I loaded her into the trunk, I couldn't help thinking the old Lindsay Latimer was checking out—permanently—and the new Lindsay Latimer was checking in.

Chapter 59 – Murder Bucket List

After six hours of blissful, uninterrupted sleep—the best night's sleep she'd had in ages—Eve rose early, showered, and changed into a fresh set of clothes.

It seemed as though her nightmares had retreated.

The previous evening, after leaving Birch and Vega, Eve had returned home late and face-planted in her pillow, not bothering to change her clothes. She had awoken this morning to the unnerving sight of Sam, motionless as a sphinx, watching her with unblinking eyes.

After feeding him, Eve made her way down to the corner deli and ordered a breakfast burrito with black coffee, then sat at a table in the far corner and dialed Andy Ramirez's cell phone, wanting to check in with him to see if he had managed to ID any of the other members of Murder School. Instead all Eve got was a recorded voice to leave a message.

Strange, Eve thought. Ramirez, like her, rarely turned off his cell. He should be at his desk at the precinct by now.

Eve ended the call and checked her emails. Between mouthfuls of burrito, she began scrolling through the long list of messages from during the night and early morning.

It was then an urgent police alert landed on her cell.

Eve's eyes scanned the alert. She stopped chewing and read it again.

Spitting out a mouthful of burrito into a napkin, she quickly got to her feet and hurried for the exit.

A torrent of ringing phones and moving bodies greeted Eve as she raced into the squad room twenty minutes later.

Ramirez's desk was empty.

"Where is Ramirez?" Eve asked Roy Beckman.

Roy gave a shrug. "Haven't seen him this morning."

"I just got the alert, what the hell happened?"

Roy handed Eve a sheet of paper he was holding. "Three murders all in the last hour or so."

Eve scanned down the page, her mind trying to comprehend the murderous rampage.

Roy pointed at the list. "Just after seven a.m., a nun was stabbed to death on the steps outside St Patrick's Cathedral just as the congregation was breaking after morning mass. No one saw a thing despite plenty of people around outside. Thirty minutes later in Times Square, a patrol officer shot dead. Again plenty of people about but no witnesses as to who shot him. Then twenty minutes later, a tourist was impaled on the horns of the charging bull at Wall Street. Plenty of office workers around and other tourists too, yet the perpetrator got away." Roy looked at Eve, shock and dismay in his eyes. "Can you believe it?" he muttered. "Someone mounted on the horns of the Wall Street bull?" Roy gave a worried shake of his head. "I've been a cop in this city, Eve, near on forty years, and I ain't seen nothing like this. Was it a full moon or something last night, bringing out all the crazies?"

"Maybe," Eve said. Things were escalating. She had to tell Hagen, let him know what she had discovered, including the involvement of Birch and Vega. He would have a meltdown, but Eve decided she would deal with the consequences later.

"Where's the captain?" she asked Roy. Eve could see Hagen's office was empty.

"He was here about thirty minutes ago," Roy replied. "Then he just took off."

They both looked up as Andy Ramirez walked in, his eyes bloodshot, a grimace across his face. "Sorry," he said sheepishly.

"Well good morning, sleeping beauty," Roy scoffed.

"What the hell happened to you?" Eve said, noticing how slow and awkward Ramirez was moving his limbs. "You look like Frankenstein."

"Late night," Ramirez replied, easing gently into his chair. "I think I've slipped a disk in my back."

Roy rolled his eyes. "Young kids these days," he muttered. "Keep this list, Eve," Roy said to her, before hurrying off to his own desk.

"Thanks, Roy." Eve turned back to Ramirez. "Well, I need you fully awake. Did you see the alert?"

Ramirez nodded, squirming as though he was sitting on a bed of nails. "Just got it."

Eve opened her desk drawer and tossed him a bottle of painkillers. "Take these," she said. "I need you alive, not looking half dead."

Ramirez swallowed two tablets then flipped on his computer. While waiting for it to boot up, he gave Eve an update. He still hadn't been able to identify any of the other members of the Murder School from Kemp's cell phone. Forensics were still at Moriarty's apartment but had found nothing of value. His laptop and cell phone had been taken and were in the process of being analyzed.

Eve rolled her chair next to Ramirez as he logged in. "I need you to find out if these new killings were done by them," she stressed in a hushed tone.

"I'm trying, really I am," Ramirez said. "I just can't get anything else."

"Then keep trying," Eve snapped, her frustration obvious. She needed to find these killers, where they were, and what they were planning to do next, otherwise more innocent people were going to get slaughtered.

She squeezed Ramirez's shoulder, her voice consoling, feeling bad for snapping at him. "Andy, you're the smartest person I know. I really need your wizardry now more than ever. See what you can find out about the other members. Get back into the chat room. I need names. Addresses. Anything that will tell us where they are and what they're doing."

Ramirez nodded, and went to work, while Eve called Birch.

Moments later Ramirez called out to Eve. "Boss, I think you should see this."

"Wait a second." Eve held up her hand. Birch's cell went straight to voice mail. She was about to leave a message, when Ramirez raised his voice.

"I need you to look at this right now!"

Eve ended the call.

Ramirez moved over so Eve could read his computer screen, and what she read made her stomach churn.

"What the hell…" Eve breathed.

"I couldn't get access to this part of the chat room yesterday," Ramirez explained. "Then all of a sudden, it opened up."

But Eve wasn't listening. She was too busy reading the horrifying words on the screen. "It's their list of targets," Eve said. "Good work, Andy."

"It's like a bucket list of people to kill, with points allocated to each person," Ramirez added.

Eve was looking at a murder list. Her eyes scanned down the page:

- A nun outside St. Patrick's Cathedral - 10 points
- New mother breast feeding in public - 15 points

- Father and daughter at the top of the Empire State Building - 20 points
- Police officer in the middle of Times Square - 25 Points
- Tourist impaled on the Charging Bull on Wall Street - 30 points
- A child at the Alice in Wonderland statue in Central Park - 40 points
- Anyone seated courtside at a New York Knicks game - 60 points

Eve quickly eliminated the murders already taken place. A new mother breastfeeding in public? What kind of sick monsters are these people? But that could be anywhere in public, she concluded. The Knicks were playing the Wizards in Washington this weekend so that ruled out Madison Square Garden.

Then, just when she thought humanity had reached an all-time low, she realized in her haste, she had skipped over an entry. She glared back up the list and at once felt a surge of pure madness course through her.

"Get this out to all the precinct captains," she told Ramirez, her teeth clenched. "Highest alert."

Ramirez started typing on his keyboard.

Eve grabbed her jacket.

"Where are you going?" Ramirez asked, seeing Eve head for the door.

"To find the Mad Hatter," Eve called out, praying she wasn't too late.

Chapter 60 – Molly

"Dad, it's me."

Thomas Birch almost collapsed to his knees as he held the cell phone to his ear. He was standing in Vega's kitchen drinking coffee after having spent the night there.

"Justin?" he gasped, trying not to fill his voice with the tears now blurring his eyes and threatening to run down his face. "Where are you? You mother called, told me you were coming to New York. Are you okay?" The questions gushed out in an unrelenting torrent, spilling from Birch's mouth, his heart soaring high above him like it had just discovered it had wings.

And yet at the same time as Birch clenched the phone, his chest swelling with newfound strength and determination at the mere sound of his son's voice, it felt as though his soaring heart was tenuously tethered only by a thin line of thread that could easily break at any time, bringing him crashing down to earth again.

"I'm okay, Dad. Calm down. You sound like Mom."

Birch smiled at the offhand remark and wiped the corner of his eyes with the back of his hand. "Sorry, it's just I was worried about you. It's so good to hear your voice again." Admittedly, Justin's voice did sound a little deeper than he last remembered.

"It's okay," Justin replied. "I'm at your boathouse by the lake. I thought you were home. Where are you?"

The thread tethered to Thomas's heart grew a fraction more taught. *So close and yet so far*, he thought. "Look, I'm not at home at the moment. I'm in the city." Birch's mind raced. He didn't want his son coming to New York. It wasn't safe given everything happening. He knew his Justin was strong willed and craved independence. And after all, he had managed to travel from Boston to Cold Spring on his own. So what were another few hours by train to come and meet him here? The train ran directly from the station in town right into Grand Central Terminal. Suddenly Birch's mind was filled with the morbid image of Tein Moriarty, slumped dead in the restroom cubicle. No it wasn't safe for Justin to come to New York, Birch decided.

"Hey, Justin, my neighbor who I rent the boathouse from has a spare key. She lives in the house at the top of the hill. You probably passed it to get to my place." There were no other houses around and it would be better if Justin stayed where he was and Birch would grab a rental and drive up. "Her name is Molly. Just knock on her door and tell her who you are. I'll call her too and let her know to expect you."

"Okay Dad, I'll go up to the house. I can see it from where I'm standing."

A wave of relief washed over Birch. Molly Gibbons was a lovely woman in her sixties who lived alone. Her son, Kip, had the misfortune of dying in a car accident a few years back, she had told Birch. He knew for a fact Justin would be in safe hands with Molly keeping a watchful eye on him until he could get up there. Also, Molly would absolutely fawn over Justin. Kip was just a few years older than Justin when he had died.

"Her name is Molly," Thomas said. "Go and get the key from her."

"You already said that Dad."

Dad. Birch could feel tears building again. It was a name he thought he would never hear again.

"Okay, okay," Birch said with a smile, "and make yourself at home. There's food in the fridge, and cable too."

"Sweet," Justin said.

"Call me when you've got the key and are inside."

"Okay, Dad…" Justin's voice drifted off.

"Justin?"

"Sorry, Dad. I can see someone coming down from the house now. I think it's them. I'll call you back when I get the key."

"Good." Thomas ended the call, then immediately dialed the landline for Molly Gibbons. Molly had a portable phone she always carried with her when she went outside, puttering in her garden or whenever she came down to visit Thomas. On numerous occasions she would stroll down at dusk to either invite him up to her house for an early dinner, or she would bring down to him a freshly baked pecan pie and a tub of whipped cream. They would sit out on the dock on camp chairs and eat her homemade pie while listening to the fish jump in the dark waters and the building chorus of crickets in forests surrounding the lake.

Thomas knew Molly was lonely, and she relished finally having someone to rent the boathouse just for the company.

The call rang out and Birch redialed. Moments later it rang out again. He shrugged, telling himself to wait until Justin called him back.

Chapter 61 – The Bat

The man seemed to appear out of nowhere.

Justin pocketed his cell phone and watched as the tall stranger approached, moving away from the house perched at the top of the hill, and down the dirt path toward where Justin stood in front of the boathouse on the lake. The man's hands were thrust deep into the pockets of a long, dark gothic-style coat he wore that billowed out behind him like a cape, giving him the appearance of a large, bat-like creature swooping down the hillside.

"Hi!" the man called out cheerfully as he got closer.

Justin raised his hand. "Hi."

"I was looking for Thomas Birch," the man said, pulling up in front of Justin. "I was told he lives here." The man was long limbed, and pale faced, with high cheekbones and intense, wide eyes.

"He does," Justin replied hesitantly. "Who are you?" Justin noted the man's eyes dart past him to the boathouse behind.

"Joshua," the man said, bringing his eyes back to Justin. "I used to work with Thomas." The man cocked his head. "You must be Justin, his son?"

Justin nodded.

"Wow, you're the spitting image of your father." The man must have seen the confused look on Justin's face and launched into an explanation. "I was a rookie cop, had joined the NYPD a few years back. Your father and I became good friends. He took me under his wing so to speak."

Justin gave a dubious frown, thinking the man looked more at home behind the counter of a comic or vintage record store than in the police. "You look kind of young. Aren't you still a cop?"

A hint of sadness touched the man's face, but there was something else there too in his eyes, like a touch of irritation, Justin thought.

"Got shot," the man said, indicating to one shoulder. "Was released from the force on medical grounds." He took a step forward. "Hey, I was sorry to hear your dad went to prison." The man glanced around, but there they were alone. "If you ask me, I thought he was innocent." The man nodded toward the boathouse. "Is that where he lives?"

"No," Justin replied, as the man walked past him, before stopping and turning back to Justin. "Oh? I thought you said—"

"I mean…that's where he lives…but he's not home…at the moment," Justin stuttered. For some reason, the man was making him feel nervous.

"I see," the man said. "I nearly got lost driving up. First time I've been here. It sure is pretty." The man rocked back on his heels, admiring the lakefront view. He inhaled deeply. "And that sweet, fresh air," he said, turning and smiling at Justin. "Don't get that in the city." The man walked back to where Justin was standing. "I kind of wanted to surprise your father, you know?" he said. "Catch up and the like." The man's eyes drifted to the ball cap Justin was wearing. "How's Boston?" he asked. "Your dad told me that's where you and your mom are now living."

Justin looked down at the dirt, a pang of hurt in his chest. "It's okay, I guess."

"He told me he misses you, Justin."

Justin suddenly looked up, the hurt he felt in his chest easing slightly. "He does?"

The man nodded sympathetically. "Terribly."

Justin looked down again, kicking the dirt with his toe, making tiny furrows. "I said some pretty dumb things to him in the past."

"We all say dumb things at times, kiddo," the man said, resting a gentle hand on Justin's shoulder. "Especially to our parents."

"That's why I came here," Justin said, looking up into the man's haunting eyes. "To see him, to tell him I'm sorry."

The man nodded solemnly.

"But my mom said I shouldn't see him because he's a criminal now, that he is no longer my father and I should just forget about him."

"So you came all the way here from Boston alone?" the man said, looking around again.

"Yeah," Justin replied gloomily. "Caught a few trains to get here. But he's in New York City. I just spoke to him. I thought he was here too." Justin felt downtrodden. He'd come all this way for nothing.

"I guess we both bombed out, then," the man laughed as though trying to make light of the situation.

"My dad said the neighbor in the house up there on the hill has a spare key to the boathouse, that I should get it and stay here and wait for him. I told Dad I'd call him back and let him know."

The man turned and looked back toward the house perched on the hill. "I just came from up there," he said. "I tried knocking on the front door but there was no answer. I don't think anyone's home."

"Oh," Justin said. All of his options were fading fast.

The man jerked his thumb over his shoulder. "You can try if you like. But I think she may have gone away." The man's brow furrowed for a while, like he was deep in thought. Suddenly his face lit up. While keeping his hand firmly planted on Justin's shoulder, as though holding him in place, he spoke excitedly. "Hey, I've a great idea! I'm heading back to the city, so how about I give you a ride so you can see your dad?" The man pivoted back and forth, waving his other hand, the tail of his coat swishing around him. "There's no point in both of us hanging around here, is there? The place seems deserted."

Justin felt undecided. If he couldn't get inside the boathouse, he didn't fancy heading back to the township to stay in some creepy motel. He wasn't looking forward to a long train ride back home either. He just wanted to see his father, to talk to him.

The man squeezed Justin's shoulder some more. "Let's head back and we can both surprise him!" he said enthusiastically. "What do you say? It's only about an hour car ride."

Justin adjusted his backpack, feeling it dig into his back. He only packed a few things, some clothes, and some cash. What the man was saying made sense. There was no point in hanging around if his father wasn't here.

"Come on," the man said, coaxing Justin with a gently shake of his shoulder. "I could use the company on the ride back. It will be fun. We can stop off on the way and grab some burgers and fries, my treat."

The thought of food suddenly made Justin feel very hungry. The last time he had eaten was when he'd managed to grab a stale sandwich on the train ride here.

"My car is just up there." The man pointed back toward the main house on the hill. "What do you say?"

Justin finally relented. "Okay." The lure of burgers, fries and a one-hour car ride to meet his dad seemed too much to pass up.

"Good," the man said, ushering Justin toward the base of hill with a sweep of his hand. "Let's go. I'm Joshua by the way, but all my friends call me Josh."

As they crested the top of the hill, Joshua Banks placed his hand again on Justin's shoulder, steering him away from the front of the house and toward where a small sedan sat parked, almost hidden among a corpse of trees. "My car is right over there." He pressed the remote and the trunk of the sedan swung up. "Might as well throw your backpack inside."

Justin slid off one shoulder strap, turning to face the yawning darkness of trunk as he did. During the brisk walk up the hill, something the man had said previously was still gnawing at Justin's mind. "You said the neighbor was a 'she'," Justin said, reaching in to place his backpack inside the trunk. "How do you know the neighbor is a 'she' if you've never been here before?" Justin asked, bending over, his back turned. It was then a low cloud broke apart across the face of the sun, throwing a dappled wedge of wavering light into the trunk of the car—revealing a blood-coated crowbar, with a clump of hair and torn scalp caught in the sharpened fork-end of the bar.

Justin's breath faltered.

If he'd had eyes in the back of his head, Justin Birch would have seen the prickly look of annoyance flash across the man's jaw, seen the cruel, cold look of contempt shine brightly in his eyes. Justin would have also seen a gun being quickly pulled from the man's pocket just before it came crashing down on the back of his skull.

It was only a slight consolation that Justin Birch didn't feel his unconscious body being swiftly upended, then dumped heavily into to the trunk of the sedan. Nor did he feel his pockets being rifled through, his cell phone and wallet taken, before the trunk was slammed shut, cutting off all daylight, and plunging him into a small, metal prison of darkness.

Chapter 62 – Eve in Wonderland

Eve dumped her car at the curb on the corner of Fifth Avenue and East Seventy-Sixth Street near an entrance to Central Park and broke into a sluggish run, cursing she didn't do more jogging for fitness.

Plunging through a narrow gate, she almost crashed into a hot dog stand on the other side. Gathering herself, she turned and headed down a left path, then took a right turn, passing ambling adults and wayward children before stopping to catch her breath. Ahead, the final path to the monument curved gently to the left through a grove of trees. The last thing she wanted was to rush in, gun drawn and scare everyone, including a possible member of Murder School. She desperately wanted to catch one of them—alive.

Eve took another deep breath, slowing her heartbeat some more, then as casually as she could, she began walking.

The path opened up into a wide clearing, the famous bronze sculpture at the very center on a circular, raised plinth. Calmly, Eve's eyes took in everything:

Alice sitting majestically on a massive mushroom, legs splayed to one side, arms held out serenely.

A woman engrossed with her cell phone while carelessly pushing a stroller one-handed, a sleeping baby bundled up inside.

Two young girls posing next to the White Rabbit, tongues poking out at the screen of a raised cell phone.

A small boy, red-faced and in tears, being made to sit on a small mushroom near the Mad Hatter, the boy's father issuing instructions at his son while holding a camera.

Three older people sitting on a park bench talking.

Eve looked away, toward the shadows under the surrounding trees.

Nothing.

No scary clown lurking in the undergrowth holding a chainsaw. No knife-wielding, Michael Myers look-a-like hiding behind a tree trunk.

Eve breathed a sigh of relief.

Then all at once came the screams and cries for help.

Chapter 63 – The Lure

Nine miles south of Cold Spring, and fifty miles north of Manhattan, Joshua Banks crossed Bear Mountain Bridge that spanned the Hudson River before curving south on US-6. He checked his speed, then placed a call using his own cell phone.

A man answered. "Did you take care of him like I said?"

"No," Banks replied. "He wasn't there." On the passenger seat sat a file Banks had been given before the drive up to Cold Spring. It contained all the relevant information about Thomas Birch, where he lived, his past, his family and details about his ex-wife and son, Justin. "He is apparently in the city, and I'm heading back now."

"So it was a wasted trip after all?" The man said, the disappointment clear in his voice.

Banks smiled, looking at Justin's cell phone on the seat next to him. "Not entirely. I have something of immense value that will lure Thomas Birch out from his hiding place."

"And what would that be?"

After Banks told the man, he was certain he could sense him gloating on the other end.

"Good, good," the man said, sounding like he was almost salivating down the phone line. "It gives us more options. I've had a change of plan. This is what I want you to do…"

Thomas Birch's cell phone chimed as a new text message landed.

"It's Justin," he said, looking at the screen. "He said my neighbor isn't home so he's catching a train to the city. He'll be here in an hour or so."

"That makes sense," Vega said, turning from her computer screen. "He can stay here if you like. It might be safer for him than just staying in the empty apartment Latimer gave you which you haven't used."

Birch looked up from the phone. "Are you sure? I thought you valued your privacy and wanted to remain anonymous?"

"No trouble at all. I've got plenty of space and I'd like to meet him. I'll just tell him I'm helping you with a missing persons case. Send him my address."

"Thanks, Beatriz." Birch texted Justin Vega's address. "I owe you one."

"You owe me plenty," she said turning back to her computer screen.

Birch dialed his neighbor's house phone just to check. Maybe Justin didn't want to stay there. After a few moments, the phone call rang out. Birch frowned as he ended the call. Maybe his son was right. Molly Gibbons wasn't home.

Paramedics had been working feverishly on saving the woman's life for almost thirty minutes now, the ground around them littered with blood-soaked bandages and torn-open plastic bags of medical supplies.

Abruptly, the paramedic doing chest compressions stopped, sat back on his haunches, and wiped his brow. After peeling off his gloves, he glanced across to where Eve was standing, and slowly shook his head.

Eve turned away, her body still flushed with the recent surge of adrenalin. Who would have believed something as innocent as a woman pushing a stroller—with a plastic toy baby inside, underneath which a massive chef's knife lay hidden—would turn out to be one of the Murder School killers.

Eve touched her gun in its holster. It still felt warm, three less bullets in the magazine. After repeated warnings to put the knife down, the woman had given Eve no choice, especially when the woman then lunged, knife in hand, toward the little boy sitting on the mushroom.

The entire area around the Alice in Wonderland sculpture had been cordoned off with police tape, and patrol officers were taking statements from witnesses. Eve wandered over to an empty park bench and sat down, and for the hundredth time replayed what had happened. The boy's father was too slow. The two young girls posing next to the White Rabbit, whose screams had first alerted Eve, scattered, while the three older people sitting on a park bench just looked on perplexed. With the foreground and background clear, Eve took the shot. It felt different somehow, shooting a woman. She was still pure evil nonetheless, and Eve doubted the woman was actually a mother, only masquerading as one so as to unobtrusively approach, then kill someone else's child.

Eve watched as paramedics covered the body before loading it onto a gurney and wheeling it past her. Pulling out her cell phone, she checked in with Ramirez, telling him what happened. Police had been dispatched to patrol the other sites on the Murder School list, and thankfully there had been no other incidents. There was nothing new in the Murder School chat room either, Ramirez said.

Ending the call, Eve breathed a sigh of relief, sat back on the park bench, and then closed her eyes for a moment, only to be roused by the sound of approaching feet. Looking up she saw two men approaching, stern-faced and methodical in their stride, badges on their belts.

Eve knew what was coming.

Wearily, she got to her feet, and glanced across to where Alice sat so peacefully and innocently on her giant mushroom—her face now spattered with blood.

Chapter 64 – You Kill Me

Birch's cell phone chimed as a text landed. "Justin is nearly here," he said to Vega. "He's walking down the street right now."

Justin had already texted a few times in the last hour, letting him know first when he was on the train, and again when he had arrived at Grand Central and was catching the subway to Vega's neighborhood.

"A Patriots fan is he?" Beatriz Vega said a few minutes later. A security camera window had suddenly popped up in the corner of her computer screen.

"I guess he is now." On the screen, Birch could see Justin standing outside under the security camera at the locked entrance door to the building. He was wearing a New England Patriots ball cap pulled down low over his head, and a backpack was slung over one shoulder. His head was tilted down looking at the cell phone in his hand, one thumb working the screen.

Birch's cell chimed again as another text landed: "Dad, I'm here. Let me in."

Vega shook her head. "Didn't take him long to switch allegiance, did it." She hit a key on her keyboard releasing the door-locking mechanism.

On the screen, Justin pushed open the door and vanished inside the building.

Moments later Vega's computer screen flashed bright red as an alarm went off.

"Why is your son carrying a gun?" Vega demanded.

"It's got to be a mistake!" Birch said, confusion flooding his head as he stared at the computer screen where bright red warning letters pulsed.

"It is not mistake!" Vega yelled. "He's got a gun on him!"

"No! No!" Birch pleaded. "It must be his phone or his laptop in his backpack." Birch could see Vega's hand hover over the keyboard, knowing with a tap of her finger the elevator carrying his son up to him would be flooded with poisonous gas, instantly killing him. "Vega! No! Don't do it. I tell you he hasn't got a gun." Birch was begging now. "He wouldn't know what to do with one let alone be carrying one on him. You must believe me."

Vega glared at Birch.

He could see her fingers hovering over the keyboard.

"Damn!" Vega said, getting up and running down the passageway and out of sight. Moments later she came running back, a handgun held firmly in her grip.

"I hope you're right." Vega ran past Birch and toward the elevator.

"It's Justin," Birch said, catching up to her. "And he doesn't have a gun. I swear."

The elevator arrived with a shudder and the doors inched agonizingly apart.

Vega pointed her gun at the occupant.

Joshua Banks smiled as he raised his hands. "Now, that's no way to greet a guest is it?"

Vega tightened her grip on the gun.

Birch stepped forward, was about to speak, but Banks beat him to it.

"You kill me, you kill Justin." Banks grinned, then pulled out his own gun and pointed it at Vega.

Vega held her aim, not wavering an inch.

"Tell her to lower the gun, Thomas," Banks said out of the side of his mouth, his eyes never leaving Vega. "Or Justin will die right now, *and* I'll kill you both, I promise."

Birch pleaded to Vega.

Vega hesitated, before finally lowering her gun, her entire body quivering with hot-blooded anger.

"Good," Banks sighed. "Let's all just calm down and no one will get hurt." His eyes darted sideways toward Birch, "I need him," before settling back on Vega, "but I don't need you."

Banks pulled the trigger and shot Vega square in the chest.

Chapter 65 – Abyss

"Are you certain you won't have anything to eat?" Carl Hagen said, looking up from where he sat alone at a small table in the corner of the empty Italian restaurant.

Thomas Birch, with a gun pressed into his spine by Joshua Banks, had entered through the kitchen from the alleyway outside where Banks had parked his car after driving from Vega's building.

"The proprietor of this place allows me certain 'liberties' so to speak," Hagen said. "Such as allowing me to conduct certain business meetings outside of normal opening hours, like this one, Thomas." Hagen reached for a wine bottle. "Come and sit down. Let's be civil about this."

"Where's my son?" Birch asked, preferring to stand, not willing to sit and drink the glass of red wine Hagen had so ceremoniously poured for him.

"Come, come, Thomas," Hagen said, dabbing the corners of his mouth with a napkin. "I had the chef come in especially early. His milk-fed veal scallopini is truly a masterpiece." Hagen looked Birch up and down. "And you look like you've lost some weight since I last saw you, Thomas. I guess that's what prison food does to you."

"Where is Justin?" Birch asked again, bunching his fists. "What have you done with him?" Birch didn't care for the idle banter. He just wanted to see his son.

Hagen took a long, excruciatingly slow sip from his wine glass, after admiring the rich red color in the candlelight.

Birch knew Hagen wanted to fully enjoy the moment, to see him squirm, to agonize over his son's disappearance.

"At least have some wine," Hagen insisted. "It's a wonderful merlot from the Clinet vineyard in Pomerol, France." Hagen gave a gloating smile. "I have several cases of it myself."

"All on a cop's salary?" Birch scoffed, not hiding the disdain in his voice. "It's wasted on someone as vile as you, Hagen."

"Let me assure you, Justin is safe," Hagen said. "Whether he remains safe is entirely up to you, Thomas."

Birch looked around at the empty restaurant. "Why did you bring me here, Hagen? What do you want from me? Let Justin go and do whatever you want to me. Just leave my son out of it." Seeing Carl Hagen for the first time in nearly three years had come as a shock and only added to the confusion Birch felt. "I have no money, Hagen. My family has left me. I have nothing. What could you possibly want that hasn't already been taken from me?"

Hagen gave a smile that reminded Birch of an alligator basking in the sun on a riverbank. Slowly a light bulb began to dimly glow inside Birch's head. Apart from Justin, there was only one other thing of value in his humble life right now.

A slow, carnivorous grin began to spread across Hagen's face. He shook a finger at Birch. "I always said you were a good detective, Thomas. Maybe too good. Have you figured it out yet?"

Birch felt a crack of despair open up under him, like a split in the earth on which he was standing, that was slowly widening in time with Hagen's widening grin.

"You see, Thomas," Hagen continued, "while you are—I mean *were,* a good detective, you always failed to grasp the bigger picture, the larger things in play. You focused too much on the small things, couldn't see the grander designs of the universe around you." Hagen took another mouthful of wine, rolled his eyes in delight, swishing the liquid around his cheeks before finally swallowing. "Ah, that's better." He placed the wine glass down again and resumed eating, not looking at Birch as he spoke. "I have bigger plans, Thomas, *much* bigger plans. Plans I can't afford to have derailed."

The light bulb began to glow brighter in Birch's mind, throwing more light onto why Hagen was doing this. Birch could feel the split in the earth under him widen into a chasm, with his feet straddling either side being pulled farther apart. Birch had been played from the start and there was no way out.

Hagen looked up and pointed his knife at Birch. "You know how you get to survive in this business, Thomas?"

Thomas could feel himself losing balance, about to tumble into the chasm.

"By staying not one, but *several* steps ahead of your enemies." Hagen smiled, revealing a piece of meat caught in between his teeth. "And I have many, many enemies, some who haven't even become my enemies—yet."

Hagen raised one hand and clicked his fingers at a shadowy corner of the restaurant. "But I also have some really important allies as well."

Birch didn't want to turn his head, to look in the direction where Hagen had beckoned, for if he did, he knew the chasm under him would open up into the Grand Canyon. But the urge was too much for Birch. He turned his head and stared into the darkness.

The shadows distorted, then a figured stepped out of the darkness and into the light, a person Birch knew had been hiding in plain sight all this time.

The woman slowly walked around behind Hagen's chair, her eyes never leaving Birch as she moved—even after she sat down—taking the seat at the table Birch had been offered. The woman then placed down on the table the object she was carrying. "Hello, Thomas," Maxine Brodie said.

Birch looked down at the green folder, the same green folder Francis Latimer had shown him in his office, the folder he had been told contained irrefutable proof of his own innocence while also condemning Carl Hagen.

The walls of the chasm beneath Birch finally wrenched apart, and Thomas Birch tumbled into the abyss.

Chapter 66 – Loose Ends

"What did he offer you?" Birch said, addressing Maxine Brodie. "It must be substantial, considering your current employer owns half of Manhattan."

"White House press secretary," Hagen replied for Brodie.

Birch couldn't believe what Hagen was saying. He already thought the man's ambition was large, but Birch had no idea he had delusions of grandeur that extended all the way to a tilt at the White House. "You're insane Hagen." Birch glanced at Brodie. "And you're insane for betraying Francis Latimer and joining this"—Birch pointed at Hagen, almost lost for words—"criminal."

"You're the only criminal here, Thomas," Brodie said with a smile. "Or have you forgotten your past?" Brodie patted the green file in front of her. "This will be destroyed, along with all the digital copies I have. Your past will remain intact, forever branded a criminal, and despised by your son."

"You mean you'll erase the truth?" Birch replied.

Hagen spread his arms. "What can I say, Thomas. Welcome to politics. I will soon wield enough power—first as chief of police, then as governor, then…who knows?"

Hatred billowed up inside Birch, and he lunged at Hagen, thinking he could reach the steak knife on the table—but Joshua Banks managed to pull him back, thrusting the barrel of the gun deeper into his spine.

Hagen looked down at the tablecloth and slowly shook his head. "You know, Thomas, I thought I would be civil." Hagen looked up, a mix of sadness and scorn in his eyes. "I offer you redemption, a chance. And what do you do? You cling to your nobility and virtuous belief in the world. As I said, you fail to understand the reality surrounding you."

"To be corrupt?" Birch snapped back. "Is that the only way to survive in the world?" Birch shook his head. "I know the world at times is filth, but it doesn't mean we all have to stoop so low and wallow in it."

"You haven't adapted to the world around you," Brodie said. "If you don't change with it, then you'll get left behind. Thomas, you need to accept this is how things now are. I did."

Hagen gestured to the last remaining empty chair at the table. "Take a seat, Thomas. I won't ask again."

"You can keep your seat," Birch said firmly. "All I want is Justin back. Nothing else matters." Birch focused on Brodie. "And what about Lindsay Latimer? What are you going to tell her family?"

Brodie gave a dismissive wave. "She really is missing. I imagine the little spoiled bitch probably had a tantrum and ran off somewhere to sulk. I don't really care about her. This whole episode with her missing has just been one huge distraction for the family. I simply went along with it for the sake of keeping up appearances. I never liked her anyway."

"And the file?" Birch said.

Hagen held up his hand. "Maxine came to me only after she had dug up what she had on me. We've known each other for a while now; she understands my political aspirations. She was already on my team well before this incident with Latimer's daughter." Hagen smiled at Brodie. Birch could see the obvious affection between the two; that, or a mutual lust for power.

"Think about all those eyes watching me on the TV and streaming services, Thomas," Brodie said. "Every day I'll be in front of more than a billion people, all hanging on my every word. I could never dream of such a role if I were to stay with the Latimer family."

"So you hitched your ride to a corrupt police officer who is just as deluded as you," Birch replied.

"It was me who put your name forward to Francis Latimer, Thomas," Brodie explained, "after researching your past, then discovering incriminating evidence against Carl, and the fact you were innocent. I saw an opportunity, that's all."

Birch felt disgusted, like he was coated in grime just from being in the same room as these two.

"You are the only threat from my past, Thomas," Hagen said. "The only person who could derail my future plans. So I told Maxine to plant the seed with Latimer to seek you out and use the information as an incentive, given what she found out about what happened in your personal life after you went to jail."

"You seemed like the perfect candidate, Thomas" Brodie added. "There was no other way we could draw you out, show you the prize while at the same time appearing to be on your side."

"Why didn't you just come to me, Hagen?" Birch asked, "once Brodie had uncovered the truth?"

"What? And use the file to blackmail you?" Brodie said, touching Hagen's arm. "Because it wouldn't have been as effective. I much prefer the carrot-on-the stick approach. We needed to dangle the hope of redemption in front of you, the chance of getting Justin back, to win your son's heart again, Thomas. That's why. It was a far more powerful motivator than just telling you that you were innocent, and I had the evidence to prove it. Same outcome but a far more powerful motivator."

"So you used my son, Justin, as the 'carrot' in this example?" Birch said with contempt.

Brodie nodded. "A more subtle, cleverer approach than having to resort to brute threats of violence."

Birch almost laughed at the absurdity of her statement. He

and Justin had both been kidnapped.

"You were never going to get the proof to redeem yourself, Thomas," Hagen said. "As Maxine explained before, all traces of the file will be destroyed. You lose—again. Like I said, Thomas. You need to take stock of the world around you. You need to follow the new rules if you want to play this game."

"Corrupt rules," Birch countered.

Brodie shook her head. "There is no such thing as corruption anymore, just differing views and alternate perspectives," Brodie replied, sounding to Birch like she was already well suited for a career in politics.

"Why are you telling me all this?" Birch asked. "You're just going to kill me and Justin aren't you?"

"No, Thomas," Hagen said, folding his napkin. "I did think about it at first, when I sent my colleague there to your home." Hagen waved Joshua Banks off and he sat down at a nearby table, the gun still pointing at Birch.

"Then I had a change of heart," Hagen continued. "There is no need to kill anyone. And there is no point in you telling the police or anyone else for that matter. Who are they going to believe? A disgraced ex-detective who is a convicted felon who seems to still be filled with resentment and bitterness over what happened to him? Or me, the new chief of police who was instrumental in bringing to justice this gang of murderous villains who have been terrorizing the city lately?"

Birch closed his eyes, realizing what Hagen was implying.

Hagen nodded slowly at Birch. "It was my idea, a sheer stroke of genius. Finding people willing to kill isn't difficult, especially in this city." Hagen leaned forward, a manic glow in his eye. "But the real genius is what Joshua came up with." Hagen nodded toward Banks.

Banks smiled. "The gamification of murder."

Birch turned and looked at Joshua Banks.

Banks spread his arms like he was preaching. "You make something, even murder, a game these days, and participants literally fall into your lap, all wanting to kill just to win. I was amazed at how many people wanted in," he said, rocking back on his chair. "I guess people these days are bored of playing computer games where they don't actually get to shoot, knife, and blow-up real people." Banks gave a heinous grin as his eyes narrowed. "They now really want to do it—to kill people for real, to feel what it's like."

"Create a campaign of fear in the city," Brodie cut in. "Fabricate the headline, invent the problem, then have Carl here swoop in and solve it. Become the hero of the city so everyone will adore and want to appoint him to higher office."

"And Eve Sommers?" Birch asked. "Leave her out of this."

Hagen gave Birch a look of pity. "It's a shame, she was a great detective. Sadly, she's going to be missed."

Birch felt sick. By involving Eve, he had inadvertently signed her death warrant. Hagen intended to tie up any and all loose ends, including Eve.

"I told you, Thomas, no police involvement," Brodie said. "But you ignored my advice and got her involved."

"She knows nothing about the file, about the arrangement I had with Latimer," Birch snarled, feeling worse by the second. It was clear now that as soon as he and Eve had left Latimer's office, Brodie was straight on the phone to Hagen, telling him about this new development.

"Unfortunately," Hagen replied, "I can't afford to believe

you. There's too much at stake." Hagen looked past Birch and motioned to Banks.

Banks slipped out his cell and started tapping the screen.

Birch whirled around. "What are you doing?"

Hagen smiled. "You created these additional loose ends for me, Thomas, by involving others. Now I need to tie them off—permanently."

Moments later, Joshua Banks looked up from his cell phone and nodded at Hagen. "It's done."

Chapter 67 – Double Agent

Birch turned, as a man, dressed in a dark gray suit, entered the restaurant dining room.

It was the same man who had appeared at the doorstep of Birch's boathouse days before. The man, whose name Birch still didn't know, gave a curt smile to Birch before addressing Carl Hagen. "Ah, Mr. Hagen. Francis Latimer would like a moment of your time," he said, an expectant smile affixed to his face.

"Who the hell let you in?" Hagen scowled.

Birch looked around, noticing Joshua Banks had slipped out of the room, and was gone.

"Why, the owner of course," the man replied as though the answer was so obvious.

Hagen threw down his napkin. "Well tell Latimer I'm busy!"

The man bowed politely, stepped aside, then gestured with his hand. "Perhaps you would like to tell him yourself—in person."

Francis Latimer swept into the room, flanked by two towering men, and stopped in front of the table Hagen and Brodie were seated at. Like two huge, stone sentinels guarding the entrance of a pharaoh's tomb, the two men—whom Birch assumed were bodyguards—stood on either side of Latimer.

Birch glanced at Maxine Brodie, expecting a look of shock and guilt on her face, now that her treacherous deceit was about to be exposed. Instead she turned to Birch and gave him a subtle smile.

"Busy doing exactly what, Carl?" Latimer replied, calm and confident.

"Business!" Hagen retorted.

Latimer smiled, looking around the room.

"You're an uninvited guest, Francis. If you and your entourage don't leave, I'll have the owner throw you all out for trespass."

Birch noticed Latimer taking a keen interest in ceiling of the room. "The owner?" Latimer replied, before affixing a cold stare on Hagen. "That would be me." Latimer remained standing, seeming to enjoy watching the blood suddenly drain from Hagen's face. "You see, Carl, people doing dark deeds tend to conduct their business in dark, gloomy places." Latimer waved a hand about the room. "Such as in a room like this one. Subdued lighting, dark walls, plenty of shadows to hide within."

Birch glanced up at the ceiling, his eyes darting left and right, wondering what Latimer was going on about.

"It's amazing what you can hide in such a room like this," Latimer continued. "My, my, if only the walls could talk…I wonder what they would say, hey, Carl?"

Birch watched as Carl Hagen seemed to shrink in his chair. His shoulders seemed a little more slumped, his face a little more droopy.

Latimer spread his hands out. "But!" he said, raising his voice. "There's no need for the walls to talk." Latimer pulled out a thumb drive from his pocket and held it aloft. "Especially when for the last six months I have recorded everything that has transpired in this very room, all in beautiful 4K color with Hollywood-production sound quality." Without being asked, Latimer pulled out a chair and sat between Brodie and Hagen. He poured himself a glass of red wine, took a mouthful, then cringed, inspecting the label on the bottle. "You always were a cheapskate, Carl. Like you, the wine looks good on the surface, but no substance underneath." Latimer pushed aside the wine glass and rested his arms on the table and regarded Hagen. "You see, Carl, I purchased this restaurant six months ago from the owner. The business was struggling, and so I offered him twice what he would have liquidated it for."

Birch smiled, as Hagen seemed to squirm in his seat.

Latimer nodded thoughtfully. "You see, Carl, I saw the underlying value in this place, what it was truly worth." Latimer gave Brodie's arm a squeeze. "When Maxine here began researching your grubby little empire, she soon discovered you were a creature of habit, and you liked to frequent this place to conduct your corrupt business dealings. So I bought the restaurant…and installed the best, low-light surveillance cameras in every room." Latimer straightened his already impeccably knotted silk tie and said to Hagen with a hushed voice, "Got them from a friend who supplies them to the CIA. But we'll just keep that fact between you and me."

Birch could see Hagen's face contort as he gripped the tablecloth in a fist. Hagen turned to Brodie. "You fucking traitor!"

"Now, now, Carl," Latimer interjected. "She cannot be *your* traitor if she was never *my* traitor first."

A wave of relief hit Birch, as he watched on. Maxine Brodie was acting as a double-agent. She had never betrayed Latimer in the first place for the sake of joining forces with Carl Hagen. It was all a ruse to make Hagen think she had jumped ship.

Latimer continued. "You must also learn to respect women…even the ones going to college." Latimer gave Hagen a knowing smile, letting the last words and their meaning sink in.

"That's right," Latimer said slowly, looking deep into Hagen's eyes. "Like I said, you are a creature of habit. Such as booking the same room at the same hotel you like to go to every Friday." Latimer sat back. "I had cameras installed in there too."

Latimer let out a chuckle. "Not that I had to buy the entire hotel to do that. I just had to 'buy' the young women you were banging there, Carl. It's amazing these little spy cameras you can buy these days. Women can so easily conceal them in their handbags and then set them up inconspicuously inside a hotel room."

Latimer's expression suddenly turned cold. "Some of those women were as young as sixteen years old, Carl. In this state, that's a criminal offence." Latimer placed the thumb drive on the table in front of Hagen. "You can keep that copy, Carl. I have plenty of copies. Perhaps you can show it to Mrs. Hagen and your children."

Hagen grabbed the steak knife from his plate.

With military speed, the two bodyguards reached for their handguns under their jackets.

Latimer held up his hand, halting the two bodyguards from blowing Hagen away. "I suggest you put down the knife, Carl." Latimer said, eyeing Hagen. "Otherwise my two friends here will turn your head into Napoli sauce."

Hagen hesitated, knife raised, looking around as though weighing up his limited options. Then slowly he relaxed, and let the knife drop onto his plate with a clang.

"Good choice, Carl," Latimer said, indicating to his two bodyguards to put their guns away.

Hagen looked down at the thumb drive but didn't touch it.

"It's all on there," Latimer continued. "All the meetings in this very room. The corrupt deals you made, the negotiations, the threats, the money passing hands, details about offshore bank accounts. Judges, city officials, prosecutors, even your own police officers. Everything, including you having sex with underage girls."

Latimer suddenly stood up. The meeting was over. Maxine Brodie gathered up the green file and joined Latimer by his side. Latimer turned to Birch, addressing him for the first time. "Time to go, Thomas."

Birch nodded and glanced at Hagen. The man looked like he had taken a beating—literally, by a more seasoned, and strategically thoughtful fighter. He cut a lonely figure now, sitting by himself at the table.

In the doorway, Birch watched as Latimer paused and turned back to Hagen and shook his head. "Mayor? Governor? Really? If anyone is going to clean up the filth in this city, then it's going to be me." Latimer jabbed his finger at Hagen. "Starting with you!"

Outside, Birch had only managed to walk a few steps before his eyes caught sight of Justin. His son was standing next to a huge, barrel-chested man dressed in a suit and wearing dark glasses. The man had a firm hand resting protectively on Justin's shoulder, his bull-like head swiveling left and right like a tank turret scanning down both ends of the alleyway while he held a gun casually in one hand. The man was easily over six foot and almost as wide as the chrome grille on the blacked-out Chevy Suburban they were both standing in front of.

"Dad!" Justin yelled, seeing his father.

"Tui!" Latimer called out toward the bull man. Latimer leaned in toward Birch as they walked. "He used to play rugby in New Zealand for the All Blacks. Apparently his teammates used to call him 'the brick.' But don't let his size and imposing look frighten you. His heart is as big as his head, but he'll tear anyone limb from limb if I ask him to."

The bull man acknowledged Latimer, and patted Justin on the back, gently pushing him toward his father.

Justin rushed into his father's arms while Latimer and Brodie were ushered into the back of a second SUV.

Birch felt his insides melt as he hugged his son. No words were needed, the tight embrace, although awkward, was enough.

"Dad!" Justin croaked, after a few seconds. "You're crushing me."

"S...sorry!" Birch gasped, fighting back tears, before reluctantly letting go, then holding Justin at arm's length so he could take a good look at him from head to toe. God, how he had grown! Justin was as tall—no, taller than him. His jaw and cheekbones were more pronounced, while his shoulders, chest and arms had taken on the strapping shape of manhood. His eyes had lost their innocent naivety, replaced with a more cautious and suspicious view of the world. Gone was the memory of the boy Thomas had been clinging to for the last two years, replaced now by the virile young man standing before him.

Parked to one side, Birch could see Joshua Bank's empty car, the trunk open, and the metal lip under-locking mechanism buckled and torn outward. It was hard to believe all that time, while Birch sat in the front seat, his son was in the trunk, only a few feet away.

Joshua Banks, though, was nowhere to be seen.

"Are you okay?" Birch asked, turning back to Justin. "You're not hurt?"

"Just a massive headache," Justin replied, rubbing the back of his head. "I woke up in the trunk and started yelling." Justin nodded toward the bull man. "Tui over there heard me and got me out. Told me you were inside the restaurant and not to worry, that you would be out soon."

Justin hugged his son again, despite Justin's protests.

"Thomas!"

Birch turned to see Latimer beckoning them through the open window of the SUV.

"Let's go."

"What's going on?" Justin asked.

Birch squeezed his son's arm. "I'll tell you everything soon, I promise."

Safely ensconced in the back of the SUV, with Justin on one side and Latimer on the other, and driving away at speed, Birch was hit with sudden bout of panic. So overcome was he with seeing Justin, that all thoughts of Beatriz Vega had been swept aside in a wave of euphoria. "We need go somewhere," he said to Latimer. "A friend of mine has been shot."

Latimer regarded Birch with a narrow-eyed expression. "A young woman?"

Birch nodded, frantically looking around outside, trying to get his bearings. "Yes! We need to call an ambulance." Birch checked his pockets, couldn't find his phone, before remembering it had been taken from him by Banks. "I need a phone." Again Birch felt hopeless, impotent, his actions stymied by his civilian status.

"This young woman wouldn't happen to be from South America would she?" Latimer said thoughtfully, slipping out his cell phone but not passing it to Birch.

In his mind, Birch conjured up a horrible image of the lifeless Vega lying dead on the floor, her open eyes staring blankly at the ceiling. Then his brain caught on to what Latimer had just said. "Yes…what?…how do you know?"

"A young lady rang me almost as distressed as you are right now. She told me you had been kidnapped. I'd guessed from her accent she was either from Brazil or Columbia."

"Peru," Birch replied, confused.

"Ah." Latimer nodded thoughtfully. "She alerted me as to

what had happened. But Maxine Brodie knew well in advance where you were being taken to for the meeting with her and Hagen. The young woman also told me to tell you that she was fine, just bruised and a little lost for breath."

"Fine?" Birch had seen Vega get shot, up close, in the chest. Surely she was dead or had been left to die on the floor by Joshua Banks.

Latimer smiled. "I'd call her back if I could and let you speak to her, but we couldn't trace the call. I guess she knew that because she said she would explain everything to you later and for you to focus on getting Justin back safely."

Chapter 68 – Sacrifice

It was late morning by the time Eve wrapped up the initial stages of the officer-involved shooting protocol with the two homicide detectives assigned to the case.

After giving her initial statement, she did several slow walkthroughs of the scene with the detectives, from where her vehicle sat outside the park gates, all the way to where she had finally stood, drawn her gun and shot the perpetrator. Evidence markers were placed where her shell casings had fallen, and where the knife now sat on the bloodstained ground.

After explaining she was currently in the middle of a very active investigation, the detectives allowed Eve to defer, until later in the day, from immediately attending police headquarters for a formal interview and to provide and sign her formal statement.

In the meantime, she just hoped the two detectives didn't confirm with Carl Hagen the fact that she had been kicked off the case—another indiscretion Eve would have to deal with later. Right now, she wanted to focus on finding the other killers behind Murder School.

Walking back to her car, Eve's cell rang.

"Ramirez, what is it?" Eve said.

"It's you...you've been added!"

Eve stopped walking. "What do you mean?"

"To the list...the murder list!" he hissed. "I'm still logged into the chat room on Kemp's cell phone. A new notification to all members has just been posted. Someone logged in as administrator and added your name." Ramirez read out the new entry, as Eve listened on, her innards slowly turning to ice.

"Detective Eve Sommers, Fifth Precinct, New York City.

One thousand points! They're coming for you Eve. You've just become the most valuable prize in the entire game!"

Eve cut the call with Ramirez and instantly looked around, wondering who was watching her right now: a male jogger, two people walking a dog, the man selling ice cream, five people doing synchronized Tai Chi on a grassy hill, the woman sitting under a tree reading a book. Any of them could be killers. Other members of Murder School would certainly have come to Central Park to claim the Alice in Wonderland prize only to stealthily withdraw to the shadows after seeing police surrounding the area.

Hastily, Eve got into her car, slammed the door and pressed the locks.

Her cell rang again, the number withheld.

"Hello, Detective Sommers," a woman said in a confident British accent, a hint of familiarity in her tone, as though they knew each other.

"Who is this?" Eve replied, looking through her side window.

"Oh, I think you know who this is."

A dull coldness seeped into Eve's chest.

"I killed Evan Brinkmeyer," the woman said, her voice sultry and provocative.

Eve felt a growing sense of uneasiness as she heard the words. It was the same creepy feeling she had at Grand Central, when she thought someone was watching her, someone close by.

"I thought we should meet," the woman continued. "I'm sure you'd like to."

Meet? Meet so you can kill me more like it, Eve thought as she scanned the opposite sidewalk, searching for a woman looking like Lindsay Latimer. Eve wasn't entirely convinced of Vega's "chameleon" theory. Lindsay was educated in the UK, and this woman clearly had a British accent. If what Ramirez had said was true, then Eve had a clear target painted on her back, yet she wanted desperately to catch the woman who had killed Brinkmeyer and Moriarty, and whoever else was involved in Murder School, even if it meant risking her own life.

"Why should I want to meet you?" Eve asked. "You could be anyone, a prank caller. I get hundreds a day claiming to have killed victims." Eve's response was a test, to see if the caller was in fact Lindsay or Victoria and, more importantly, if she knew Ramirez had hacked into the Murder School chat room. If Eve admitted to knowing about Murder School, or made out she was fearful to meet because she knew thirty or more ruthless killers were right now hunting her—including the woman on the call—then the connection would be severed, the members would all go to ground, vanish, and any chance of Eve catching them would vanish too. Eve had to play it cool, calm, nonchalant, as though she knew nothing.

"Just call the Fifth Precinct and talk to the desk sergeant," Eve replied, sounding bored. "You can leave your statement with him, goodbye."

'Wait!' The woman almost shrieked in Eve's ear.

Eve let out a mock sigh of impatience while fervently glancing out of the passenger-side window and windshield. It was impossible for the caller to know where Eve was at this exact moment. Unless…

"My name is Victoria Christie, Eve. I killed the man at Grand Central Station too. It was me you ran into outside the men's restrooms."

Eve sat perfectly still, cell phone to her ear. Eve had only shared that piece of information with Birch and Vega.

The decision to meet was sealed.

Chapter 69 – Off Grid

After agreeing on the location and time, Eve ended the call with Victoria Christie, then immediately called Birch again.

The call went straight to voicemail, so Eve left a message for him to urgently call her back.

The location Christie had chosen, while being out in the open, with plenty of people about, didn't lessen the huge risk Eve was taking. There were plenty of people about when Even Brinkmeyer was killed. The same with Tein Moriarty. But it was too good an opportunity to catch her as well as find out what really happened to Lindsay Latimer. Plus Eve knew she had a distinct advantage compared to the two previous victims: she was expecting Victoria Christie to try and kill her. What did puzzle Eve, however, was how did Christie get hold of her cell phone number? It was something Eve tended not to give out unless it was related specifically to a case. Otherwise she would be inundated with a deluge of crank callers.

Eve tried Birch again and got the same voice mail and ended the call.

"She will kill you," Eve's left side of her brain was telling her, in a logical, orderly tone. She didn't like being bait, yet what other choice did she have? Wait for more people to die? There were no other immediate options, other than to walk into what effectively was a trap.

"Dying is an occupational hazard, honey," replied the right side of Eve's brain, in a passionate and inspired tone. Police officers all over New York—all over the world—took that risk each day when they left their front doors carrying just their badge, their gun, and the hope of seeing the day through.

Glancing in the rearview mirror one last time, Eve cautiously pulled out from the curb and entered the traffic flow, her mind occupied by Victoria Christie's call. Something just niggled at Eve, like the missing piece of a puzzle which had fallen under the sofa. She could see it there, in the shadows, but couldn't quite reach it.

Pulling quickly to the curb again, Eve turned off her cell, slid off the back cover, removed the SIM card, and reassembled the phone, keeping the SIM card in a separate pocket.

She would talk to Birch later.

The last thing she wanted now was anyone tracking her. One psychopathic killer and a desperate, ex-detective was about as much as she could handle on her own.

Chapter 70 – Pulling the Plug

Victoria Christie cut down West Thirty-Third Street, ignoring the lewd stares from a group of construction workers dressed in bright orange and yellow shirts who were sitting on a low concrete wall eating lunch.

"You've got killer looks, babe!" one worker jeered, looking up as she walked past.

"More than you could ever know," Victoria whispered under her breath. She crossed the intersection at Tenth Avenue, then dialed a number on her cell phone.

"Where the hell have you been?" Joshua Banks snarled. No formalities. No niceties. Just all snarl. "I've been trying to reach you since we last spoke yesterday."

"I've been taking care of business," Victoria replied. "Been busy."

"What? Too busy to return my texts and calls?"

Victoria rolled her eyes. She wasn't answerable to anyone. "What's up?" she asked, resisting the urge to hang up.

"Wot's up? Wot's up?" Banks parroted back, in a poor rendition of a British cockney accent. "I'll tell you what's fucking up! Moriarty is dead! That's what's up!"

Victoria smiled, "Really?" feigning surprise.

Banks lowered his voice to an accusatory growl. "Did you kill him, Vicky?"

There it was again, Victoria thought. Her name abbreviated. How she hated when people did that. "No, I didn't *kill* him," she lied. "But I see you've added a new target to the list. Detective Eve Sommers. Gave her top billing too. Why did you do that, Joshua?" Victoria always felt the best form of defense was to go on the attack, turn the tables. "Is there something you're not telling me? Some kind of hidden agenda you'd like to share?"

"Er...what?"

Victoria could sense she was right. "Why is Sommers suddenly on the list? Who is she to you?"

"She's no one. I thought I'd throw her in there for fun."

Victoria shook her head. He was up to something, changing the direction of the game for his own personal gain. Unless... "Or are you taking instructions from someone else, Joshua?"

Banks didn't reply. Victoria could almost hear him thinking on the other end, trying to come up with a suitable lie. She didn't wait for his response. "Well, you'll be pleased to know"—Victoria checked her watch—"in about twenty minutes, Sommers will be removed for the list."

"Removed?" Banks replied. "What do you mean?"

"I called her. We're meeting for a little chat."

"Chat about what? Where are you meeting her?"

Victoria told Banks the location where she agreed to meet Eve. "How else was I going to find her before anyone else? I'm on my way there now. She's mine."

Banks went silent on the line. When he came back, his voice was serious. "Stand down, Vicky," he said sternly. "Stand down now, right now."

Victoria frowned. She could sense the panic in his voice. "What's going on, Joshua?"

"Leave Sommers for someone else, Vicky. I'm shutting it down, pulling the plug on everything."

"And if I decide not to 'stand down' like you say?" Victoria could feel her initial suspicion now being replaced with growing anger. "She's mine. No one else's. You put her on the list in the first place, so I'm taking her out. She's my prize. One thousand points to me."

"Don't do it Victoria. Walk away. It's too risky. Something doesn't seem right. You can't—"

Victoria ended the call. Suddenly she looked around, thinking about what Banks had said. She switched off her cell, then strode toward the building that was her destination.

She was damn sure about one thing: no one was going to stop her from killing Eve Sommers.

Ten blocks to the south, Joshua Banks glared at his cell phone. "Bitch!" he hissed.

He paused, his mind racing. He was breathing hard, having run three blocks just to get away from the restaurant, when Latimer and his entourage of gun-toting henchmen had turned up. He didn't need that kind of heat. He knew exactly who Latimer was and the huge power and influence he wielded. Carl Hagen was small fry compared to Latimer and the fire and brimstone he could rain down on him. The money, the infamy Hagen had promised, now seemed to have evaporated.

Shutting down the game was the right thing to do. It was all over. Banks would go to ground, hope Francis Latimer and his private little army wouldn't find him.

But he couldn't shut it down right away. He had to tie up a few loose ends.

One in particular.

A vindictive smile broke out across Banks' face as both his thumbs feverishly went to work on his cell phone. "If that's how you want to play, Vicky," he breathed, "then two can play at this game." He pressed a button and sent the notification.

He then hailed a cab.

Chapter 71 – Notification

Andy Ramirez sat at his desk in the squad room, having spent the last thirty minutes or so logged into the Murder School chat room trying to identify who the systems administrator was. But he was having no success.

Since Eve had been added to the murder list, the chatter between members had increased significantly, yet from what he could tell, no one knew where she was. If anyone did, they were probably not going to share with the others, Ramirez guessed.

He wondered if any would have the guts to turn up here at the precinct. The desk duty Sargent had said Eve had logged her status as 'out of office' and that was what would be told to any walk-in visitors. But it didn't stop Ramirez worrying about his boss. After he had told her of being added to the murder list, she had abruptly ended the call.

Getting off his chair, Ramirez stretched and immediately regretted it. The bruises on his wrists would eventually vanish, but his lower back and spine left him feeling like an overly knotted pretzel. Victoria had been particularly 'enthusiastic' last night, almost as though she were taking out some deep-seated anger on his body. Several times he had to pry her fingers from around his throat because she was almost choking him during the throes of her passion.

He walked slowly over to the coffee machine and refilled his cup, popping two painkillers in his mouth as he did, washing them down with the coffee. Bending the window blinds, he glanced out into the street below. Everything looked normal, but it depended on what you considered "normal" for New York City.

The computer chimed, and Ramirez turned and went back to his desk. "Target location?" he muttered, staring at the screen as more details came through. An address. Near the Lincoln Tunnel. Hudson Yards. A building on the corner of Tenth Avenue and West Thirty-Third, level one hundred.

The hot coffee he had drunk turned into an iced latte in his stomach. Someone had posted the exact location of where Eve Sommers was going to be.

Ramirez tried Eve's cell phone, only to get an inactive signal.

He dialed again.

Now came the robotic voice message, telling him the cellular service was unavailable.

Ramirez cursed as he quickly typed Eve's cell phone details into the "Track and Trace" software he had used to locate Tein Moriarty at Grand Central.

Ramirez drummed his fingers on the desk impatiently while he waited for the search. "Come on!" he groaned.

The latest location signal from Eve's cell came up on the screen—it was over thirty minutes ago, near Central Park.

That couldn't be right, Ramirez thought. She must have pulled her SIM card. Now she couldn't be tracked, but it didn't matter. All the members of Murder School knew where she was going, and Ramirez had no way of warning her.

Chapter 72 – The Edge

At the very edge of the Edge, where the two glass walls came together to form a peak, like the slanted bow of a glass ship floating in the sky, a woman stood alone.

Beyond the edge—nothingness, except air, the sky, the wind, and a plummeting drop of one hundred stories to the street below.

There was nowhere else for Eve to go, nothing further.

This was the end.

Again, the devil took him to a very high mountain and showed Him all the kingdoms of the world and their splendor. Now Victoria Christie had brought Eve to the highest platform in the Western Hemisphere, with New York City spread out below in all its magnificence.

The lone woman standing at the edge tilted her head, as if sensing Eve approaching. Then she turned fully, and for the very first time, Eve faced her enigma.

They stood just out of arm's reach, contemplating each other.

For Eve, the resemblance was astonishing. She was looking at Lindsay Latimer, and yet she sensed she was encountering Victoria Christie.

Eve's eyes narrowed. "It was you who was watching me at Grand Central. I couldn't see you, but you were there." Eve thought she would feel fear. But she felt nothing, just a morbid curiosity. After all, the woman was an enigma, a ghost, who had so clinically and brutally killed two people, and would many more if given the chance. "Why did you kill them?"

Victoria Christie smiled her trademark lopsided smile. "Brinkmeyer was just for fun," she said. "But Moriarty... because I had to."

"Had to?"

"He had a device, a bomb with him. He was going to kill dozens of people."

Eve tensed, looking around.

"It's perfectly all right," Victoria assured Eve. "It's someplace safe. I don't intend to use it. It's not my style."

Eve turned back. "Not your style?" They had found nothing at Grand Central, just Moriarty dead in the toilet cubicle, the gruesome handiwork of the woman standing in front of her. Eve thought back again, but still couldn't pull anything additional from her memory of the brief encounter. Perhaps Victoria Christie was carrying bag or wheeling a case.

A young couple stood off to one side, keen to get their photos taken in the exact spot where Christie was standing. Christie motioned to Eve, and they began to move away from the edge to a quiet spot farther along the glass wall. But not before Christie accepted the proffered cell phone from the young woman, who asked in broken French if she could take their picture.

Eve watched as Christie then gave impromptu directions to the young couple on how to stand and when to smile as she snapped several photos. Beatriz Vega was right. Christie was a true chameleon, capable of adapting to any situation.

Joining Eve away from the crowds, Christie turned to face her. "Don't worry," she said. "If I wanted to kill you before now, I would have done so before you reached your car outside Central Park."

Chapter 73 – Steak Knife

"Excuse me," the man caught the attention of a passing server. "I don't seem to have a steak knife."

The female server stared on either side of the man's plate, certain there was a full cutlery setting on the counter a few moments ago before she had placed his meal down in front of him. "My apologies. I'll get one right away."

"Thank you," the man said. From where he sat at the bar of the Peak Restaurant, he had an uninterrupted view of the Manhattan skyline looking south, and of the triangular observation deck one floor below. But it was not the view he was interested in. It was the woman who was standing outside on the triangular wedge-shaped deck. She was perhaps mid-forties, mousy blonde hair, rather bland-looking in his opinion. More of a typical soccer-mom type, running her kids back and forth to school and sports, rather than a NYPD detective chasing killers. Soccer Mom was talking to another woman, slimmer, younger, fitter, who had her back toward him.

This should be easy, the man thought, glancing at his cell phone again, studying the photo of the woman on the screen. Satisfied it was indeed Soccer Mom, he pocketed the cell phone and smiled.

The server returned with a clean streak knife wrapped in a napkin, apologizing profusely before leaving the man to his enjoy his meal. Blood oozed from the strip steak as he sliced into it. Extremely rare, that's how he liked his meat. While he ate, he kept a watchful eye on Soccer Mom and the other woman outside. Both seemed to know each other and were involved in a deep conversation.

When he had finished eating, the man carefully placed his

knife and fork together, dabbed the corners of his mouth with the napkin, and motioned to the server behind the bar for the check. After paying in cash, he eased off the bar stool and made his way toward the exit door that would take him outside, and down to the observation platform.

Reaching the door, he slid one hand into the pocket of his leather jacket and wrapped his fingers around the wooden handle of the steak knife he had taken.

Soccer Mom's day was about to get a whole lot worse.

Resuming their meeting, Christie pulled out a set of keys and dangled them in front of Eve. "Here, take them." She gave Eve the address of a Local Locker site near Hell's Kitchen. "Moriarty's intentions I found crude, vulgar."

Eve took the keys and memorized the address. "So, is stabbing someone in the thigh or sticking a cocktail stick in their brain more humane?" Eve asked, with a hint of sarcasm. "Less crude and vulgar?"

Christie smiled. "I was thinking of something more… eloquent."

Eve shook her head. The woman was obviously intelligent, composed, supremely confident and…clearly insane.

"It's extremely difficult to hit the Femoral Artery on your first attempt," Christie explained. But there was no bragging in her voice, just a clinical, matter-of-fact explanation. The woman lacked any empathy, any shred of moral dilemma.

"So I've been told," Eve replied.

Christie gave Eve a quizzical look, like she was deciphering her. Then she nodded. "Ah…yes. How is Dr. Maya Zin by the way?"

Eve tensed again. How did she know of Maya? Her name had been deliberately withheld from the public, for Maya's own safety. Eve answered the question by asking one of her own. "How did you get my cell phone number?"

"I know more about you, Detective, than you could possibly believe."

The answer was unsettling, and Eve didn't like being unsettled. So she took a verbal shot of her own, wanting to elicit a reaction, to break the woman's confidence.

"Was Moriarty going to win the game?" Eve asked. "Is that why you killed him? You couldn't stand losing, so you took him out? Victoria Christie was the only name worthy of being at the top of the leaderboard?"

The barest flicker of surprise danced across Christie's face.

Eve pressed on. "Murder School, Marcus Kemp, Tein Moriarty, and you. I also know a lot more about you and your murderous little game than you could possibly believe."

"Don't worry, Detective." Christie regained her composure. "I don't intend to kill you. You're safe."

"Spare me the lies, Christie." Eve edged forward. "Or should I call you Lindsay Latimer? Which is it?"

Christie's eyes flared more noticeably this time.

"I'm going to arrest you," Eve continued.

"If you attempt to, you'll die trying, I assure you," Christie countered, her eyes suddenly darting sideways.

Eve noticed Christie's attention had drifted past her, over her shoulder, at something behind her.

Christie's expression hardened, her eyes narrowed and she turned her attention back to Eve. "I told you not to bring anyone else with you!" she said, switching to a low, guttural growl.

"I didn't tell anyone," Eve replied, turning around.

"Vicky?" came a male voice.

Eve felt dread grip her throat as she saw Andy Ramirez hurrying toward them. He pulled up suddenly, keeping his distance when he saw Eve staring dumbfounded at him. "Boss?" Ramirez looked from Eve to Christie. "Victoria, what are you doing here?" With a look of panic, Ramirez turned back to Eve. "Boss, they all know where you—" But Ramirez didn't have time to finish his sentence.

Out of the corner of her eye, Eve caught an explosion of movement, then felt a bone-jarring thump as Christie struck her in the side of her face with a raised elbow. Eve collapsed sideways into the glass wall barrier and slid to the ground, pain blooming in her skull. Dazed, she turned and looked up just in time to see Christie rushing at Ramirez, a sharp needle-like object in her hand, and plunging it deep into Ramirez's throat just under his chin.

"Noooooo!" Eve heard a woman's wild scream, only to discover it was her own. Struggling to get to her feet, Eve watched in horror as Ramirez, wide-eyed in shock, sank to his knees clutching at his throat, bright red spurting out between his fingers.

Chapter 74 – Needle

Eve staggered to one knee, holding on to the glass wall for support, shaking her head to clear the doughiness she felt.

Her vision rippled like heat waves. She blinked hard. Slowly the rippling cleared, and everything came back into sharp focus. Her eyes searched, then found Victoria Christie. She was standing over the body of Ramirez, smiling down at him. With her eyes firmly locked on Christie, Eve drew her gun from under her jacket, brought it up and carefully took aim at her in the foreground, while shapes moved and danced in the background, people screaming and scattering.

Something large moved in Eve's peripheral vision, a dark shape growing in size. Her eyes flicked toward the shape. She saw a man dressed in a leather jacket making a direct line toward where she knelt, his powerful arms pushing aside panic-stricken people as he thundered forward. Maybe it was an off-duty cop. Maybe it was a brave, concerned citizen taking matters into his own hands.

But her hopes were dashed when he pulled a long knife from his jacket and sped up. Instantly she changed her assessment of him. Getting to her feet, Eve switched her aim toward the man—then back at Christie, then alternating her aim between the two, her legs wobbly.

Finally she decided on the man with the knife, the more imminent threat. She held her breath, and settled the front sight of her gun over his swelling shape. Her aim wavered as pinpricks of light crowded the edges of her vision.

In the foreground the man seemed to grow by the second, while the background was cluttered with the mass hysteria of innocent people. Unlike Central Park, Eve didn't have a safe shot, nor full command of senses. If she missed, she could likely hit and kill an innocent bystander.

The man kept coming, bearing down on Eve, face contorted, bloodlust in his eyes, a heinous grin across his jaw, the knife in his hand glinting in the sunlight.

Shoot him! Eve's mind screamed. She hesitated.

The man was nearly on her.

The world turned dark and the glint of the knife burned brighter.

Eve fired.

The man half spun as the top of his shoulder burst into a cloud of misty red and tattered leather.

His momentum faltered, then recovered. He kept rushing forward, slamming into Eve, jarring her backward.

Eve hit the ground hard, the man on top, crushing the air from her lungs. He was straddling her, pinning her down, his eyes wild, his mouth drawn, growling like a dog as viscous, ropey strands of saliva hung from his lips.

Eve tried to bring her gun up, but her forearm was pinned under his knee. She struggled, thrusting her hips and buttocks upward, trying to buck him off. But he was too heavy, too strong.

Eve felt thick fingers take hold of her neck, crushing her throat. The knife came up high in his fist. She struggled some more. Couldn't breathe. Couldn't move.

"You're mine!" the man hissed, staring down at Eve, drawing the knife back farther, ready to plunge the serrated blade into her forehead.

Eve heard a voice. "No she's not."

The man's eyes burst wide, as a long, thin needle of steel slid out from his gapping mouth, piercing his tongue before skewering his bottom lip like some weird human kebab.

For a moment, the man didn't move, he just sat frozen, straddling Eve. Slowly he toppled sideways, revealing a long needle protruding from the base of his skull.

Victoria Christie stood over Eve, a look of hard-earned satisfaction on her face.

Scrabbling to her feet, Eve retreated along the ground, her hands searching for her gun.

"You dropped this," Christie said, holding up Eve's handgun between her finger and her thumb like it was a dead rodent. She tossed the gun at Eve and it landed in her lap.

Eve looked down at the handgun, then back up at Christie.

Stepping over Eve, Christie crouched down next to the dead man, withdrew the needle of steel with a long, drawn-out grating sound, wiped it on the man's leather jacket, then slid it back up into her own sleeve.

Christie turned to Eve. "That's how it's done."

Chapter 75 – Loss

Getting to her feet, with her gun in her hand, Eve stumbled to where Andy Ramirez lay.

Sliding her gun back into its holster, she knelt down next to him and gently lifted his head into her lap, tears filling her eyes.

Ramirez smiled up at Eve, his teeth stained red. He made a gurgling sound, convulsed, then coughed up blood. It dribbled from the corners of his mouth, down his chin and neck. "Sor…sorr…sorry," he rasped.

Eve stifled a sob before slipping her hand under his head, feeling the warm wetness there. She thought she would be tougher, more composed, but seeing her partner like this was overwhelming. To Eve, it was okay to cry. At times, when she was alone, she knew she wasn't as strong as she made herself out to be, admitting it to herself. Every day it was a battle to stop her fragile nerves from shattering. All people saw was her outside, not what was going on inside her.

Eve sniffled, wiping her tears on the back of her hand, noticing that it was coated in blood, unsure as to whose blood it was. Taking Ramirez's hand in her own, she squeezed it. His whole arm felt loose, boneless.

"Hang in there, Andy," she pleaded. "Help is coming. Don't you fucking die on me…Detective!" she half laughed, half cried, knowing how much he wanted to hear being called that, thinking it would bolster his will to live. "Hang in there. I want to be there when they give you your shield."

Eve's words brought another gritted red smile from Ramirez. More blood bubbled up as he tried to speak. "I'm…sorry." He pushed the words out in a trail of bloody red. "Couldn't call…you. S…someone gave your…location away." Ramirez's body tensed, then relaxed as Eve could feel him fighting against the pain. "I always wanted to…be a…detective…like you. Be your…partner."

The warm wetness Eve felt on her hand as she cradled his head increased. She could feel the life beginning to seep out of him faster. "You *are* my partner." Eve knew he was dying, and telling him whatever he wanted to hear was all she could do to ease his suffering.

"Vic…Victoria," he struggled. "Girlfriend…I didn't know."

Eve nodded, squeezing his hand harder, pulling him closer. This wasn't the way his mother envisaged her son dying, Eve thought. "It's okay," she whispered. "It doesn't matter." Eve glanced around, silently cursing as to where the police were. Then she felt his hand in hers beginning to slip, to let go.

Ramirez opened his mouth and in one final gasp, whispered, "K…Kil…her."

Eve held Ramirez tighter, not letting go, not even after the life completely faded from his eyes.

Chapter 76 – Unhinged

Eve could see Victoria Christie in the distance.

She was standing with a man, arguing it seemed, her actions animated, her face contorted. The man then forcefully grabbed Christie's arm, pulling at her, urging her to leave, but Christie twisted away, then yelled something at him.

Gently, Eve eased the body of Ramirez off her lap, and placed him to one side, arranging him as best she could. She tried to keep this head from lolling to one side, yet his neck was flimsy, his limbs disobedient. Tears of frustration streaked down Eve's face as she wrestled with the head, as though the most important thing in the entire world right now was to make Andy Ramirez not look dead.

Eve cursed and wiped both her cheeks, unintentionally smearing the blood on her hands across her face, creating the look of red war paint.

Satisfied with her efforts, Eve knelt over Ramirez. "Sorry," she whispered as a red tear dripped from her chin and landed on his cheek. It was a quiet moment between them. For reasons Eve couldn't explain later, a sensation of calmness settled over her, made her feel at ease, safe, not fearful. It was the gentle simmering before boiling point. The silent gap between lightning and thunder. A lonely neutron traveling serenely toward the mass of uranium.

She felt a gradual disconnect with what was happening around her, as though her mind was untangling itself from her body, setting her free to do what needed to be done, without judgment or repercussion.

She gave his arm a squeeze. "I'll be back soon," she promised.

"I just need to take care of something first."

Then finally, Eve stood up and the veil of controlled calmness slipped from her shoulders and fell to the ground.

The man next to Victoria Christie turned toward Eve, was looking straight at her. Despite not knowing him, never seeing him before, she sensed something in his gaze—something dark and sinister. It was in this moment Eve realized the man was the cause, the root of all this evil, the devil at the heart of the murderous chaos she had witnessed. No pity in his eyes. No empathy. Just a cold loathing with a mouth brandishing a cruel grin. Christie had also turned toward Eve and was in the process of slipping out from her sleeve the needle-like weapon she had used to kill Ramirez.

In tandem, both advanced toward Eve.

Without conscious thought, Eve drew her gun—then put three bullets into the grinning face of Joshua Banks, wiping the features clean off his head.

From the neck up, everything of him vanished in a mushrooming blizzard of red. With robotic plodding steps, Banks continued forward, his body upright. Then, as though his legs had discovered an invisible set of stairs in the ground, his erect body gradually sank to one knee, then both knees, before toppling over.

Almost casually, Eve turned her attention to Victoria Christie—and stopped.

Christie stopped mid stride.

For three breaths, both women stood motionless, eyes locked on each other.

Eve watched as Christie tilted her chin down, narrowed her eyes, and launched into a dead run at her, a demonic look spread across her face, the sharp needle in her hand held out in front, aiming it directly at Eve's heart.

Eve blinked hard, tasting blood in her mouth—not her own blood, but Ramirez's. She came awake, out of her trance-like state, remembering everything as the rage poured into her. It came on like a red, raw tsunami of emotion, flooding all her senses at once. Boiling point, thunder, critical mass, all simultaneously detonating inside her head.

Christie was closing the gap between them fast.

Waiting for the last possible moment, Eve stepped off to one side, swung her arm back, then brought it around in a sweeping arc, smashing her gun into the side of Christie's head, near the temple, narrowly avoiding the thrust of the needle.

Christie staggered, tried to pivot, to turn fully back toward Eve, but her feet stumbled, her killing impetus lost from the blow to the head.

As Christie tried turning, to reengage, Eve smashed her again, this time on the side of the jaw, with a more measured, targeted crushing blow. Reversing her grip on the gun, holding the barrel this time, and using the chunky grip like the head of a hammer, Eve struck Christie on the top of her head, repeatedly hammering her skull, face, jaw, raining down a barrage of pulverizing blows.

When exhaustion finally set in, Eve stopped her onslaught, her chest heaving, the gun in her hand slippery with blood.

With her head misshapen, her face distorted, and blood streaming from her nose and mouth, Christie teetered, only just managing to stay on her feet. One side of her jaw hung loose, almost unhinged from her face. The whites of two eyes glared out from a hideous, bloody mess at Eve. Christie's lips drew back, forming a rictus snarl, and she lunged at Eve.

They fell together, in a tangle of thrashing arms, Christie on top.

The gun slipped from Eve's greasy grasp. She brought her hands up, saw the needle repeatedly spearing toward her eyes, jabbing up and down like a sewing machine, Christie's ruined face filling Eve's vision, her eyes wide with fury.

Clamping Christie's wrist with her own hand, Eve stopped the needle's jackhammering motion. The sharp point hovered just inches from Eve's left eyeball.

Christie snarled again, like a rabid dog, the top row of her teeth bent horribly inward. She pushed with her other hand against her bunched fist that held the needle, as though trying to drive a wooden stake into Eve's chest.

Eve grimaced, rotated her hips, throwing Christie sideways. Without pausing, she clawed on top of Christie, pinning both the woman's arms with her knees. Balling her right hand into a fist, Eve drew her arm back and brought it down squarely on Christie's already broken face.

"You!" Eve screamed.

She hit Christie a second time—harder.

"Killed!"

A third time—harder still.

"My!"

A fourth time.

"Fucking!"

A fifth time.

"Partner!"

Eve's hand broke.

Chapter 77 – Christie's Journal

Eve watched as Vega came softly pattering down the passageway and sat cautiously back on the sofa, noticing the slight grimace as she did.

"He's still asleep," she said to Birch and Eve who sat opposite her.

"I'm not surprised," Eve replied. "What the poor kid has been through." It had been three days since everything that had transpired, and they had gathered at Vega's fortress home.

"He's a good-looking young man, not a kid," Vega said, turning to Birch. "Are you sure you're his father?"

Birch gave Vega a tired look but said nothing.

"Well, like I said before, you can both stay here as long as you want. I've got plenty of space."

"Thank you, Beatriz."

Eve sat cradling a cup of Vega's special brew and thought about what they had just been discussing. Molly Gibbons—Birch's neighbor—had been found. Local police were dispatched and soon discovered her unconscious and barely breathing on her kitchen floor. She was rushed to the ER and was diagnosed with a fractured skull, but was expected to make a full recovery.

After being freed from the trunk of Josh Bank's car, Justin had spent that night in hospital under observation and was discharged the next day. Birch had said he was planning to remain in New York for a few more days, to spend some father-and-son time together. See the sights and maybe catch a ball game.

Eve had fared a lot worse but had refused to stay any longer in hospital after the bones in her hand were set by the doctors.

"How's the hand?" Vega asked.

Eve looked down at the plaster cast. "I guess I won't be punching any psychopathic killers in the face anytime soon. How's the chest?"

"Just one broken rib," Vega said, shifting gingerly on the sofa. "It should take six weeks to heal."

"I still can't believe when you went to get your gun when Joshua Banks appeared, you had time to slip on a body-armor vest under your shirt," Birch said, shaking his head. "I thought you were dead."

Vega shifted again before clutching her chest, another grimace on her face. "I'd be dead if I hadn't." She let out a slow breath. "It wasn't that I didn't trust you, Thomas, when you said Justin wouldn't be carrying a gun—which was true, because it wasn't him in the elevator. I just trusted more what my security measures were telling me."

"Maybe you should take some time off," Birch suggested. "To recover."

"No, I'll be fine."

"What about you, Eve?" Birch said, turning to her.

Eve shrugged. "Maybe. I have a cousin who is a sheriff in Lacy, Colorado."

"Lacy?" Birch asked.

"It's a small town up in the Rocky Mountains. My cousin, Claire, says it's a quiet place, nothing much happens up there. Maybe I'll go and visit her. It will certainly make a change from here." In all honestly, Eve didn't know what the next few weeks held for her. She hadn't shared with the others that she had received a notification this morning from Internal Affairs to present herself for an interview in two weeks' time. It was something she wasn't looking forward to. However, she had crossed the line so many times in the last week, IA were always going to come calling.

"I'm really sorry about your partner, Ramirez," Vega said, with sadness in her eyes.

Eve gave a thin smile, still feeling raw with guilt and remorse. If she hadn't removed her SIM card from her cell phone, Ramirez could have called her. Instead, he risked his life and died making the ultimate sacrifice by coming to warn her in person. And if she had told him about Lindsay Latimer, and about the other line of inquiry she was pursuing with Birch and Vega, he would have seen her photos and would have been alerted about his girlfriend, Victoria Christie. Instead, Eve kept it all to herself, for fear Hagen would find out.

It still made Eve sick to her stomach knowing Christie had only befriended Ramirez so she could pump him for police information and details specifically about Eve.

"So as you were saying before, Beatriz," Eve said, "you condone what Victoria Christie did?"

Vega reached for Victoria Christie's journal and placed it back on her lap. "That's not exactly what I said. I don't fully *condone* what she did. She became Lindsay Latimer in order to survive, to hide from her past." Vega held up the leather-bound journal. "It's all in here. However, Christie still is a psychopathic killer."

"Murderer," Eve corrected her. "Everything she did was premeditated, with intent. Let's be very clear. She is a cold-blooded, calculating murderer."

"No argument from me," Vega added.

Eve could tell the young woman didn't fully agree, that reading the journal of a murderer somehow gave Vega an acute insight into Christie's behavior and reasons for her killing spree.

"And what do you think?" Eve asked, nodding at Birch.

"I'm perfectly happy to let the two of you argue semantics as to what Victoria Christie is or isn't," Birch said with slight indifference. "I'm not a psychiatrist. I'll leave it to the experts. Have you had a chance, Eve, to interview her yet?"

"No. I was told in no uncertain terms that she's off limits to me. I have no access to her." It didn't surprise Eve, given she'd almost pummeled Christie to death. However, she was still involved in parts of the wider investigation. Yet over the last three days, Eve got the distinct feeling she was being slowly pushed aside by the higher powers at One Police Plaza. "Let the shrinks line up to prod and poke her if they want," Eve added. "As long as she remains behind bars, that's all that concerns me." Eve did know, however, Victoria Christie—after being fully treated for her injuries—would be transferred to a secure psychiatric facility pending her sanity evaluation. "I think the Feds are getting involved with hunting down the rest of the Murder School members as well as identifying and dismantling Hagen's corrupt network."

"I don't think they will ever truly find everyone involved," Vega said, flipping the pages of the journal.

"Hagen's network or Murder School?" Birch queried.

"Both," Vega replied, not looking up. "Some will go deep into hiding, just vanish."

"Could be the perfect job for you, Beatriz," Birch said with a nod.

"What? Me?" Vega paused turning the pages before glancing up.

"Don't tell me you haven't thought about it," Eve added, "going after the rest of the Murder School members?"

"We'll see," Vega said, with a slight glow in her eyes. "I'm more interested in Victoria Christie at the moment." Vega resumed her skimming of the journal.

"At some point I'm going to have to book it into evidence," Eve said, noticing how Vega was clinging to Christie's journal as though it contained her own closely guarded secrets. Eve had found the journal while searching Christie's own apartment with a police team. She had given the journal a cursory glance and thought it would shed some light for Birch and Vega on their chameleon theory. She owed them that much, for them to take a proper look at the journal first. Taking it was another indiscretion to add to the long list Eve was mentally compiling in her head as mounting grounds for her dismissal from the force.

"She is a master of illusion," Eve said. "Take her own apartment for example. I was expecting something more palatial, given the money she had access to." The police discovered Victoria Christie had maintained a second apartment, paid for in cash using funds channeled from Lindsay Latimer's bank account where her allowance was deposited each month.

"Maybe she was having trouble reconciling herself to Lindsay's life," Vega said. "She wanted to assimilate into Lindsay's wealthy, privileged lifestyle, but was still clinging on to her childhood beliefs."

"Maybe she saw the hypocrisy of it," Birch said. "Hundreds of pairs of shoes and dozens of expensive handbags."

"Exactly," Vega said. "It was never about the money…it was what money could give her. Freedom, the opportunity to escape. Not the material trinkets." Vega thumbed through more of the pages in the journal. "I was up all night reading this. It is fascinating."

Vega glanced up at Eve. "Perhaps you should read it too."

"I think I'll pass," Eve said curtly. She felt no empathy for Victoria Christie.

"But in it, she explains her motives for doing what she did," Vega continued. "She was sexually abused not only by her uncle, but also by her father."

Eve rolled her eyes. "Spare me. It's no excuse for what she did. Don't use her abused childhood to justify her killing spree. It's a lazy assumption." There was no moral dilemma for Eve. In her mind, it was clear cut: Victoria Christie was a murderer.

"I'm not using her childhood as an excuse," Vega disagreed. "She is more complex, much more complex than we may ever truly know. Her abuse may be only one of her many motives, a convenient one. However, I can sympathize in part with her."

"Sympathize?" said Eve. "With a monster?"

"*In part*, I said." Vega located a particular page, one of many she had tagged. "Here she states her mother did nothing when she first confided in her that her uncle began raping her as a ten-year-old."

"Look," Eve said, her expression softening slightly, "I get it. I get the young, innocent version of Victoria Christie when she was a child. I understand it. But somewhere along her journey to adulthood, she became a sociopath, a product of her environment. Plenty of young girls and boys who suffer sexual abuse don't go on to become homicidal maniacs. The only killing they tend to do is of themselves—suicide."

"I know Eve," Vega said softly. "But aren't you at all interested in why she became what she became? Why she killed Lindsay Latimer, then assumed her identity?"

"Greed! Jealousy!" Eve said throwing her hands up in the air. "Want of a better life."

"That's partially correct."

Eve studied the young Peruvian woman for a moment. Maybe she had been a little harsh on her, yet as she let out a sigh,

Eve knew none of them were ever going to be the same again. This case had become personal, to all of them. "I don't need to read her journal to know Christie is insane and deserves to spend the rest of her life in prison."

"Is that why you didn't kill her when you had the chance?" Vega looked at Eve. "You thought it would be too quick, too easy for her. Subconsciously you want her to suffer long and hard, like how the families of those she has killed will suffer."

The air in the vast space suddenly went very still. No one said anything for a few moments.

Then Eve spoke. "Perhaps. Maybe I do want Christie to rot long and hard in prison." However one unanswered question was plaguing Eve ever since coming face-to-face with Christie: why the woman hadn't tried killing her when she had the chance? She had done the exact opposite, had saved Eve's life by killing another Murder School member who was coming at Eve. "If we were slightly farther south, in Virginia, Christie would be getting the death penalty."

"Maybe she still will," Vega said.

Eve sat upright. "Why? What have you found?"

Birch suddenly seemed interested too in Vega's cryptic comment. "Yes, what did you find?"

Vega leafed through the pages. "I've only read parts of it, but I think she's killed more people than what we know."

Eve slid forward to the edge of her seat.

Vega looked Eve directly in the eye. "A lot more."

Chapter 78 – Not My Face

"Did you kill the nanny?"

Silence.

Thomas Birch sat alone on a chair, his face pale under a single, grime-covered fluorescent bulb hanging from above, the watery light only enough to penetrate slightly beyond the steel bars, and certainly not enough to illuminate where someone sat silently on the cot, cloaked in darkness.

But, she was there, looking at Birch. He could feel her eyes on him. He could sense the dark smudge of malevolence pushed up into the far corner of the small prison cell, like an inhuman black hole, absorbing all warmth, all compassion.

"Do you know what I think?" he said. "I think the nanny, the woman who then became the housekeeper, knew there was something different about you—not *you* in particular, but Lindsay." Birch strained his eyes, tried to pierce the curtain of black inside the cell. "I think she noticed something was different about Lindsay when she returned. Her suspicion of you, in turn made you suspicious of her."

Birch paused again, expecting a response.

Nothing.

Then he thought he saw a ripple of movement, a nocturnal stirring from deep within. But there was nothing, just the nasally whistle of labored breathing.

"After all, according to Lindsay's father, the nanny practically raised Lindsay from a child. She would have known her intimately. Any distinguishing features, mannerisms, those little nuances that made her who she was both physically and socially. Things you couldn't simply mimic from the information you ruthlessly gathered from Lindsay—with the exception of the scar on her arm of course. That was a nice touch."

Still nothing.

Birch slowly shook his head. "That really must have taken some doing, for you to disfigure your own flesh."

Silence.

"The nanny probably knew her better than her own mother did."

The frame of the cot creaked.

"And then, when the nanny had seen enough, and was convinced you were not Lindsay, but an imposter, she confronted you didn't she? It was then you killed her to protect your secret. She didn't fall did she? *You* pushed her out of that window in Lindsay's old nursery, made it look like an accident."

Another creak.

"I imagine you're an expert at making things look like 'accidents', aren't you? You did a good job imitating Lindsay; after all, you looked very similar to her, maybe just a few pounds heavier though," Birch continued, deliberately choosing the past tense 'looked,' wanting to elicit a reaction.

Another creak, louder this time, weight shifting on old, rusty hinges. Then the darkness spoke, a slurred voice that sounded misshapen, warped, vowels slightly skewed. "I'll tell you where she is."

Birch squinted through the bars to where the voice had come from. There—the barest outline of a shape against the darker backdrop.

A slow, gloating laugh. "That's right. I'll tell you where she is if you get me out of here."

Birch felt his chest heave. Was Lindsay still alive? The journal said Christie had killed her. Or was she now tempting him with a cruel riddle designed to give him and the family a glimmer of false hope?

"Is she alive?" Birch sprang up and grabbed the cold steel bars with both hands. "Tell me now! Is—she—alive?" He shook at the bars as though it was he, not she, who was imprisoned.

Next came a giggle, childlike. Maybe she was completely insane after all, Birch thought.

"I'll take you to her. Just get me out of here. I'll make a deal. Her life in exchange for mine."

"She's dead. Has been for some time now. You killed her."

"You don't know that for certain, do you?" the voice slurred, the tongue making wet, smacking sounds. "I'm sure the family would want closure either way—to know what actually happened to their loving daughter." The outline shifted, grew in size, like an animal emerging slowly from its darkened lair. "It must be excruciating for them…not knowing."

As Birch clenched the bars, he cast his mind back to the image of Francis Latimer clutching his sobbing, inconsolable wife, her pleading cries for him to bring Lindsay home, to find out what Victoria Christie had done with their daughter. Francis Latimer had made peace with himself, he had told Birch. He was resigned to the fact Lindsay was dead and felt partly to blame for allowing a monster like Victoria Christie into the family. Then he told Birch that no matter the cost, he wanted him to find his daughter. Those were the terms of the original deal. Finding what had happened to her wasn't good enough. Birch had to actually find Lindsay, dead or alive. Deep down, however, Birch knew she was dead. Victoria Christie suggesting otherwise was just her being her manipulative self.

"Where is she, Victoria?" Birch asked. "Where did you bury Lindsay?" It was the only logical question he could possibly ask.

Another childlike giggle. "Far from where anyone could possibly find her if you don't help me."

Birch sat back down, struggling to maintain his composure, not wanting to appear desperate—which he was. "The guards told me you requested the mirror be removed from your cell," Birch said, ignoring Christie's offer for a deal. Two can play at this game. "But they refused. I guess you didn't want to give yourself a fright by looking at your own reflection."

"Sod off!" Christie snarled out of the darkness, reverting to her English slang, her tone instantly abrasive at the mere mention of her face. "There *was* no mirror in my cell, asshole."

Good, Birch thought. He wanted to get under her skin.

"I'm willing to make a deal with the D.A.," Christie said, annoyance clearly in her voice now. "Get my sentence commuted and I'll tell you where darling little Lindsay is."

Birch ignored her. "I spoke to the surgeon too. He told me you'll be having your fourth round of facial surgery in a few days. He said your face took a real beating, the worst he's seen. The bone damage is so significant, you will never really look the same again."

"I will kill her!" Christie hissed.

"Who will you kill, Victoria?"

"The bitch who did this to me. You know her name."

"Not from inside a prison cell you won't. Do you really think they're going to let you out no matter what you tell me? You killed four people, one of them a cop."

Christie was silent for a moment, then to Birch's surprise, she switched tone again. "Europe is such a big place," her voice dreamy and soft. "So many places where Lindsay could be."

"We found your journal. It makes for interesting reading."

"You know nothing of me, who I really am!"

Birch wanted to see her, see her face. Up until now Victoria Christie had been a myth, a theory of Vega's, someone not real, hiding beneath the skin of another. Birch wanted to see the real Victoria Christie in the flesh. "I think we have a fair idea of who you are, or should I say, 'what' you are."

The chair made a grating sound on the cement floor as Birch stood. "We're done here. Have a bad life, Victoria," he said. "We will not be meeting again until you tell me where Lindsay Latimer is."

Suddenly the darkness inside the cell parted and Victoria Christie stepped through and into the insipid light, her feet soundless as she seemed to float like a wraith up to the bars of the cell. "You'd better take one last look at me, then," she whispered through the gap between the bars.

Birch took an involuntary step back. Under the low light, part of Christie's face was in shadow, but what Birch could see of the rest was enough to make him recoil slightly. One eye, while completely swollen shut, bulged outward as though her eye socket had swallowed a baseball. The other eye, watery and stained red, the resulting hemorrhage of a broken blood vessel, swiveled like a Cyclops, staring straight at him. Her head was encased from the neck up in a birdcage-like brace, secured in place by a metal headband around the top of her hairless skull. Thin metal rods speared inward from each corner of the headpiece into her cheekbones at the front, and into each side of her jaw. Her face had lost all of its symmetry. It appeared to Birch to have been sheared down its central axis causing one side to droop lower than the other, giving the appearance that two halves from two different faces had been haphazardly fused together by uncaring hands. The nose was gone, replaced with a flap of discolored skin, grafted from another part of her body

Birch imagined, with two pencil holes for breathing. The lips were purple, drawn back into a permanent snarling grin by the rubber bands of an orthodontic brace. The top row of her teeth was completely gone, leaving just the pinkish wet ridge of the upper gums. Saliva, viscous and glistening, dribbled down her chin, and the front of her prison overalls were damp with drool.

For a moment Birch felt a tinge of sorrow, of compassion for how she looked, and the enormous pain she must be in. Then as quickly as his compassion had manifested itself, it vanished, leaving him feeling a deep sense of justice.

"Questa non e la mia fascia," Christie said with a wet, smacking lisp, her tongue slithering over her top gums.

Birch tilted his head questioningly. Italian? He could tell it pained her to talk, to form the words, her mouth straining against the brace holding the bones of her jaw in place. She spoke like a bad ventriloquist.

"This is not my face," Christie translated the Italian, more drool dripping from her chin. "They say love is the most powerful emotion of them all," Christie said. "But I disagree. Let me tell you, love goes out the window when fear comes barging through the front door. Fear will always conquer love, Thomas. Fear drove me to do what I did, nothing more, pure and simple." Christie paused to wipe the drool from her chin.

"Playing the victim doesn't wash with me," Birch replied, "to justify what you did, the people you murdered."

The Cyclops eye widened; the red stain seemed to throb darker. "I'm not playing the victim, Detective. Where were you when I was being repeatedly raped as a ten-year-old child?"

Birch had no answer. There was no suitable answer.

Christie looked around at the cell bars, as though wondering if they could really contain her. She took a sip of water, making a gurgling sound. Birch watched in morbid fascination as some of the water leaked out of the sides of her mouth and down the front of her prison overalls. She didn't seem to care.

"I killed out of fear. But I'd be lying to you as well as insulting your intelligence if I didn't admit I started to enjoy it...the killing."

"Why did you kill the hooker and throw her in the dumpster with Lindsay Latimer's purse?" It was another mystery Birch had a suspicion about.

"You tell me, Thomas," Christie said. "You're the detective."

"Because you were getting ready to run again," Birch replied. "To hide. So you planted the purse to make it seem Lindsay had been mugged, possibly killed by the hooker. You made it look like Lindsay's possible killer was then killed themselves."

"And the dead don't talk," Christie said. "Especially not after what I put in her mouth."

"So any police investigation would focus on finding who killed Lindsay's killer, being the hooker, after assuming the hooker killed Lindsay. You skillfully created another killer who does not exist for the police to chase and then removed yourself as the link. They would never find Lindsay's body, because she, being you, would vanish again."

"Correct, Detective man," Christie replied, tilting her head in acknowledgment. "Lindsay is the gift that keeps on giving."

"But why run now?" Birch said. "After all the careful planning and effort it took for you to assume Lindsay Latimer's life, why throw it all away?"

Christie's single, watery red eye swiveled over Birch's face.

Then it dawned on him. It was something Vega had said. "You hated her didn't you?"

Christie made a wet, sucking noise.

"Deep down you loathed Lindsay Latimer and all she represented." Birch paused, thinking, before speaking again. "A strange choice for a young woman—who is a multiple murderer—to be reading about, don't you think?" he said, referring to the book he had found in Lindsay Latimer's apartment with the postcard from Naples.

The single, watery red eye narrowed.

"Inequality, class struggle, the unfairness of society, the widening divide between the rich and powerful and the poor. You thought money would bring you freedom, but instead it made you feel trapped. You came from a poor background didn't you? Life for you was a struggle, with hardship and suffering."

"You know nothing about me!" Christie hissed, more drool dribbling from her mouth.

"So you thought you would rise up, rebel just like how the pigs did in the book, overthrowing the farmer, the ruling class. But then you soon realized after assuming Lindsay's life, you were becoming like her, becoming everything she was, everything you despise."

Christie made gurgling noises and for a moment Birch thought she was choking on her own drool. But then he could see she had cupped one hand below her chin, allowing the drool to gather in her palm before hurling it through the bars at him.

The phlegm-laden drool fell pitifully short of hitting him.

"I was going to kill them all," she slurred.

"You will never be released," Birch said before turning in disgust and walking away, his footsteps echoing through the cellblock.

"Take one last look at my face so you don't forget me!" Christie called out after him.

Birch didn't stop, didn't look back, just kept walking. His

skin, his face, his hands, his lungs felt dirty, as though he'd touched or breathed in something poisonous, something so utterly contaminated. Victoria Christie's face wasn't a sight he was going to forget anytime soon.

And, if they were ever going to find where Lindsay Latimer was, then they were going to have to make a deal with the devil.

Chapter 79 – Hiding Evidence

You could tell from the jogger's labored, gasping breath, their awkward, plodding footfalls, and their hunched shoulders, with one wrapped hand held protectively against their chest, that they were *not* a true runner.

Shrouded by the cowl of their hooded sweatshirt, the jogger moved slowly along the waterfront, like a stooping monk shuffling to prayers in some dark abbey.

The jogger stopped, turned their head, and looked over their shoulder, causing the edge of the hood to fold back slightly, revealing a woman's pale-skinned face, a wisp of hair the color of winter wheat, and brilliant green eyes that scanned the surrounding shadows. At this time of night, and along this stretch of neglected shoreline, solitude was her only companion.

The woman set off again, finally stopping when she reached the skeletal remains of an old pier that jutted out over the water, where the air stank of decaying things, of rotting mud and spilled diesel.

She looked around one more time.

The only sound came from the water lapping below at the ancient wooden pylons supporting the pier, and the perpetual, deep hum of the glittering metropolis on the opposite side.

Reaching into the front pocket of the hoodie, she retrieved a small, cylindrical object made of carbon steel. Clutching the object in her left hand, she drew back her arm and hurled it out across the dark, cold expanse. The throw was difficult, clumsy, given she was naturally right-handed. But the motion was effective nonetheless.

The object sailed out into the darkness, and seconds later,

confirmation of its final resting place floated back with a watery 'plunk.'

Like most modern handguns, especially those carried by the NYPD, it is a simple task to swap out the steel barrel, to replace it with another. For it is the barrel itself, that imparts a unique and traceable imprint, like a fingerprint, on a fired bullet allowing it to be linked directly back to the gun—and then to its likely owner.

Satisfied, the woman turned and began to jog away, her stride more certain, her shoulders less hunched. For she now possessed a newfound confidence in knowing her nightmares about Uri Goff had finally come to an end—by her own hand.

Chapter 80 – Failed Father

"I failed her as a father, Thomas."

Birch sat next to Francis Latimer on the park bench. Both men gazed out from Liberty State Park across the Hudson River toward the colossal view of Manhattan glinting in the bright morning sunshine.

"I've accepted the fact that she's dead," Latimer continued, his mood somber. "But my wife…" his voice trailed off. "She is another matter entirely."

Birch had already briefed Latimer on his meeting with Victoria Christie, a meeting Birch could have never envisaged happening if Latimer had not intervened. Latimer had personally called the D.A., who in turn called the Commissioner of the Department of Correction. And so it came to pass, Thomas Birch, ex-NYPD homicide detective, and soon to be exonerated convicted felon was granted a one-hour meeting with Victoria Christie.

After reviewing the extensive photographic analysis Beatriz Vega had undertaken of Lindsay's photos, and the contents of Christie's journal, Francis Latimer was left with no doubt Christie had befriended, then killed his daughter. She had then placed her body in a luggage case, wheeled her out of the hotel they were staying at in a small town in Italy, and had driven her to some unknown location to dispose of the body.

"I should have known it was not her," Latimer said, his face etched with self-loathing. "What kind of father must I be if I can't recognize my own daughter?" Latimer shook his head. "I never paid her the attention she deserved. If I had, I would have known something was wrong, that it wasn't her." Latimer closed his eyes, and for a moment, and Birch thought the man was going to cry.

"I let a monster play the role of my daughter without realizing it, Thomas," he said, his voice catching in his throat. "It sickens me to think I couldn't recognize it wasn't Lindsay, my own flesh and blood."

Birch watched as ferries crisscrossed the expanse of water, the mournful sound of their horns echoing off the tall edifices of glass and steel. The air was clear, the sun warm, and Birch thought back to what Victoria Christie had said—or had not said—wishing he could have drawn the truth out of her as to what she had done with Lindsay's body. The matter of finding her body had been turned over to the police, who were working in conjunction with their European counterparts. Maybe one day they would find her body, or what remained of it. Then perhaps they never would. Birch knew in cases such as these, there were no guarantees of closure, no promise of everything being neatly tied up with a bow. Many victims were never found, their families condemned to a lifetime of never finally laying them to rest.

Victoria Christie was refusing to tell NYPD about her past. This didn't surprise Birch, who doubted if it was in fact her real name. Maybe she had several 'pasts,' all layered one on top of another, burying her real identity in some dark, satanic hole. It was going to take time to dig down, uncover those layers, and discover who she truly was and where she had come from. According to Eve, Italy's state police, the *Polizia di Stato,* were investigating the Italian angle, while Scotland Yard in the UK were looking into tracing Christie's history there.

Latimer cleared his throat and regained his composure. "I love this city, Thomas," he said looking out at the view. "With all its flaws, all its imperfections. But I want to make it a better place. I want what's best for this city." He turned and affixed Birch with his stare. "It's why I'm running for political office, for governor of this state."

"Is that why you went after Hagen?" Birch asked, thinking about why Victoria Christie killed Moriarty. "You saw him as your closest competitor?" In a sense, Birch believed Latimer had deliberately "killed" Hagen's career, his name, his life, simply because he saw the man as a future political opponent he may encounter.

Latimer vehemently shook his head. "As I told Hagen, Thomas, I want to clean up this city, starting with him first."

Birch nodded but didn't believe Latimer. There were plenty of other places you could start with to clean up crime in this city. Not that Birch was ungrateful. Latimer had already given him a full copy of the green file and had told him his own legal team was working on his case in conjunction with the D.A.'s office as part of the wider prosecution of Carl Hagen. They had already submitted an extensive appeal that—based on the sheer weight of evidence in the file—would result in Birch's conviction being quashed.

"Why me?" Birch asked. "Why did you choose me to find Lindsay?"

"I thought the answer was obvious, Thomas. You featured heavily in the file Max had compiled on Hagen. Part of the reason why Hagen's corruption had flourished unchecked was because he set you up. Everyone else he bought off, except you. He knew money, or a slice of the power it brings, didn't interest you, Thomas. Your file told me that. So Hagen fabricated the case against you. What better person to look for my daughter than someone who had lost everything, including his own son? I needed someone with high enough emotional stakes on the line, who had nothing to lose and everything to gain. Money can't buy that kind of determination."

Both men sat in silence for a moment. Then Latimer spoke. "I'd like to meet Justin, some day—properly that is, after all this has blown over." Latimer reached inside his jacket pocket and pulled out a bulging envelope. "That reminds me." He placed the envelope on the bench between them.

Birch looked down at the envelope but left it untouched. "I don't want any money."

Latimer stifled a laugh, his mood improving since they had switched the topic of conversation away from Lindsay. "It's for Justin, not you."

Curiosity got the better of Birch and he peeled open the envelope. Inside were two New York Yankees lanyards, attached to private suite passes.

"Anything you need, Thomas, anything you need to keep your son here, with you, and not returning to Boston, just ask."

Birch nodded. "Thank you."

"You have a powerful friend in me now, Thomas. I want you to know."

Birch did know…and it truly scared him.

Chapter 81 – The Calling

Eve could feel her cell phone vibrate.

As she read the text message, a deep sense of foreboding wrapped its arms around her and gave her an unwelcome squeeze.

"What's up?" Maya Zin was staring at Eve. "You look as though Victoria Christie has just escaped."

"Almost as bad," Eve said with a mock grimace.

They had gathered at Death & Co, to celebrate and commiserate Andy Ramirez. It had been gut-wrenching for Eve to attend the funeral that afternoon and watch as his casket was lowered into the cold earth. Having Birch and Maya standing next to her during the service, though, had given Eve a strange, yet unifying feeling. Like comrades in arms, they had jointly suffered and endured.

Vega decided to stay at home, preferring to remain anonymous from the prying eyes of the huge NYPD contingent in attendance. In her absence, Vega had sent a beautiful floral arrangement of white roses and lilies, speckled with brilliant pink flowers, which she explained to Eve, were called *flor del Inca*, or "flower of the Incas," and were commonly found in the high valleys of Peru.

After much effort, Eve had managed to coax Beatriz Vega away from her computer and come out for the evening, telling the usually agoraphobic woman that Eve's friend, the woman she had wanted to buy a drink for, Maya Zin, would be coming.

The mood had started off somber, but as the drinks began to flow, so did the conversation. It warmed Eve's heart, as she looked around the table, eavesdropping on some of the conversations, to see such an eclectic group of people come together who shared one common goal, in a place so aptly named.

For Eve, the passing of the last two weeks had taken the edge off some of the raw pain she had felt. It wasn't completely gone. That would take time and being surrounded by people she now regarded as close friends.

Eve's hand was better, Beatriz's rib was on the mend, and Maya seemed to be returning to her old self. Beatriz and Maya, initially hesitant with each other, appeared to have become instant friends once the subject of Marcus Kemp arose. Soon they were swapping alternate more, gruesome ways he could have been killed.

And Birch—who had spent the last two weeks with his son Justin in New York—seemed much happier. With his melancholia gone, and his spirits much higher, to Eve he seemed like a different person compared to when they first met. Apparently Birch and his ex-wife, Suzanne, had come to an amicable agreement for Justin to visit his father on a regular basis.

"Anything important that we should know about?" Birch asked.

"It's nothing," Eve said, quickly putting her cell away. She stood up and began shuffling out of the booth.

"Where are you going?" It was Beatriz Vega this time.

"Just outside for a few minutes," Eve replied. "I need some fresh air." Eve knew this moment would finally come, and it had. It was impossible to avoid, given the mayhem she had created. Her first Internal Affairs interview two days ago hadn't gone well, which made Eve all the more concerned after reading the text message.

Birch looked up. "Will you be back?"

Eve hesitated, unsure as to how to answer the question. Finally she said, "I'm not going anywhere."

"Good," Birch said, draining his beer glass. "It's my turn to buy the next round."

A small chorus of cheers went around the table and the remains of drinks were quickly downed.

Eve lingered at the booth for a moment longer.

"Aren't you leaving?" Vega asked.

Watching the small group, Eve couldn't help but feel happy, with a tinge of sadness. Happy she had gotten to know Thomas Birch, and now Beatriz Vega. Yet sad that Andy Ramirez couldn't be here with them too.

Out front, in a No Parking zone, a large black SUV sat idling at the curb. A man dressed in a dark suit was standing by the rear passenger door. He smiled at Eve as she approached, before opening the door and ushering her inside. "This way, Detective."

The interior of the SUV yawned dark and uncertain for Eve, with a faint glow of internal lights, not enough to reveal the occupant. Taking a deep breath, Eve braced herself, then stepped inside, the door closing solidly behind her.

In the semidarkness, ensconced in one of the plush leather seats, sat Valentine Brady, Chief of Detectives. "Hello, Eve."

Eve sank into the leather seat. "Sir." Eve had never met Brady but knew him by reputation as a trailblazer: fair, big on action, short on words, and was someone who despised all the politics that went with the job. As chief of detectives, all investigatory elements of the entire NYPD were unified under him. His oversight covered all seventy-seven precincts, across all five boroughs of New York City encompassing all fields from

Homicide to the Gang Squad, including the highly regarded specialized units of Forensic Investigations, Criminal Enterprise, and SVU or Special Victims Unit. In essence, Brady was the boss of every detective in the city.

"This will not take long," Brady said, staring straight ahead. "How's the hand?"

"It's on the mend, sir" Eve replied, trying to get a read on Brady's face. "Where are we going, sir?"

Finally Brady turned and made eye contact, his expression blank, half his face in shadow. "We're going to stay right here on the curb, Detective. This meeting is more about where *you* are going."

Eve steadied herself, ready for the severe reprimand that was sure to follow. She was either going to be demoted from detective first grade to detective third grade—or, worse still—be kicked off the force entirely. Eve closed her eyes and nodded. "Sir, I would personally like to apologize for—"

"Be quiet for a moment, Detective."

Eve opened her eyes.

"The repercussions of what happened have already started," Brady continued, his voice soft, measured. "As you already know, Carl Hagen has been arrested, and it's only a matter of time before his associates in his corrupt network are too. As expected, there will be some blowback on the department from the media, and from others.

Eve listened just wishing Brady would deliver the bad news, so she could return to the bar, be with her friends, drown her sorrows—and start looking for a new job in the morning.

"You've received a lot of good and bad publicity lately, Eve, as a result of your behavior, your actions."

Here it comes, Eve thought.

"Your total disregard at times for following proper departmental protocols," Brady began, listing off Eve's indiscretions. "Willfully ignoring the mandated chain of command and stipulated investigative guidelines." He turned and looked at Eve directly in the eye. "Not to mention removing police evidence and passing it on to civilians, as well as revealing confidential information about an ongoing police investigation you were in charge of."

Eve sat silently.

"You went totally off the reservation on this case, Eve, displaying such maverick qualities I rarely see among the team of detectives whom I'm responsible for." Brady let out a sigh, as though saying any of this gave him no pleasure whatsoever. "Not to mention the feathers you have ruffled of some of the other chiefs, as well as a few of the deputy commissioners."

Eve swallowed hard. It was all true, her crimes. But, deep down, she had no regrets and was willing to face the consequences. It was the price you paid for working within such a large organization bound by so many rules and regulations, even if those rules and regulations, if followed all the time, would result in more people being killed.

Brady straightened his tie. "But frankly, I don't give a damn what the other chiefs think, nor the deputies."

Eve felt her chest tighten.

"Because you work for me, not them."

Eve watched as his stoic expression softened, then as a mild smile creased the corners of his mouth. "We're setting up a new task force, Eve, a new specialized unit. If Murder School has taught us anything, it's that we need to tackle this breed of villain head-on. Go on the attack and stop playing catch-up."

Eve was confused, bewildered by this sudden turn of narrative.

"Even if it means breaking the rules," Brady grinned. "Because these types of criminals don't play by any of the rules and we're losing this fight."

Eve nodded, still afraid to speak.

"This directive comes straight from the Commissioner, Eve, under my recommendation. We want you to head up this new unit. It will be small, and nimble, and you'll have our full and direct support so you won't be hindered by bureaucracy and departmental red tape."

"So I still have my job?" Eve asked tentatively.

Brady gave a dismissive wave. "As of now, your previous job no longer exists, Eve. The everyday, 'garden variety' homicides you have been involved with can be easily handled by the existing pool of detectives." Brady angled himself toward Eve. She felt her pulse quicken and could see the excitement build in his eyes. He spoke in a low, haunting tone. "We want you to go after the monsters, Eve. We want you to hunt down the worst of the worst, the truly evil who live among us, the criminals who are hell-bent on racking up the body count by doing the most harm and damage to the good people of this city."

For the first time since stepping into the back of the SUV, Eve felt excited too.

"And you will have complete say as to who you choose for your team," Brady went on. "With approval by me of course," he quickly added. "We want you to draw upon a range of disciplines—both officer and civilian candidates." Brady reached into his jacket and pulled out a small, black bifold and held it out. "This goes with the job."

Eve looked at the bifold, then took it—with both hands. She opened it up and immediately felt her throat swell up. She didn't need to flip on one of the internal lights to see what was inside.

On the left, a pair of single gold collar bars glinted in the subdued interior lighting. On the right, sat a dazzling blue-and-gold shield. If she accepted this new role, she would leapfrog from detective, over sergeant, and land straight into the position of lieutenant. Lost in the gravity of the moment, Eve said nothing for a few seconds, as she held on to the shield tightly, not willing to hand it back.

Brady gave a wry smile, almost sensing her silent decision. "Good decision…Lieutenant."

Eve finally found her voice. "Thank you, sir," her words almost cracking, "for your trust and faith in me."

"You're welcome," Brady replied. He glanced out his window as though appraising the city around him. "At the end of the day, that's all this entire department wants." He turned back to Eve. "The trust and faith of the people of this city. Without it, we are nothing." Brady gave a slight bow of his head. The meeting was over.

Despite the good news, there was still a smudge of darkness hanging over Eve, and Brady seemed to pick up on her indecisiveness to exit the vehicle.

"The Internal Affairs investigation?" he said with a tilt of his head.

Eve gave an awkward nod.

"It will run its course," Brady said, "as it should. However, it looks like you're in the clear."

"I shot an unarmed man," Eve replied.

"You were confused, Lieutenant, still feeling the effects of the concussion you had suffered. After all, you had just witnessed your partner brutally murdered by Victoria Christie and had fought off a male member of Murder School. When Joshua Banks approached you, again you feared for your life, and for the lives of others, the public, the innocent civilians around you. Joshua Banks was the ringleader of this murderous group of cold-blooded killers while Carl Hagen was the puppet master, hiding in the shadows, pulling everyone's strings for his own political gain. He appointed Joshua Banks to manage his campaign of fear and bankrolled it—ten thousand dollars per kill—from the fruits of his own corruption."

"Murder for hire," Eve muttered.

"Plain and simple," Brady agreed. "There was no righteous cause, just political greed coupled with financial greed. God knows, Eve, what would have happened up there on the Edge if you hadn't intervened. Many more innocent people could have died." Brady's jaw tightened. "You did the right thing, in the moment. You take out the Night King, and the entire army around him suddenly falls—and it did. Don't forget too, thanks to the keys you provided for us, we also found the storage locker containing the bomb Tein Moriarty had acquired. Joshua Banks may have been able to detonate it remotely. You didn't know that at the time, so you acted in the public's best interest."

Brady leaned toward Eve. "You did the right thing, correct?"

Eve said nothing while replaying in her head the scenes Brady had just described. Her sudden burst of violence had shocked her. She didn't recognize the person she had become during those brief moments of extreme aggression. It worried her. Perhaps some of Victoria Christie had rubbed off on her, and she too had acted out of pure fear for herself and for others. Upon reflection, she wasn't exactly proud of what she had done.

Brady cocked his head at Eve. "Correct?"

Eve broke out of her introspection. "Yes," she finally said. "Correct."

"Good."

Eve opened the door and stepped out onto the sidewalk again.

Brady leaned across and looked up at Eve. "Start thinking about those you want on your team, Lieutenant."

Eve closed the door, stepped back and watched as the SUV pulled out into the traffic and disappeared.

In the window of Death & Co, Eve saw Maya Zin, Thomas Birch and Beatriz Vega. They were laughing and pointing accusing fingers at each other.

Eve smiled to herself.

"I already have."

THE END.

About The Author

Jack Ellem is the Amazon #1 Bestselling thriller author in the US and in the UK.

His crime, mystery and suspense books have rocketed to Number 1 globally in the categories of Crime Fiction, Thriller Fiction, Financial Thrillers, Heist Crime, Kidnapping Crime Fiction and Noir.

His cutting-edge stories are unpredictable, multi-layered with sub-plots, twists and turns that readers cannot see coming and his books have garnered thousands of five-star reviews.

Jack splits his time between the US, the UK and Australia.

So whether you like crime thrillers, mystery and suspense thrillers, psychological thrillers, domestic thrillers, or just enjoy an addictive read, then pick up one of his books today in e-book or in paperback.

But BE WARNED! You might just find yourself up until 4:00 a.m., reading them.

Printed in Great Britain
by Amazon